LEAGUE OF UNWEDDABLE GENTLEMEN

Books 4-6

TAMARA GILL

COPYRIGHT

League of Unweddable Gentlemen
Books 4-6
To Be Wicked with You
Kiss Me, Duke
The Marquess is Mine

Cover Art by Wicked Smart Designs

ISBN: 978-0-6450581-5-4

TO BE WICKED WITH YOU

League of Unweddable Gentlemen, Book 4

Evie Milton knows she'll never marry. But that doesn't mean she can't celebrate her sister's betrothal to Finlay Stone, Duke of Carlisle. Until the bride-to-be runs off with the wrong man, that is. Now, if they have any hope of avoiding a devastating scandal, Evie and Finlay will need to bring the runaway bride to heel. And Evie will have to somehow ignore her growing attraction to the handsome duke who can never be hers …

In order to avoid disinheritance, Finlay needs a wife, and he requires one now. Finding a match wasn't terribly difficult. Keeping her, however, was another story. Going after the chit was his last option. What he never expected was how he'd start to feel for Evie. She's beautiful, kind, mature…and an entirely unsuitable bride. If only he could convince his heart of that …

. . .

All it takes is one spontaneous kiss to scatter their best intentions to the wind. But as secrets emerge and truths are revealed, can Evie and Finlay find their way to happily ever after—or is their wicked liaison doomed to end in heartbreak?

CHAPTER 1

1827, Marlborough, Wiltshire

Finley Stone, Duke of Carlisle, stared blankly at his solicitor. He would not believe what he'd been told. His father would not control his life, even after death. His decree would not be borne.

"Excuse me, Smithers, but can you repeat what you just said? I'm sure I did not hear correctly."

His solicitor cleared his throat, lifting the parchment yet again. "You have been the duke for one year, may your father rest in peace. However, I am now at liberty to tell you that your father put in a stipulation to his will. If you do not marry within one year of his death, you have sixty days from the anniversary of his death to do so. If you fail this stipulation, the bulk of your fortune, the money, and any assets not entailed, will revert to your cousin, Andrew Stone of Kent."

Finn leaned back in his chair, running a hand through his hair. His mind balked at the idea of marrying. Not to mention what men were supposed to do with the opposite sex. The idea of being forced into that occupation both terrified and excited him. It terrified him more.

"So I would keep Carlisle Hall in Wiltshire, but will have no money to keep the estate running other than the income it produces, which we all know is not enough."

"That's right, Your Grace. As the owner of several profitable estates, to lose those to your cousin would financially impact you severely. And have devastating consequences for those who rely on your estates for their livelihood. I would suggest you marry posthaste, retain your assets, and secure your future as soon as possible."

A wife? His stomach clenched, and he turned to stare out the window. He couldn't lose his home, the only place he'd ever loved. God knows his wicked father had been too busy carousing London to care about his family at home.

His mother had passed when he was eight, and his father had rarely bothered with him. Finn had promised to be a better person than that. Someone his servants and friends would respect, a landlord who was reliable and not flippant.

"Well then, I suppose I have to return to London and find a bride."

His solicitor cleared his throat, and Finn looked up, meeting his gaze. "Is there something else that I should be aware of, Smithers?"

"Your father has decreed that you are to find a wife here in Wiltshire. Someone local to Marlborough is preferable. He's decreed you marry a woman from your home county as he thought it would be better for the staff if they have a mistress who is familiar with the area and the local peoples."

Finn stared blankly at his solicitor. Was his father mad? Quite possibly, before his death and his wayward ways in London. Finn certainly had thought his sire had lost his mind. But a wife from Woodstock? There were only two noble families living close by, if he could call them that at all.

One family had several daughters, all of them under the age of ten. They would never do. The second family, The Miltons… Finn tried to remember the dynamics of the family. The father was a gentleman, living off the income from his small estate. He doubted there was any dowry for any of the girls. They did, however, have a son, although he was still in short coats.

"In effect my father is stating I need to marry one of the Milton girls, whom if I remember the number correctly is a total of two."

Smithers nodded, coming to sit in the chair before his desk, rustling through the paperwork in his leather satchel. "That's right, Your Grace. The eldest Miss Milton is beyond marriage, but her younger sister, Lucy, is not."

"Who is the oldest Miss Milton again?" Finn asked, a face echoing through his mind from last season when he was in town.

"Ah," Smithers said, searching further through the paperwork. "Miss Evie Milton. I believe she is friends with the Duchess of Whitstone and her social sphere."

A vision of a dark-haired beauty that was well on her way to being on the shelf entered his mind. He'd danced with her if he recalled, their conversation somewhat awkward since she'd been less than engaged to speak. Surprising really, considering her and her friends were some of the most opinionated women in the *ton*.

"Does not Miss Milton live in London in Marchioness Ryley's townhouse?" He frowned, certain he'd heard that after the marquess's marriage, the marchioness had allowed her friends to remain in her London townhouse. Miss Milton being one of them.

"That is correct, Your Grace."

"Hmm." Finn leaned back in his chair, wondering what the younger Lucy Milton looked like. If she were as striking as her sister, she would do very well indeed. She was young still, from a respectable family, and the local area. All requirements that would satisfy his late father's will.

"Do you expect Mr. Milton has any dowry for his daughters?" Not that it mattered, he was beyond wealthy and could afford to have a wife who came with very little or nothing at all. Even so, providing for female children on the off chance that you do not produce an heir told Finn a lot of a man's character. Whether they were loving, forward-thinking, and honorable. All the characteristics his father was lacking.

"Two hundred pounds per annum. The elder Miss Milton came into her stipend when she turned twenty-five. Of course, they assumed she would be married by then, and well, that did not occur. The younger Miss Lucy is two and twenty years of age."

"Very good. Well then," Finn said, standing and bringing this meeting to an end. "Tomorrow I'll commence my courting of Miss Lucy Milton and have it all settled by month's end. I will call for you when everything is in place."

Smithers bowed. "Very good, Your Grace. I wish you well in your endeavors and look forward to hearing the happy news."

"Yes, well..." Finn said, sitting back down and watching his solicitor stride from the room. Happy news may be too much of an exaggeration. More like resigned would fit in this context.

Finn pulled a piece of parchment toward him, picking up his quill and scrawling a letter for Mr. Milton to expect him tomorrow at eleven. He would not tell the gentleman as to why, merely let them believe it was a natural attraction and courtship that will bring him to offer for Miss Lucy. That would be best.

One thing he did comprehend was that no bride wanted to hear her betrothed only asked out of necessity. Or, in this case, the pain of disinheritance.

CHAPTER 2

Three weeks later, Marlborough Wiltshire

The carriage turned into the short drive of her family's home on the outskirts of Marlborough, her sister's hastily written letter the week before burning a hole in her gown. It was pure luck that it had taken her a week to organize travel to Wiltshire from London, for she needed a week to prepare herself for the realization that her younger sister was getting married.

The last time she had heard from Lucy, she hadn't mentioned a word about His Grace, so now to be engaged to him was out of nowhere. Her sister, although high-spirited, was not a silly woman prone to hasty decisions. To be marrying the wicked rakehell, Duke of Carlisle had made her think her sedate, intelligent sister had lost her mind. She would speak to her parents when she arrived, ensure for herself that they too had not lost their minds regarding their daughter marrying a duke.

No doubt, they were overcome with joy at the thought of Lucy marrying into such a lofty title. The duke was their closest neighbor, but never before had he ever shown an interest in the family. Evie glanced out at the passing oak trees that lined the driveway. She'd danced with him in London, had been a little distracted at the time with her friend's tribulations that evening, but she could still remember his scent. Sandalwood and spice. His hands had been large and strong against the small of her back. She'd had to look up to meet his gaze, and the memory even now made her shiver. One glance from the wicked Duke of Carlisle and one's knees went a little weak.

So handsome with his cutting jaw and perfect, straight nose. His smile was deadly, and his intense, heated stare worse. Not that she had been on the receiving end of such a look, oh no, he'd shown little interest in her. In fact, he'd seemed bored and uninterested in her attempt at small talk to pass the minutes of the dance, Evie had eventually pretended to be having a lovely time in his arms while counting down the minutes to the end of the dance. She had watched him at times in the *ton* and envied the women who did capture his attention. How lucky they would be to have such a rogue caught by their loveliness.

That her sister had captured his heart left her at odds. She was happy for her, of course, but a part of her also wished she'd found such a man herself. To marry, to love and be loved in return. Evie sighed, slumping back into the velvet squabs. She supposed it would not happen now. Not at her age, but at least she could content herself with being an aunt someday. Spoil her nieces and nephews to her heart's content.

Her sister deserved all happiness bestowed on her. She was the sweetest person who Evie knew, other than her favorite friends in London.

The carriage rocked to a halt before her family's Georgian manor house. Evie stared up at the golden stone home that shone like a beacon in the afternoon sun. The many windows glistening and welcoming her home.

A footman opened the door, and she stepped down, taking his hand for assistance. "Thank you," she said, starting for the house. A horse stood tied to one of the hitching posts near the front of the residence, and a dreadful thought entered Evie's mind.

Please don't be the duke's beast. She needed to speak to her parents and talk to her sister alone. Ensure this was a welcome marriage. Not merely because a duke offered for a woman who only lived close by. Their lack of a substantial dowry at least told Evie that the union was based on affection.

Evie pulled off her gloves as she strode toward the entrance, glancing up as the door opened and Lucy stood before her, taller than she remembered, but just as beautiful with her golden locks and lithe figure. Evie smiled. "Lucy," she said, laughing as her sister all but ran toward her and threw her arms about her back. "You've grown!" she said, her voice muffled from all of Lucy's abundant locks.

Lucy chuckled, hugging her tighter before pulling back. "It is so good to see you. I cannot tell you enough how much I need you here. We have so much to discuss."

Evie cast a glance toward the house, linking arms with her sister. "I gather the duke is here now?"

Lucy nodded. "He is. They're in the drawing room having tea. I heard the carriage and said it would be you. They are waiting to see you. Mama is very pleased that you'll be home with us for some weeks."

"I'm pleased as well." They started toward the house, entering the foyer where Evie gave a waiting-maid her pelisse and bonnet.

"Come, Evie, time to meet my betrothed."

"This is all so fast. I did not know he was even courting you." Evie watched Lucy and noted the light blush kissing her cheeks. Had the duke seduced her? She would not put it past the gentleman. His kissable lips were what made up women's fantasies in town.

"He arrived three weeks ago to call on Papa, something about land or some such, but it was during his time here that we were introduced. He was very kind and attentive and has been back often since then."

"So it's a love match then?" Evie asked, hoping that was true. The duke's reputation made it impossible not to judge and wonder if his motives were honorable.

"I like him very much. He's very kind. I think you'll like him too, Evie."

Evie didn't bother to mention that she already knew His Grace, no need muddying the water for something so small. In any case, he danced with many women in town. It was highly unlikely that he would remember her.

They walked into the front parlor, a small room, especially with her mother's crafts and knitting and her father's many books. The room was where they congregated most evenings before and after dinner, and it was nothing like the parlors of grand homes that dotted the English landscape. This one held few, and with the tall, dominating presence of the duke, the room appeared smaller still.

"Evie," her father said at the same time as her mama as she appeared. They both started toward her, arms outstretched and she hugged them both in turn. "We're so delighted you're home with us for some time. We've missed you, our dearest."

She smiled, pulling back from her mama and her comforting scent of lavender that always reminded Evie of home. "I'm happy to be home. I missed you all."

She glanced over and met the duke's calculating gaze.

He was staring at her, and Evie looked back to her father to make the introductions.

"Oh, forgive me, my dear. May I present my eldest daughter, Miss Evie Milton. Evie, this is His Grace, the Duke of Carlisle. Lucy's betrothed."

Lucy blushed as she went to stand beside the duke, her shorter height against his taller frame making her appear even more dainty and delicate. Beautiful and perfect for him.

The duke bowed. "Miss Milton. How very good to see you again."

Evie dipped into a neat curtsy. "I… It is, Your Grace." She watched him a moment, and as if remembering his fiancée stood beside him, thrust out his arm for Lucy to place her hand atop his.

"How is London, Evie?" Lucy asked, bouncing beside her betrothed, her golden curls springing beside her face.

"Busy. Everyone who is everyone is in attendance. Molly and I have taken to riding in the park most days to keep our sanity. We've become excellent riders I think, much better than we used to be in any case."

"Oh, I do worry for you, my dear," her mama said. "Is Miss Sinclair still ensconced at Marchioness Ryley's former home?"

"She is, Mama," Evie said, talking of Willow's former companion who now chaperoned Evie and Molly about town. "I would not be able to stay there if not."

"That is very true," her father said, gesturing for her to sit before the fire.

Evie did as he bade and held her hands out toward the heat, grateful to be out of the carriage and home. She turned toward her sister and the duke, studying them as they too took their seats.

"I suppose congratulations are in order. I'm very happy

for you, Lucy. Your Grace," Evie said. They were a strange pair, even if they portrayed or at least tried to portray otherwise. The duke sat as stiff as a rod beside her sister who, compared to him, was relaxed and bubbly as per her nature.

Maybe he liked women who were more outgoing than he was, although that went against everything that she knew about him. One would think that a consummate rake, a man who seduced the fairer sex with wicked intentions, would not look so uncomfortable with her sister.

Evie's eyes narrowed, taking in his features. Was he sweating?

"We're so pleased you'll be here for the nuptials, Evie. His Grace is going to have his good friend Marquess Ryley stand in for him, and I would like you by my side if you're willing."

Pleasure filled Evie at the thought of helping give away her sister on her big day. Even though there was a relative age difference between them, they had been close as children, and as all young women do, they dreamed of meeting their husbands and having a memorable wedding. "Of course. I would be honored." She glanced at the duke and tried to ignore his intense inspection upon her. Evie shot a look to Lucy, but her sister seemed oblivious to the duke's attention. Evie cleared her throat, unsure what the duke was about or why he found her so very interesting. Evie reached up to check that her hair had not slipped from its pins, or that her fichu was missing from her gown. No, all was in order. "Where is the wedding to take place?" she asked, wanting to remain engaged and excited about her sister's upcoming nuptials.

"At my estate," the duke said, cutting off her sister's reply. "The drawing room at Stoneheim Palace is very large and will accommodate the guests we intend to invite."

Evie adjusted her seat, warmer now. "I'm curious as to how you met. Will you tell me?"

"I had business with Mr. Milton and called one afternoon," the duke answered before anyone else could get a word in. "A delightful outing that turned even more so when I ran into your sister, Miss Milton. I asked to call again, and from there, we found we got along very well."

Lucy smiled at Evie, but there was something in her sister's eyes that gave her pause. The light within them was a little less bright when her betrothal was spoken of. Evie's eyes narrowed, and she wondered why that was. Outwardly her sister seemed happy and excited about the forthcoming marriage, but Evie wasn't convinced. She knew her sister better than anyone else in the world, and she wasn't as happy as she was pretending to be. Why, however, was the question.

"That is a lovely story. I'm very happy for you both." Evie smiled at her sister and promised herself when they were alone, she would ask that all was well. That her suspicions were incorrect, and her sister was merely nervous. To marry a duke was no small matter, especially to women such as themselves who may have a gentleman father, but little else to offer other than their person.

Lucy grinned. "I did not know you had met His Grace, Evie. How long have you both been acquainted?"

Evie looked to the duke as she tried to remember exactly when they met last.

"Midway through the last Season, I believe. I danced the cotillion with Miss Milton at the ball I hold annually in London."

Lucy's eyes widened at his exactness of detail and glanced between the duke and herself. Evie stared back, having not expected him to remember, certainly not to that detail. She knew she'd danced with him at his ball, but what that dance was precisely was lost on her. She had not thought he even remembered her name.

"I think you may be right, Your Grace. I admit you have a better memory than I," Evie said, making light of the situation.

"It was a pleasant spell about the dancefloor. One I will cherish always now that we're to be brother- and sister-in-law."

Lucy met Evie's eye, a question in her blue orbs. Evie shrugged, not knowing the duke remembered their dance so well.

Their mother cut in and started to discuss the weather and who would preside over the wedding, and Evie let the conversation flow over her. The duke and Lucy were a stunning pair, no matter that Lucy wasn't titled. She would have expected the duke to marry a lofty, titled woman, not a younger daughter of a penniless gentleman. But here they were, discussing invitations and where the happy couple would go on their wedding trip.

Evie listened and partook in the conversation when she could, but a part of her could not help but be a little jealous of her younger sister. At the age of seven and twenty, she had assumed to have been married and a mother by now. It wasn't so, and highly unlikely to occur now. But at least her sister would be happy, and that was a comfort at least.

❧

THE FOLLOWING day was a perfect summer day. Evie sat outside on a setting that looked out over her father's modest gardens. They were not as grand as the duke's at

Stoneheim Palace, but then few places in England were as grand as his country seat.

Evie watched as the duke and Lucy strolled the gardens, every so often stopping to talk of a particular rose or tree. Her sister outwardly looked content and happy, but she was not at ease with the duke, and Evie couldn't help but wonder why. What was her sister hiding?

"Did you have any inkling at all, Mama that Lucy had feelings for the duke or that he, in turn, had feelings for her? We have never circulated with that family. Even I in London only really knew of the duke due to my friends and their elevated marriages. Do you not think Lucy may be a little out of step with him? Open to ridicule due to her lack of connections?"

Her mother finished her sip of tea before placing her cup down on the table before them.

"I did have my concerns, of course, regarding those matters, but I'm sure the duke is a good man and will not let Lucy suffer from any nastiness or jealousy that may arise at her lofty marriage accomplishment."

Evie didn't want to upset her mama and tell her that Lucy would be targeted and for quite some time by those in the *ton* who thought her marriage to the duke was above her reach. They would make her pay for marrying a man who only the worthy should have taken off the marriage mart.

"As for her feelings for the duke, I believe they like each other very much. I even hope that in time the duke will come to love our Lucy. I believe she already loves the duke."

Evie shot a look at her mama, not believing that for a moment. "Lucy loves the duke. Has she told you that?"

"Well, no," her mother said, casting a glance at her youngest daughter. "But look at her, the way she studies the duke, how she hangs on to his every word. Oh yes, I do believe she loves him very much."

"Mama," Evie said, her tone comforting, "I also look up at gentlemen when I speak to them, that does not mean that I'm in love with them. They have not known each other long, and I worry that Lucy may not like being a duchess. You know how much she loves her freedom, her life here in Wiltshire, and the people we know in Marlborough. She would not be able to circulate in that sphere any longer when she becomes the Duchess of Carlisle."

"Oh, the Duchess of Carlisle, how well that sounds, do you not think?"

"Mama," Evie chided. "Lucy will miss her friends. She has never tried to be anything more than what we were brought up to be. Daughters of an untitled gentleman with no dowry. Do you not think it's odd that the duke just arrived one day, supposedly regarding estate business and the next moment he's engaged to our Lucy? That is odd. I do not care how well Duchess Lucy sounds to you. I find it strange."

Her mama turned to her, reaching out to clasp her hand. "My dear, I know it is hard to see a younger sister wed before you, and to such a high position, but do please be happy for Lucy. She loves you so very much and will need your guidance and support during the next few weeks."

"I'm not jealous, Mama, if that is what you're implying. While I have hoped that marriage may become a possibility to me, something that is looking less and less an option at my age, I am happy for Lucy. I merely want to ensure that Lucy is satisfied and appeased. Once I'm certain of this, then I will throw myself into the wedding preparations with such enthusiasm that even you shall be sick of me."

Her mama laughed, and Evie smiled, but as she turned back to watch Lucy and the duke, the niggling doubt would not abate. Something was off. None of this hasty courtship made any sense, and she would satisfy her concerns before she allowed her little sister, someone she always promised to protect, to marry a man whom she did not love.

"Thank you, my dear," her mama said. "And do not despair. Now that your sister is marrying a duke, it is only a matter of time before a gentleman will wish to be associated with the Carlisle family and offer for your hand. This connection will throw you into the path of men of substance and breeding, I am sure."

"I do not think–"

"You will see, Evie," her mother said, cutting her off. "You too will be happily married by the end of next Season. The Duchess of Carlisle's sister cannot be a spinster."

Evie groaned, picking up a sugar biscuit and taking a substantial bite. "I never set out to be a spinster, Mama, as you well know, but neither will I allow anyone to parade me like a new, shiny goose ready to be plucked."

Her mama gasped, and Evie met her gaze, wanting her mother to know what she was implying. Just because her sister was to be a duchess did not mean anything. Not to society. Some of her closest friends were married, one to a duke, the others to a marquess and an earl. That had not changed Evie's or Molly's position. It simply gave them access to balls and parties that would otherwise be closed to them. No man of substance or breeding had bent the knee before her and offered for her hand simply because her friends were well placed in society.

It would be no different with her sister being a duchess. Having a sister so high on the social sphere did not change her circumstance. She was, after all, still a woman of no rank, no inheritance, and seven and twenty years. Gentlemen, unfortunately, were immune to seeing her or women like her for what they could give. A priceless prize worth so much more than anything else.

CHAPTER 3

Later that evening, Evie sat in her room alone, brushing her hair. The door swung wide, revealing her discombobulated sister. "You have to help me, Evie," Lucy blurted as she stormed into her room, shutting and locking the door behind her. "I cannot marry the duke."

Evie stared at her sister a moment in horror. Had she gone mad since she'd left her in the drawing room, not an hour before with her family? "What! Why ever not?"

Lucy came over to where she sat before the fire, drying her hair after washing it. Her sister slumped onto the chair across from her, her cheeks and lips a ghostly white. "He arrived here not a month ago and has courted me ever since. Mama was so very pleased and happy that I did not want to upset her. You know she's not been well these past months, and it was nice to see her animated again."

"Mother has been ill?" Evie had not known that. Why did she not know that? "She never wrote to me about such a thing. I hope it's nothing serious."

Lucy frowned, marring her otherwise perfect forehead. "I do not believe so. I think a lot of mother's forlorn countenance has something to do with Papa not wanting to travel to Bath this Season. In any case, she was happy and lively, and the duke was attentive and kind, and before I knew it, he was bowing before me and asking me to be his wife."

Evie sighed. It was just like her sister to get herself into such a pickle. "You did not have to say yes, Lucy."

Lucy made a sound representing an injured dog. "I know I did not have to say yes," she moaned, "but I felt compelled. He's so wealthy and powerful. He owns most of the land surrounding Papa's estate. I did not want to offend him, and I just blurted yes before I thought about it. But I cannot marry him. I don't want to be a duchess."

Evie snorted, unable to believe such a thing. Women in town would do almost anything to wear a ducal coronet atop their heads, but then this was Lucy, and she had never cared for such things. "There are very few who would not want to be a duchess. Are you sure you're not the one who is ill?"

"This is not a jest, Evie. I cannot marry the duke because, well, because I'm already in love with someone else."

"What!" Evie shot to her feet, the brush in her lap clanging onto the floor. "You cannot be in love with another man and have given your hand to the duke. Whatever were you thinking, Lucy?"

Lucy stood and started to pace back and forth from the bed to the fire. Her fisted hands at her sides telling Evie that her sister was upset and unsure of what to do. Evie took a calming breath, needing a clear mind to think about what was to be done.

"If you remember last year, Mama took me to Gretna to visit her cousin. What she does not know was that I was seeing Mr. Anthony Brown, you know, the gentleman farmer on the other side of Marlborough. He's been courting me for some months and Evie," Lucy said, coming over to her and clasping her hands, "I love him so very much. He is everything that I've ever wanted, and when I'm with him, I care for nothing else."

"You've lain with him?" Evie shut her mouth with a snap, knowing she was gaping at her sister. How and when had all of this occurred? And how did she not know of it? She should have been here for her sister. To guide and help her through this. Although father would not have wanted either of them to marry a farmer, if he had seen his daughter's happiness with the gentleman, he may have relented. Neither of their parents was hard or so unforgiving.

"No, of course not. Mr. Brown is a gentleman, but I do wish to be his wife and he has asked for my hand. Secretly of course, no one can know of our love as yet. Papa will never approve." Her sister sat again, clasping her hands in her lap. "I will admit to kissing Anthony, but nothing more. I promise you."

That was something, Evie supposed.

"So you see, I cannot marry the duke, and if Anthony finds out that I agreed to marry the Duke of Carlisle as well he'll never forgive me. Father is going to have the banns called. My life will be over if I lose Anthony. Please, Evie. Please help me."

Evie bit her lip, at a loss as to what to do. What did one do in situations like these? Her mind jumped from idea to idea, each one dismissed as soon as she had it. The only thing left to do was tell the truth, no matter how difficult that may be. "You will have to tell Mama and Papa the truth and break off the understanding with His Grace. That is your only choice."

"No," Lucy gasped, her hand rushing up to her neck.

"I'll be ruined if I do that. The whole town will think me a scheming minx with no regard to the duke. When they find out that Mr. Brown was already my betrothed, they will shun and hate me. The duke may be so enraged that he may try to injure father financially to seek revenge. No, no one must know that it was me who cried off. We need to keep father from posting the banns, and you need to seduce the duke into thinking he's asked the wrong sister to marry."

"Me?" Evie asked, pointing at herself. "I cannot seduce a duke. I'll be ruined. Think for a moment of what you're asking, Lucy."

"You're a confirmed spinster. I did not think you would mind."

Anger replaced the compassion she had for her sibling. "I may be unmarried, but I'm not a whore who'll ply her trade to repair an error that is of someone else's making. You need to tell the truth. You're the one who lied to both men. You need to make this right."

Lucy kneeled before her chair, clasping Evie's hands. "I'm sorry, Evie. I'm desperate. Please, please help me," her sister begged, gripping her hands tighter.

Evie shook her head, staring at her sibling, whom she had started to wonder if she knew at all. Whatever was she thinking about, getting herself into such a lie? "I wouldn't know the first thing about how to steal him away from you, and he's asked you to marry him. He likes you, not me. That idea will never work. You must own this mistake, I'm afraid."

"You're far prettier than I am. It'll be no problem at all. Just show him more attention than I will. I'll distance myself over the coming days, be unavailable or away whenever he calls, and you shall take my place. He only ever talks in any case, he has not tried to kiss me, thankfully, and he's boring." Her sister pursed her lips, turning her head in thought. "London gossip paints him as a libertine, a rogue, and yet I do not believe it. He's never tried once to seduce me. I'm sure, though, he'd try and kiss you. As I said, you're much prettier than me."

The idea of the duke kissing Evie made heat pool at her core, and she slumped back onto the chair, her stomach in knots. "If I try and steal him away, he'll think the worst of me. No one does such a thing to a sister, and he's a gentleman, he would not do that to his betrothed."

"No, no no no, he'll simply believe that the feelings he had for me were misplaced. As you said, you've met before. Surely you can work with that. He does not love me, that I do know, and so it won't be so awful for him in the end. You do not have to marry him, merely pull his attention away from me long enough that he'll decide to end the betrothal."

"But what if he then offers for me? As you said, I've resigned myself to my lot in life. I don't know if I could marry a man who could be so fickle with his feelings."

"Evie, my actions toward the duke, my marriage, could ruin the family if he should find out. You need to make him turn his head toward you, fall in love with you if possible, but you need to do it soon. Please help me."

"Lucy," Evie sighed. "When is he to call next?" she asked, resigning herself to tell the duke the truth herself, no matter what Lucy wanted her to do. She could not seduce him. To do so was an abhorrent thought. Not because he was not deadly handsome, what with his chiseled jaw and straight, cutting nose, no. He was so very charming to look upon, but because she could not seduce a man away from her sister, even if asked to do so.

It was impossible to imagine, and he would question her loyalty toward her family if she tried such a thing.

He'd think her a horrible person.

And she would be a horrible person. No, she would tell the duke the truth and have Lucy own her mistake. It was what was best for the family. The duke would surely understand. As Lucy said herself, they hardly knew each other. It wasn't like their marriage was a love match. All would work out, and tomorrow she would solve this problem, and they could all get back to their normal lives.

CHAPTER 4

Finn had ridden hard to make his afternoon call to Miss Lucy Milton. He'd been held up with his steward regarding a letter from his attorney who queried about his marriage. Namely, when it would take place and reminding him of the time restraint he had on his person.

He pulled his mount up before the sandstone, modest estate, and sighed, running a hand across his jaw. What was he doing? He was marrying a woman whom he did not love and all for the sake of money.

Granted, it was a lot of money, and funds that were required to keep his many estates and the people who relied on him for a living. Even so, the thought of marrying a woman he did not care for grated on his conscience. Miss Lucy Milton was a delightful young woman, bright and happy, and seemingly very much in love with him. He ought to be satisfied he'd found a wife, a local girl who was not only the daughter of a gentleman but from his home county. Just as his father decreed in his will, but he was not.

He didn't love her past that of a passing acquaintance, no more than a friend.

The image of Miss Evie Milton flittered through his mind, and his blood stirred. He'd not thought to see her so soon, having expected her to stay in London. The fact that she'd returned home early to partake in her sister's wedding preparations hadn't occurred to him.

Stupid mistake and now one that haunted his dreams.

Evie was a little older than Lucy. Part of a friend set of some of the most powerful and influential women in the *ton*. And damn it all to hell, she was beautiful. Had she been a little younger, he would've courted her instead of her sister, but she was nearly thirty by his calculations—her breeding years long behind her.

She was not for him.

He needed a wife who would give him sons. A young wife was more suitable for that position. If he had to marry at all, he at least would ensure he had children and soon. To have an heir would at least be one thing less that he had to concern himself.

Finn jumped down and handed his horse to a waiting stable lad, throwing the boy a ha'penny for his trouble. The boy thanked him profusely, and Finn walked to the door, steeling himself to act the besotted fiancée that he was anything but.

The door opened, and he glanced up, expecting to see the young footman who also served as the butler. The person before him was most certainly not a man. Miss Evie Milton was all woman. Voluptuous, and curved in all the right places. His hands started to sweat in his gloves at the thought of running them over every portion of her body he could. Her cheeks reddened, her eyes wide and bright, and he steeled himself not to act the rogue he was rumored to be, and drag her up against him to kiss her soundly. Take those full lips and meld them with his.

Finn swallowed, remembering to bow. "Miss Milton, good afternoon. I hope I find you well today."

She stared down her nose at him, her gaze sliding over him like a caress. He shouldn't be reacting to her in this way. She wasn't for him, and yet, there was something about Miss Milton that made his blood burn. Had always made him burn even when he'd promised to never act the cad like his sire. He could only guess how many bastards lay littered about London his father had produced before his death last year.

"Your Grace, how very opportune this is for me. I was just about to go for a walk to ensure that my dog is well. She is expecting, you see. Perhaps you'd like to join me," she asked him, stepping down onto the lower step and closing the door at her back.

Finn ought to move aside to give her space, but he couldn't budge a foot. He was a bastard and one who may be more like his father than he wanted. "I thank you for the offer, but I must make my addresses to your parents and Miss Lucy."

"Oh, they're not home at present. Lucy wished to visit Marlborough, something about acquiring a new hat and traveling case, I believe. So, you see, it's only me here today."

She slipped past him with little care as to whether he was following her or not. The sound of her footsteps on the graveled drive loud in his ears as she walked away. Finn stood there a minute, debating his choices and decided a walk would do well enough so long as they stayed within the grounds of the house and were in view of the home. Her lack of chaperone could be overlooked.

"Very well, I shall join you, Miss Milton."

She stopped and turned, pulling a loose bit of hair out of her eye that had slipped across her face. Finn swallowed.

The action should not be seductive at all, nor fill him with a longing to be the one to slip the stray piece of hair behind her ear, but it was.

He was the worst type of fiend and ought to be horse-whipped thinking of his betrothed's sister in such a way. He'd had the opportunity last year in town to court Miss Milton, and he'd chosen not to. Marriage had not been a thought to trouble him with. Stupidly he'd imagined he had time to choose a wife. While their dance had been memorable, to him at least, it had not caused him to lose his head and declare undying love.

Rallying himself to control wayward thoughts, he clasped his hands behind his back and raised his chin, all seriousness for their stroll about the garden. A damned hard feat when Miss Milton strode purposefully down the drive, heading out of sight of the home and at a pace that made it impossible to continue his sedate stride he'd started with.

"What is the rush?" he asked, catching up next to her. A light blush stole over her cheeks, and she pointed ahead of her.

"My wolfhound is in labor, or so Ben our gardener said this morning, and I want to be with her."

"You have a wolfhound?" Finn asked, his steps faltering. He wasn't an enthusiast of the canine breed, never trusting the beasts. Small dogs he could tolerate, but a wolfhound, those things were as beastly as they came.

"I do," she said, gifting him with a smile. "Her name is Sugar."

Sugar? His lips twitched at the farcical name, and yet he continued to walk with her, curious now to see Miss Milton's pet. "I'm hoping this Sugar is friendly."

"Oh, yes. Sugar has the sweetest temperament. She'll be fine with you since you're with me, she'll have no reason to distrust you. Normally she would be with me in the house, but due to her condition, Mama wouldn't let her stay inside until she'd had her pups."

"You allow the dog to live inside your home?" Pets were nonexistent in his life growing up. They had the odd barn cat, but they were wild and would leave a respectable scratch if anyone ever tried to catch them. As for dogs, his father had loathed them. Horses were the only animals allowed, and only because they served a purpose.

"Of course. Sugar sleeps on my bed whenever I'm home, and I miss her, but I'm also very excited to see her pups." She studied him a moment, working her bottom lip between her teeth, and the sight of it sent a bolt of desire to his cock. He clamped his jaw, looking away to remedy his nonsense. What on earth was wrong with him? He'd been away from town too long, and the bed of willing women, or he'd liked Miss Milton more than he'd admitted to himself. Not a helpful revelation since he was about to marry her sister.

"You never had pets as a child, did you, Your Grace?"

He kept his attention straight ahead and spotted a kennel of some sort near a small cottage. "You're very astute, Miss Milton."

"We have mutual friends, Your Grace. I do know you a little. Talking of such, would you like to call me Evie? I do prefer it to Miss Milton."

Pleasure thrummed through him at the thought of such a thing, but he couldn't allow it. Not until he'd married Miss Lucy, then he could be on more familiar terms with Miss Milton. Until then, he would not be calling her by her given name. "I think it would be best to remain Miss Milton and Your Grace if you do not mind. When I marry Miss Lucy, then I believe we may be on more familiar terms."

"Out of curiosity, however, what is your first name, Your Grace? If you're willing to disclose that, of course."

He cleared his throat, not sure he ought to tell her. To do so really defeated the purpose of his rule only a moment before. "Finlay, but close acquaintances call me Finn."

"I must admit," she said, chuckling a little. The sound as sweet as any he'd ever heard. He shouldn't find it so very carefree and relaxing to be around Miss Milton, and yet he did. More so than when he was with his betrothed. It was blasted inconvenient, and not to mention wrong. "I imagined a much more severe, stern type of name for a duke."

"My mother named me," he said without thinking. He rarely spoke of his mama, whom he'd lost when he was young. To think of her always made him melancholy, and yet, with Miss Milton, he seemed to be able to talk of the one parent who showed affection for the short amount of years that he had with her with no melancholy at all. Only pride and love.

"What name do you suppose a duke should have, Miss Milton? I'm curious to know."

"Hmm," She threw him a teasing glance and continued toward the kennel. "I do not know. I suppose perhaps George or Arthur, or even William. Finlay seems a carefree, happy type of name. I think it suits you," she said, meeting his gaze.

He smiled despite himself, enjoying this little stroll, not to mention her. He was enjoying her so very much as well. More so than he'd enjoyed his many strolls with Miss Lucy Milton. When he'd gone on walks with his betrothed, they would often go minutes at a time without speaking, and sometimes, Finn had to wrack his brain to think of things to talk about. The conversation did not come easy with Miss Lucy. He'd put it down to her being a little shy around him, he was a duke after all, and often brought on such reactions when around the fairer sex. Miss Milton, however, seemed to be a paradox.

Evie was easy to speak to, and a little niggling doubt crept into his mind that he'd made a mistake in choosing the younger sister. That he should have taken more time to see who would suit him as a wife. Instead, he panicked and picked the first gentleman's daughter in his home country who was appropriate. The debate on the matter reminded him why he'd dismissed Miss Milton in the first place. She was mature of age to be an agreeable wife. He needed a bride who would give him heirs. Miss Lucy would fill the role well. She still had ample years ahead of her to provide him with children.

By the time they arrived at the kennel, a man that Miss Milton introduced as Ben was waiting for them. From his worn clothing, dusted with mud and grime, Finn marked him as the gardener whom she had mentioned before.

Miss Milton went into the kennel, large and under-cover, and Finn followed at a slower pace, not wanting to stress the dog at his presence. The enclosure was large, needed to be for a wolfhound, and the brown-haired dog lay on a bed of straw, four little pups suckling milk already from their mother.

"She's had them already," he said, kneeling beside Miss Milton, keeping his hands well away from the dog or her puppies.

Miss Milton did not. She slumped onto the floor beside Sugar's head, patting her face and leaning down to kiss her head before she reached out and ran one finger over the new puppies' backs. An adoring smile slipped onto her lips, and something inside Finn ached.

What it would be like to be looked upon in such a way. With utter adoration and love. He supposed it was similar to what occurred when a woman had a child of her own. Unconditional love for her offspring the moment she saw her new babe. His father had not cared for him at all. His main priority was who his next bedding partner was to be. His son was the least of his troubles, so long as he was home, healthy, and out of the way, his father was content.

"Let Sugar smell you, and then you can probably sit closer if you like. She knows I'm relaxed with you, and so knows you are not here to harm her or her puppies."

Finn slowly placed the back of his hand near Sugar's nose, and she sniffed him a moment before lying back and putting her head on Miss Milton's lap. Having seemed to pass the little test, he sat on the straw bedding beside Miss Milton, merely watching the little puppies fight for a teat.

"They're charming, I will admit."

"When they're weaned, you may have one if you like. I have several friends who wanted a pup from Sugar when we bred her next, but I can hold one for you if you wish." She studied him a moment. Her head cocked a little to one side. "I can see you with such a grand dog. A duke should have a wolfhound."

He glanced at the puppies, having never given the idea much thought, even though he supposed he could have a pet if he wished. His father had not allowed them, but that did not mean that he could not do as he wanted now. Perhaps if he gave the canine breed a chance, he might like them better after all.

A novel thought and one he would consider.

"I shall ponder it," he found himself saying, reaching forward to run a finger across the back of a black pup that seemed eager for milk. "Do you think Sugar will have any more today?" he asked, having never seen a dog give birth before. That's what he told himself was the reason he wished to stay in this warm kennel, patting puppies.

Though, he knew it was because he wanted to spend more time with Miss Milton, away from her family and society as they had been in London.

His good friend, the Duke of Whitstone spoke highly of her, and he could see why. She was no fuss, intelligent, and sweet. She adored her massive dog and cared for her sister and family. There was little one could not like about her.

The fact that she was beyond pretty also made his time with her easy. To look upon such beauty all day was never a chore.

EVIE PULLED the duke from the puppies after an hour of cooing, holding, and patting the adorable little mites before they returned to the house. Her family was due home at four, and it was well past three by the time they returned themselves to the house.

They sat in the front parlor, which gave Evie a view of the front drive, taking tea and biscuits that cook had prepared for them on their return.

She studied him as she ate a slice of carrot cake. The Duke of Carlisle sat straight and tall in his chair, all proper again, no longer the relaxed nobleman she had talked to in the kennel only half an hour before.

How she supposed her sister thought that she would be able to seduce such a fine specimen of a man away from his beloved was an absurd notion. While they did get along, seemed on friendly terms, that did not mean he found her handsome as much as she found him.

Why she'd never even kissed a man before, so how was she going to seduce a seasoned rogue? It was an absurd notion that her sister even asked. No, if Lucy's happiness depended on breaking the understanding with the duke, then Lucy had to tell him the truth. Tell him that she loved another and would not marry him. That was the best course and the one Evie would make her walk when they returned home.

She frowned down in her tea. What would the duke do after the fact? Would he return to town? Marry a woman much closer to him in wealth and situation? The idea left a sour taste in her mouth, and she reached for more sugar to put in her tea.

"I thought to hold an engagement ball in some weeks. Do you think your sister would welcome such an event?"

The question brought her out of her dispirited thoughts and back to the duke. "I think she would like that very much," Evie lied, knowing her sister would hate that above anything else. To be paraded before all of the duke's closest friends as if she were in love with the man. No, she could not allow it to get that far. She would make Lucy put a stop to this madness.

"I shall need help in drawing up a list of guests to invite. Would you and Miss Lucy like to call on me tomorrow next, and we shall get a start?"

Evie placed her teacup down on the small table that separated them on the settees. "Perhaps we could join you for luncheon and start collating a list after that." Not that any lists or balls would be occurring. When Lucy returned home, the duke would be released from his offer, and everything would return to normal. Other than her sister marrying Mr. Brown that was.

"I think that will do very well." He threw her a small smile, his eyes lingering on her lips a moment before slipping away back to the biscuit he held in his hand.

A flutter of delight thrummed through her at his interest before the sound of carriage wheels on the drive outside caught her attention. Evie glanced at the window and spied her mother and father alight from the vehicle, her mother's countenance one of distress. Evie stood, the pit of her stomach tightening with impending doom.

Just as the front door swung wide, she met them in the foyer, leaving the duke alone in the drawing room.

"What has happened?" she asked her mother, whose face was pale, her eyes red-rimmed as if she'd been crying for a long time.

The absence of Lucy made her pause. "Is Lucy well, Mama? Where is she?" she asked, turning to her father, who merely stood looking at her as if he'd lost all sense and feeling.

"She's gone," her mama screeched, her eyes filling with tears and loud, wailing sobs filled the room.

"What do you mean she's gone? Tell me!" Evie demanded, shaking her father a little by his arm. "Father, tell me what happened." All terrible thoughts entered her mind that her sister had befallen a terrible accident and was no longer alive. Surely not. The idea did not bear thinking about.

"She's gone," her mother said again, more wailing that made Evie's legs start to shake that her little sister had indeed passed away.

"She's run off. With…with…Mr. Brown! You know, the farmer who lives west of Marlborough. Lucy asked to look at some cloth for a new dress, and I said that I would be along shortly as I had run into Ms. Oyster, my friend. I thought to meet her at the seamstress' store, run by Ms. Clay, but when I got there, not five minutes later, she was gone. The shopgirl handed me a missive. It was from Lucy and contained her apology and plans for her life."

"What did the note say exactly?" Evie asked, anger replacing her fear over what her sister had done. How could she do that to their parents, whom she knew would worry no end about her until they saw her again? As for Mr. Brown, he ought to know better than to act in such a selfish way. She would have some very stern words for him, too, when she met with him next.

"Not so very much. She asked us to notify the duke of her change of feelings and told us to release him from his duty to her. To marry another."

"I beg your pardon, Ms. Milton?" the duke said, striding from the drawing room, frowning down at her parents as if they were wayward children. "What has my betrothed happened to do?"

"It seems Lucy has run off, Your Grace. Run away to be married to a farmer we're acquainted with here in Marlborough. I'm very sorry," Evie said, turning back to her parents and leading her mama into the drawing room where she could sit. "At least Lucy intends to marry, Mama. I'm sure all will be fine by the time she returns home."

"She's ruined herself, and for what? That Mr. Brown. He's a farmer, Evie. I had hoped that Lucy's esteemed marriage would help in settling your private circumstances, but it seems this will not be the case. Mr. Brown has no social standing, and you'll forever be an old maid."

Evie sat beside her mama, taking her hand to try to give comfort. The fact that the duke heard everything that her mama just said was mortifying enough than to make a scene about it. "You know I do not care about my circumstance in life. I shall get along well enough. Our concern now must be for Lucy."

"You're right," her mama said, clasping her arm. "We must hope she marries and is happy."

"What are you going to do about her actions?" the duke demanded, striding to stand before the fire and looking down at them all with displeasure. At some point, her father had also come into the room and sat on the settee aside them.

"We do not know where they have gone, Your Grace," her father said, his voice weary. "Lucy will return home when she's married, I believe. I see little point in chasing after her and making a scandal out of the situation."

"She's my betrothed. I suggest you ought to do a little more about it than that."

Evie rubbed her mama's back as the duke's words brought forth another bout of hysterics. "We are sorry for your loss, Your Grace, but there is little we can do, save going after her. She could be anywhere by now. Had run off in any direction. I'm sure in time, your heart will heal, and you'll marry again."

"That is what we shall do. Go after your sister and inform her that she signed a contract to marry me, and she'll damn well abide by it, or I'll ruin your family even more than this escapade will."

"I beg your pardon?" her father said, standing and going forehead to nose with the duke, who was much taller than her sire.

Evie sighed. If her father meant to intimidate the duke, it did not seem to be working, if his thin lips and unimpressed glare were any indication.

"Apologies, Mr. Milton, but you were there when the contracts were signed. Contracts that bestowed upon you a large sum of money to ensure the marriage took place within sixty days. That money is now due since your daughter has run off with another man. So, unless you have that thousand pounds in your desk to reimburse me for my trouble, I suggest you do as I ask and go after your offspring."

"Father cannot travel far these days, Your Grace. His

doctor has recommended he stay close to home," Evie said, feeling as though she needed to defend her parents, who were innocent as the duke in all this. Not that Lucy had told her of her latest plan. She had no idea that her sister would take such drastic action to end her betrothal. She was supposed to tell the duke the truth, not elope with Mr. Brown.

Oh dear, this was all such a mess.

"He has a bad heart," her mother said, hiccupping for effect.

The duke strode to the window, muttering under his breath before he turned, facing them all. His eyes were a little wild, and Evie shivered at the sight of him. When displeased, there was something oddly attractive about the man. He was much less refined, less the duke, and more the man.

A very delicious man who was once again free for the fairer sex to pursue.

He gestured toward Evie. "Your daughter will accompany me. To give Miss Lucy respectability when we return her home. They could not have gone far, and we shall return in a day or two."

"Evie is not going anywhere with you, Your Grace," her father said, his face going a little ruddy with his aggravation. Evie stood, going to him before leading him back to his chair.

"Sit, Father. You know the doctor said he did not want you to stress yourself in any way."

"You cannot go off with a man in a carriage. You'll be ruined, and then you'll never marry."

"I'll take Mary with me, and you forget that I'm already known in London as a spinster, Father. The duke will ride a horse outside the carriage, will you not, Your Grace?" she said, looking to the duke for agreement. "All proprieties will be met, I promise, should you allow me to go, that is."

Her father glanced at her mother a moment before his shoulders slumped, and he sighed. "Very well. You shall travel with the duke to fetch Lucy home. If you leave today, there is a chance you may catch them before nightfall." Her father clasped her arm, holding her firm. "She must not marry Mr. Brown, my dear," he whispered for her ears only. "I do not have the money to pay back the duke. Should Lucy marry Mr. Brown, it will ruin us financially, and we'll lose our home."

Evie sighed, her heart a little less full at her father's troubles. However, not all was lost. They shared mutual friends. Perhaps the duke could be persuaded to offer that money as a loan and allow her father to repay him over time should Lucy get her way and marry before they caught up to her. Evie could ask this of him. He was their neighbor after all in Wiltshire.

She nodded. "I shall, Papa," she whispered, before bidding them goodbye. She started for her room, needing to pack a valise and organize her maid Mary. There was much to do and very little time to do it in.

CHAPTER 5

The road toward London was arduous and lengthy, doubly so since she'd only just traveled it only two days before. Her maid sat across from her, her skin turning a darker shade of gray with each passing mile. It did not bode well for Mary being unwell so soon on the trip. They had many, many days ahead of them.

"Are you ill, Mary? You're quiet and pale," she asked, leaning forward to clasp Mary's hand, shaking it a little when she didn't respond. "Mary?"

The young woman leaned back against the squabs, taking a deep, calming breath. "Oh, Miss Milton, I feel so very poorly. I thought now that I'm one and twenty that my childhood traveling difficulty would have ceased to trouble me, but it has not."

"You feel as if you may be sick?" Evie asked, slipping to the side of the carriage to lower the window a little. They were traveling in the duke's carriage, a highly sprung, opulent equipage, and the last thing Evie wanted was to see Mary's stomach contents all over the floor or silk cushions. She doubted the duke would be appreciative of the gift.

"I do, miss." Mary curled forward, clasping her stomach. "Stop the carriage. Please, Miss Milton."

Evie yelled out to the driver through the window, and within a moment, the carriage rocked to a halt. No sooner had Mary stepped one foot outside did she cast up her accounts, only just missing her boots, but not, however, missing the duke's horse's hooves.

The horse stared down at Mary with a look of disdain, if horses were capable of such things. Mary was oblivious to all of them, merely continued to heave copious amounts of fluid all over the ground. Evie glanced up at the duke and noted he, too, had an inpatient, disdainful scowl across his brow that matched his horse.

Evie jumped down from the vehicle, going over to Mary and rubbing her back, giving comfort in any way she could. Thankfully she'd stopped heaving and was merely taking deep breaths, trying to calm her stomach.

"Do you feel a little better?" she asked, standing up and taking stock of where they were. Through the trees ahead, Evie spotted what looked like the start of their next town, Hungerford. On her way from London, they would typically change horses here, but they had not been traveling long from Marlborough. She supposed they could stop for luncheon, even though it was a little early for that.

"We shall walk into Hungerford. It is not far, and I think it's best that Mary doesn't get back into the carriage just yet. We could break our fast, which may help her unsettled stomach. Do you not agree, Your Grace?" she asked, catching his gaze.

His lips thinned, but he relented and nodded. "I agree. I shall ride ahead and order lunch for us all. Charlie," the duke said to the footman who sat at the back of the carriage, "walk with Miss Milton and Miss Mary to the Bear Inn. I shall meet you all there."

Evie helped Mary to walk toward the inn, and the closer they became to the town, the more the color appeared in Mary's cheeks. Her demeanor improved. Her eyes brightened, all good signs that a walk was just the thing to make Mary feel better. "I do believe the carriage was what made you unwell, Mary. We shall have lunch, and with any optimism, you'll be well enough to continue this afternoon toward London."

"I think I shall be well, Miss Milton. I'm so very sorry for being such an inconvenience. I thought my sickness whenever I traveled was past me. It seems it is not."

"No, and we didn't have time this morning to have a hearty breakfast before we left, so that may not have helped you at all, either." Evie spied the whitewashed inn in the bustling market town and started toward its front door. It was a large, coaching inn, many people bustled about it, and all of them looking very busy with their employment. A pretty bow window ran from the first to the second floor and made her think of Whites in London and its famous bow window.

The duke, who must have been watching them from indoors, stepped outside and into the sunshine, and a little flutter of pleasure settled in her stomach.

He was such a handsome man. Her sister was either addled of mind or she indeed was in love with Mr. Brown to have thrown a duke over for a farmer. Evie could not see herself parting from the duke should he offer for her hand. Had he chosen her to be his bride, she would've made him fall in love with her, no matter how long that may have taken. The duke watched them walk toward the inn, and Evie shivered as his gaze took in her appearance, sliding over her like a caress. If he thought she had not noticed he was mistaken. There was little that she did not discern when it came to the duke.

Did he like what he saw? She supposed now that her sister had run off with another man, she no longer needed to worry about Lucy's plea for Evie to steal him away and force him to end their betrothal. Evie could only hope that her sister was married by the time they caught up with them. The duke may be disappointed for a time, but surely his heart would heal. That's if his heart was ever involved regarding her sister, and sometimes, the way he spoke and the way he looked at her, she could not help but doubt that was the case.

They came to stand before the duke, and he bowed, holding out his arm for Evie. "Miss Mary, you look much better already. Miss Milton, I have lunch served in the private parlor."

The inn inside was as busy as it was on the outside. The taproom was full of tables and people taking repast. Some sat at the bar, eating and drinking and busy discussing all sorts of matters while they waited for the next stagecoach or change of horses.

Her maid stared as if she'd never seen such a sight before, and Evie pulled her to where the duke was leading them. He opened a door and gestured for them to enter. The private parlor was a bright, airy room that overlooked the pretty River Dun. The table was full of bread and cold meats, cheese, and a steaming pot of tea.

Evie's mouth watered at the sight and she went forward, sitting down across from the window so she could watch the goings-on on the river. "This looks wonderful, Your Grace. Thank you for the delicious lunch."

He sat across from her, filling his plate with a selection of what lay before them. "Of course. It is no trouble."

Evie poured herself a cup of tea and sipping her dark

brew, sighed in relief at having a cup. "How refreshing. I do not think I could survive without tea. Do you not agree, Mary?"

Mary giggled, and the duke smiled, cutting a large piece of cheese and placing it on his plate.

"I do not, Miss Milton."

"We're to travel to Reading next. It will be several hours in the carriage on rough, uneven roads I'm afraid. We will not make the next town until nightfall. Do you think you'll be well enough to continue, Miss Mary?"

"I believe so, Your Grace. Now that I'm having something to eat, all will be well, I'm sure."

IT WAS NOT THE CASE. Finn stood beside his horse, who grazed the grass at the side of the road while Miss Mary heaved up her luncheon for the third time in as many minutes. Not a mile up the road and the carriage stopped so the maid could be sick. It wasn't to be borne, and it would not be able to continue. If he were to catch up to Miss Lucy Milton before she eloped with her preferred gentleman admirer, they had to travel swift and without issue.

He needed to marry Lucy. And he needed to marry her soon before he ran out of time and lost all his wealth to his cousin, bar his estate.

Impatience ate at him, and he sighed, his mind furiously working with what to do. "That's it. This cannot continue. Miss Milton, you shall ride behind me on my horse until we reach Reading. Dickens and Charlie will escort Miss Mary back to Hungerford in the carriage and organize a private carriage to return her home to Marlborough. It is obvious that she will be unable to travel the full distance to London, nevertheless Gretna, should we need to go that far. I do apologize, Miss Milton, but we cannot dally any longer."

"But I'll be unchaperoned," Miss Milton said, her eyes wide with scandal.

She would be, unfortunately, but there was little he could do about it. The maid could not travel with them. Her stomach was not built for long distances, obviously. "We will go as brother and sister until London, and from there, we will take an unmarked carriage north to stop curious eyes.

"Dickens," he said, turning to his driver. "We shall wait for you in Reading."

"Right ye are, Your Grace," Dickens said, climbing back up onto the box.

"How long do you think we'll be in Reading? What if we run into someone we know? I'll be ruined."

"It is a risk we must take to bring back your sister. I'm sorry, but my mind is made up."

Miss Milton's lush mouth thinned into a displeased line before she turned to Mary, taking her maid's hands. She was very kind to her lady's maid, talking to her more as an equal than a woman who was her servant. As a duke, he'd never much thought about the people who worked for him, so long as they went about their duties and acted acceptably due to their position in a ducal household. He was always fair and kind, but not friendly. It was a novel thing to see.

"What are your thoughts, Mary? Are you happy with this plan?"

Mary nodded, her hair falling out of her many pins after a day of casting up her accounts. "I cannot continue, Miss Milton. I'm so very sorry to do this to you."

Miss Milton helped Mary back toward the carriage,

her hand idly rubbing the maid's back in comfort. "It'll be well, Mary. I just hope that the ride back home is not too taxing for you."

"As do I," Mary said, stepping up in the equipage. "Thank you, Miss Milton. Your Grace," the maid said, before leaning back on the squabs and closing her eyes.

"Ensure Miss Mary is safely stowed on a private carriage back to Miss Milton's estate. Pay handsomely that should she need to stop, that the driver does so whenever required. We shall meet you at Reading tomorrow."

"Very good, Your Grace," the driver said, clicking the reins to turn the equipage about, before they started back down the road they'd just traveled.

"Come, Miss Milton," Finn said, holding out his hand to help her up onto his horse. She cast him a glance, taking in his horse, and her eyes widened. No doubt the idea of riding his high beast and traveling all the way to Reading the least of her desires.

She turned and waved the carriage away and then did as he bade, striding over to him and holding out her hand for him to clasp.

The moment he wrapped his fingers about her own, heat crept up his arm and into his chest. He heaved her onto his horse, wrapping her hands about his stomach and securing them before him. It was not necessary that she hold him so tight, but against his better judgment, he helped her to. She leaned into his back, hugging him tight and the feel of her legs, her arms wrapped about him, made his mind seize with notions. Other imaginings of them together, wrapped close and tight.

He closed his eyes, steeling himself for the long-spun afternoon ride to Reading. Without further ado, he turned his mount and kicked it into a canter, needing to distract himself from the woman behind him. Finn soon realized his mistake of placing Evie behind him. She undulated against his back with every step, and he now knew the feel of her breasts. Soft and full and not his to touch.

He was marrying someone else, he reminded himself. The woman behind him was his betrothed's sister. She was prohibited to him.

The hours loomed ahead of him. Hours of torture mixed with pleasure.

He would not survive it, of that he was certain.

CHAPTER 6

Evie's bottom had gone numb hours before, and she was no longer aware of her legs. They too ached, and with every step of the horse's hooves, she cringed, wanting to get off the beast and never, ever to get on another one.

To ride so many hours when one was not used to the exercise was not to be borne. An outing around Hyde Park was one thing, but miles on the back of a horse, over uneven, slippery, and sometimes rocky terrain was quite another. She would be thankful for the carriage again tomorrow, and not only because her bottom would thank her for it. She questioned she could last another day seated behind the Duke of Carlisle without her hands doing something uncomely, like caress his chest.

She glanced over his shoulder, her eyes moving to take in his profile. For all the pain her bottom was currently experiencing, her body suffered nothing but pleasure. One that the duke wrought within her.

He was so very fetching. His straight nose and chiseled jaw and sweet-looking lips left her breathless and aching and not just her behind. The idea that should her sister's plan to marry another be thwarted and the duke became her brother in law, Evie knew she would have to limit her time with her sibling from the day of their marriage.

There was something about the duke that she liked, and deep down, wanted for herself. Silly of her, really, as she'd never thought too much about him when they were in London and circulating within the same set of friends. But now, out in the country and headed toward London, there was little else to imagine. It was all she thought about.

Evie flexed her hands, feeling the hard, muscular lines beneath her fingers before clasping them together to stop her inappropriate caress. He stilled at her touch, something he'd done often during the trip north. Her breasts felt heavy in her traveling gown; her nipples hardened points from slipping against his back. For a time, she'd leaned her head against his spine, merely trying to grapple with the pleasures she was taking from the duke while she could.

He was so overwhelming that if they did not stop soon, she would be tempted to rub up against him like a cat seeking a satisfying pet.

A carriage rumbled past them, and Evie glanced ahead to see the beginnings of a substantial village. Relief poured through her that she'd been soon on her feet. For all the delightful reactions that the duke brought forth within her, she would be thankful to stand.

Within a short amount of time, the duke pulled up his horse before the Crown Inn, a redbrick building with a stable yard to one side. He reached around, holding out his arm. "Here, let me help you down," he said, meeting her gaze.

Evie diverted her attention to his hand and clasped it

tightly. Why did he have to be so consuming? So generous and charming?

So unavailable.

Well, at least in his opinion, he was. He was right at this moment, chasing after her sister to beg her to marry him still, even though she was in love with someone else.

The thought of him doing all that he had set out to achieve filled her with despair, and she slipped from the horse. She had expected her legs to hold her upright, but instead, her knees gave way, and she continued her downward spiral until her bottom hit the dirt and rocky courtyard.

"Miss Milton," the duke shouted, jumping from his mount and bending down to assist her. He clasped her hands and helped her to stand.

"Thank you, Your Grace," she said, reaching behind her and trying to massage her bottom without being apparent to those around them. "I seem to have sat too long today."

The duke frowned down at her, all seriousness. "I should have asked if you were accustomed to such lengthy rides. I apologize for the lapse in care, Miss Milton."

"Evie, please. Miss Milton makes me sound like a spinster."

He threw her a small smile, before handing his horse to a waiting stable lad and leading her indoors. "You may call me Finn then in return. Especially since we're to be brother and sister for a time."

"That is true," she said, returning his smile before taking his arm.

They headed inside the inn and stopped in the taproom. It, too, was similar to the one they had luncheoned at earlier today in Hungerford.

"Two of your best rooms, if you please. For one night."

The publican rubbed his hands down his grimy apron and studied them both. "I only have one room left. 'Tis the best I have." The publican's eyes narrowed on Evie, and she stepped closer to the duke, hiding a little behind his arm.

"My sister and I need separate rooms. I will pay handsomely."

The man shrugged, crossing his arms across his broad chest. "Canna help ye, I'm sorry. I ave one room. Take it or leave it."

Evie glanced at the duke and didn't miss the pained expression that crossed his features. She supposed it wasn't her he wanted to be alone with but her sister. No matter what Lucy thought of the duke, Evie had no idea if his feelings were genuine. Everything that she'd seen of him when around her sibling told her they were.

Perhaps he was heartbroken that her sister had run off with another man.

"We'll take the room," he said, his voice bored. "Have a maid bring up a hip bath for my sister, and we'll be looking for a substantial dinner, with wine. Also, extra bedding as I'll be sleeping on the floor."

The publican's eyes brightened, sensing the man before him was of some means. "I canna bring up a mattress that we have spare if ye would like. Ye may place it before the fire to keep warm."

"That will do very well. Thank you."

The man bellowed out for a Masie, and a young, disheveled woman ran into the taproom, her cheeks ruddy from exhaustion, a small line of sweat across her brow.

"Take the gentleman and his sister up to our best room and then come back to me for further instruction."

The young woman bobbed a curtsy and gestured for them to follow. "Of course, Papa." She took in their appearance and then gestured for them to follow. "This way, if you please."

They climbed a short flight of stairs and walked along a narrow passageway before Maisie unlocked a door and pushed it wide, showing off their best bedchamber for their guests. The room had a stoked fire set and ready for the next guests to occupy the space. The maid quickly went over to it, and using a tinder box lit the kindling.

Two chairs sat before the hearth. A large, wooden bed lay in the middle of the room and beyond that a small antechamber with a door. Evie walked over to inspect where the door led and found a water closet and small hip bath inside. Evie supposed they at least could bathe and take care of their personal needs without the other hearing and seeing anything.

A small mercy since they had to share the same chamber.

Evie waited at the end of the bed until the maid left. The moment the door closed behind the servant, she went over and pulled the bedding back, checking the sheets for lice. The bedding was clean and smelled of lemon and was thankfully free of bugs.

"You may have the bed. I'll sleep before the fire on the mattress they're bringing up."

She strolled about the room, looking out the bank of windows that overlooked the main thoroughfare of the town, the bustling carriages, and people. Had her sister even traveled through here on her way to London? Did they go to London first, or did they travel north by some other means? Their journey north may be a waste of everyone's time, especially if Lucy was already married to her Mr. Brown. Or worse, was hiding somewhere like Bath.

Movement out the corner of her eye caught her attention, and she turned to see the duke pulling his shirt up over his head, throwing it haphazardly on top of the wing-back chair before the now-crackling fire. His cravat, waist-coat, and coat already discarded.

Her mouth dried at the sight of his chiseled body. Never before had she seen a man in such a near-naked state. Her fingers itched to run down the center of his chest, the slight decline that pointed toward his breeches a road she'd certainly like to travel. She bit her lip, all delicious, wicked thoughts entering her head. What would his skin taste like if her tongue was to poke out and lick it? Was the modicum of chest hair coarse? Would it tickle her face if she were to lay her head against him?

Evie turned to look out the window. Wherever did that thought come from? She shut her eyes a moment, disgusted at herself for the wayward contemplation. If he caught her ogling him, the spinster sister of his betrothed, it would not be borne. No matter how much she may wish to be of interest to him, she could not be. He was meant for another, and she would have to remember that until she saw her sister was indeed married and happy with her choice.

The realization struck her mute, and she stared out the window, wondering what she would do about the truth. Her sister had asked her to help break off the understanding, but to do so without him knowing that Lucy was in favor of this plan made her look like an evil, villainous sister.

But then, he was aware that her sister had run off with another man, so he must at least have had the thought that Lucy did not want him as he'd hoped. Not that Evie dreamed of marrying the duke herself, but she certainly wouldn't mind a stolen kiss or two from the handsome beast. And if that kiss led to more, or they found that they suited better than he did with her sister, there was nothing wrong with that. Indeed, never before had her stomach fluttered, or her heart raced as much as it did when she was around His Grace.

The very sight of him without his shirt had made her ache in places she hadn't known could and made her long for things she'd thought lost to her. Maybe her sister running off and breaking her betrothal was a sign, a possibility that Evie may have a chance at happiness after all.

She stole a glimpse of the duke, who was now hunting through his traveling bag, looking perhaps for a change of clothes. All of this, however, depended on whether he saw her in a romantic light, which at present, she did not think he did.

"I'm going to go wash up," he said, striding past her as if walking about half-naked in a room with a woman who was not his wife was a natural occurrence.

The rogue…

A knock sounded at the door, and Evie bade the maid enter. Two burly men brought in hot buckets of water that they placed near the entrance to the water closet, along with a hearty meal and wine that they set up on a small table before the fire.

"We'll be back in an hour to clean away the dishes and to make up the second bed," the maid said, bobbing a quick curtsy before leaving.

Evie sat before the fire and poured two glasses of wine, the smell of lamb and vegetables making her stomach rumble. The duke joined her, dressed appropriately once more, but still as handsome as sin.

A self-satisfied growl left his lips at the sight of the food, and she fought not to react to the sound. She was not herself with him. Never before had she reacted in such a way to a man, so why was she doing so with the duke? When in London she hadn't crooned like a besotted debutante when dancing with him, but then in London they had not been alone, and she had been only too busy trying to remember the steps of their dance than worrying about what he thought of her. If at all.

"I'm ravenous," he said, smiling at her as he took a sip of his wine.

Evie knew the feeling well and not always for the food that was before her. She nodded, smiling. "The stew and bread do smell delicious. Thank you for all of this, Finn. I shall repay you my fare to London when I'm able. I apologize that my father was unable to before we departed."

"I understand your father's predicament. This is not a mammoth expense. I think I can withstand a few days on the road with my *sister*," he said, his mouth twisting into a wicked grin.

Evie chuckled at his remark against their lie to the landlord of the inn that they were related. She picked up her fork, stabbing at a potato. The stew burst a kaleidoscope of flavor onto her tongue, the meat tender and flavorsome, the vegetables cooked to perfection, and not overdone. The bread hot and spiced. The red wine complemented the lamb and left Evie's tired muscles soothed and relaxed as if she'd soaked in a deep, hot bath.

"I've never traveled to Scotland before. I just hope the carriage arrives by tomorrow, so I don't have to ride behind you again on your horse. I do not believe my body is capable of that many hours again on the back of your mount."

He smiled. "I do apologize again, Evie. I should have asked you if you were able to ride for such a distance. I will not make that mistake again."

She shrugged. One of the main reasons behind her discomfort was the fact that she'd had to hold on to him for so many hours. Even now, her fingers could feel the contours of his body, the heat from his skin, the smell of sandalwood, and clean, pressed linen. Now that she'd seen him without a shirt, well, that image was imprinted into her mind and didn't help her body recover from being pressed up hard against him for hours on end.

"Please do not feel as if you have to sleep on the floor on my account. The bed is large enough for both of us, and as you know, no one knows you or I here, even if caught together." Evie snapped her mouth shut, unsure where the scandalous thought came from. Or perhaps she did know. From years of wishing to find a husband like her friends had, who would love her as passionately and devotedly as they were. Her body, at times, physically ached with the need to have what they did. To be as happy as they were.

Even so, she and the duke could not share the same bed. The floor would have to do for him.

He shook his head, sipping his wine. "I cannot do that. You're an unmarried maid and my betrothed's sister. It would not be right."

Evie thought about his response. He needed to know that his chances of marrying Lucy were nil now that her sister had run away with another man. Surely, he could see that. "Lucy is probably married by now, and even if she isn't, surely you do not wish to marry a woman who is in love with someone else." The duke deserved happiness, like everyone else. There was no reason why he could not take his time in courting another and then marrying them. He was only young and had plenty of time to choose a bride.

"You do not know that she's married."

"No," she agreed, understanding too well that Lucy did not want to marry the duke even if there wasn't a Mr. Brown involved in her sister's elopement.

"Of course, I do not want to marry a woman who had

thrown herself at someone else, but there are other things at play."

"What things?" Evie asked, studying him as he sat forward, adjusting his seat.

"Many things. Money has been changed hands between your father and myself. Marriage contracts have been signed."

All true, unfortunately, but even so, until the vows were spoken, no one was obligated to follow through on the agreement. "Lucy and Mr. Brown are a day ahead of us with travel. For all we know, they could have gone on horseback instead of a carriage, making them faster than we are in a carriage. He may have secured a special license, and they plan on marrying in London. You may be too late."

"I may be too late, but I have to try."

"Why?" Evie asked, curious now. He went to adjust his cravat that wasn't there, not after the stripping of his shirt earlier. Instead, his action brought her gaze to his neck and the shirt that was only partially buttoned. He had a lovely throat. She looked down at her meal, needing to distract her view of him.

"We had an agreement. I'm a duke. Who turns down being a duchess for heaven's sake?"

"Finn," she said, her tone a little chiding. "I feel I should warn you that should my sister still be unmarried by the time we meet with her, she may not wish to marry you, and I shall not force her. Nor will I allow you to do so." Especially when she knew that Lucy did not want to marry the duke at all. What a terrible mess this all was.

He stared at her a moment, his eyes narrowing. "I will not force her either, but I think I am owed an explanation and or at least an apology. I do not like scandal and strife. I've had enough of that to last me two lifetimes, and I will not see my name dragged down and gossiped about London as the latest *on dit*, all because of your sister's actions." He paused, wiping his mouth roughly with his napkin. "If she does not wish to marry me, I will ensure she is married, and therefore, my name cannot and will not be associated with her again."

Evie placed down her fork and leaned back in her chair, exhaustion swamping her all of a sudden. "I fear you may have no choice in that."

"I fear you are wrong," he said, digging back into his meal with gusto.

Evie stood, starting toward the private water closet they had. "I'm going to pour the buckets of hot water into the hip bath and freshen up."

"Oh, let me help you with those," he said, standing and striding toward the buckets before she had a chance of telling him she was more than capable. Evie stood back and watched as he poured the four buckets into the tub, the muscles on his back flexing whenever he bent over and tempting her yet again.

"Thank you." Evie stood aside as he passed.

"You're very welcome." He stopped beside her, and she looked up, meeting his deep-blue orbs that were heavy-lidded and made her skin prickle in awareness. "Enjoy your bath, Evie." His voice was deep and husky.

Evie forced her legs to move toward the room, but stopped at the threshold, throwing him a glance over her shoulder. "I shall…Finn."

CHAPTER 7

Finn was in hell. Literally. The sound of the hip bath water splashing in the adjacent room, the moans and sighs from Evie whenever she relaxed in the small tub was torture. His mind filled with images of her naked, sweet form, of her breasts turning into a rosy-pink hue from the warm water. Her skin supple and fragrant from the soap.

She would taste delicious, and he wanted to kiss every part of her. Fill himself with her flavor and gorge himself until he could not sustain any more.

He leaned forward on his chair, clasping his head in his hands. He was betrothed, damn it. He was supposed to marry Evie's sister.

The thought gave him pause. He was running out of time to court and marry anyone else from his home county. Not that he had many to choose from. Lucy Milton was the only one who suited his needs and his father's decree in his will. Young to bear children and born from a gentleman's family.

The elder Miss Milton could substitute for her younger sister, he supposed, but she was much older. Less likely to give him sons. She was a spinster well on her way to sitting with the matrons of the *ton* each Season, watching over their young charges instead of being a new wife.

He sighed, hating the thought of Evie being shelved in such a way. She may not be suitable for him, a duke who needed healthy sons and soon, but she would be suitable for a rich gentleman, or even a lord.

In truth, he needed to think about what he would do should Lucy be married. Why she agreed to marry him in the first place if she was in love with someone else was beyond him, but that didn't matter now. If he could convince Miss Lucy to relent on her current course, return to Wiltshire and marry him instead, all would be well. Before his sixty days were up and he was left penniless. Not that the idea of marrying the chit filled him with any sense of expectation now. She'd made her choice, as absurd as it was, and she should live with it. No, he would ensure she was married so he could ask another to be his bride, return home and find one posthaste.

The door to the water closet opened, and Evie moved into the room. With each footstep, her shift swayed against her legs and gave him a delightful view of her ankles. She had donned a long dressing gown, giving her discretion, and yet, still, his blood heated at the sight of her.

Her hair was no longer pinned up but lay against her shoulders in dark, loose curls. Her lips pinkened from the bath, and her skin was glowing. He tore his gaze to the fire. He didn't need to look at her any more than he obliged to. She was too tempting, too sweet and innocent for him to be having such thoughts about her. Of what he'd like to do with her.

Of how he'd ravish those full lips, kiss her neck and suckle upon breasts that would haunt his dreams from this night onward.

She sat in the chair across from him and unable to deny himself, he took his fill, from her bare feet to her delectable lips.

"Are you sure you wish to sleep on the floor? You are paying for the room. I feel bad for you having to sleep so rough."

At the mention of his bed that will be on the floor, a knock sounded on the door. Finn bade them enter and stood when a young manservant carried in a mattress, a maid following on his heels with linens and blankets.

"Here you are, sir," the maid said, helping the young man set up the bed before the hearth. Finn and Evie stood aside and watched as they quickly set the bed up on the floor. "Will there be anything else, sir?"

"No, that will be all. Thank you." He followed them to the door and threw the bolt across as their footsteps echoed down the hall.

Evie stared at his bed a moment before meeting his gaze. "Well, if you're sure then. Goodnight, Finn."

"Goodnight, Evie."

He didn't watch as she settled under the blankets or look to see when she fell asleep and rolled onto her back. At the sound of even, deep breaths, he took her in, a smile quirking his lips as he noticed that she slept in the center of the bed, one of her arms laying out to the side and taking up most of the spare room.

Finn sat for several more hours before the fire, watching as the wood turned to ash. He stoked it high for the night, before settling himself into his makeshift bed. Surprisingly it was warmer than he thought it would be, and yet sleep eluded him. The soft exhales coming from the other side of the room made him crave things he should not want, and it wasn't to be borne.

He was in hell.

. . .

SOMETIME IN THE middle of the night, Evie shivered awake. She sat up, groping to find her blankets that she had kicked off and that lay heaped at the end of the bed. The room was dark, save for the few slivers of moonlight that came in through the closed curtains.

She glanced toward where the duke slept, a mound before the fire that glowed with hot coals but no wood. Evie slipped out of bed, making her way carefully over to the fire. She picked up one of the coarse logs that were stacked neatly at one side and threw it on, the wood added to the hot coals sizzled and spat a moment before it caught alight and delightful heat chased the chill away.

Checking that the fire grate was in place, she tiptoed past the duke. For a time, she would sit in the chair and warm herself before returning to bed. There was a draft in the room and one that had chilled her to her bones.

Her foot caught on his mattress, and she tumbled, unable to right herself. Evie came down hard onto the duke, buffeting her fall with her hands as much as she could, even so, the feel of his solid, naked chest against her palms made her body burn. "I'm so sorry, Finn."

"What on earth are you doing?" he said, his words slurred with sleep.

She cringed, could just imagine what he was thinking. That she was throwing herself at him, quite literally. It was bad enough that she'd had thoughts to do precisely that, nevertheless doing so without his approval. "I was stoking the fire, and I tripped on your bedding. I do apologize."

His hands came around to settle on her waist, and he lifted her off him, setting her to one side of his bed. "Are you well? Did you hurt yourself when you fell?"

Only her pride. He probably thought she'd fallen on

him on purpose to make him manhandle her. Heat bloomed on her cheeks, and she was thankful that the room was filled with shadows so he could not see her embarrassment. "I am well. I do apologize," she stammered, moving toward the side of the bed to go back to her own.

"Wait." His arms ran over hers, warming her more than any fire would. Evie stilled, biting back a sigh of pleasure at his touch. "Your skin is as cold as ice."

His statement pulled her from her thoughts. "That's why I came over to the fire. I was going to warm myself in a chair for a time."

He pushed down his blankets and patted the space beside him. "Come, lie by me. I'll keep you warm. No one will know, and no harm will come to your reputation. I promise you that."

She stared at the space beside him with longing. She would like nothing more than to be near the duke and all his sweet handsomeness, but she could not. To lie beside him was a temptation she did not think she could deny herself.

"I shouldn't." She hesitated, her voice breathless. There was no hope for her. Whenever she was around him, she acted like a silly little fool who was experiencing her first turn about a ballroom floor with a man.

"But you will." He clasped her hand, pulling her down to lie beside him before righting the blankets to cover them both. His arm sneaked out about her waist, and he hoisted her up against his chest.

Evie stared into the darkness of the room, his chest a solid length of muscle against her back. Comforting warmth seeped into her chilled veins, and she could feel her eyes grow heavy with sleep even though her body thrummed with need.

She wiggled, getting comfortable, and his grip tightened. "Be still." His breath tickled her neck, and she bit her lip, tempted to wiggle some more to see what the duke would do.

"Sorry, I was trying to get comfortable." Evie fell to sleep with a grin on her lips.

EVIE WOKE with a sense of contentment. Sometime during the night, she'd turned in the bed and was now draped over the duke. Her head lay nestled on his shoulder, her leg laying over one of his and her arm slumped across his chest where she could feel the steady beat of his heart.

She should move, slip out of bed, and dress, and yet she could not. She didn't want to. To lie in a man's arms, held tight against him in sleep was a delicious experience that she'd never had before. It was new and kind of lovely. Who would not like such a way to start the day?

He shifted a little beside her, pulling her close and laying a soft kiss atop her head before he stilled. Evie wondered at the unexpected gesture; sure he had not meant to kiss her.

"I do apologize, Evie. Sleep always makes me a little hazy come morning. I did not mean to accost you so."

She glanced up at him and met his gaze. Her heart beat a little faster in her chest at his heavy-lidded inspection of her. For the life of her, she could not move. If he were like any of the other gentleman who prowled the *ton*, surely he may lean down and kiss her? Make use of the opportunity when it arose. She wanted him to kiss her. Her first kiss and possibly her last ought to be with a man like the duke. If she were not ever kissed again in her life, at least she would have experienced one kiss with a man who she valued and liked.

He sighed, rolling onto his back to stare at the wooden-beamed ceiling before he left the bed, striding toward the chair where he'd left his clothing the night before.

His back flexed as he hastily pulled on his shirt, his waistcoat, and threw his cravat about his neck untied. "I'll go downstairs and order breakfast and check on the whereabouts of our carriage. I shall return presently."

Evie sat up, holding the blankets to her chest and stared at the door as it slammed closed, leaving her alone. Was his hasty exit due to his reaction to her? Reactions that he had not counted upon. They were going to be around each other for some time yet, weeks perhaps, if he became satisfied that Lucy was married and no scandal will darken his name, maybe he would look for another to be his wife. They certainly rubbed along well enough and had things in common, not wealth or connections, but where they were born, duty to do the right thing, and mutual friends. They suited better than the duke and Lucy did, at least Evie thought so.

What she felt whenever around the duke was new and nothing like the lackluster emotions that other men had produced in the past. Her body seemed to come alive, to yearn to be near him, to want to listen to his authoritative, commanding voice speak. The way he had held her last night and his impromptu kiss this morning had to mean something.

Did it not?

CHAPTER 8

An hour later, after a hearty breakfast of bacon, ham, and coffee, they were on the road, heading toward Slough. He hoped they would make London by nightfall, especially now that upon entering the taproom, the landlord of the inn jovially notified him that their carriage would momentarily arrive.

Finn was thankful for it. He wasn't sure how he was going to survive another day with Evie behind him on the horse. Her chest bouncing up against his back, her hands slipping to sit at the tops of his breeches and making him wish her grip would move lower to caress him. The very thought of having her had filled his dreams, and he'd awoken unsure if his dreams had not come pleasantly true. Without thought, he had kissed her and pulled her into his arms like a lover after a good romp. Before sense had rocked him back into reality.

No, at least in the carriage, he would be able to think straight and keep a safe distance from the delectable Evie, who was not suitable as a bride, no matter how comely she was. A spinster well in the making who was past her childbearing years. If he was being forced into marriage, his wife must be a woman five years his junior at least and not the same age. Even a debutante would do if he could find one from Wiltshire and near his home in Marlborough.

They pulled out of the inn's yard and through the high street of the town. His betrothed had run off with another man, could be at this very moment married to Mr. Brown, ending his ability to marry her before his sixty-day deadline.

What to do? Should he continue north from London to chase down Miss Lucy, it would all but stop his ability from courting someone else in time to marry unless he threw away his conflicting thoughts on Lucy's sister and wooed Evie instead. He would seek out his doctor in London and ask him his opinion on older mothers and their ability to have children. The Duchess of Whitstone and the Countess Duncannon had both birthed children last year, and they were of the same age as Evie. Maybe her time to be a mother wasn't behind her after all.

Finn frowned down at the carriage floor, his gaze slipping to Evie's traveling boots, which were worn and in need of new soles. Each moment he was around Evie, he was tempted to ravish that pretty little mouth of hers. A mouth that occupied his thoughts more than Miss Lucy's had ever done so.

The carriage rumbled on the gravelly, uneven road, only the sound of the wheels on the ground and his driver talking to the accompanying footman could be heard. Evie was unusually quiet. A thick book open in her lap, and yet he'd not seen her turn a page for the past five minutes. He could not but wonder what she was thinking on, or pretending to read. Was she thinking of him? Finn inwardly groaned at the sight of her bottom lip clenched tight between her teeth in thought. Evie flummoxed him, tempted and intrigued him more than he was comfortable with.

How had he not noticed her in London these past years? Miss Milton had been no more than a passing acquaintance, a mutual friend through the Duke of Whitstone. A conundrum and a shameful one, really.

Because she wasn't high enough on the peerage ladder for you to look.

Finn ground his teeth at the little chiding voice that whispered in his mind. And the voice was right. He'd always planned to marry a woman of wealth and position and not anytime soon. He had his father to thank for rushing him to the altar. Evie and her sister were neither of those things, and yet his scandalous, nefarious father was no doubt laughing down on him, or up on him perhaps, at the position his son was now facing due to his own stupid will.

Now he had no other option but to marry a woman such as the Milton sisters.

Tonight they would reach London. It would be late, a fortunate occurrence, and one that should stop anyone from seeing them together and without a chaperone. They would break in London and head off for Gretna in an unmarked carriage. The less conspicuous they were on the road, the better.

Finn leaned back against the squabs, watching Evie. Warmth seeped into his bones on the chill morning at the thought of having her under his roof. He'd never had a woman sleep in his home before. Not since his mama was alive, at least.

Evie was a temptation he doubted he could ignore for long, and so it made sense to satisfy his father's will that his attentions would have to turn to the woman before him. There was no time left to find anyone else more suitable for his needs, and he liked Evie. She was sensible and beautiful, and as a duke, he could never marry someone who was nonsensical.

A short time later, his carriage pulled to the side of the road. Finn checked their location and in the distance could see Windsor Castle and Eton College nestled on the hills beyond. They were not far from Salt Hill.

The carriage dipped as his coachman climbed down from his box before he came up to the window. "The horses need a rest, Your Grace. This is a pretty view as any if ye wish to stroll for a time, break your fast with the picnic the innkeeper packed ye."

"Perhaps we should break for lunch, Your Grace? I am a little starved."

Finn glanced about and noted the open fields to both sides of the road and the forest that circled those fields farther away. "Of course," he said, opening the carriage door and stepping down. He turned and helped Evie outside, and the moment their hands touched a shock of awareness ran up his arm, and he had to force himself to let go of her hand before his coachman noticed his peculiarity.

Evie walked out onto a grassy field that gave an unimpeded view of the grand Castle and school for boys. "This is a good a place as any to set up for lunch."

Finn joined her, crouching down to sit with her in the grass. The ground was warm, if not a little damp. He'd not had a picnic like this since he was a child, and his nanny had taken him. "We're only a few hours from London from here. We shall break overnight at my London home before setting off for Scotland in a day or so. If we make good time, we may catch up with your sister before she ruins herself any further."

Not that he was going to save her now. Miss Lucy had

made her choice and it was not him. She would live or die by her own sword. But he would ensure that Mr. Brown married the silly chit and by doing so, eliminating his association with Miss Lucy. He would not allow anyone of the gossiping *ton* to use his family as fodder for their amusement ever again. He'd endured such an existence when his father was alive. He would not do so again.

Evie sighed, and he glanced at her quickly, wondering what that sweet sound meant and hating the fact that his body reacted to it without warning or sense. "Why are you sighing and not saying anything, Evie? Is there something wrong with my plan?"

She opened the picnic basket that she had carried from the carriage, taking out two bread rolls and handing him one. "I'm curious as to why you would continue to chase Lucy when she's run off with another man. As a duke, I would think your choice is endless, and you may marry whomever you choose."

If only it were that simple. "Miss Lucy is from my home county and is young, and I thought unattached. She is from a good family and would have suited me very well." He paused. "However, I have given some thought to what you've said these past two days, about Lucy and her actions, and I no longer see a future between us. My travels north are now to ensure she marries, and neither mine or your family suffer the consequences socially of her choice."

"When it comes to matters of the heart, do you know that you speak with very little emotion? You sound as though you did not care for Lucy at all, or minded that she had run off with another man."

"I'm not a man of fanciful emotions or words," he stated, hating the fact that he was termed as someone without feeling.

She bit into a piece of ham, and his attention snapped

to her mouth. Dear Lord, she chewed with the utmost sweetness.

"My father is a true gentleman, but we're not nobility. We're not rich nor are we part of the *beau monde*, and so I find it strange your courtship of my sister. Out of nowhere and without warning, I received a letter from Lucy that she was engaged and with you. A duke."

Evie was far more intelligent than he initially thought, and if he didn't watch his answers, he had no doubt she'd find out that he'd only offered for Lucy because he'd had no other choice. Why would he speak with emotion when he had none when it came to Lucy?

He was a bastard, and he should have fought his father's will instead of allowing his absurd clause to run his life.

"It is as you already know. I had business with your father and met Miss Lucy. She was a pleasant and jovial type of woman, and I thought she would suit as my bride." The lie tasted sour on his tongue.

He met Evie's steely, rich-brown eyes, and he had the overwhelming feeling that she could read his lie as if he'd written the word across his forehead. One eyebrow arched and he fought not to fidget where he sat. "Lucy has chosen another. Are you so set on your original course?"

"I cannot marry your sister now. Not after what she's done," he admitted. "I will not be part of such a scandal—a nefarious start to one's married life. But as a gentleman, I shall ensure she is married and limit the scandal on you and your family. Women who run away with their lovers always impact those who are left behind."

"I suppose London will have a juicy time with what Lucy has done, and I shall be talked about until the next scandalous thing occurs and takes their interest elsewhere." Her dejected tone did something odd to him inside, and he threw a piece of bread into his mouth less he be tempted to pull her into his arms and soothe her hurt.

The idea of Evie being talked about, taunted, and given the cut direct wasn't something he ever wished to see. For one, she did not deserve it and two, he had been right where Evie now sat. His father was forever causing scandals that were talked about for months. His friends at Eton would ask him of the stories, taunt and laugh at him. He'd not let that happen to her.

He poured them both a glass of red wine, handing one to Evie, determined to remove the dejected, sad expression that had befallen her features.

"What about you, Evie? You live in London and circulate in the same society as I do. I would have thought that a woman as attractive and intelligent as yourself would have been married by now." Finn swallowed a robust sip of wine. Today he seemed determined to bury himself in inappropriate compliments.

Her cheeks pinkened, and Finn had to admit that sometimes saying things that were not the way of a gentleman, or what he should talk to an unmarried woman about was worth it. Certainly, if he made her blush and made her porcelain skin turn a pretty shade of pink.

"No, there is not," she said, refusing to look at him. "I live in London with Molly and have not walked the same path as some of our friends have. My age doesn't make me the most sought-after woman at a ball, not that it ever made much difference when I was younger. As you know my family is not titled or rich. We're known more in Bath than in London, and I suppose I was found lacking."

"You are not lacking in any way," he said, cringing at his use of more inappropriate words. Soon he'd be as infamous as his father. He studied her a moment, watched as she chewed her sandwich of bread and ham. She tempted him. In fact, he wanted to do wicked and delightful things with her.

Since his father's death, he'd lived mostly in Wiltshire, looking after his estates and business dealings. Seeing Evie again, spending time with her, more time than he'd spent with Miss Lucy, all that occupied his mind since leaving Marlborough was what the woman before him would look like under him in his bed. Her long, chocolate locks spread about his pillow. Her sweet moans whispered against his ear as he brought her to climax.

"I'm sorry that we did not get to know each other well in London. We have mutual friends, have been to numerous balls and parties together and yet we have never spoken as honest and open as we have these past two days. I'm sorry for that." And he was. Never had he said anything more true. If he was to change his plan and court Evie to suit the clause in his father's will, more conversations such as these were what they needed. Evie required to like him in return and trust him.

A small smile played about her mouth, and he wanted to close the space between them and kiss her. To see if her lips were as soft as he imagined. It had been all he'd imagined last evening when he'd pulled her into his bed and hoisted her up against his chest. Her father would have him horsewhipped should he ever find out what he'd done, but he could not help himself. He'd wanted her in his arms for a night and so he'd pushed aside his dislike of scandal and had indulged himself.

Still, the thought of doing it again made him grin back at her. He'd suffer the wrath of anyone so long as he got to hold her again.

"I'm sorry too," she said, watching him. "Now tell me more about your estate. I've never been to Stoneheim Palace, but I hear it is lovely."

"My great grandfather built it and made a study of Blenheim Palace, hence the closeness of the name and design of the home. In fact, they're almost a mirror pair." They spoke for some time about each of their homes, and the local country near Marlborough and for the first time in his life, Finn did not feel as if he were putting on a mask or airs but was being merely himself. It was a heady feeling indeed and one he could get used to.

CHAPTER 9

They did not make London as planned after one of the carriage wheels lost a supporting bolt and threatened to fall off. Their journey into Salt Hill was slow, and it wasn't until the sun was low in the western sky that they arrived at the busy Windmill Inn. It was a setback that they did not need, not if they needed to ensure Lucy was indeed married and not just living in sin with Mr. Brown. Tomorrow they would push for London and travel on from there.

Even though the inn was busier than their accommodations of the night before, they were able to get separate rooms. The private dining room, unfortunately, was occupied, and so they had to break their fast in their accommodations.

Evie bade the duke goodnight just as the innkeeper's wife brought up their dinners of roast beef and vegetables along with red wine for her and ale for the duke, as his request.

The duke's room was across the hall from hers, and as the innkeeper's wife bustled about in Evie's room, setting her table for dining, nerves fluttered in Evie's stomach as she stood across from the duke about to bid him a good evening.

Something had changed between them today. Her body no longer felt itself, certainly not when Finn looked at her as he was right now, heavy-lidded and a slither of contemplation in his blue orbs. She shouldn't want him. He was still her sister's betrothed, sort of, she supposed. Even though he did state that he would not marry Lucy any longer and Lucy had said herself, she did not want the duke.

There was nothing, therefore, wrong with Evie finding him attractive, wondering what if… If he were willing.

"Do you think the carriage will be repaired in time for departure early tomorrow morning?" she asked, stepping aside as the innkeeper's wife went into the duke's room to prepare his table for dining.

"I should think so. There is a carriage maker here in Salt Hill, and he has promised to have it fixed for us posthaste. We will make London tomorrow as planned."

Evie thanked the innkeeper's wife as she bade them good night. For a moment, Evie stared at the duke, her body a riot of emotions, of wants and needs. She took a calming breath, pushing down the urge to throw herself at him and see where it would lead. If anywhere. "Well, thank you for the lovely day. I shall see you in the morning."

"Goodnight, Evie. Sleep well."

"Goodnight," she said, closing her door before the duke went back into his room.

Evie bathed and dressed for bed, climbing under the covers and wishing she were home where she could sneak down to the library and choose a book to read. Or merely huddle before her fire in her comfortable room and think about anything but the man who occupied the room across the hall from her.

What was wrong with her that he occupied so much of her mind? He never had before. They had barely spoken in London, there should be no reason at all that he did so now, but he did. He was a duke. She was an improvised spinster. They could not be more opposite.

And yet, he made her heart thump loud in her chest and her skin to prickle with awareness. She'd never had that with anyone before in her life, and she was loathe to lose it.

But maybe she didn't have to. If her sister was married and the duke looked for another to be his wife, maybe that another could be her.

The thought thrilled and scared her equally.

Evie sighed, rolling to her side and staring over to her window. She'd forgotten to close the curtains, and the moonlit night bathed a small square of the room's floor in light.

The bellow of a man out in the corridor, followed by running footsteps on the wooden floorboard planks, pulled her from her thoughts. Evie gasped, sitting up.

Had she locked her door? A female voice joined that of a man's, and she sat still, listening to the altercation. The man's voice shouted over that of the woman's, something about her sleeping with the baker and how he was going to kill the bastard by choking him with his own bread.

A light knock on her door made her start, and getting out of bed, Evie searched her room, spotting the chamber pot behind a privacy screen. She picked it up, holding it at her side as she padded over to the door. "Who is it?" she asked, hoping her voice sounded more confident than she felt.

"It's me. Finn. Let me in."

The fear of the couple arguing left her in an instant, and another fear flowed through her. What did the duke want? What did she want to do if she were to have him to herself another night? Alone.

She reached for the handle, happy to find she had locked the door after all. Opening it a fraction, she took in the duke in all his glory. He wore only his shirt that was gaping at his neck. His hair was askew as if he too had just been pulled from sleep. Thankfully he wore breeches, and yet she could not stop her inspection of him like a person starved of sustenance. Her eyes took in his bare feet and she bit back a grin. He looked like he'd jumped from his bed to her door and it did odd, delicious things to her insides. "What is it, Your Grace?"

"Let me in, Miss Milton. There seems to be a domestic quarrel going on, and I need to ensure you remain safe."

Evie glanced down the hall and spotted the couple arguing, the husband or lover, or whoever he was, paced that end of the corridor, his hands gesturing while the woman tried to appease him.

She stepped back, opening the door wide, and the duke stepped inside. He closed and locked the door, leaning on it a moment. "I thought tonight would be better for you, but this inn seems to have people who like to argue with no regard or care to others who are staying within its walls. I do apologize, Evie."

Evie sighed, walking over to her bed and sitting on its end. "I'm not bothered by it, truly." Evie took in his state of undress, his shirt that gaped at the front, teasing her with glimpses of his muscular chest. Warmth thrummed between her thighs and she crossed her legs.

His gaze burned into her, his attention traveling over her like a tempting caress. Evie's breathing fastened, and she bit her lip, wishing her thoughts to be a reality. She was turning as scandalous as her sister.

He sat beside her. The bed dipped a little, and she fell into him. He shot a glance at her as if she'd startled him.

"I, ah, I just wanted to ensure you were safe," he said after a time, his voice a deep, husky rumble.

"I am perfectly well. Their argument did not wake me, however. I was already awake," she said, needing to stop talking now before she started blabbering nonsense. "I think she had an affair."

"Yes." He glanced at her, and the breath in her lungs seized. He was so very handsome, with his beautiful, blue orbs and chiseled jaw. How was this man not already someone's husband? Someone's lover? Although, she supposed he was already someone's lover. What duke didn't have a bevy of women chasing after his coattails.

For all the inner strength of self she possessed, nothing could tear her eyes from his. She could lose herself with this man. There was something about him that drew her in, captured her attention and made her want to stay.

"It seems to have quietened outside. You should probably leave," she whispered. Why, however, she could not fathom since they were alone.

"Yes," he whispered, not moving.

Nor did she want him to. She wanted him to kiss her. A need tore through her and Evie stood, facing him. He stared up at her, the longing in his eyes a reflection of hers she was certain.

"I'm going to kiss you, Finn." Evie swallowed her fear, having never been so forward or demanding in her life. She wanted her first kiss to be with this man. This honorable, sweet duke who was chasing after her sister simply to ensure the scandal was not too great.

Evie shoved all thoughts of Lucy aside. Her sister had

made her choice. She was in love with another man and was probably already married. Had asked Evie to ruin her understanding with the duke. There was nothing wrong with her stealing her first kiss.

She leaned down, closing the space between them and their lips touched. The last, flittering thought she had was that indeed his lips were as soft as she suspected.

FINN DID NOT FEEL like himself. His body seized with need, with a desire to ravish the woman kissing him with such sweetness that his heart ached.

Without thought, he reached up, clasping her face. He deepened the kiss, thrusting his tongue against hers. She didn't start or seize in fear at his action. No, she did none of those things. Instead, she kissed him with the same frenzied need. Wrapped her arms about his neck and pushed herself against his chest.

Her shift was no barrier and the contours of her body, her breasts… Good God, luscious, heavy breasts teased his chest. Her long, thin legs that stood between his made his body ache. Fuck, he wanted her. Wanted her as he'd never wanted anyone in his life.

Their kiss deepened, turned incendiary, and she pushed against him, tumbling them back onto the bed. She came over him, their kiss never breaking, and hunger roared through him like a fever.

He was ravenous for her. Wanted her so much that had he been thinking rationally, it would scare him, but logical thought was a long way off at present, and so he let himself go. To simply enjoy her and her sweet mouth.

Finn rolled her onto her back, coming over her to settle between her legs. His cock rigid, his balls tight. He reached down, lifting one of her legs against his hip and pushed against her hot cunny.

It would be so easy to lean back, rip his front falls open, and thrust into her wet, welcoming heat. She undulated against his manhood, and he groaned, mimicking her and eliciting a delicious gasp from her sweet lips.

A loud crash sounded outside, and they started, the kiss ended. Like a bucket of cold water washing over them, Finn took stock of the position he was in and with whom. What was he doing? He had yet to decide if Evie was even a contender as his wife. He had planned on talking to his family doctor about Evie's chances of giving him children at her age. And here he was, hard as stone, poised to rip his breeches down and take her anyway.

This was not right, and not only for that reason. Two days ago, he'd been poised to marry her sister. He could not touch Evie until he was certain Lucy was married to Mr. Brown. What he would do after that, who he would marry, he had yet to decide.

Finn gazed down at Evie, her cheeks flushed red with exertion, her lips full and a little bruised from his kiss. She looked ripe enough to eat, and the thought of losing himself in her was a temptation hard to deny, but he had to.

"I must go. I'm sorry," he managed, crawling off her and ignoring the sight of her lying pliant and ready for a lover—his loving.

He adjusted his clothing, before opening the door and watching as the drunken man stumbled wobbly down the hallway before disappearing into a room. "Goodnight, Evie," he said, not looking back. To do so would mean one thing. That he would not leave, and that was not an option.

Not now, at least.

CHAPTER 10

Evie bathed and dressed early after sleep eluded her. Last night when the duke had come into her room, she'd seemed to have lost all control of self. Her body had burned with a need that she'd never experienced before. It ached for his touch, for his kiss, for things that no unmarried woman should ache for. She'd wanted nothing more than to rip down his breeches, take him in hand and make him hers.

She'd wanted to be filled and inflamed, wanted more of his delectable, deep kisses that left her head spinning. What her sister Lucy did not see in the duke, she could not fathom. He was a duke to start, above whom either of them ever thought to marry. He was kind and loyal; his helping of their family to ensure Lucy was married before moving on with his life was proof of that.

Even so, after last night, Evie knew for the first time in her life what it felt like when one wanted something they could not have. She didn't just want to divert the duke away from marrying Lucy as her sister had asked. Oh no, now she wanted him for herself.

But how to make a duke see her more than a spinster—a woman who was far beneath him in rank and riches.

Evie packed up her things, placing them in her small valise and left the room, heading downstairs. The carriage was hitched and waiting at the inn yard by the time she arrived. The wheel once again adequately attached to the carriage with the correct amount of bolts. Evie placed her small bag inside the vehicle, wanting to go for a short walk before they left.

The duke was nowhere to be seen, and so Evie found the carriage driver. "Dickens, I'm just going to go for a short walk down high street. I shall not be more than a few minutes."

The carriage driver tipped his hat. "Right ye are, Miss Milton. I shall inform His Grace when I see him."

"Thank you," Evie said. She left the bustling inn and started walking down the main town's thoroughfare. There were a few stores, a bakery, numerous houses and other inns that looked as busy as the Windmill. Few people were out at this early hour, and she took her time, enjoying the solitude and exercise that she would not get again for several hours.

Today's journey to London should not take as long as yesterday, and with any success, they would not have any issues with the carriage that could hold them up. In London, the duke had stated he would inquire as to whether Lucy and Mr. Brown had traveled through or stopped. A small part of Evie hoped they had continued on to Scotland. They would be near impossible to find in London, and if they were still on the road, Evie could spend more time with the duke.

Alone.

After last night, the crisp, fresh country air had helped clear Evie's thoughts. Her sister did not want the duke, so if she were to pursue him, make him see her more than his scandalous ex-betrothed sister, there was nothing wrong with that. It was not against the law.

The kiss they shared told her more than anything they would suit. His kiss had lit a light within her, a light she could not see ever going out. It was not a sweet, chaste kiss on the cheek or lips, but a total ravishment, one that left her mouth tingling, her body longing long after he'd left her room.

She wanted more, and Evie was anything if not resourceful when she wanted something.

"Miss Milton, is that you? Miss Milton!"

Evie glanced across the street and stilled at the sight of Miss Emma Malcolm, an heiress who lived in the same square as she did in London and newly betrothed to Earl Mcfarlane. The young woman was sweet of nature, but a terrible gossiper. Evie looked back toward the inn, and inwardly sighed at not being able to make her escape before being besieged.

"Miss Malcolm, how very nice to see you here. What brings you to Salt Hill?"

The young woman chuckled, coming to stand before her on the street, her maid a little way behind. "Oh, my father's estate is but a mile from here. We've been home preparing for my marriage to the earl but will be returning to London tomorrow, in fact. What brings you to Salt Hill?"

Evie furiously thought of what to say. She supposed she could tell the truth. That her sister had run off with a farmer after agreeing to marry a duke, and now she and that said duke were chasing after her. "I too, am returning to London. Today in fact. I have been home visiting family in Wiltshire."

"How lovely for you. Only yesterday I ran into your

sister, I believe. You introduced me to her last Season when she came up to London for several weeks if you remember." Miss Malcolm frowned, pursing her lips. "However, she did not have a maid, and she was traveling with a man who did not seem her equal if you do not mind my saying. He was not dressed as smart as Miss Lucy was, and seemed distracted, almost as if he was expecting someone to come up behind him or something."

Evie fought not to clasp Miss Malcolm's arms and shake more information from her. She'd seen Lucy, and only yesterday! Which would mean they were likely in London today. Perhaps they would halt their travels north a day or so and give Evie and the duke time in catching up to them.

"Ah, yes, Lucy was traveling ahead of me. I shall meet up with her in town tomorrow."

"Your cousin said as much," Miss Malcolm said.

"My cousin?" Evie queried.

"Well yes." Miss Malcolm chuckled, but even Evie could hear the thread of nervousness that entered her tone. "The gentleman with Miss Lucy. He introduced himself as your cousin. A farmer, which I suppose thinking about it, would explain why he looked so poorly dressed."

Miss Malcolm's pretty face drained of color. "I do apologize, Miss Milton. I did not mean to be so rude."

Evie waved her interpretation of Mr. Brown aside, her mind whirring with news of Lucy. She had to return to the inn and tell the duke. This was good news. "I must leave you now, Miss Malcolm, but I wish you safe travels to London tomorrow and do wish you very happy with your upcoming nuptials."

The young woman beamed, pleasure written across her features. "Thank you, Miss Milton. I'll be sure to send you an invitation."

Evie dipped into a curtsy. "It will be a pleasure to attend. Good day to you." Evie waved goodbye and started back toward the inn at a clipped pace. Of all the towns to run into someone from London, and not just anyone, but a dedicated gossiper was beyond unlucky. And Lucy too. But the news on Lucy was just what Evie needed to hear. At least they had traveled the same way, and they were only a day behind her. A niggling concern of Evie's had been that Lucy and Mr. Brown had gone to Bath and traveled north from there. The journey was much quicker and smoother on the great north road, but there had been no hint as to which way they would go.

She rounded into the inn-yard, and her steps faltered at the sight of the duke, pacing behind the carriage, his great-coat flying behind him like a cape. Pleasure replaced all thoughts of her sister a moment, and she just enjoyed the sight of the duke, his tall athleticism on full display for any who were watching him.

"Where did you go?" the duke demanded, coming to a stop and pinning her with his gaze. "I thought something terrible had befallen you."

Evie came to stand before him, tipping up her chin to meet his gaze. "I went for a walk, and I have news of Lucy."

"You do?" All annoyance at her stroll disappeared, and he pulled her over to the carriage, helping her inside. The duke joined her, seating himself across from her.

"What are you doing?"

"I'm traveling in the carriage. I do not feel like riding today."

"What about your horse?" she asked, looking out the window as their coachman walked the duke's horse past the carriage window.

"He's being tied to the back of the carriage. He'll be fine there."

Evie wasn't sure what she thought about the duke being in such close confines to her once again, especially after last evening. The carriage was opulent and roomy, but he was overbearing, took up too much room of the space.

The trip to London would be lengthy indeed…

He studied her a moment, and she fought not to fidget with the sleeve of her dress. "Tell me of this news of Miss Lucy. How is it that you found out this information?"

"I wanted to go for a walk, as I said. I knew we were going to have a lengthy carriage ride today, and I wanted to exercise before we departed. I ran into Miss Malcolm. You may have heard she's recently engaged to the Earl Mcfarlane."

He nodded, turning to stare out the carriage window just as the equipage dipped as the coachman climbed up onto the box. The duke knocked on the roof, and the carriage lurched forward. "I had not heard that news, no, but tell me more of your sister. She was here in Salt Hill. Recently I presume."

"Only yesterday. Miss Malcolm ran into her and Mr. Brown, so at least we know that they are together. They were traveling to London and are only a day ahead of us."

The duke rubbed his jaw in thought. "With any luck, they will halt their progress in town before traveling north. We may not have to go all the way to Gretna, after all, to ensure your sister marries this Mr. Brown."

"That was my hope too." Evie didn't feel like traveling all the way to Gretna, not any longer at least. Days on end in a carriage and nights at inns where not all of them were guaranteed to be comfortable nor clean. It was not ideal. "What is the plan once we arrive in London?" she asked.

"We shall return to my townhouse. I will send out my

man of business to try and locate Miss Lucy and Mr. Brown. See if they are still in town or have traveled north."

"I can return to my home in London if that suits. If we're to be in London a day or so, I should probably not be staying under your roof." Not that Evie didn't want to spend more time with Finn, she did, desperately so, but it wasn't right, and she didn't need to bring any more scandal onto her family. Her sister had done enough of that already.

"About last evening, Evie."

Evie held up her hand, not wanting him to profess how much he regretted their kiss or to chastise her over instigating her lack of decorum. She didn't want to hear how it was wrong and why it would not happen again. "There is nothing to discuss."

"I would disagree with that summarization."

Evie swallowed the nerves that fluttered in her stomach at the near mention of them kissing. She met his gaze, resigned to hear him out. "Very well, you want to discuss our kiss?"

His attention dipped to her lips, and nerves skittered across her skin. The air seemed to evaporate in the carriage, expectation thrumming through her.

He cleared his throat. "Yes, the kiss. I wanted you to know that I hold no ill will toward you over your conduct. I've thought about it and have concluded that you were upset over the argument outside our rooms and required comforting."

Evie's lips twitched, and she couldn't hold back a chuckle at his reasoning. "That wasn't why I kissed you, Finn." The kiss had a lot more to do with her wanting him than it did about anything else.

He stared at her, his face an unreadable mask. "Why did you kiss me then?"

"I kissed you because I wanted to kiss you. Not because I was scared for my safety. I like you and the way that you were looking at me last night," Evie said, shrugging. "I thought that you might like to kiss me too."

A muscle in his jaw clenched, and he turned to look out the window. It was not the response that she wanted to see, but then she'd never thrown herself at a duke before, there was no telling how these aristocratic men would react. "Honor dictates that I ensure Miss Lucy is married before anything can happen with anyone else. I know that my understanding with your sister was at an end the moment she ran off with Mr. Brown, but still, I should not have kissed you. It was wrong, and I apologize."

Evie pushed away the stab of pain his words caused and settled back into the plush, leather seat. "Had you ever kissed Lucy, Your Grace?" she asked, reverting to titles since his kiss with her was wrong. The fiend. It had not been wrong. It had been wonderful, and if he only could admit that, there may be hope for them after all.

"Of course not." His words came out a little scandalized and she wondered why. Why would kissing his betrothed seem so undone. "I have not known Miss Lucy for very long and did not feel she was open to such affections," he said, rubbing a hand over his jaw.

Evie watched his hand slide against his face, marred by only the slightest shadow of impending stubble. The memory of those lips upon hers, her skin abraded by his ardent kiss, bombarded her, and she wiggled on her seat. Perhaps, at her advanced age of seven and twenty, she had long run out of patience and wanted more. Wanted a husband who could kiss her, love her as much and as often, as she wanted.

"I suppose I understand now why Miss Lucy was not interested in kissing me. I was not her choice."

"I am sorry my sister has done this to you, but I cannot be sorry for her choice. Had you married Lucy, she would not have been happy, and your marriage would have suffered for it. I think any couple who marry must respect and like each other and have a mutual desire if they're to endure a lifetime. I know that is what I want when I marry. I want to desire my husband, to want to be near him as much and as often as I'd like."

The muscles on his jaw tightened, and his eyes heated as they watched her. Her words held more meaning than face value. Scandalous talk that the duke did not like, but Evie could not help it. He maddened her no end. "We have many hours ahead of us in this equipage. Did you bring your book today, Evie?"

"I did not, no," she replied. Now that they were alone, on the road to London, all she could think of doing was kissing him again. Of having his hands on her, his body pushing against hers in the most inappropriate fashion. His disapproval of the action only made her want to do it more. "A game of cards perhaps. Did you bring a pack, Your Grace?"

He cringed. "I did not, no," he said, mimicking her words.

"Well then," Evie said, grinning across the space at him. "You'll just have to kiss me again to pass the time. That will be just as diverting."

CHAPTER 11

Finn cleared his throat, wondering if he'd just heard correctly. Had Evie told him to kiss her again after he'd just told her they could not do such things? She was a temptation he could not deny, no matter how many times he told her or himself that he should leave her alone. A small part of him felt that if he dallied with her, it was wrong. He was still to decide if he would pursue her as his future bride, but after last evening the idea of having Evie in his bed for the rest of his life was an idea that made sense to him. Even now, he wanted to wrench her onto his lap and take that sweet mouth with his. Touch her, lose himself in her willing heat.

Finn inwardly groaned. He'd turned into his father—a man with no self-control.

Her wicked, teasing grin that beckoned across from him was not helping him in the slightest, and the minx damn well knew it. He'd hardly slept last evening, having tossed and turned all night. For a time, he'd debated taking himself in hand and releasing his aroused state.

There was something about Evie that drew him in,

made him question everything that he thought he'd wanted. A bride some years younger than himself, from a wealthy, noble family. Evie was none of those things, and yet still, it was she that made the blood in his veins pump at a heady beat.

God damn it, he needed to get a grip on himself. He shifted on his seat, his cock coming to attention when her pink tongue slipped out and wet her bottom lip. "Tell me you did not just ask me to kiss you again," he said in the sternest voice he could manage. "Have you not been listening as to why we cannot kiss again?"

"I have been listening," she said, no shame in her voice. "I'm not engaged, and after my sister's decision two days ago, neither are you. We're not doing anything wrong if we were to pass the time in such a delightful way. No one need ever know, so it is not scandalous to act on our desires."

Delightful?

He found her kisses just so as well. "Whether kissing was delightful or not, we should refrain from doing so again. For a time, at least."

Finn stilled when Evie leaned forward, and the sight of her breasts in her traveling gown caught his attention. She was dressed today in a dark-navy gown and cream pelisse, and she was utter perfection.

He forced himself back into the squabs, away from her delectable, tempting self. "You should not throw yourself at gentlemen like you do. You may find one day a gentleman will take you up on your teasing and ask for more than you're willing to give."

"If that happens, then he is no gentleman. And I do not throw myself at anyone. Indeed, my friends can attest to the validity of my statement. That is, until now, with you. Why will you not kiss me again? Did you not enjoy yourself?"

Enjoy himself? He'd reveled in the delight of having her in his arms. Of losing himself in her kiss, her little whimpers, and sighs. "It was adequate."

"Adequate? Oh no, we cannot have that."

Before Finn knew what was happening, Evie was beside him on the seat, staring up at him, a wicked, teasing grin on her pretty visage. She was a handsome woman, with her long, dark chocolate locks and rose-colored lips. It made him wonder why she'd never been swooped off her feet and carried to the altar. How was it that she had not become someone's wife a long time ago?

"Why are you not married, Evie?"

"Me?" she asked, taken aback at his question. She sat back a little, and Finn breathed deep once more. Having her so near did odd things to his mind, made it cloudy and thick and not at all like he usually was, thorough and clear of thought.

"Yes, you. You're a handsome woman, your father is a gentleman, and your friends are highly placed in society. Why is it that you have never married?"

"You're trying to distract me from kissing you again, are you not, Your Grace?"

He didn't like being back to titles, but perhaps it was necessary. They should not be kissing and fondling each other. Not yet, at least.

"Have you never been courted?" he asked, refusing to answer her question.

She leaned back in the squabs and glanced out the window a moment before she said, "I was sent away to school in France. I met my friends at Madame Dufour's Refining School for Girls, before they had married into the *ton*. I suppose over the many years of watching them all be courted and then married, I have missed my chance at finding love.

"Before Willow inherited Viscountess Vance's fortune, I had to return to my father's small estate at the end of each Season. Some years my family could not afford to send me to London to join my friends in the Season, and so I spent that time away from society and opportunities to meet new people. Time went by, and now I am seven and twenty. An old maid to some."

"I feel we have missed an opportunity with us both being in Wiltshire and having never met there." He'd been so distracted with trying to distance himself from his father, keeping the estate running while his sire had sown his seed all over London, creating scandals wherever he went, that he had not looked up to see who was around him. Even in London he'd known of Evie, had danced with her, and still, he'd walked away from her without a backward glance. A foolish mistake. "I have not spent much time in London these past years. And then the death of my father a year ago has kept me busy."

"I did hear that he passed away. I'm very sorry for your loss."

"Don't be," he said automatically. "He never cared for his family, only his whores. Even now beyond the grave, he is trying to rule my life."

"How so?" she asked, glancing at him curiously.

Finn started, realizing that he'd said too much. An easy feat when talking to Miss Milton. When she was not trying to kiss him, she was a very good listener and spoke common sense, no silly debutante who giggled and blushed every time one spoke. He liked her maturity. It suited him and his character better than Miss Lucy ever had. Evie's younger sister had been a little bit of giggler and smiled a little too often for his liking. Not that he didn't want a wife who smiled, but he would've preferred one who did not grin like a lunatic at everyone she came in contact with.

"I only meant," he continued, "that his reputation has tarnished my own. No matter what you may have heard about me, Evie, I am nothing like my father. Not in any way other than the title that I inherited from him."

She reached out and clutched his arm, squeezing it a little before letting him go. "You're an honorable man, Finn. No matter what, nothing can change my opinion of you." The moment her hand slipped from his arm, he missed her touch. He liked Evie touching him, and little else occupied his mind of late. He was not like his father, he repeated in his mind. Kissing an unmarried woman did not make him debauched like his sire.

"Thank you," he said, her words meaning more than any he'd heard from anyone before.

The carriage turned and, glancing out the window, Finn took in the less-pretty landscape of scrubby acreage that was marred by gravel pits. "We'll luncheon at The Magpies at Uxbridge. The fare is satisfactory there."

"I stopped there on my way home. Their beef pie is tasty indeed," Evie said, leaning over him to look out the window even though she had one on her side. "Perhaps we can spend our time occupied in other ways after all, Finn. You may not have to kiss me again if we're to keep up such lively conversation such as the one we just had."

Finn chuckled, yet inwardly he could not stop thinking about every which way he could instigate another kiss with the delectable Evie. Lively conversation be damned.

Evie woke with a start several hours later after a hearty lunch at Uxbridge, as promised. The carriage rolled to an abrupt halt. She sat up, rubbing her neck and realized that she'd been sleeping on Finn. She threw him a small smile and glanced out the window. This was not her house, and from the look of the massive Georgian mansion they'd pulled up before, this was most definitely the duke's.

As promised, the duke had not tried to kiss her again on their journey into town. Instead, he had purchased a pack of cards from the inn where they had broken their fast, and they had played several games of *vingt-et-un* before she'd begged for a reprieve to simply relax and enjoy her last few hours with the duke.

It was only a matter of time before she'd grown tired from the rocking of the carriage and had fallen asleep. That she'd woken up with her head in the duke's lap was not what she'd imagined when she'd closed her eyes.

Evie sat up, the duke stilling as she came to sit up next to him. She glanced at him and saw that he too looked like he'd just woken up from slumber. "I do apologize, Finn. I did not mean to make use of your lap in such a way."

He adjusted his seat, rubbing a hand over his jaw as he tried to take in his surroundings. "Do not trouble yourself, Miss Milton. No one shall ever know that we've slept together."

Heat rushed up her neck to settle on her cheeks. She glanced at him quickly and read the horror that his words wrecked on his visage.

"I do apologize, Evie. My words came out wrong. I merely meant to say that our napping in the carriage was perfectly normal and not in any way untoward. We're fully clothed, are we not?"

Evie glanced down at her gown just to make sure she was indeed fully clothed. "We're stopping here for the night?" she asked, wanting to change the subject. How could she have fallen asleep with her head in the duke's lap? Her mother would suffer apoplexy if she knew. As for her father, he would demand a wedding. "I thought you were taking me to my home with Molly."

"We are," he said, seemingly thankful for her change of subject. "It is very late, and I did not want to throw your household into an uproar at your return. My staff is expecting us, and they will have a room ready for you. No one will ever know you stayed here. It is only for one night. I shall return you to your home tomorrow should we not need to travel north after your sister."

Evie was too tired to argue with his plan and simply took his hand, thankful for his support as she stepped out of the carriage for the first time in as many hours. Her back ached, and she leaned back, trying to loosen her tight, sore muscles. "May I have a bath brought to my room, Your Grace. I am terribly sore and tired."

"Of course, I shall have one ordered at once."

"Thank you." They made their way indoors, and Evie couldn't help but be awed by the grandeur that met her. Marble-lined the walls, a spiraling oak staircase led upstairs and large, family portraits hung along the walls, all of the dukes of the past staring down and judging her for the commoner she was.

The butler bowed, taking the duke's greatcoat. "Your rooms are ready, Your Grace, and we have dinner waiting for you whenever you're ready to eat."

"Thank you, George," Finn said, he too rolling his shoulders. "A tray in our rooms will do very well, and can you have a bath brought up for Miss Milton?"

The butler bowed once more. "Of course." He gestured toward the staircase. "Would you like me to escort you to your room, Miss Milton?"

Evie glanced at the duke, and he smiled in agreement. "Goodnight, Miss Milton."

"Goodnight, Your Grace." Evie went with the servant

up the long flight of stairs before walking down a well-lit passageway that too was lined with family portraits and an abundance of hothouse flowers.

She'd seen similar opulence in Ava's, Willow's and Hallie's homes, and yet to see the man whom she had been kissing the past two days was as fortunate as her friends filled her with unease. Of course, she'd always known he was a duke, but she'd never seen just how wealthy he was. It made his betrothal to Lucy, and her dreams of having him for herself seem feeble, if not impossible. Made her feel inferior and unworthy. There were so many rich noblewomen who would suit him better, who had been raised to marry such a man. She was not one of them.

The butler opened the door to her room for the night, and Evie was unable to stop the gasp of delight at seeing her chamber. The walls were painted a light, bright cream, but the bedding was a rich green, the dark, wooden furniture giving the room a masculine feel, but so very beautiful. Evie stepped across the threshold, going to the bed to run her hand along the silk cover.

Just as promised, Evie broke her fast and then soaked in a bath that two footmen brought up for her. She sat before the fire, drying her hair when a light knock sounded on her door. Nerves fluttered in her stomach, and she pulled her dressing gown closed before opening it.

Evie cracked the door a little to find Finn standing before her. "Is there something wrong?" she asked, searching for words and unsure what to say now that they were alone once more and in his house. No one to interrupt them.

"I, ah..." he stammered, his attention moving over her shoulder to take in her room. "I hope you find your accommodations are to your liking."

Evie nodded, glancing back into the space, her bed like

a beacon of temptation, more so now that the duke was standing before her. "It's lovely. I don't think I've ever had such a beautiful room before."

"You should always have beautiful things," he said, his voice low and gravelly.

Her heart twisted at his sweet words, and for a moment, she could not move. She wanted to lean up and kiss him, to take more of what she knew he could give her, but she did not. Her brazenness had seemed to have deserted her after today when he'd gone above and beyond in keeping his distance. Maybe he did not want to kiss her anymore, and she'd been fooling herself into thinking that the one kiss they had shared meant anything at all. To the duke, at least.

The thought left her depleted, and she stepped back into the room. A hand shot out and clasped her arm, pulling her back.

"Goodnight then, Evie," he whispered, closing the space between them, his lips but a feather width from hers. Her knees threatened to give way as he closed that small space between them and kissed her. She was sure he'd meant it to be a chaste kiss, merely a goodnight between friends, but it was not chaste in any way.

The moment his lips touched hers, he deepened the kiss, his tongue twisting with hers and sending her wits to spiral. Evie reached up, clasping his shoulders to stop herself from falling to the ground at the pleasure of it. She'd wanted him to kiss her, wanted so much to be back in his arms, and for him to kiss her this time left a heady feeling spiraling through her blood. He stepped against her, walking her back until she came up against the wall beside her door. Pleasure and need shot through her, her body not her own, but his to have.

Evie had never been with a man before. Something

told her this was the desire her friends had spoken about when they had discussed their marriages. How one look, a touch or small smile could send their wits spinning and make them follow their spouse to see where their interlude would lead.

"I shouldn't want you as much as I do," he said against her lips before kissing her again. The kiss was unlike any she'd ever known, not that she'd known any before, but chaste was not what was going on right now between them.

He kissed her as if he were starved of her touch. As if he wished to devour every ounce of her flesh. She shivered at the thought of him kissing her elsewhere, of his tongue that now tangled with hers, tasting her skin, her body, in the most private of places.

"Do not stop," she begged, kissing him with as much desire as she could. Still, she could not get enough of him. And then his hands slipped down her body, past her breasts to settle on her hips before skating behind and clasping her bottom. He wrenched her up against his body, undulating against her core. Evie moaned, liquid heat pooling between her legs.

"Finn," she gasped, clutching at him like a lifeline. Never had she felt as she did right now. As if she would wither and die if he did not continue what he had started. And he had started this. He had kissed her this time.

The sound of footsteps on the staircase sounded, and Finn pulled away, going to stand out in the hall just as the butler came toward them. "Your Grace, your steward is here, as you requested."

"Thank you, George. Please tell Mr. Cleavers I will be down directly."

"Of course, Your Grace," the servant said, leaving them as quickly as he arrived.

Finn sighed, turning back toward Evie. "I should go. I

need to speak to my steward about your sister and Mr. Brown. See what he can find."

"Of course," Evie said, taking a calming breath and hoping he did not notice that her heart beat a thousand times too fast. "Let us hope they are in London, and we can find them."

"Yes." The duke stepped back into her room and kissed her yet again. Evie gasped, reveling in his touch, before he wrenched free, striding down the hallway to meet his steward. Evie closed the door and slumped against it when closed. A small smile slipped onto her lips. After those two kisses, it would seem the duke was not so unaffected as he'd claimed. Perhaps there was a chance for them, after all.

CHAPTER 12

The following morning brought news that her sister and Mr. Brown were indeed in London and had not traveled north to Scotland. The report was both pleasing and worrying at the same time. Did Mr. Brown intend to marry Lucy at all, or was he simply enjoying his time with her away from the security of her family?

Evie sat at the breakfast table, the duke reading over the paper beside her, and she could not help but think that this is how a married couple may break their fast. The duke had told her of the news he'd found and was now reading the paper.

"We need to travel down to St. Giles and see if we can flush them out. Would you come with me?" he asked suddenly, looking at her for an answer.

Evie set her cup of tea down, unsure she'd heard him right. "You wish for me to come with you?"

"I do." He folded his paper, placing it to his side. "Which brings me to something else that I wanted to discuss with you. Regarding your accommodations while in London."

Evie frowned, having thought they had already discussed where she'd stay. "I thought I was returning to my normal place of residence in London."

He studied her a moment before he said, "I want you to stay here, Evie. With me. No one knows we're in London trying to chase down your sister to limit her ruination. If it becomes known that we are, that we are here and why, it will only make the situation worse for everyone. I have spoken to my staff and steward and notified them all that as far as they are concerned, we're both still in Wiltshire and will not be back in London for several weeks yet."

Evie took in his plan and could see sense in it. The thought of staying under the duke's roof, hiding themselves away from the world with only themselves for company. "Very well, but what if we are seen? My reputation will be ruined."

"It will not be. I will not let it." The determination in his tone soothed the small amount of trepidation at his plan.

"If you're sure. I will stay here with you." Evie pushed back from the table, starting for the door. "If we're traveling into St. Giles, I need to go change."

"What is wrong with your gown?" the duke asked, calling after her.

Evie paused at the threshold of the room, turning to face the duke. "You should change as well. If we want to blend into those who live in that seedy part of London, you had better take off those highly polished hessian boots and superfine coat. You'll be mugged before we take two steps from the carriage door.

FINN GRINNED at Evie as she disappeared out into the foyer. Warmth seeped into his bones at the knowledge she was going to stay in his home for some days. Just the two of them, nestled away from the *ton*, and only themselves for company.

At this point, he was becoming less and less troubled by Miss Lucy and Mr. Brown, finding them, or the scandal all of this would cause if people found out. He'd promised Evie's father he would help in ensuring his daughter was not ruined, but other than that, there was little between him and his ex-betrothed.

Finn pushed back his chair, starting for his room to change, as Evie suggested. Under an hour later, they were in the carriage and heading down toward St. Giles. The area where his steward had heard word that Miss Lucy was staying.

Evie sat beside him in the carriage, her lip clasped between her teeth as she glanced outside. The streets of Mayfair soon gave way to the more impoverished areas of town, showcasing the struggles that the poor faced every day.

"Do not worry, Evie. I have brought a flintlock, and I'm not incapable of looking after myself."

"But are you capable of looking after us both should we get in trouble?" She glanced back at him. "Did you bring any money? I cannot pass a child in need and not give them anything."

He nodded and tapped the pocket on his chest. The jacket he'd borrowed from one of his stable staff was surprisingly comfortable and befitted this expedition. "I do. You may give it all away if you wish."

She wrapped her arm about his, pulling herself close to his side. "I knew that you were a good man. A trait that you keep proving to me time and again." Her sweet face tipped up toward his and did odd things to his insides. Finn took the opportunity to lean down and take her lips.

His body roared with possession, and he took her mouth, sliding his tongue against hers. She tasted of tea and the honey that she'd put on her toast this morning. The idea of having this woman always occupied his mind as much as the idea of her in his bed, and it would not abate. Evie Milton suited him, was of similar character and sensible. She would make a good duchess and wife, even at seven and twenty.

Her hands clasped the lapels of his coat, pulling him closer, and he took the opportunity to touch her. Her dress was coarse wool, nothing like the clothes she usually wore. In fact, breaking the kiss, he took in her gown, frowning.

"What is it you have on? That cannot be comfortable," he said, taking in the coarse wool and ill-fitting cut.

"It's one of the scullery maid's gowns. I paid her to use it and she was more than happy to part with it then." She took in his own attire. "You're looking very handsome yourself. I think I like seeing you look so very rugged."

He chuckled, sitting back against the squabs but not before taking her hand and holding it in his lap. A simple, sweet gesture that felt as natural as kissing her did.

The carriage turned around a corner, and Finn gauged their location. "We should be there soon."

"Do you think we'll find Lucy today?" Evie looked up at him with expectation, and he wished he could tell her they would, but he wasn't sure. His steward had said that although there had been sightings of the couple, the exact location of their quarters was not yet known.

"We'll walk about the streets where I was told they had been seen. Maybe they will be out and about and we shall spot them." Finn had taken the precaution of having two burly stable men on the back of the carriage who would be with them, and his driver was not unarmed. He'd not usually take a woman into this part of town, but Evie was the only one of them who knew what Mr. Brown looked like. He himself had never met the fellow.

A little while later, the carriage pulled up on Newman street and Finn helped Evie alight. He took in their location and those who took note of their arrival. He pulled her close and started up the narrow, cobbled street, clothing hanging across the space above their heads and children running about, their feet bare.

Evie reached into his pocket, taking the few coins he'd brought and gave one to a little girl who held out her hand. "I hate seeing children with so little. Our government should do more to help the poor."

Finn couldn't agree more, and he often gave to charities and orphanages. The task of pulling the poor out of their substandard living needed more than one's duke's funds. It required everyone to partake in their rise.

They took in the people they passed, Evie looking up and down the alleyways they crossed. The area became dank and of worse conditions the longer they walked about. "I cannot believe Lucy would stay in such an area. Mr. Brown was a farmer. Surely he had some funds to pay for better lodgings than those this area offers."

"It would seem he did not." Finn hated telling Evie such truths, but for Lucy to be living in such conditions, away from her family and friends, there was a good chance that she had ruined herself beyond repair, and they may not be able to keep her actions private for long.

They turned up an alleyway, Evie handing out more coins to a group of children who all jumped and hooted at their windfall before running off. The lane opened up to a circular group of two-story houses. All of them were of wood construction, windows broken, and wood rotten and missing in some places. There was a decided odor of urine and human feces and Finn cringed.

Evie gasped, her body stilling beside him, and he glanced at her quickly, seeing her widened eyes and pale skin. "What is it?" he asked, taking her hand and shaking it a little when she did not answer.

"Someone threw something onto my dress from above." Her eyes filled with tears, and Finn glanced up, seeing a smirking, large woman leaning out the window.

"'Ave a good day, my lady," the woman said, tipping her chamber pot over the windowsill once again to ensure it was empty.

Finn glared at the lady before she disappeared inside. "Come, we'll return home. There is always tomorrow."

"I cannot get in your carriage with this muck on me, Finn. The smell will never come out."

"Never mind that. I'll buy a new carriage." He pulled her back to where they came, never seeing Lucy or Mr. Brown on their wanderings. It did not matter, they would be found soon enough, and then Finn would ensure the blaggard married the woman he stole from her home or he didn't know what he would do.

One thing he was certain was that he would not let Evie suffer the fate of her sister's actions. He would not allow an ounce of scandal to touch himself or Evie.

They arrived back at the mews of his townhouse, and Finn helped Evie return inside, ordering the house staff to bring up water for a bath. He fought not to cringe at the scent permeating off her clothing, which would have to be burned.

"I'm humiliated," she said beside him as he helped her up the stairs. Thankfully the urine had missed her hair and had merely hit her back first before running down the rear of her gown. "I'm so sorry, Finn. Your carriage may never smell the same again."

He chuckled, taking her arm and pulling it around his own. "You'll be clean soon, and the carriage is nothing. It wasn't your fault that it happened."

"Thank you, Finn."

Finn walked her to her door, opening it for her. "I'll send a maid up to help you undress and prepare for your bath. It will be up soon, and then you'll feel better."

"Since I'm a woman, standing before you and smelling of someone else's bodily fluid, you're very sweet to say so."

He tipped up her chin, leaning down and kissing her, not caring if any of his household staff saw them. "Enjoy your bath, Evie. I'll have lunch sent up to you on a tray if you wish."

"Thank you," she said, stepping into the room and gifting him one last look before closing the door. Finn took a calming breath, pushing away the thought of her stripping off her clothes and stepping into the hot, fragrant bathwater.

Naked.

He groaned, forcing his feet to his room to change. He could pursue her without impediment once Lucy was married and voiding his understanding with her once and for all. And then, *then*, he could pursue what was becoming a little bit of an obsession.

Evie.

CHAPTER 13

Evie stared a moment as the door closed, separating her and duke once more. It was becoming harder and harder to keep her distance from him, from asking him if what she was starting to suspect was between them was only on her side.

She did not think that was the case, but it was hard to tell what the duke was thinking most of the time unless those times were when he was kissing her, and then she knew what he was feeling.

A knock sounded, startling her, and she opened the door, a little disappointed to see footmen carrying a large hip bath and buckets, a maid behind them also with drying linens and a cake of soap. Evie stepped back, bidding them enter and watched as they set it up before the stoked fire, giving her inspecting glances now and then.

She supposed she deserved their inspection. She was, after all, an unmarried woman living under the same roof as their master. They probably thought she was his mistress, but the way she felt right at this moment, she did not feel very mistress-like. She felt like a cesspit.

The maid helped her undress, and Evie dismissed her, asking her to burn the gown immediately. Both Lucy and she were used to bathing on their own and not needing anyone to help. The water was fragrant and smelled of lavender, and she tested the heat with her foot before stepping into the bath, lowering herself.

Bliss was the first thought that slipped into her mind. Utter bliss. Evie lay back in the bath, sliding the soap through her fingers as she lathered it. She leaned forward, washing her shoulders before lying back and raising one leg to clean it. The terrible stench that had followed her from St. Giles was gone, and she was thankful for it. How anyone could throw such contents on an unsuspecting person was beyond her.

Her mind whirred with thoughts of the duke. Her hands slipped over her skin, and she closed her eyes, thinking of his hands on her flesh, teasing and caressing her body, clasping her breasts and kissing her nipples.

She sighed, wanting him in such a way. No one kissed someone as the duke kissed her. Not unless they were lovers or at least on the path of becoming so. The idea of taking the duke to her bed was not such a scandalous thought, not anymore at least. The night at the inn when he had laid upon her on the bed, his hardness teasing her wet flesh made her breathing hitch. Oh, to be back at the Bear Inn once again. Alone with the duke.

"Evie?"

The sound of his voice so close behind her rent a squeal from her and she sat forward in the water, covering herself. "Finn," she said, using his given name. "What are you doing here?"

"I apologize, I thought you would've been out of the bath by now."

She turned and noted he was just inside the door, and

yet so lost in her own musings, she didn't hear him enter or close the door behind him.

"I was covered in human excrement. I may be a little while in the bath." Evie dipped into the water to try to cover her nakedness. A pointless exercise. She could see her nudity under the clear water, and she had little doubt that the duke could as well.

"I did consider it, and then I ignored that consideration."

Evie looked over her shoulder, meeting his gaze. She shivered at the longing she read in his blue orbs. He looked wretched, lost, and confused, and her heart did a little flip in her chest. The past few days had been some of the most enjoyable of her life. She could not understand why Lucy would throw over this wonderful, honorable man for someone else.

The duke was a catch to any woman, and yet he was in her room, alone, and she was naked. Her friends would be scandalized should they know the improper thoughts that were running through her mind. Of all the things that one could do with a man that no woman of intact virtue ought to know.

But she'd read enough books in her seven and twenty years to know what happened between a man and a woman. To do those things with the duke made her shiver and ache in places she'd never ached before.

She reached for the drying cloth on the nearby chair and standing, wrapped it around herself before turning toward the duke. "What do you really want, Finn?" she asked, not just for tonight, but always. Did he want a rich, noble wife to be his duchess, or would a woman from Wiltshire with no money and no connections satisfy his aristocratic blood?

"I want you," he said at length, striding across the

room and hoisting her up in his arms. Evie gasped, letting go of her inhibitions and her towel and simply held on to him, wrapping her arms about his neck and kissing him as fiercely as he kissed her.

His clothing was rough against her nakedness, but changed now back into clothing that was suitable for a duke, his attire was soft and smelled fresh and clean. She wrapped herself about him, hooking her legs around his back and pressed her aching sex against his.

He moaned through their kiss, spinning her and walking backward toward the bed. He carried her as if she weighed nothing at all and deposited her on her bed. She bounced once, and she giggled.

The duke didn't move from the end of the bed, his gaze hungrily devouring her form. He ran a hand across his jaw before stripping off his coat and tearing at his cravat. "I want you. No one else. Only you."

His words sent a bolt of heat to lick up her spine, and hope bloomed in her chest. Did he truly mean it? She hoped that he did. She kneeled on the bed, reaching out to help him undress. She wanted him too, ached with the need of him.

Together, they stripped him of his jacket, waistcoat, and cravat, his articles of clothing pooling about his feet. The sight of his muscled chest made her mouth water. Evie ran her hand over the corded muscles that flexed under her touch and each ragged breath the duke took. Finn was warm, his heart beating a fast crescendo of need. She had done that. Made him want her, and no one else.

"We shouldn't do this, Evie." His words were breathless and held a hint of regret in them. He was torn between doing what was right and expected of a gentleman and what they both wanted. And right now, Evie wanted him and be damned what etiquette they were breaking.

"You do not want me?" she teased, her hands dipping to his breeches to unhook the buttons keeping all of him from her.

He leaned his forehead against hers, his breath rasping against her face. "Damn it, yes, I want you, but we're not married. This is wicked."

Evie met his gaze as her fingers slipped the first button on his breeches free. "We're consenting adults, Finn. There is nothing wrong with what we're going to do." She needed this, even if for one night. To lose herself with a man who made her blood sing and her body yearn.

He raised one brow, not moving to push her hands away. "Are you sure you wish to do this?" he asked, his hand stemming hers as she undid one more of the buttons on his breeches.

"Oh yes, we're doing this," she replied, slipping the button free.

He leaned forward, kissing her neck. A shiver rocked through her, and she slid her hand inside his breeches, touching him for the first time. His manhood was ridged, long and wide, and yet the skin was the softest she'd ever felt before, like steel encased in velvet. His hand clasped over hers, showing her without words what he liked.

What she liked too.

"You enjoy that?" she asked, when he moaned, nipping the skin on her neck.

"Fuck yes," he groaned, the use of the word shocked and pleased her. He wasn't so much the proper duke. Not always. Not with her and not like this.

They tumbled onto the bed, and she slipped her legs about his waist, wanting the weight of him, his body against hers. His chest brushed her breasts, her nipples hard little peaks that ached for his touch. Evie pressed against him, wanting him to soothe the ache that he made.

"You're so beautiful," he said between kisses as he made his way down to her breasts, his tongue tasting her skin, his teeth giving sweet little bites along the way. She could lose herself in the arms of this man. Envy and jealousy rippled through her that he had been betrothed to her sister, that had Lucy not run away with another man, that right now it could be her sister in his arms.

Evie pushed the unhelpful, troubling thoughts aside. She would not think of such a horror. The duke was kissing her, had her beneath him in her bed within his home. She would fight for what she wanted, and she wanted him—all of him tonight and every night after.

She spiked her fingers through his hair as his mouth covered one nipple, his tongue laving at her sensitive flesh. Evie held on to him and let go of all her troubles, her secrets, and simply let herself enjoy.

Finn.

FINN WAS GOING to hell and heaven from the feel of Evie beneath him. To seduce a woman only days after his betrothed had run off with another man was not the act of a gentleman. Yet nothing save a natural disaster would tear him away from Evie's delectable body right at this moment. Her breasts, in particular, were the perfect size for his hands.

Evie gasped his name, a husky pant that told him more than anything that she enjoyed his touch. She rubbed against him, a siren stretch that pushed her soaking mons against his aching cock, and for a moment, his mind went blank. He pressed against her, giving her what they both wanted, and he fought not to guide himself into her sweet cunny.

"You're teasing me, Finn. Stop teasing me," she gasped, her fingers tangling into his hair and pulling a little.

Oh, how he loved the sound of his name on her lips. Of how she undulated, thrust, and kissed him with such abandonment, not caring that he was a duke, a wealthy peer of the realm. She saw him as a man who could give her pleasure and company. He would marry this woman once her sister was settled with Mr. Brown. He'd not always wanted a woman of similar age to his, but he could not see himself with anyone else but Evie. That she was from Wiltshire, his home county, and fulfilled all of his father's decree was not to be overlooked either.

He reached down between them, placing himself at the tip of her wet cunny and pushed into her heat. She was so warm and tight that he bit back a groan. Impatient minx that Evie was, she lifted her hips, pushing him a little farther into her. He gasped at the pleasure of it, fighting the urge to thrust all the way in.

"Damn it, Finn. Take me. I'm aching for you. Surely you can feel how much I want you."

"I feel it, love," he said, ignoring the endearment that slipped naturally from his lips. He was merely caught up in the moment, nothing more. He soothed the part of him that wanted to panic at such blandishment. She moved again, and this time he thrust into her, making her his. She threw her head back, moaning at his intrusion. Finn breathed deep, bracing himself and kissed her neck, taking his time to suckle on the little vein that ran down from her ear to her shoulder.

Her skin was sweet and smelled of springtime, of jasmine and delicious honeyed things. So good. He wanted to lick and taste her all over. He thrust deeper still, hoisting her legs high on his hips to take her fast and sure.

"Finn," she moaned, her hands sliding down his back to caress his ass. "Oh yes."

For a moment he lost all ability to think straight, he thrust hard and deep, giving her what she wanted, and he too. The slap of their skin sounded loud in the room, a symphony of desire or pleasure and the most satisfying sound he'd heard in an eon. He wasn't a rakehell, a rogue who slept his way through the widows of the ton, or the whores who plied their trades at Covent Garden. He'd kissed women, yes, had one mistress whom he'd parted with once he'd heard he had to find a wife and within sixty days, but never before had he wanted to please a woman as much as he wanted to please Evie.

Not just here and now with her beneath him, with him ruining her completely, but with other things too. He would make her his duchess. Some would say he was an ass to go from one sister to the other, but he was under a time constraint, and Lucy did choose another to be her husband. He couldn't marry someone of his ilk, of his rank or wealth, but nor did he want to. Not after getting to know Evie better.

He wanted her.

Evie rolled him onto his back and straddled him. Finn gasped, not having expected her to do such a thing.

"I want to try it this way." She wiggled a little on his cock, and he sucked in a breath, fighting the urge to come. She stilled above him. "Oh, I did not hurt you, did I, Finn?"

God no she did not. There was no pain between them, only pleasure, satisfying pleasure ripping through him. "No, not at all. By all means, please continue."

Her palms pushed down against his chest, and she levered herself up and down on him, sending his wits to spiral. He had not expected her to be so astute or so adventurous for her first time. Not that he was complaining, he would take all and everything that she offered him.

His cock was like steel, his balls ached with the need to spend, and the sight of her breasts rocking above his face did little to stem his desire to fuck her, take what he wanted until he shot his seed deep into her.

Finn clasped her hips, anchoring her to him and helped her to ride his cock. She fell into a rhythm, and he bit the side of his mouth, trying to stem his release. "Fuck that feels good," he said, thrusting into her each time she slipped down onto him.

Their joining became frantic, and then the most perfect, most beautiful sight he'd ever beheld in his life blossomed above him. Evie threw back her head, moaning his name as her sex tightened and contracted about his cock, pulling his release to mix with hers.

He spent his load, enjoyed her milking him of every little ounce before she slumped onto his chest, the beat of her heart coinciding with his.

"Well," she gasped, her head nestled under his chin. He felt the lightest kiss on his chest, and he closed his eyes, reveling in her touch. "That was simply exquisite and something that I do believe I'd enjoy doing again."

He chuckled, rolling her to the side of him before hoisting her up against his body, keeping her close. "Do you now," he said, teasing her and knowing full well that now that he'd had her once, he would have her again. And again, and possibly again after that before he had to return to his room in the morning.

"Oh yes," she said, glancing up at him. This close, he could see her luminescent brown orbs and the little flecks of copper in them. Something in his chest thumped hard, and he reached out, slipping a piece of her hair behind her ear that had fallen over one eye.

"Well then, as a gentleman, you know that I can deny you nothing. If that is your wish, then I am at your command."

A wicked little grin slipped onto her delectable mouth, a mouth he would never get tired of kissing, he was sure. "Hmm, at my command. How much I like to hear those words. I shall keep you accountable to your offer, Finn."

He leaned down, unable not to taste her again. Their kiss lingered, heated, and his cock stirred. Damn it, he was a rascal. He'd just deflowered a virgin. He could not have her again so soon. He ought to be horsewhipped.

"Please do, I look forward to a repeat performance."

"As do I," she said, kissing him anew and stripping him of all sense and gentlemanly manners.

EVIE WOKE the next morning late, turned to glance at Finn and found nothing but a cold bed and linen that was decidedly empty of one gentleman duke. She sat up, glancing about her room. The small table before the fire was set with a delicious-looking breakfast of warm bread, ham, and eggs. A pot of tea steamed, all but begging her to the table. Evie pushed the blankets aside, slipped a shift over her naked self, and started toward the table.

The fire, newly stoked, radiated warmth. Evie smiled down at the food, knowing Finn had not been long in here, looking after her after their night of bliss. A night she was decidedly hopeful would be repeated often.

How wonderful it was to be in his arms, to be loved and caressed, adored, and kissed until she did not think she could bear much more of it. Evie sat on the chair closest to the fire and picked up the pot of tea, pouring herself a cup, adding a drop of milk just as she liked. That he'd had sent up such a delicious breakfast for her told her more than anything else that he cared.

Could his caring for her lead to more? That she did not know, but she was an always optimistic person, and she would fight to make him like her as much as she feared she was starting to like him.

The door to her room opened and in Finn walked. Dressed in tan breeches and blue jacket, he had forgone a waistcoat and simply wore a shirt and cravat. His hair still damp from his wash that morning. "Good morning," she said, unable to hold back the little grin his presence brought forth on her face.

He tipped her chin up with his hand, leaning down as if to kiss her. Her blood heated at his nearness and the thought of repeating everything they had done the night before flittered through her mind.

"Good morning, Evie," he said, placing a soft and too-short a kiss on her lips.

He sat across from her, spooning a hefty serving of ham, bacon, and eggs onto his plate and pouring himself a cup of tea."

"I have a proposition for you." His voice held a hint of trepidation, and Evie met his gaze, wondering what he was thinking.

"What sort of proposition?" she asked, the idea that he'd ask her to be his mistress souring the taste of her tea in her mouth.

"I want you to be my wife."

CHAPTER 14

Evie stood in the front drawing room of the duke's townhouse, staring at the busy Mayfair street beyond and thinking of Lucy. Where was she? Was she safe? Was she married? She stayed behind the sheer curtains so no one could see her and thought of what they would do next. How they would find Lucy and ensure her marriage before it was too late. How to stop her from ruining herself beyond repair.

If she wasn't already.

"Pacing and chewing off your fingernails is not going to make Lucy appear before you, Evie. Come away and join me for tea," the duke said, standing from behind his desk and going to where the butler had not long left a tray of tea and sweet biscuits.

"They could have left for Scotland by now," she said, turning toward him. "We may have missed our chance here in London."

"We have not. I have men watching the White Horse Cellar Coaching Inn. I will know within the hour if they pass through there."

"What if they travel north by other means? Whatever will we do then?"

"They will not," Finn said, coming over to her and taking her hand, moving her toward the settee to have a cup of tea. "Everyone travels through the White Horse. They will, as well."

A ruckus in the foyer sounded, and Evie glanced at Finn as the distinct sound of her sister's voice rose above that of the butlers. "That's Lucy," she said, standing and all but running to the front door.

"Lucy," she called, not believing that her sister was here. At the duke's home, safe and well. Lucy stilled, turning toward her, relief replacing the ire on her usually pretty visage.

"Evie," she said, her shoulders slumping in relief. "You are here. Oh," she sighed. "I'm so glad."

Evie closed the space between them, and the nearer she came to her younger sister, the more she noticed her disheveled appearance. Gone was the clean, pressed gowns, her hair always up and in perfect order, even her face had little smudges of grime upon it.

"Lucy, I'm so happy to see you." Evie pulled her into a tight embrace, and she could feel her sister's tension in the line of her back. "What has happened? You're upset. I can see it."

Her sister's eyes filled with tears, and Evie walked her back toward the drawing room, Finn stepping aside as they came into the room. "Come, have a cup of tea. It looks like you're in need of sustenance."

"Oh, Evie." Her sister hiccupped, the tears falling down her cheeks unheeded. "I've been such a fool, and I fear when I tell you what has happened, you'll never forgive me, or the duke."

The mention of Finn did little to help Evie's nerves. The fact that her sister was also without her betrothed or husband was also of great concern. They made their way inside the drawing room, and Finn closed the door, giving them privacy from himself and the staff.

Evie pulled Lucy to sit beside her on the settee, pouring her a cup of tea and handing it to her. That her sister was without Mr. Brown left Evie with an uncertain, sinking type of feeling in her stomach. If Lucy was not married, then she was ruined. This was not what she had hoped for her vibrant, enthusiastic sister.

"What happened, Lucy? Tell me everything. Where is Mr. Brown?"

"Oh, Evie," her sister said, wailing into a fit of tears, her teacup rattling on its plate. "It's all such a mess. I made a complete muddle of everything." Lucy sniffed, and Evie reached into her pocket, passing her a handkerchief. Another oddity as Lucy always carried a handkerchief, and anything else she thought one would require during any situation.

"You know that I ran off with Mr. Brown, Anthony, and all was going splendidly, but when we arrived in London two days ago, he ran into some friends from Bath, and everything changed. We were staying at a lodging house in St. Giles, and he started to go out at night, leaving me behind. Saying that it wasn't correct that I should join him if we were not married, and so I did not. But then last night, he returned, well into his cups and..."

"He did not force you, did he, Lucy?" The idea that her sister was assaulted wasn't a thought she ever wanted to contemplate, and Mr. Brown would want to be many miles from here if he so much as touched one strand of hair on Lucy's head.

"No, no, nothing like that, I assure you, but he did return, declared that he was going to travel abroad with his friends. I thought he was a farmer, settled and happy in Wiltshire. Whatever happened to his love of the land or his county or his love for me for that matter?"

"And so you have not married him?" Evie squeezed Lucy's hand when she did not reply, although, by her pale countenance and a red nose from too much crying, Evie already knew the answer to her question.

"We did not marry. He left me this morning, and I used the last of my money to travel here to the duke's home. I knew, you see, that you were looking for me. I saw you yesterday walking the streets in St. Giles, and I'm sorry, Evie, but I hid from you."

"Lucy, we were only trying to ensure Mr. Brown did the right thing and married you. We were not going to send you home if you did not wish it."

"I know," she said, tipping her head down. "I tried to return home via coach, but I only had enough funds to make Mayfair. I was going to write to Mama and Papa to send someone to collect me, but now that you are here, I am saved."

Evie sighed, wishing that were true, but her sister had not thought too much about her circumstances or what they meant for her. Circumstances that Evie thankfully would not need to worry about herself since the duke had asked for her hand. Evie had promised him she would marry him once her sister was married and settled. To see Lucy now unmarried and decidedly ruined was not what she'd wanted to face.

"The duke wanted to ensure that you were married. Papa sent us to follow you, you see. You will have to return home, and in time, hopefully, the scandal will pass."

Lucy glanced about the room, taking in its decorative

walls covered in silk wallpaper, the many books, and marble fireplace. A smile spread across her pretty face. "I will not be ruined, Evie. The duke coming after me proves that he cares. I shall simply marry him instead."

Evie stilled at her sister's words. Marry the duke? What was her sister thinking!

"The Duke of Carlisle is with me to ensure Mr. Brown did the right thing and married you. Now that he has not, all that can be done is to bring you home and try to limit any scandal. Fortunately, our family is not well-known in town, and you may escape too much social shaming."

Lucy patted her tears away with Evie's handkerchief, her countenance brightening with each minute. "I went with Mr. Brown because I thought the duke did not care for me as much as Mr. Brown did. But I was wrong. He's come after me, no doubt, to try to stop my betrothal. I had thought that he was merely offering for my hand because I was there and of age, but I think that estimation was incorrect."

"What are you saying?" Evie asked, the pit of her stomach churning, the room spinning at her feet.

"There will be no scandal, Evie, for I'll marry the duke. To society he is still my betrothed. He's a gentleman," Lucy continued, "he would not cry off from an understanding, not when contracts have been signed."

Evie swallowed, unsure she was capable of words right at this moment. "You wish to marry the duke? Still? I do not think that is an option, Lucy." A terrible thought, but Evie could not allow the duke to marry her sister. Not now, not after she had given herself to him. Had fallen in love with him and she hoped, with all her heart, that he too was in love with her. He had asked for her hand in marriage after all. There had to be affection between them.

"Of course, he shall have me, Evie." Lucy laughed, but

even Evie could hear the nervous tone to her words. "You will see. His honor and his hatred of scandal will ensure such an outcome."

Evie did not wish to see that at all, and she was a terrible person to think that about her sister. Over the past several days that they had spent together, she had come to respect and care for the duke. He was a good man, sweet and amusing, and, as Lucy said, honorable.

Knowing that the woman he betrothed himself to had not married, had, in fact, made an error of judgment, would he marry her still? If he was to do such a thing, what did that mean for her? What was she going to do if the man she loved married her sister?

"You will have to speak to the duke, but you ran off with another man, Lucy. It is unlikely he will forgive such folly and marry you still. While he came after you to ensure that your reputation was kept intact and that you had not made a mistake, I do not believe he will allow you to be his wife."

"Why are you not helping me? Defending me? The way you speak, you sound as if you do not wish for me to become a duchess at all." Lucy stood, going to the window and looking out past the curtains. "I did care for the duke, you know. I may not have loved him, but I did agree to be his wife."

"You also asked me to seduce him away from you. Have you forgotten so quickly what you were willing to ask me to do so you could marry your Mr. Brown?"

Lucy turned, staring at her with innocent, widened eyes. It was as if she had forgotten her request and was now scandalized by it. Whatever was her sister up to? "Please tell me you did not. You know that I only said that in jest. I would never want you to throw yourself at the duke for my sake. You did not, did you, Evie? You did not seduce my betrothed away from me."

Evie took a calming breath as the world around her started to spiral out of control. "Lucy, I never seduced the duke away from you." Which was true. When they had finally come together, it was mutual and with the understanding that Lucy would be married by the time they caught up to the eloping pair. The duke had long thought his understanding to her sister over. Lucy's actions had ensured that. They had done nothing wrong. Evie did not set out to break her sister's engagement. Lucy had done that herself. To now turn about and chastise her, beg her to tell her something that she did not want to hear, even if she had asked her to do so in the first place was unfair. All of this was unfair.

"Of course, I did not take it as a jest, but I did not seduce him away from you, Lucy. You left him for another man. You were going to marry Mr. Brown."

A knock on the door sounded, and Evie stood, going to open it. The duke stood on the threshold, his gaze slipping over her shoulder to her sister, who sat in the room beyond. Evie stepped back, opening the door wider so he could enter. The duke glanced across the room, and like a shutter on a window, his demeanor changed. He stood straight, the smile wiped from his handsome visage and replaced with that of the duke's, all proper and schooled.

"Miss Lucy, good of you to join us."

Lucy burst into another pool of tears and stood, running over to the duke, throwing herself into his arms. She wrapped her hands about his back, holding steadfast. "Oh, Your Grace. You've saved me. I'm so very sorry. Mr. Brown led me to believe that he loved me and that I was special. I was a fool to follow him. He is the worst of people. Please tell me you forgive me. Tell me that I have not lost your affection."

Evie closed the door. As much as she loved her sister, had always protected her from the world, her actions right at this moment reeked of a spoiled, rotten child. What was her sister thinking throwing herself at the duke as if he was free to marry her still? At least, Evie hoped he was not free, or her hopes and dreams with him were over.

"You're not married?" the duke asked, setting Lucy away from him a little, holding her at arm's length. The sight of Lucy in the duke's embrace did not sit well, and Evie narrowed her eyes, all hope that there may be a future for her and the duke slowly dissipating before her very eyes.

"I made a mistake. I was tricked, you see. Mr. Brown was not who I thought he was. Please tell me that I have not lost you. As a gentleman, I know that you would not leave me to the wolves."

Evie watched with horror as Lucy stared up at Finn, her eyes filling with tears. She looked crestfallen and lost, in need of support. Evie should want to help her, and she did, truly, but she did not want her to have Finn. She had chosen Mr. Brown. Was supposed to be at this very moment married to him. Not standing before the very man she loved and adored asking for him to honor his marriage proposal.

Finn stared down at Lucy, seemingly lost for words. Evie willed him to tell Lucy no. No, he would not marry her, not after being thrown over for another.

"You signed contracts to marry me, Your Grace," Lucy said, using his title for the first time since she'd seen him again. "I know I have done you wrong, and I promise never to be persuaded elsewhere in the future, but I do not wish to bring scandal down on my family if I can help it.

And your family too," she added, walking over to Evie and picking up her hand. "Is that not right, my dear? Both His Grace's and our family will be forever talked about should we not marry."

"The banns have not been called as yet, Lucy. No one need ever know that the duke offered for you."

"Oh, well, after Mr. Brown left me last evening, I wrote to Papa and asked him to announce our betrothal. I do hope you do not mind, Your Grace. With the contracts signed, your honor, and my apology, I did hope that we could marry and have a happy life together. Just as we planned."

Evie stared at Lucy and was unable to believe what she was hearing. Had her sister gone mad? To think the duke could just forgive her after her indiscretion was absurd.

"You had the banns called?" Finn met Evie's gaze, and she saw the disappointment within them. A disappointment that she too felt.

"Lucy, how could you do that to the duke?"

Her sister gave a nervous laugh, and yet Evie could not see anything amusing in the situation.

"How could I not?" Lucy looked between them, her eyes narrowing in thought. "The duke is in London trying to catch up with me, is he not? No doubt because he still cares for me and wants to marry me. I am sorry for the trouble I have caused. I do wish to marry His Grace if he will have me. You will have me, won't you, Finn?"

"I, ahh," he mumbled, looking at Evie, somewhat stricken.

"Lucy, will you please leave us? I wish to speak to His Grace alone. Ask the butler in the foyer to take you to your room."

Lucy looked between them, before nodding and,

without another word, started for the door, but not before stopping beside Evie.

"Please help me convince the duke, Evie. I know you love me and will do this for me because we're sisters and have always supported each other. I truly am sorry for all the trouble I caused."

Evie walked Lucy to the door, closing it behind her sister without another word before rounding on the duke. "You cannot marry Lucy. I love her, I do. She's my sister, and I will do everything to protect her, but this? No, not this."

"The scandal will be atrocious, for both our families if I do not make right on my proposal and marry her."

"I think after what she has done, and you as well, Finn that be damned the scandal. What about us? What about the offer of your hand to me?"

The duke ran a hand through his hair, pacing before the hearth. "It never occurred to me that she would not be married. I had hoped we could marry once we were satisfied that Miss Lucy was settled with Mr. Brown, but it does not seem to be the case. No matter how much we may dislike the situation, I am, in fact, betrothed to your sister."

"And you ruined me," she said, unable to hold back that truth, even though she hated saying the words. It was not the duke's fault that they had fallen into bed together. It was just as much Evie's fault as it was his. A mutual desire that was acted upon.

"I must marry, Evie, and I'm running out of time to do so. If your sister holds me to the understanding, it is her that I must marry. No matter how much I wished it would be you."

She took a calming breath, thinking on his words before recollecting what he said. "What do you mean you're running out of time to marry? Are you ill and must beget an heir before your time runs out?" The thought made her want to cast up her accounts. She could not bear it if Finn were sick.

"No," he sighed, running a hand through his hair. "I am not sick. What I have failed to tell you is that my father decreed in his will that if I were not married a year after his passing, I had only sixty days to do so, or I would lose monetary funds that are required to run Stoneheim Palace and my other properties."

Evie paused at his words, his hasty actions in securing her sister's hand finally making sense. "You offered to marry Lucy because you did not wish to lose your inheritance?"

"I did," he said, pacing still, his hair further on end.

"You could have married anyone. Why my sister?"

"Father had also decreed in his will that I must marry a woman from my home county and who was a gentleman's daughter. Your family met my requirements." The duke sat, staring at the fire, lost in thought.

"Why did you not think of me as your prospective wife when you first called on Papa?" They had known each other in London after all. Granted, they did not know each other well, but they had mutual friends, circulated within the same social sphere, to choose her sister seemed odd to Evie. Or, perhaps, he had not desired her in that way. The thought left a hollow feeling deep in her core.

"Because you're my age. I'm a duke. I require a wife who will give me an heir. I feared that your age would be an impediment to this."

Evie felt her mouth pop open at his words, and for a moment, she was unable to respond. She was too old? There was no mistake that she was older than Lucy, a few good years in fact, but she was not yet eight and twenty. Women older than her were still having children. Why Ava had a child only last year, and she was two years older than Evie. What had he been thinking?

"So why offer for me if during this whole time I was too much of a crone for your exacting standards."

The duke looked up from his chair, understanding dawning on his face. He stood and came over to her, reaching for her hands. Evie stepped out of his reach, wanting to know the truth. All of it, even if it were as ugly as her sister's actions from earlier today.

"You know I care for you, Evie. We've been intimate. It would be wrong of me not to offer for you."

"But you cannot now, can you? You're already betrothed to my sister and now that she will be ruined should you not marry her, create a scandal which you loathe to endure, I am left alone. Left looking like the biggest fool in history, but I shall survive," she said, rallying herself not to cry. "I am, after all, a woman and capable of weathering any storm."

"I want you. You know that I do," he said, reaching for her. Evie moved farther away from him.

"Do not fear, Your Grace. Society would never imagine such a virile, powerful duke such as yourself would waste his time with a woman who was of his age. How uncomely and vulgar."

"Evie, that is not true, and you know it."

She shrugged, heading toward the door. "None of it matters now. You require a wife, and your betrothed is now yours once more. She's young and will give you heirs. I may not. Not to mention your dislike of scandal will be averted should you do as you originally planned."

"Evie," he said, coming over to her and turning her to look at him. "We've been intimate. I cannot abandon you."

"I have always put my sister above anyone else, cared, and looked out for her her whole life. I'm not about to let her fall on her own sword. Even if that was of her own making. You will marry her, and I shall be fine. We will not speak of this time again, and from the moment I walk out of this house, what has passed between us is to be forgotten. Do you agree?"

He stared down at her, his beautiful, aristocratic face that she had kissed with abandon no longer going to be hers to have. A lump lodged in her throat, and she tried to swallow past it.

"How are we to go on as if nothing has happened between us? I cannot marry your sister under such circumstances. It would not be right."

"You will tell her nothing. You cannot. To do so will ruin my reputation and hers because she would call off the wedding if she knew the truth."

"Evie," he said, frowning, his hands tight upon her shoulders. "How will I stay away from you?"

"Because your family has been through enough scandal to last it two lifetimes, you said so yourself. You will have a happy marriage with my sister and will keep your distance from me because you have to. That is how you will stay away from me."

A muscle worked at his temple before he stepped back, the chasm between them growing wider and wider by the minute. "I will return to my London home with Lucy. Mama and Papa can travel to London for the wedding. Your nuptials must be seen as a joyous and much-celebrated event. A marriage all the way in Wiltshire will not do."

The duke nodded but said nothing, merely watched her. "I'm sorry, Evie," he whispered.

Evie walked to the door, hoping that the duke would stop her, while all the while praying that he did not. They could never be. Not now, at least. "I'm sorry too," she said at the door, before she opened it and left him behind her.

Evie went upstairs and packed her things, explaining the situation to Lucy before heading out the front of the duke's townhouse and hiring a hackney cab. Leaving her heart inside.

CHAPTER 15

Finn started to make the usual circulations that were required of him whenever he was in town, and the Season was in full swing. He'd attended numerous balls, had played the doting fiancée, and yet he'd never been more sorry for himself.

How on earth was he to marry Miss Lucy when Evie was in the world, an impossibility that he could not stomach. The past three weeks had been torture. To parade a woman about town as if they were the happiest couple in England made him want to cast up his accounts. Made him want to storm across the ballroom floor right this instant and demand Evie to see sense. To forget what everyone thought, what scandal his marrying her instead of her sister would create and live a long and happy life together.

He wanted her back. Hated that she'd reverted to the proper English lady who was courteous, commandeering, and sweet—helping her sister prepare for the wedding and only too happy to give him and Miss Lucy time together whenever he called. He didn't go to her London home to see his betrothed. God forgive him, he went there to see Evie.

Finn stood beside his friend, the Duke of Whitstone, sipping a whiskey while His Grace watched the Duchess of Whitstone dance a minuet with Viscount Duncannon.

"Miss Lucy will make a sweet wife for you, Finn. I will admit to being surprised to hear you're marrying the younger Milton girl. I always thought you and the elder Miss Milton suited better in temperament. At least, when we've been together in London, that is what I gathered."

Finn was well aware that he suited Evie better than anyone ever before in his life. Hell, even now, as he spied Evie across the room, speaking to her group of friends, laughing and smiling, he was conscious of how much he missed her.

Loved her.

The past three weeks in town had been hell. Sleep eluded him. It would seem that he could no longer rest alone, missed having her beside him, someone to reach over and pull into his embrace whenever he wished.

He drank down the last of his whiskey, steeling himself to speak the words that he'd tried not to these past days. "I've made a grave error, and I do not know how to fix my circumstance."

The duke glanced at him, his brow furrowing. "Tell me everything. Perhaps I can assist you," Whitstone said, watching him with something akin to pity. As if he suspected already that he longed for Evie instead of his betrothed Miss Lucy.

Finn sighed, hating himself beyond measure right at this moment. Whatever was he going to do? "I have offered to the wrong sister, and now there is little I can do about it."

The duke nodded, turning back to watch the dancers on the floor. "I know something of what happened between you and Evie. Ava has disclosed some particulars. Whatever made you agree to marry Miss Lucy after she threw you over for another man? You are not obliged to marry her after she treated you with so little respect."

"I know I am not, but she had written to her father, asking for the banns to be called after her Mr. Brown high-tailed it to the Continent. Not to mention, she begged Evie to help her in gaining back her betrothed. Should I have called it off, the scandal would've been great. All of London would've talked about my name for months. I could not endure that again."

"And so, you'll endure a lifetime of misery in a marriage you do not want?" the duke scoffed, before clearing his throat. "If you believed Miss Milton that she is content with this decision, you're fooling yourself. A woman in love does not want her love to marry her sibling."

Hearing it spoken out loud made his blood run cold. It also left him wondering why the hell he'd agreed to such an action. Miss Lucy had no feelings for him or respect by what she had done, whereas he had an overwhelming notion that what he felt for Evie, was something that he could not live the rest of his life without. He cared for her deeply. More than he'd ever cared for anyone else in his life. Her opinion was what he valued most, and so when she demanded he save her sister's reputation, he could not deny her.

"You think that Evie loves me still?" Finn closed his eyes a moment, needed to break his view of Evie across the other side of the room. "I do not know how I'm to keep myself from her. To think of all the times ahead of us that she will visit Lucy at Stoneheim Palace. Have Seasons with us here in town, and I'm to be distant, unaffected by her presence. It's an impossible thing to ask of a man."

"An impossible thing to ask a man who is in love."

Love?

The word reverberated around in his mind once again and he fought not to panic at the decision that he had to make. His marriage was to take place next week. How could he go through with such a thing? He could not, but did that mean he loved Evie? Finn looked to where she stood with her companions, just as she glanced up and stared in his direction. Their eyes met. Held. Time stilled, and the music drifted away, and all that was left in the room was the two of them.

Regret, savage, and brutal, tore through him, and he fought not to stride across the ballroom floor and take her in his arms, tell her that he was sorry. That he'd made a mistake, not just in London but when in Marlborough too. That he should have thought to ask her to be his bride. He'd always liked Evie, had known her through their mutual friends, why he'd allowed his narrow-minded views on women and their age to impinge on his decision he could not fathom. A mistake that he would forever regret, but at least he could do something now about it. Before it was too late.

She turned back to her friends, severing their contact, and the action cut him like a blade. Finn summoned a footman, in need of another drink. "How does a duke cry off from a wedding? Tell me, Whitstone, how I have managed to get myself into this position? My father was the man who London watched and gossiped about for his antics, never me. How have I allowed this to happen?"

Whitstone clapped him on the shoulder. "We are human, Finn. We may be dukes, but we do make mistakes.

Take myself and Ava. I lost her for years because I followed my parents' decree and believed them their lies. Do you think you should accept Miss Lucy's lies, her treatment of you, and lose the only woman you've ever loved? You cannot and you do not need me to tell you that for you already know what is right. Be damned the scandal that it will cause. You're the Duke of Carlisle. Who is to naysay or ridicule you? No one."

Finn thought over Whitstone's words, knowing them for the truth that they were. His friend was right, of course. He could not marry Miss Lucy. He did not love her, nor could he marry a woman who had run off with another man, no matter what crying off from their wedding would do to her reputation. She cared naught for him when she had chosen Mr. Brown.

His gaze landed on Evie once more, and warmth seeped into his bones for the first time since she had left his townhouse three weeks ago. He could not marry Miss Lucy, not when he loved Evie.

Loved her so very much that all he could think about was to make things right, to have her in his arms and love her for the rest of his days to the best of his ability.

"You're right," he said to Whitstone, a weight lifting from his shoulders at the sound of those words aloud. "I will make things right, and I will marry the woman I love. Not the woman whom I'm betrothed to."

"Good man," Whitstone said, taking a whiskey from a footman and clicking his glass against Finn's. "Congratulations on your forthcoming marriage. I know you shall be very happy. You will not regret this choice."

Finn smiled, sipping the amber liquid. "I believe I shall not. To love," he said, toasting the emotion.

"To love," Whitstone agreed, smiling at their antics.

THE FOLLOWING afternoon Evie sat in the front parlor of the London home she shared with Molly, her parents were seated before the fire, discussing Lucy's marriage next week. Evie tried to ignore their chatter, their excitement that their youngest daughter was marrying one of the wealthiest, most highly situated men in England.

Evie had already decided what she would do once her sister was married, and Molly had agreed to go with her. They would travel abroad, visit Europe and see all the beautiful things that they had never seen before.

She could not stay in England to see her sister start her life with the man Evie loved. She could not. To do so would be the veriest torture, not to mention impossible to bear. The last three weeks that they had been in town had been unbearable. To watch her sister hang off the duke, play and tease him as if she had never run off with Mr. Brown had changed her opinion of her sister forever.

Of course, she would always love her, but she no longer respected her so much. How she could do such a thing to the duke, a good man, not faultless by any means, but still a good man overall, was beyond her.

Her stomach twisted, and the ever-present nausea wracked her. She had been progressing more and more each day with illness. Her trip abroad could not come soon enough. She needed to get away from seeing the duke and Lucy together. It was making her unwell.

Or something was.

There would be other adventures in her life, other gentlemen admirers, and perhaps even a man who would love her as much as she feared she loved the duke.

The door to the parlor opened, and their butler announced the Duke of Carlisle.

Evie stood, curtsying as he entered before sitting back down. Her parents stood, going to the duke and fussing over him for several minutes. During their conversation, Lucy joined them, her golden locks bounding about her shoulders, her pretty blue eyes throwing the duke a coquettish look whenever she thought he was watching her.

Evie glanced back down at the knitting in her lap. She should have guessed that he would call this afternoon, he called every afternoon. She should have gone to her room or disappeared in the upstairs parlor, but she had not. Her foolish heart lived for his visits, to hear his deep, seductive voice speak of nothing of import for an hour or so before taking his leave.

The times with him here reminded her of when they were together on their travels to town. That time seemed a million years ago now, and never to be repeated. She could not wait until she left for Europe with Molly. No longer could she call London or Wiltshire home. Not if that meant she would have to see almost weekly her sister's happiness that came at the price of her own.

Her stomach cramped, and she stilled, hoping she would not be ill in front of everyone. Her travels abroad could not come soon enough for another reason as well. This very morning she had visited a doctor on Harley Street, and she'd been informed that she was with child.

Evie clutched her stomach, a sense of rightness, and also fear, filling her. Molly said she would help her abroad with the baby and help her on their return home to settle her somewhere in the country. A plan they were going to be discussing with the Duchess of Whitstone when she arrived shortly.

As if the very thought of Ava conjured her, she waltzed into the room, as pretty as ever, greeting everyone.

"Good afternoon," she said, smiling at those present

before coming over to Evie. "I'm so very sorry to do this to you all, but I must beg a private audience with Evie. Please do excuse us."

Ava clasped Evie's hand and pulled her from the room, heading for the upstairs parlor. "What is it that's so important? When I received Molly's missive, it left me fearing the worse. Are you ill?"

"I will explain everything when we're alone." Evie took Ava into the private parlor and was glad to find Molly already in the room, reading a book. Evie checked for servants before shutting and locking the door. She leaned against the wood, knowing the best way to announce her news was to the point and without any hesitation.

"I'm pregnant with the Duke of Carlisle's baby."

Molly, as expected, did not react. The duchess, however, stood from her chair, her mouth agape but without any words. "Tell me that is not true. Evie. Surely you are joking." Ava looked between them and slowly lowered herself back onto her seat when Evie and Molly remained quiet.

Evie came to sit with them both. "Please do not be cross, Ava, you're making me more nervous than I already am."

Ava stared at her, her usually perfect brow marred with a scowl. "He's marrying your sister next week. You have not forgotten that have you, my dear?"

How could she forget? Had she not been carrying the duke's child, she may have learned to live with her sister's marriage to the man she loved, and she did love him. More than she'd ever thought to love anyone in her life. She had thought marriage, courtship, and affection would never be hers to have, but she'd been wrong. With the duke, she had all of those things, and now he was marrying someone else.

"That is why I'm traveling to Europe above anything else, even though I've longed to return to France and visit other locales. We shall stay away for a good year before returning home."

"What shall you do when you return to England? I think if you're carrying a child about with you, people will notice. The duke and your sister above anyone else."

"That is where you come in, I hope," she said, steeling herself to ask for help. She wasn't used to having to be reliant on anyone for anything, but she would need the help of her friends if she were to survive this change in her circumstance.

"Me? What would you like me to do?" Ava asked.

"We need you to see if you have an empty cottage that Evie can live in on your estate. Away from society, but close to a community that she may be able to bring up her child without the censure of anyone we know," Molly said, answering for Evie.

Ava did not reply for several moments. "Well, of course, I shall help you, but I will not lie to Whitstone, and so he will know the reason as to why I'm hiding you on our property."

Evie could understand that well enough and nodded. "Very well, so long as His Grace does not tell anyone of my whereabouts or why I have disappeared from society. They do not need to know, and the Duke of Carlisle certainly does not need to know."

"Hmm," Ava said, narrowing her eyes on Evie. "Are you certain about that choice? If you told Carlisle of your circumstance, I think you would find that he would break off his engagement with Lucy and marry you. You do love him, do you not? Why not fight for him instead of running away to Europe?"

"Could you imagine what society would think if they

found out what I had done. To them, I slept with my sister's betrothed and fell pregnant with his child. I cannot let anyone know what I have done, not if I'm to protect the child I'm carrying from being labeled a bastard, among other things."

"People will ask questions. Are you prepared for those?" Ava asked.

"I will have some months to prepare myself for those questions while we're in Europe. If I have to see my family or Lucy and her husband, I shall ensure my child is safe at home, and I shall only visit sparingly. I cannot see them together. Even to imagine Finn lost to me forever is a pain that I cannot bear."

"You love him so very much, Evie. Please tell him the truth. I know the duke shied away from society, the gossip and scandals all because his father was normally the very one who created them, but he would throw all of that aside if he knew that you were having his baby. He loves you, I'm sure, and does not wish to marry Lucy. You really ought to give him the opportunity to choose."

"I did give him the opportunity to choose, and because of my sister's scheming, her reminder of the scandal, the duke chose her. No child in my womb should alter his choice. He either wishes to be with me, or he does not."

"He does love you, though," Molly said. "The other night at Lord and Lady Hood's ball, I watched him most of the evening. He did little but stare at you, his eyes following you about the room like you were the only woman present."

"I know the duke cares for me, but he has chosen to honor his understanding with Lucy, and no matter what Lucy has done, I do love her and never wish to see her shunned by society. Not simply because she was fooled by a man who lied to her."

"I like your sister too, Evie, but she chose to run away. Had her beau not run away, she would already be married to him. The duke and yourself need to remember that when you're deciding to live separate lives. Why should you both suffer the consequences of someone else? Yes, Carlisle should not have offered to Lucy, but neither did she have to agree to his offer when all along she was in love with someone else."

"And had no intention of marrying the duke," Molly put in, her lips pursed.

"What do you mean by that?" Ava asked, looking at Molly before turning to Evie.

Evie sighed, knowing Ava deserved to know the whole truth. "The night before Lucy ran away with Mr. Brown, she asked me to seduce the duke, or at least convince the duke that he'd made a mistake in asking for her hand. She asked me to help her break off the understanding in some way."

Ava gasped, her hand clutching the pearls about her neck. "Tell me this is not true. Your sister asked this of you, and you're still willing to let her marry the man you love and who loves you in return. I cannot allow their marriage to occur. It would be a mistake and one they both will pay the price for the moment they're expected to consummate the marriage."

The idea of Lucy sleeping with the duke made Evie's stomach turn, and she took a calming breath. "All that you say is true, I know that, but it doesn't change anything. The duke may love me as much as I love him, but he offered to Lucy first, and now she is in need of his name to save her reputation. I will not stand in the way of that."

"You also need the duke's name to save your reputation, Evie. And if you think for one moment that Carlisle will be pleased that you did not tell him that you're carrying his child, you are acting a bigger fool than you already are."

"Ava," Evie said, a shard of hurt piercing her heart at her friend's words. "That is unkind."

"I'm being honest. Carlisle will hate the fact that his child is now illegitimate because you did not tell him the truth. He will find out, Evie. The truth always has a way of coming out."

"That is very true," Molly said, nodding in agreement.

Evie looked between her friends. They meant well, but Lucy was her sister. How could she ruin her sister's only chance of keeping her reputation intact? No one knew outside their friend set that Evie had been intimate with the duke, loved him beyond reason. Her reputation was safe, so long as she could disappear into the wilds of England with her baby somewhere, never to return.

"I know what you're saying, and I love you for your honesty, truly I do." Evie reached out and clasped both of her friends' hands, squeezing them a little. "But I have made up my mind, and I'm determined to allow the duke and Lucy to continue on with their plans for a future together. I will be happy to remove myself from society and not be in anyone's way."

Ava shook her head, her lips pulled into a disapproving, thin line. "I do not agree with this. You're Evie, our impulsive, fun, determined friend. You ought to fight for your heart and happy future."

"I may have lost the duke," Evie said, loving her friends for their support and honesty. "But I shall not be heartbroken. I will have a little part of him when our child is born, and that child will be my greatest love. A sign that what we had together was real, even if it were only fleeting."

Molly sighed, smiling wistfully. "That is truly lovely, but

we still do not agree. You need to tell the duke the truth and now, before it's too late."

"I agree," Ava put in. "And if you do not, Evie Milton, be warned, that I shall."

CHAPTER 16

Finn paced Earl Tinley's drawing room at His Lordship's yearly ball, the muffled sounds of music and conversation seeping into the room. The ball was far from an enjoyable night out, it was a crush out there, too many people in attendance, the stifling heat from the compacted bodies and the numerous odors were enough to make him want to leave, get on his horse, and return to Wiltshire.

He swore, running a hand through his hair. Tomorrow was his wedding day. A day that he could not go through with. He'd tried to do as Evie asked him, to steel himself to marry Lucy, but he could not. He could not marry a woman he did not love, nevertheless know.

Especially when the woman whom he did love was right at this moment gracing the ballroom he'd just left, her eyes bright with excitement as she talked with her friends, her face as sweet as he remembered it. The time that they had been apart having been torture, and he would no longer be a party to such pain.

He loved her.

Wanted her and damn it all to hell, he'd damn well marry her, no matter what she thought on the issue. No matter that he'd made a mistake in asking Miss Lucy to be his bride. He should never have worried about Lucy's reputation or the scandal to their families should he cry off. She'd run off with another man, for heaven's sake. He was a fool to even think to salvage such a union.

The door to the drawing room opened, and he turned to see Lucy, giggling and clasping the hand of a gentleman he had not seen before. The moment she saw him, her steps faltered, her cheeks turning a bright red that did not suit her at all.

"Your Grace, I did not know you were in here."

He raised one brow, staring down at her and not giving the gentleman a second glance. "So it would seem," he drawled.

Lucy glanced between the man at her side and Finn, working her bottom lip between her teeth. She oozed guilt, and Finn's temper stirred.

"Pray do tell me, Miss Lucy. Who is your acquaintance?"

Lucy's eyes welled with tears, and within a moment of his question, she was seeking a handkerchief from her pocket, her cheeks wet with tears. "I'm so very sorry, Your Grace. This is Mr. Brown and the man that I love. He came back for me, you see."

"Did he now?" Finn drawled, fisting his hand at his side before walking up to the tall, spindly looking fellow. He punched him straight on his nose, sending him careening backward before he landed hard on his ass. Lucy screamed, kneeling beside her fallen rogue, her handkerchief now in use of cleaning up the bastard's bloody nose.

"You broke my nose," the man mumbled, his fingers pinching the bridge of his nose.

"You broke his nose," Lucy gasped, dabbing at the man's face with little effect.

Finn flexed his hand, shrugging. "I do apologize, but I think it was long overdue."

Lucy stood, fisting her hands on her hips. She glowered at him, reminding him of Evie for the first time since he'd met the chit. His stomach clenched, knowing he'd lost Evie and all because of this fickle little troublesome wench before him. He should have thrown being a gentleman aside, allowed her to ruin herself due to her foolish actions, and married Evie as he wished.

Instead, he'd allowed Evie to shoulder her ruination by herself. He did not care that she was of similar age to him, or if she could not give him children. He only wanted her, and if Miss Lucy did not cry off the understanding between them, then he damn well would.

"I cannot marry you, Your Grace. I love Mr. Brown, and he shall be my husband."

Finn chuckled, more than happy with her words. He bowed. "As you wish, Miss Lucy. And let us all hope that this time nothing else calls your Mr. Brown away from you before you marry the rogue. Because this time," he said, leaning close so only she could hear, "I will not be standing to the side to save you, no matter how many tears you shed."

Finn left Lucy gaping after him in the drawing room with her favored Mr. Brown and started for the ballroom, determined to seek out Evie. He needed to find her, to tell her he was sorry and that he was a bastard for not throwing her trouble-making sister to face her ruination, one of her own making, and marry Evie instead.

His actions made him look like a bastard, and he wasn't uncertain that he wasn't one. All he could hope was that Evie would forgive him, allow him to show her that he'd made a mistake, a colossal one, and he was sorry.

❧

Evie having had enough of the ball and watching her sister fawn over the Duke of Carlisle as if she were in love with him, left the ball and stood in wait while the footman hailed a hackney carriage for her. When one came around the corner, she thanked the servant before giving the coachman her address and stepping inside.

No sooner had she sat on the seat, the carriage lurched to one side, and she watched in both equal parts horror and shock as the Duke of Carlisle joined her, slamming the door closed and tapping the roof to signal they were ready to leave.

She glared at him. "What are you doing here? Have this carriage stopped and get out, Your Grace." He reached for her, and she pushed him away. "Do not touch me, Finn. You have no right to touch me. Not anymore."

"Please, Evie," he pleaded, the sight of his sweet face tempting her more than ever to throw herself into his arms. The thought of Lucy stopped her, and she crossed her arms over her chest to halt her impulsive actions.

"I made a mistake, Evie. A colossal mistake that I hope you'll forgive me for. Give me another chance."

"You're marrying my sister. There is nothing left for us to say."

"There is so much more to say. Please let me try."

Evie stared out the window on Mayfair, watching as the large, opulent homes slipped by. She shouldn't want to give him a chance. He didn't deserve one. Not really. He'd chosen her sister, simply because she cried. Evie sighed, that may not have been the only reason, but even so, she wasn't sure she wanted to allow him to tell her more things that would probably only hurt her.

"Let me explain. I will not leave you alone until you do. I will follow you all about London if I have to."

Evie shook her head at his insistence, but then she supposed she'd never be able to sleep if she did not know what he wanted to say. Never be able to move on with her life, travel abroad, and have her baby if there were things left unsaid between them.

"Very well, what is it that you have to say?"

He gave her a small smile before seemingly steeling himself to speak his truth. "I just spoke with your sister, and our understanding is over. For two reasons. First, before I caught her with Mr. Brown, I had decided to end our betrothal."

"What!" Evie wrenched forward. "What do you mean you just caught Lucy with Mr. Brown? Where? At the ball?" She banged on the roof. "Back to where you picked us up from," she yelled out the window to the driver.

The carriage slowed and turned at the next available corner as Evie turned back to the duke. "You caught Lucy with Mr. Brown? Why ever did you not come and get me? Where is she now? Was she going to run off with him again?"

Finn frowned, holding on to the carriage strap as the vehicle rounded another corner. "I do not know, Evie. She was too busy helping him with his bloody nose."

"Mr. Brown had a bloody nose? Was he injured?"

"Yes," Finn said, clasping her arms and wrenching her to sit beside him on the seat. "Because I bloodied it. First for running away with an innocent woman and then for leaving her alone to find her own way home. I bloodied his nose because he threatened both your and your sister's reputation by acting like a cad. I would bloody anyone's nose who thought to injure you by their actions."

His words trickled into her mind, and Evie forgot about Lucy a moment and more about what he was saying. "You punched him? For me?"

"I did, and I will ensure that this time he does not take flight to Paris before marrying your sister. I will not see your family name tarnished, and yours along with it, due to his behavior."

The carriage rocked to a halt across the street from Lord Hood's home, and Evie heard her sister's voice before she saw her. Lucy was standing on the sidewalk, Mr. Brown beside her, still holding a handkerchief to his nose.

Evie inwardly chuckled at seeing the fiend in such a state. He deserved so much more than a bloodied nose, that was certain. She pushed the window down, leaning out. "Lucy, have Mr. Brown escort you here. I need to speak to you."

Her sister spied her and, pulling Mr. Brown, started across the road, her steps faltering when she spied the Duke of Carlisle inside the carriage. Evie opened the door, without words telling Lucy she needed to get inside.

Lucy sighed but did as she bade, seating her and Mr. Brown across from Evie and the duke. The duke slammed the door closed, wrapping on the roof for the driver to return to her London address. The carriage lurched forward, and so too did Lucy's tirade.

CHAPTER 17

"The duke punched Mr. Brown. Without any warning or need to do so. We deserve an apology."

Evie wondered when her sister became such a little termagant. She'd never been so selfish or self-indulged, but over the past three weeks in London, she had been. Lucy's confidence that the duke would take her back, simply because she bade it, was unlike her. Or at least the girl Evie had known before her flight from Wiltshire with Mr. Brown in any case. Her actions tonight were proof that she never really cared about Finn or anyone but herself.

"His Grace will not be apologizing to anyone, Lucy. I think it is you who needs to apologize and explain what you're about. What is Mr. Brown doing in London? I thought you hightailed it abroad to travel with your friends, sir?" Evie said, staring down her nose at the gentleman. Her attempt at chastising him, reminding him of his error, did little good. Mr. Brown seemed as blind as her sister to the wrong or trouble they had both caused.

"I made a mistake and came back to the woman I love. I only got so far as Devon and turned around."

"How very gentlemanly of you," the duke drawled, watching them all with a disinterested affair.

"Lucy, do you still wish to marry, Mr. Brown? And what of your understanding with the duke?"

"There is no understanding, certainly not after Mr. Brown told me what he learned about His Grace. Not that I care any longer, since the man I do love has returned for me." Her sister crossed her arms, pouting like a child. Evie sighed.

"What did you learn?" the duke asked. Evie felt him stiffen beside her, and she shot a look toward him, noting his hard stare and tense jaw. There could not possibly be any more to this horrendous story that she didn't already know.

"What did you learn, Lucy?" Evie steeled herself, despite not knowing what her sister was about to say. With Finn tense beside her, she couldn't help but think it was severe and not what she wanted to hear.

Lucy smirked, pursing her lips. "Well, as to that, before Mr. Brown left for Devon, he met his traveling companions at Lincon's Inn. He was having lunch and overheard a conversation between Mr. Smithers and one of his work colleagues. You know who Mr. Smithers is, do you not, Your Grace?" Lucy asked, smirking. "They were talking about a time constraint that their client was facing and how it may be solved. That client was the Duke of Carlisle."

"A very interesting conversation." Mr. Brown leaned back on the squabs, a triumphant look crossing his face. "Stating that the Duke of Carlisle required a bride from his home county of Wiltshire and one born from a gentleman or gentry if possible. Mr. Smithers also mentioned that the duke only had sixty days to make it all come to fruition, or he would be facing financial ruin."

"I was that required bride," Lucy put in. "I'm just so very happy that my Mr. Brown came back for me before I married a man who only offered for my hand to keep his thousands of pounds."

"You did not have to say yes, Lucy," Evie stated, wanting to remind her sister that she was just as much to blame for all this mess as the duke was. Not that the news that the duke needed a bride or faced financial ruin was news to her. No, she'd found out that unfortunate information already. She had hoped, however, to save Lucy from that truth.

No woman wanted to hear that any prospective husband only chose her out of necessity. The knowledge that his affections toward her had been due to his fear of losing his fortune left an ache in her chest. They had spent so much time together, had been intimate…that could not have all been false. The duke was capable of love, Evie was sure of it. If the duke was certain of that fact, however, it was another matter entirely.

"You already loved Mr. Brown before the duke offered, you only had to be honest, Lucy."

Lucy gestured toward the duke, who unnervingly remained quiet. "He's the Duke of Carlisle. Who says no to such a man?"

"You should have." Evie digested all this information as the carriage rumbled through Mayfair.

"I must say you're acting very high-handed yourself in all of this, Evie. You knew that I did not want to marry the duke. You agreed to try and dissuade him from me just as I asked."

"You knew that Miss Lucy did not want to be my wife?" The duke stared at her as if he were seeing her for the first time, a stranger he hardly knew instead of a woman who had shared his bed, been a companion. The disappointment in his blue orbs left a hollow feeling inside and she winced. "Why did you not tell me?" he asked.

Evie glared at her sister. How could Lucy involve her in her falsehearted scheme? "I told her to tell you the truth, but before I could make her do so, she'd run off. I agreed to help her, but I was never going to go through with it, I just let her think I would."

"I would not have traveled after your sister had I known that Mr. Brown was indeed who she wanted. I would've let her face the repercussions of her own choice."

"I never asked you to chase after me. I thought that when I ran away, that would've been enough for you to break the understanding."

"Unlike your Mr. Brown, I'm a gentleman," Finn rebuked. "A duke. We do not act in such an ungentlemanly way. We had signed marriage contracts, and unfortunately, I needed a bride and within a short time constraint. You were my only option, and so I had to see if you were sure Mr. Brown was who you wanted before looking elsewhere."

"Well, it certainly seems like you found a replacement with my sister. Have you offered for Evie yet, Your Grace? Or is what Mr. Smithers said about the Milton girls true?"

"What did he say?" Evie demanded, leaning forward. She hated the thought that people were talking about her family, or that others like Mr. Brown could overhear those very conversations.

"That because I was the younger of the Milton sisters, I would suit better since I am of child birthing age. You, a spinster at almost eight and twenty, were past your fertile years. Or so the duke thought."

Evie gasped, her stomach roiling and not only because of her sister's truth but because of the very child she carried that she supposably was too old to bear. How dare the duke be so cruel? So dismissive of a woman who, by the way, was the same age as he.

"No more, Lucy." Evie met her sister's eye and was glad her sibling shut her mouth and lay back, seemingly understanding that she had heard enough. "Your marriage with Mr. Brown will take place next week instead of marrying the duke. A small affair is better, I think, and then you shall retire to Wiltshire and Mr. Brown's farm. Away from Society and any ramifications that you may face due to your actions."

"Why should we hide?" Lucy whined, glaring at the duke. "The duke was more at fault than I was."

"I would have to disagree with that notion." The duke's low, steely tone broke into their conversation, and Evie didn't miss the warning in his words. "I traveled far too many miles these past weeks trying to ensure that your reputation was saved. I did not have to do this. I could have let you throw yourself away, your reputation, and your life. I did not."

"Only because you needed a bride due to financial implications. Not because you cared for my family or me. Your honor and motives are not pure, Your Grace."

"Enough," Evie said, looking between her sister and the duke. The carriage rolled to a halt before her townhouse, and she opened the door, stepping out onto the cobbled footpath. Her sister followed, marching into her home. Mr. Brown went to pursue, and Evie stepped in front of the carriage door, stopping him. "You may call on my sister tomorrow afternoon. Good night, Mr. Brown," she said, ignoring her sister's protests before she disappeared inside, grumbling about the unfairness of life and older, interfering siblings.

The duke alighted from the carriage, shutting the door with a decided snap. "I need to speak to you, Miss Milton."

"Tomorrow will do very well for you as well, Your Grace."

The carriage rolled off down the street, and Evie turned, needing to go inside and digest all that she'd learned about the duke, and her sister, whom she decided she did not like very much at the moment. The young woman upstairs did not represent how they had grown up or the morals she thought they both had.

"Please, Evie. Let me come inside."

Evie halted on the step at the duke's plea. Damn her for being weak when it came to him. To want to hear him explain his actions away. She glanced up and down the street, and not seeing anyone and hoping no one was watching from their darkened windows, relented. "Very well, but not for long. I'm fatigued, and in need of solitude after the night we've just endured."

The duke followed her into the house, not saying another word as they reached the front drawing room. Evie closed the door, glad to see that the fire still burned in the room. Molly must have not long retired for the night. She sat before the hearth, clasping her hands in her lap and readying herself to hear the duke out.

He paced before the fire before coming to sit beside her, but still, he said nothing.

Evie had no issue in breaking the silence. "Did you ask for my sister's hand simply to secure your fortune?"

"I did," he said after a moment, shame seeping into his blue orbs before annoyance replaced that emotion. "And did you agree to try and persuade me to end my betrothal with Lucy? Neither of us is innocent in this."

"I know that," Evie said, hating the fact that she ever agreed to help Lucy. Not that she ever planned to follow through on her scheme, she had planned on making Lucy tell the truth. Not that the duke would believe that. Not now, after the fact. "But I did intend on making Lucy break the engagement that she did not want. She left before I had a chance to make her do so. That is the truth."

The duke rubbed the back of his neck, watching her. "This is madness, Evie. I do not want to quarrel with you."

"Nor I you, but you offered for my sister out of necessity, not because you had any emotional response to her. Was your offer to me the same? How much time do you have left before your father's clause comes into effect?"

"I have only a few weeks before I lose what I need to keep my estates running. I will be left with land and property, but no money."

"So I shall do well enough since my sister is no longer willing or perhaps not, since I'm in my dotage and unable to bear children."

"Forgive me for thinking such a thing. I do not believe that to be true, and I do not see you as a spinster or a woman in her dotage. The assumption was made irresponsibly. My father married in his thirties to a woman ten years his junior. I was only of that opinion because it is what is done, but it is not what I wish to do."

She raised her brow, looking down her nose at him. Not the easiest feat when he sat beside her and even in this position dominated her with his height. "Do you care for me at all, Finn? Or is what I feel for you one-sided?"

"No, of course it is not only on your side." He paused, running a hand through his hair and leaving it on end. "I still require a bride, desperately so, and my father decreed that it must be a woman of good family and from my home county of Wiltshire. I have no doubt the stipulations were so very concise because he wished for me to fail at the quest. He never cared for his son, probably why he stopped coming to my mother's bed once I had been born. He cared only for himself and his whores. He was an infamous rogue that London loved to hate."

The duke reached out and picked up her hands, holding them firm. "What I feel for you, Evie, is nothing like what I felt for your sister. While I liked her, it is you that I long to see, to hear, and spend time with. It's you that captured my heart."

She wanted to believe him. The time that they had spent together, she had lost her heart to the duke. In fact, she feared on their first night at the Bear Inn, where he'd held her close during the night, allowing her to keep warm was when she'd first suspected her heart had been touched.

Even so, it did not change the fact that he'd chased down her sister simply to marry her to satisfy some will. Of course, a duke needed funds to run his estates, but to make a woman believe she was desired, wanted when not, was not the act of a gentleman. How could she trust him to be telling the truth now? That she was different. That she was desired and loved.

"You lied to me. To my family."

"I was not alone in my untruth," he shot back, silencing her. "Did you and your sister plan how to end the understanding? Did you think to seduce me? Were your actions in my bed all feigned?"

Evie gasped. How dare he ask her that. "I would never do such a thing, and if you knew me at all, you would know that for the lie it is."

"Evie," he sighed, squeezing her hands a little. "Why did you not tell me that Lucy was in love with someone else? All the time we were together I felt as if I were being torn in two. Between honor and what I desire, what I want. I repeatedly chastised myself for the choice I made, for it was the wrong one. If I knew that my concern was not warranted, that I could act on my desires, my wishes, without feeling like I was replicating my father, a scoundrel who enjoyed scandal and acting without honor, our time together could have been so much better."

"You were set on bringing her home. Your reminding my father of the money you paid him along with the marriage contracts was always in the back of my mind. How could I tell you? I figured that once you did see Lucy, married and happy, that it wouldn't matter what she asked me to do for her actions made her plan moot in the end."

"I have long forgiven that debt. I will not be making your father repay me if that is your concern."

"I did not think you would," Evie admitted, wanting to tell him that there was more to say between them. That she was carrying his child, but she wanted him to choose her for herself, not because he needed a wife. "What do we do now?" she asked, hating the trepidation in her tone. For all that had occurred, she did not want to lose the duke, but nor would she marry him simply to ensure his riches.

"What indeed," the duke drawled, meeting her gaze.

FINN WANTED to pull Evie into his arms and kiss away her fear, her doubts. He needed her to know that he adored her and only her and bedamned his father's will and clause overshadowing his life, turning it upside down.

"Evie," he said, kneeling before her. "Know that what I'm about to ask you is done so because to my very core, it is what I want. Know that what I'm about to ask you is asked because I love you, more than any inheritance, or honor a man can have. I ask you this because I want you and no one else, and had I realized that sooner I could have saved everyone a lot of trouble and strife."

She shifted on her chair. Her beautiful dark eyes focused on his every word. "What did you wish to ask me?"

So many things, more than he could count. "My first question would be, Evie, from this day forward, will you do me the extreme honor of becoming my wife? Marry me and be my duchess just as you should always have been."

His heart beat fast in his chest, beating a crescendo that he was sure she could hear. The clock on the mantle clicked the seconds away, and still, she did not speak. The fire crackled in the grate, and he fought for patience, needing to know what she was thinking. "Evie? Will you marry me?"

She threw him a small smile, and a little part of him rejoiced. Hopeful that she would give him a second chance. Everyone deserved one, surely. "Are you certain that I'm not too old to be your bride? What if I'm unable to have children?"

"I do not care, so long as I have you. You mean more to me than anything I do not have, already have, or may never have. Did you hear what I said, my love?" he asked when she remained quiet. "I love you. I want you. From this day forward and forever. Tell me you feel the same and pull me from this torture that I have been living with these past three weeks."

She smiled, her eyes warming upon him. "I'm so glad that you said what you just did, for I too feel the same way."

Finn leaned forward on his knees, coming eye level with her. "Marry me. Marry me as soon as I can gain a special license. I do not want to spend another night away from you."

She slipped her arms over his shoulders, and heat licked down his spine. He'd missed her. So very much that at times he thought he would go mad with want of her. A life with Evie would forever be an adventure, just as their travels had, and he could not wait to start the journey.

"I will marry you," she said, at last, closing the space between them and kissing him gently on the lips. The embrace was short and chaste and nowhere near what he needed, wanted from his future bride. "I love you too," she admitted.

Finn pulled her into his arms, never wanting to let her go. He took her mouth in a searing kiss, one that had been building for the past weeks back in town. Her tongue melded with his, and his body shot to life for the first time since she walked out of his life.

"I want you," he said, kissing his way across her cheek to nibble on her ear. She had the prettiest ears he'd ever seen, and tonight with the little diamond pendant hanging from them, they made her look even more beautiful if that were possible. "Under me and in your bed tonight. I do not want to leave," he whispered into her ear, feeling a slight shiver rake through her body.

"I want that too." She gasped as his hand cupped one breast, his thumb and finger finding her nipple and rolling it between the two pads. "This is wicked, you understand. Are you certain you do not want to wait until we're married?"

"I could not keep my hands from you these past weeks. I'm not about to start doing so now. You will be my wife in a day or so. I see no harm in us coming together."

"Hmm," she said, standing and pulling him up to stand before her. He towered over her, and he could not help but run his hands over the soft, delectable flesh of her face. Hell, she was beautiful, sweet, and his.

All his.

He scooped her up into his arms, ignoring her protests that they would be seen and strode from the room. "Where is your bedroom?" he asked when they made the top of the stairs, Evie turning a deep shade of red when they passed a startled footman.

"Second door on your left," she said, playing with the hair on his nape.

Her touch drove him insane, and he breathed deep, calming himself. They would be alone soon, and then they could take all the time they wanted. And before this week ended, she would be the new Duchess of Carlisle. Just as she always should have been.

Her bedroom door was ajar, and he pushed it open, kicking it shut with his foot. Relief poured through him that he was hers, and she was his, and soon no one and nothing could rip her from him again. Not family, scandal, or steadfast honor.

Nothing.

CHAPTER 18

Evie stood beside the Duke of Carlisle in the beautiful St George's Parish church in Hanover square and exchanged vows with His Grace. As promised, he'd secured a special license, and two days after asking for her hand, she was marrying him. Her friends stood in the pews behind them, each of them unable to hide their pleasure, just as Evie was unable to stop the smile on her lips.

The duke turned and repeated the vows the priest spoke, and warmth flowed through her veins. He stood beside her, dressed in a superfine coat of dark blue. His cravat highlighted his sweet face, and it took all of her concentration not to throw herself into his arms, just as they had been doing the past two days. He'd insisted she traveled with him to Doctor's Commons in London to get the special license from the Archbishop of Canterbury. Being back in the carriage with His Grace alone for some time ended up being quite an enjoyable ride.

The priest announced them husband and wife, and he took her arm, turning to smile at their friends.

Married at last.

LATER THAT MORNING, they stood in the gardens of the duke's London home, celebrating their wedding ceremony. Tomorrow they were returning to Wiltshire to inform her parents of their marriage and to see her sister wed. Lucy had returned home the previous day, having stated that she wanted to marry Mr. Brown in their family church in Marlborough. Her mother and father had traveled with Lucy and her betrothed, wanting to ensure that Lucy did, in fact, return home to be married.

Evie had not told her parents of the duke's offer. They would find out soon enough, and she did not need them at her wedding. When she returned home, there would be time for a celebration.

"What a handsome husband you have," Molly said, passing Evie a glass of champagne and smiling over to the duke, who spoke with Whitstone, Lord Duncannon, and Marquess Ryley.

"Isn't he?" Evie agreed, hoping their wedding breakfast would be over soon so she could be alone with him. She had not told him of the child, but she would today. He'd married her without knowing that she was pregnant. She didn't want to state her vows with any doubt that he was making her his wife because he loved her, not because she was carrying his child. "I'm so happy, Molly, and sad too. We will no longer be living together."

Molly waved her concerns away, sipping her drink. "Never mind that. You know that I'm more than happy to visit my family in Hertfordshire. Then, as planned, I shall be traveling abroad to France. I wish to see Paris again, and then when I am home, perhaps you shall allow me to follow you all about during the London seasons, so I shall have something to occupy my time. I may be unmarried and have two or three strands of gray hair on my head, but there is still plenty of fun to be had, and I'm determined to have it."

"And you shall," Evie agreed, linking arms with her oldest friend. "You are more than welcome to stay with us during the Season or whenever you wish. My door is always open to you. I cannot thank you enough for being my companion and support these past weeks. I know I have not been the sanest person at times."

"You thought that you had lost the love of your life. That is enough to make anyone a little mad."

"Who is mad?" the duke asked, wrapping his arm about Evie's waist and holding her close to his side.

"I was, husband, when I thought that I had lost you."

He leaned down, kissing her promptly in front of their friends. The kiss, a sweet embrace, lingered longer than it ought and a few muffled chuckles from about them brought them to their senses. "You will never lose me, my darling. I promise you that," the duke whispered so only she could hear.

Ava, Hallie, and Willow joined them. All of her friends here made the day more special, and she was thankful for their love and support.

"Well," Willow said, a teasing glint in her eye. "Now, there was only one."

"One what?" Molly asked, looking at them all in turn.

"One of us left unwed. Whatever shall we do, ladies? I suggest that next Season we promise to all be in town to ensure our darling Molly finds the gentleman of her dreams," Ava said, grinning mischievously.

"I beg you not to do such a thing," Molly said, shaking her head. "I'm traveling abroad, as you well know. I may not even be back before next year."

"You will be, we'll make sure of it. There are some

acquaintances of Whitstone's that I know are suitable and honorable for our Molly. I shall hold a ball and invite them."

"Please do not." Molly shook her head, her face paling somewhat. "I will not be bargained off like a prized mare of yours, Ava."

Evie smiled at her friends as they planned and schemed for Molly. Finn took her hand and pulled her away toward the house, her friends so caught up in their conversation they did not notice their parting.

"What are you up to, Finn?"

"I think our friends have had us for long enough. It's time for you and me to become better acquainted as husband and wife."

She raised her brow, unable to keep a smile from her lips. "Really? How very naughty of you."

"You have no idea." Finn pulled her through his townhouse without, thankfully, passing a servant. To see them, it would not be hard to know what they were about. Evie chuckled at the thought just as he pulled her into the ducal apartments in the home, closing and locking the door with a decided snap.

He leaned against the painted wooden door, slowly dragging the cravat from his neck before throwing it aside. The top button on his breeches was next, and heat licked across her skin, expectation thrumming through her core.

"You are impatient."

"I am." He pushed away from the door and came up against her within a couple of strides. He hoisted her in his arms, kissing her soundly as he made his way to the bed.

Evie expected him to throw her onto the opulent bedding, but he did not. Instead, he set her on her feet, turning her, so she faced the bed. "Put your hands down to support yourself."

She did as he bade, expectation flowing through her. She could feel herself grow wet, and she wiggled her bottom against Finn, wanting him with a desperation that left her breathless.

Cool air kissed her legs as his large hands clasped the hem of her gown, sliding it up to her waist. Evie bit her lip, thinking how delightful married life was already.

Naughty indeed.

FINN'S COCK had been in a state of semi-erection since he'd seen his beautiful Evie walking up toward him to become his wife. He'd chatted and entertained their friends in the gardens for as long as he could, but all he could think about was when he'd have his bride to himself.

Alone in his bed. His duchess next to him in the ducal apartments.

The duchess, of course, had her own suite of rooms both here and at their numerous country estates, but he wanted Evie to sleep with him. To only ever be within an arms reach of his side.

His wife mewled as he glided his hand up her thigh, slipping it against her mons and teasing her wet cunny. She was hot and ready for him, and with his other hand, he freed his cock, taking himself in hand.

"I'm going to fuck you, Duchess," he said, lifting the last of her gown and thrusting his cock against her sex, teasing her with slow, delicious strokes.

"Oh yes," she gasped, her hands fisting into the bedding. She slid back onto him, teasing him in turn. "Fuck me, Finn."

Her taunting words maddened him, and without waiting, he thrust deep into her. His hands anchored on her hips, holding her as she took each thrust. She was so tight, grinding down on him, and he breathed deep, wanting to pleasure her as much as she did him. He could not get enough of her.

Finn pushed Evie onto the bed. "Get on your hands and knees, my darling."

She scrambled to do as he asked, and he came over her. He slipped into her again, and exquisite pleasure made them both moan. From the first time they had been together, each time was the same. The enjoyment they wrought was something he would never tire of. Finn thrust his cock, finding a fast, delectable rhythm Evie liked. She panted and moaned before him, dropping to muffle her noises in the bedding.

He pushed her toward a climax, teasing himself in turn. Her cunny wrapped about him like a glove, milking him and his breathing seized. She was so beautiful, so willing and his.

The word *mine* reverberated about in his mind, and he held himself deep in her, smiling as she undulated against him, seeking him, wanting him to fuck her.

"What are you doing? Stop teasing me, Finn."

Finn came down over her, one hand slipping down her bodice to clasp her breast, tease her puckered, erect nipples. They fit into his palms and he was impatient to kiss them, lick his way down her delectable body to between her legs and take her to climax with his tongue.

So many things to do and now they had all the time in the world to do it in.

Not willing to wait any longer, she pushed back onto him, fucking him instead. His body seized, and he groaned, pumping her anew. Their lovemaking became frenzied the closer they came to pleasure.

Finn moaned as the trembling contractions of her

release pulled and tightened about his cock, and he came, hard and long, fucking her until she collapsed on the bed, still dressed in her wedding gown, but satisfied beyond reason.

He slumped beside her, chuckling at their dressed state and what they had done. "At least this way, we can return to the wedding breakfast, and no one will be any the wiser."

"Really?" Evie said, sitting up and pulling the pins from her hair.

"What are you doing?" he asked, unable to form enough energy to stop her progress.

"We're not going back to the breakfast, husband. You're going to make love to me all day and all night. If you did not already know, I'm seven and twenty. I have some years to make up for being without a husband."

He grinned, pulling at his cravat. "Well, I cannot say no to that."

She came down over him, kissing him before moving down his neck. "No, you cannot. And now that I have you right where I want you, there is something else that I'd like to try."

"Hmm? What is that?" he said, closing his eyes and enjoying her touch.

"Well, what I want to kiss next is in your breeches, so please, Your Grace, do lie back, and let me explore what is now mine."

Finn groaned, his cock twitching at the thought of seeing Evie take him in her mouth. The idea alone could almost make him come. He lay his arms behind his head, grinning. "I'm all yours, Duchess."

"Yes, you most certainly are," Her Grace agreed.

Evie woke the next morning, her stomach cramping and protesting the new day. She pushed back the blankets and flew out of bed, running toward the chamber pot behind the screen and retched. Only just making it in time. Her stomach roiled as it always did during this time of the morning and she slumped back against the wall, hoping that the nausea would pass sooner rather than later.

However, she would deal with such an unwelcome side effect to a most precious gift.

"Evie? Are you poorly?" Finn came around the screen and kneeled before her, reaching out to touch her forehead. "You are a little warm and clammy. Was it something you ate?"

He helped her to stand and then swooped her into his arms, walking them both back toward the bed. Evie basked against his warm, calming presence, before he laid her down on the bedding, tucking her back in. The perfect husband, he poured her a glass of water, handing it to her. "Do you wish for me to ring for a tisane? A bath? What will make you feel better, my darling?"

Evie reached out, pulling him to sit beside her. "Nothing will make me feel better for a little while at least. You must prepare yourself to be putting up with such annoyances for some weeks still. Or so my doctor advised me when I met with him the other week."

The duke frowned down at her, his face a mask of confusion. "Whatever is wrong? There must be something we can do. You cannot be ill like that every morning, surely."

Evie chuckled, sipping her water. "The sickness the doctor advised will pass, Finn. He says by the fourth month I shall be quite myself again." She was being vague, wanting him to guess their happy news, which if his widened eyes and gaping mouth were anything to go by, he'd figured out her secret.

"You're pregnant?"

She nodded, tears welling in her eyes at the welcome news. A baby. Their baby. "I am. I know I should have told you earlier, but I was fearful. Silly really," she said, wiping at her cheeks. "I should have trusted in your love."

"You thought that had you told me I would have only married you out of obligation, out of necessity due to my father's ridiculous will." Finn joined her in bed, pulling her up against his chest. "I'm glad you did not tell me. Now not you nor anyone else can ever think that I married you out of such reasons. I married you because I love you." He kissed her soundly, taking her cup of water and placing it on the table beside their bed. "I adore you. I cannot tell you how happy this news makes me."

"Truly?" she asked, clasping him tight. "I'm so glad. I was a little worried you would think it was too soon."

"No," he said, meeting her gaze, the love that shone in his blue orbs making her heart squeeze. "A child with you, to start our family, would never be too soon."

Evie reached up and touched his jaw, feeling the short stubble against her palms. He was so very handsome and dishevelled after their night of lovemaking and sleep. How she adored him. "I'm so glad you said that, my love for I couldn't agree more."

"We should travel back to Wiltshire. You need to rest and my housekeeper at Stoneheim will know exactly how to make you comfortable, so you do not suffer unduly."

The idea of returning home was appealing. The country air, her mama to help her through the coming months. "I would like that very much."

"Wonderful." Finn jumped out of bed, racing to ring for the servants. "We'll leave today if you agree."

"I most definitely agree," Evie said, before another cramping pain took hold in her stomach and she raced out of bed for the second time that morning.

The duke came about the screen, rubbing her back. "On second thought, maybe when your sickness calms down, we shall return home. There is no rush."

Evie nodded, heaving once again into the chamber pot. "I think that may be best."

EPILOGUE

The Season, London – One year later

Evie rocked the cribs of Marcus Finlay Stone, Marquess of Lexington, and Lady Marigold Stone in their newly decorated London bedroom. She had just read them a bedtime story, and tonight she and Finn were going to attend their first ball of the Season since their marriage. Evie bent down, giving her wolfhound, Sugar a big pat and scratch before taking her leave.

They had not returned to town after they had traveled back to Wiltshire, preferring to stay in the country for the duration of her confinement and because the duke had long lost interest in the *ton*.

But, duty called, and she had promised her friends that she would attend next year's Season if only to ensure their friend Molly found a husband as wonderful and sweet as they all had.

"Are you ready, my dear?" Finn said, stepping into the room, his skintight black breeches and superfine coat with a silver embroidered waistcoat made him look beyond handsome. Nerves fluttered in her stomach, and she had the urge to pinch herself that he was hers—all hers and no one else's.

"I'm just putting our babies to bed. Are they not adorable?"

Finn smiled, coming into the room and kissing each of their children in turn. He pulled her from the room, wishing the nanny a goodnight and telling her where they could be found if they needed to return home.

"I know you're nervous about leaving them, but all will be well. They're safe and happy and about to go to sleep. Nanny will look after them and I need to look after you. You deserve a little fun and to see your friends again. It's almost been a year."

"I know," Evie said, walking down the stairs and taking a shawl from a waiting footman. Finn helped her into the carriage, and he rapped on the roof. The carriage rolled forward, and Evie glanced back at the house, praying all would be well.

"You're a wonderful mother. I'm so very happy that you're mine."

Warmth spread through her, and she turned toward Finn, snuggling up against him as they so often did when traveling alone. "And you're a good father. Thank you for the wonderful, full life that you've given me."

Tears pooled in her eyes and she sniffed, knowing that not all her emotion was due to her love of Finn, but also being away from her precious babies for the first time. She took a calming breath, repeating what Finn had told her. That all would be well. The children were well looked after.

"Are you really going to try and match Molly with a gentleman that you ladies believe is suitable? I could not help but feel she is less than enthused to be a party to your plan if her words the other afternoon at tea were anything to go by."

Evie shot a look at the duke. "Really? I thought she seemed quite open to our helping her."

Finn scoffed, smiling. "You are all blind if you think that is the case. Molly looked like she could spit fire, not to mention I have heard rumors."

"Rumors? What kind of rumors?" Oh dear, Evie hoped there was nothing wrong with her friend. She had not spoken much about her trip abroad, only that it was pleasant and something that she would love to do again.

"Rumors that she was somehow involved with a certain duke in Italy. He's English, has lived abroad for many years, indeed, has houses in both Italy, Spain, and England. A rogue, of course, never married and unlikely to do so, but he's in London for the Season, and it's quite the scandal."

"He's here? Whatever brought him back to England, do you think?"

Finn grinned down at her, winking. "What brought him back to England indeed? Can you not guess, my dear?"

Evie stared at her husband a moment, hardly able to believe it. "Molly?"

The duke kissed her, smiling. "Yes. Molly."

KISS ME, DUKE

League of Unweddable Gentlemen, Book 5

Molly Clare is living her dream. Being a guest in a gorgeous villa while she explores Rome is everything she could've hoped for and more. The man who owns the villa is equally charming—and entirely too tempting. At least, that's what he appears to be. The truth of who and what he really is…well, that's infinitely more complicated.

Lord Hugh Farley is living a nightmare. Ruined by rumors of indiscretions he didn't commit and betrayed by his own family, his only option was to leave London. But any hope he had for a quiet Roman exile is destroyed when she arrives. Molly is everything he's ever wanted…and nothing he can have. But keeping his mind—and hands—off her quickly proves impossible.

Can Molly and Hugh find a way to clear his name and build a future together? Or is their happily ever after nothing but a fantasy?

CHAPTER 1

Rome Italy, 1829

They had arrived. Finally. Molly stepped out of the carriage and stretched, basked in the warm Mediterranean sun that warmed her blood and healed the many aches and pains from weeks of travel. Rome. Just the thought of where she was sent a thrill down her spine and expectation thrumming through her blood.

So many wonderful places to visit and see, and thanks to her wonderful friends back in London, and the Duke of Whitstone, month-long lodgings at the Villa Maius had been secured for her. The gentleman who resided here was from home, but his servants would care for her and her companion for the short time they would be in the city.

The front door to the villa opened, and a gray-haired, voluptuous woman came out onto the street, her smile as warm as the sun shining down on her back.

"*Signora*, Molly Clare, welcome. Welcome to Rome. Come, we shall serve refreshments for you. You must be exhausted."

Molly smiled, relieved to be welcomed so lovingly at the home. She did not know anything of Mr. Farley, who lived here, other than he was friends with the Duke of Whitstone. There had always been a little niggling concern within her that the staff may be annoyed at her arrival, being unknown to them as she was, but it would not seem to be so.

"Thank you for having me. I hope it is not too much trouble that I'm here." She walked in off the street into a small foyer that led onto a large, rectangular room partly roofed. A fountain sat in its center, a naked cherub squirting water from his mouth. Looking up, Molly noted the opening in the roof sat directly over the fountain, and in ancient times, it would be the place the villa would have collected its water for the family.

"Oh, no no no. We're very happy to have you here." The servant ordered a tall, dark-haired man to attend to the luggage while she walked them toward a set of stairs. "Mr. Armstrong is not here. He is away in Naples for the duration of your stay, and we have been expecting you. He informed us all before he left last month to care for you well. You have mutual friends, yes?"

Molly looked about the villa. Mosaic-tiled floors adorned the space, images of Roman life, of agricultural scenes and animals. All lower-floor rooms had their windows open, the curtains billowing with the warm, Mediterranean air. The breeze smelled of salt and spices, of oranges and freshly cut grass. She stopped a moment, taking in the view from one of the windows she could see through a doorway. The courtyard garden, full of olive trees, beckoned her to sit and savor its beauty.

"We do, yes. The Duke of Whitstone. Although I have never met Mr. Armstrong, I am very grateful to him for allowing me to stay here."

The housekeeper beamed, seemingly well pleased at her compliment of her employer. "He is the best of men whom I'm sorry you shall not have the honor of meeting." The woman started up the stone stairs. "I'm Maria, my dear, the housekeeper of Villa Maius. Should you need anything at all, merely let me know, and I shall do all that I can to make your stay enjoyable."

"Thank you." They climbed the stairs, the second floor opened up to a large, rectangular room with reclining wicker chairs. A balcony stood at the end of the room. Molly could not pass without taking in the view. She stepped out onto the balcony, the breath catching in her lungs. The view overlooked the street they had entered on. At this height, it gave her a better vantage point of the city beyond. Rome. Its glory spread out before her like a gift from the gods. Her fingers curled around the stone balustrade, anchoring herself so she would not run from the villa and see firsthand the ancient city. Sounds wafted up to tease her and urge her to leave and explore.

Soon, she promised. As soon as she had bathed and had a restoring cup of tea.

"The center of Rome is only a short walk from here. At the other end of the villa is another room similar to this that overlooks the river Tiber. I can always have the carriage put at your disposal, however, if you do not want to walk. To see the Vatican, you shall have to avail yourself of the vehicle."

Excitement thrummed through her veins, and she leaned out over the railing, spying a few people out on the streets, some taking in the sights while others plied their trade. "What a magnificent city. I have always wanted to tour, and now I can. I cannot believe it."

"I am dreading the return journey, however," her companion, Miss Sinclair said, joining her and staring down at the city with a disgruntled air. "Shall we have tea?"

Molly was reluctant to leave the magnificent view, one she longed to be part of, and nor would she allow Miss Sinclair's dislike of the distances they had traversed to dampen her excitement. If her companion did not wish to see Rome, she could stay here at the villa. Molly went about London most of the time on her own, it would not be out of character for her.

"Yes, let's, and then I can get started on exploring this wonderful city."

"Would you like to have tea on the balcony, *Signora* Molly?"

"Thank you, yes," she replied, seeing the outdoor setting and sitting. Servants bustled about the home, bringing up their trunks to the rooms. Molly could almost pinch herself just to confirm that she was indeed here in Rome. Her time was precious, only a month, and then they would be on the return journey back to England. Travel would take several weeks, and she wanted to visit some other cities on the continent before returning to London and the new Season.

The tea was sweet and refreshing, and lovingly the housekeeper had made some biscuits with almonds through them, which squelched her rumbling stomach.

Molly leaned back in her chair, placing down her napkin, well-sated after the fleeting repast. "Shall we finish the tour of the house, see our rooms and then decide where to go first?"

"Of course, Miss Molly," Miss Sinclair said, yawning.

It had been a long day, but Molly was too excited, had waited too long to be in Rome to lie down for the afternoon. She wanted to explore, walk the streets, visit the markets, and be part of the culture here in this ancient city.

"If you're tired, Miss Sinclair, I can always go out without you. I do not mind."

Miss Sinclair's lips pursed into a disapproving, thin line. "No, that would never do. You need to have a chaperone and company to keep you safe. I will simply have to endure it."

"I do not wish for you to endure Rome. I want you to enjoy it as much as I intend on doing."

"I do not believe that will be possible, Miss Molly. I have an aversion to heat, and if it did not escape your notice, it is very hot outside."

Molly turned toward the balcony, the slight breeze wafting in through the doors cooled her skin. Yes it was warm, but England was always so very cold. How could anyone not make use of such beautiful weather and explore it?

The housekeeper stepped forward, catching Molly's eye. "We have a manservant here, Miss Clare. He would be more than happy to escort you about Rome so you may see some of our wonderful city."

Molly smiled at Miss Sinclair. "See, I shall be perfectly safe. You may have this afternoon to rest and recuperate, and we shall come together for dinner this evening before tonight's ball."

"You intend to attend Lord and Lady Dalton's ball this evening? Even though we only arrived today?"

"Of course I intend to go." Molly shook her head at her companion, having gained the sense that she did not want to go or do anything while they were here. The prospect was not helpful, nor would it be possible. Molly had four weeks to visit this wonderful city, and she would simply have to ignore her companion's complaints about seeing everything they could in that time.

"Maria, will you show me to my room, please?"

The housekeeper bustled down a wide passageway until she came to a room that overlooked more of the villa grounds, lawns, and gardens that swam with a variety of colors. The tinkling sound of water carried up to her, and she looked for the fountain but could not see it from her room. She would have to go downstairs to find it herself.

Her room was a tiled mosaic floor that was made out in a variety of blossoming flowers. Her bed was large, opulent with its coverlet and abundance of pillows. She, too, was partial to lots of pillows on beds. It somehow made them look complete. Perfect.

A small writing desk occupied the space before one window, and a large settee sat before her fire. Although she did not believe she would need that at all while she was here in Rome. Not with it being so warm.

"There is freshwater and linens behind the screen for you, Miss Molly. When you're ready to go out, come downstairs, and I shall fetch Marcus for you. He will keep you safe and show you all the best sites Rome has on offer."

"Thank you so much. I cannot tell you how thrilled I am about being here."

The housekeeper smiled before leaving her to her ablutions, the sound of Miss Sinclair's voice as she was taken to her room echoing down the hall.

Molly walked to the small balcony her room had and glanced down at the garden. She raised her face to the sun, breathing deep. What an idyllic location to live. One could get used to such a place and never return home to rainy, dreary old London.

CHAPTER 2

He wasn't supposed to be in Rome. He'd promised his close friend the Duke of Whitstone that he would leave Miss Molly Clare alone for the month she was visiting the ancient city. But he could not. Not because he wished to meet the chit—he'd long thrown away any notion of making a grand match or even trying to court a lady.

Business brought him back to Rome a month earlier than planned. A letter from his brother's steward in London never bode well. What had his brother done now that was so very bad that the black sheep of the family had to be notified?

Lord Hugh Farley, younger brother to the Duke of St. Albans, pushed through the small door off the street that led into his Roman villa and strode through the gardens, headed for his office. He waved to a couple of his staff who were picking vegetables, ignoring the fact they looked a little shocked at his return. His housekeeper Maria doubly so when he strode into the atrium.

"I shall have lunch brought into my office, please,

Maria." He half-laughed at the woman's expression. "Do not look so shocked at my being here. I do live here as you well know."

The housekeeper made an awkward chuckle before following close on his heels. "You have Miss Molly Clare here, *Signore* Hugh. Do you not remember she is to stay a month?"

"I have not forgot, but I received a letter from my brother's steward that I must attend to." His man of business in Rome had sent word to him, telling him to return from Naples as soon as possible. It was unfortunate that Miss Clare was here at the same time as he, but this was his home, and she had a companion, it would not be too scandalous, surely.

"I do not intend to ruin her, Maria. Do amend your distress."

Another awkward laugh from his housekeeper rent loudly in the room. Hugh glanced up at her, not missing that she was now wringing her hands in her apron. "You disapprove."

"She's unmarried, *Signore*. You, too, remain unmarried. We could weather any storm of her being here when you were not at home, but now that you are, tongues will wag. Whether those tongues are in Rome or London."

"Let them wag. I have business to attend to, and she has a companion. There is little we can do about it. I shall not allow society to rule my life." God knows he'd allowed enough of that in London along with his family. The thought of his brother, his mother, soured the taste in his mouth. He picked up his penknife and sliced open the missive.

"Lunch, Maria. If you please."

As if remembering herself, she bobbed a quick curtsy and left the room. Hugh opened the parchment and read.

His blood ran cold at the black, cursive words that lay out before his eyes.

His Grace, the Duke of St. Albans, had passed away after a carriage accident. We here inform Lord Hugh Farley that you are now the Duke of St. Albans, heir to St. Albans Abbey in Kent, Brentwood House in Surrey. and Clare Castle in Ireland.

The rest of the missive blurred at the thought of his brother no longer living. This letter was already a month old. Hugh leaned back in his chair, staring blankly at the wall before him.

It could not be.

Henry was dead? His only brother. Another letter sat on his desk, the neat, flowing script that of his younger sister, Sarah. He tore it open, not bothering with the penknife. She was less diplomatic, having never been very good at making her words less blunt and to the point. Her letter contained details about their brother's demise, of his foolhardy bet with the gentleman who formed his London set. They had planned to race a curricle from London to Southampton, and Henry had overturned the vehicle, killing himself instantly. She implored him to return to London post-haste and take up the position as the Duke of St. Albans.

Hugh scrunched up the letter, throwing it onto his desk. London could go hang. The fickle *ton* may very well forgive him the scandal that dogged his every move in that city, but he would never forgive London.

The bastards.

The amused, excited voice of a woman flittered downstairs before the boots on his staircase echoed in the foyer. From where Hugh sat, he could see who came and went in the atrium outside his tablinum. In the past ten years that he'd lived in Rome, he realized that there had never been a woman under this roof, save the servants of course.

He watched the threshold of his door, wanting to see what this Miss Molly Clare looked like. His friend, The Duke of Whitstone, one of only a few he had left in the world, had written to him asking for assistance in housing Miss Clare. He could not refuse.

Every year, Hugh traveled to Naples to his vineyard there, so there were no problems offering his Roman villa while he moved to his estate in the country.

A woman in an azure-colored dress stepped into his line of sight, and the breath in his lungs seized. She wasn't a young woman as he thought she may be, but a woman, her figure filling out her day gown in the most promising way.

Her hair was inky black and tied up into a motif of loose curls, some of which had already fallen out and bounced about her slender shoulders. A bonnet hung from her wrist from a vivid-blue ribbon, and a pelisse lay over her arm. Everything about her embodied what he had left behind in London. Had he stayed in England, he could now be married to a woman as appealing as Miss Clare. Had a family, children playing about his hessian boots. A pang of nostalgia thrummed through him over everything that he had lost by leaving London to live in Rome.

By following the rules and doing what he was told.

Not that it was his fault that he had to come away, his brother Henry had ordered him to take the fall for his wayward actions. Hugh had refused of course, until both his mother and brother had told him his ruin was done. That the *ton* would not accept him from that moment onward. His choice was clear, leave England or face being cut off socially and financially.

A younger son of a duke, he had money, of course, but not enough that would keep him for long. He had not studied law or the church as one might to live. A stupid mistake.

With nowhere else to turn, he had made some demands of his own. His brother would fund his living here in Rome. Purchase him a villa and house in Naples, a locale he had enjoyed when on the grand tour only two years before. A small price for his brother to pay since Hugh was the one losing everything, and his family.

Miss Clare slipped on her bonnet, laughing at something Marcus, his manservant, said to her before they both walked from the atrium. "Maria," Hugh called, catching his housekeeper's eye.

Maria bustled into his office, a small smile playing about her mouth. "*Signore*? You called."

"Where is Marcus taking Miss Clare?" He placed the letters from his brother's steward and Sarah into his drawer, locking it away.

"She wished to visit Trevi Fountain. I think they will then walk to the food market, Piazza Navona after that."

"I shall dine with her tonight, explain the reasons why I'm back in Rome. I'm sure she'll understand that business has brought me home." It'll also allow him the opportunity to ask her about London and what the latest *on dit* was. He'd not dined with a woman in an age. In fact, he could not remember the last time he'd slept with one either. Too long, not that he was looking to Miss Clare to scratch that particular itch, but even so, she was attractive with her womanly curves, pretty eyes, and warm laugh. Dinner this evening may be an enjoyable affair and a good distraction after the news he'd just received.

"Of course, *Signore*. I shall get your luncheon right away."

"Thank you, Maria."

Hugh slid a piece of parchment before him, picking up

a quill and dipping it into the black ink. He started a reply to his brother's steward. He wished he could feel an ounce of despair, sorrow even, at the death of his brother. He did not. He would write to Sarah, and console her as best he could. Even with the thousands of miles that separated them, she had never turned against him at least, had believed his side of the story, especially since she knew all too well what a reprobate Henry was. Even so, she would be hurting right now, she had loved them both being her only brothers, her only family left, no matter how wild or vexing Henry could be at times.

Hugh wished he could be sorry, but his brother having joined in with the *ton* allowed the lies to percolate through society until his name was mud, and not admitting to his wrongdoing in the whole sorry mess was something Hugh could not forgive.

And now he was the Duke of St. Albans. A title and responsibility he'd never wanted.

Damn it all to blasted hell.

MOLLY RETURNED to the villa late in the afternoon after a day of walking the streets of Rome. The Spanish Steps, the markets, and the beautiful, awe-inspiring Trevi Fountain. Marcus had allowed her to visit whatever seized her attention while keeping her safe. It had been the perfect first day in Rome, and she could not wait until another commenced tomorrow.

She entered the villa, the cooler air inside the atrium a welcome reprieve after a day in the sun. Molly slipped off her bonnet, perspiration moistening her hair and sticking to her neck. She would need to bathe before dinner. Her stomach rumbled at the thought of food as she stepped on the first stair heading upstairs.

"Miss Clare, how very good to meet you."

The deep, gravelly baritone startled her, and she gasped, turning to see where the voice had come from. She felt her mouth pop open at the sight of the man before her. His tall, athletic frame was enough to turn any woman's eye, but his face was beyond stunning. His cheekbones seemed chiseled from marble, similar to the statues she'd seen this afternoon. His raven colored hair was longer than it ought to be, was tied back off his face, and the shadowing of an unshaven jawline made her mouth dry. Her whole body shivered at his presence, and she swallowed, hoping her voice would still work.

Molly stepped off the stair and walked toward him, giving her a moment to compose herself. She met his clear, smoky-black orbs, and something inside her thrummed, came alive at his proximity.

She jerkily held out her hand for him to take. "Sir, I do not believe we've been introduced." His mouth lifted into a delicious grin, and she bit her lip, unsure what to do with herself when he smiled. Heat crept over her face at her wayward thoughts. His eyes roamed over her features, and she schooled her emotions, willing her racing heart to calm.

"I'm Mr. Armstrong. I live here. The Duke of Whitstone, I believe, is a mutual friend of ours." He picked up her hand, kissing her gloveless fingers. The feel of his lips on her skin sent a bolt of awareness up her arm, and she stepped back, placing well-needed space between them.

"Oh yes, Mr. Armstrong. How do you do? Thank you so much for offering me your home during my stay here. I hope you did not mind that his grace asked on my behalf for accommodations."

"Not at all." He gestured toward the stairs. "I shall return you to your room. I'm sure you wish to freshen up before dinner."

"I would yes," she said, starting up the stairs and hoping he hadn't noticed her disarray too much. "Have you known the duke for long?" Molly hadn't queried too much how the duke and Mr. Armstrong were known to each other, even though she was so very grateful they were. She had not wanted to stay in a hotel here in the city. She'd wanted to visit Rome and stay in an ancient villa if she could. Being here would probably be the only time she would visit the city in her life, and she had wanted to make it memorable.

"We were in school together at Eton and socialized in the same social sphere." He walked beside her, his hands clasped behind his back. She surreptitiously took in his attire and liked what she saw. He seemed to have the air of a titled gentleman, but that wasn't the case from what she did know.

His tan breeches and highly polished buckskin boots went well with his casual attire—no superfine coat or waistcoat for this Mr. Armstrong. A simple shirt and loosely tied cravat were all that he needed. It suited him, and she liked the casual way of life here in the city.

"Whitstone stayed here when he traveled abroad a few years ago."

She nodded, listening to him talk of their friendship, savoring the sound of his voice, like rich, delicious chocolate that melted on one's tongue. Molly cleared her throat, not sure why she imagined Mr. Armstrong in such a way. "Are you staying in Rome for some time, or are you just traveling through? I understood that you were going to be away from home for several weeks."

"I was going to be away, but I had an urgent letter from

London that brought me back. I hope you will continue to stay here, Miss Clare, even with me ensconced under the same roof. You have a chaperone, I understand."

The thought of having Mr. Armstrong under the roof sent a thrill down her spine, and for a moment, she regretted her decision to bring a chaperone with her to Rome. Molly was, after all, a woman well beyond her first blush. It would be unnatural for her to look upon such a handsome specimen of a man and not imagine all sorts of naughty things with him. She'd read enough books on anatomy and the art of lovemaking to know that she would not be adverse to a man such as the one who towered beside her, taking her to his bed. His strong, athletic build, well-defined arms, and large hands displayed a healthy, active gentleman well in his prime.

"I do have a chaperone. Miss Sinclair is her name. I'm sure with her being here with me, nothing untoward can be said about you being back in Rome." Molly let out a self-deprecating laugh. "Not that anyone cares what I do in any case, save my friends."

"Why is that?" he asked, frowning and halting his progress at the top of the stairs. "Why would no one care what you do? I cannot believe such a statement."

Molly stopped and glanced up at Mr. Armstrong, losing herself in his comforting stare. "While I may have friends who are well placed in society, I am not one of them. My family was good enough to help me achieve my dream of traveling to Rome, but there will not be another such venture. I'm not certain what I shall do when I return to England."

"You do not wish to marry?" Mr. Armstrong ran a hand through his hair, cringing. "Apologies, Miss Clare. I should not ask you such personal questions. It is not my place."

She smiled, reaching out and clasping his arm. The moment her hand touched the bare flesh, she knew it for the mistake it was. To feel his warmth, the sprinkling of coarse hair beneath her fingers shot longing through her body. Only made her want to touch more of him.

"I do not mind. If you're to be here with me and we're to spend more time together, you will learn soon enough that I am who I am and have no issues with being truthful. I cannot stand it when women dissemble, say things that one has to try to puzzle out. I think some women of my acquaintance think such a thing is amusing, whereas to me, it's merely annoying."

Mr. Armstrong barked out a laugh, taking her hand and placing it on his arm as they started back toward her room. "I think, Miss Clare, that you and I shall get along well. I, too, am opposed to disassembling and falsehoods. It is why I live in Rome. I could not live in London with the despicable gossipmongers who live to ruin other people's lives."

Molly stared down at the mosaic-tiled floor. His words held a hardened edge to them as if he were cut by the *ton* itself and knew firsthand what could happen to an unsuspecting or vague fellow in the *ton*.

"I hope your letter from home was not bad news, Mr. Armstrong. I should hate to be an inconvenience," she said, hoping to change the subject away from London, and the pitfalls one could sink into without too much trouble.

He stopped at her bedroom door, and the scent of wisteria floated through the air. "You are not an inconvenience, not at all. I'm glad that you're here and I intend to show you about Rome myself. It has been too long since I took the time to enjoy the city, the people. I will have no argument on the point, either. You're my guest to spoil, and spoil you I shall."

Molly stood before him, taken aback by his kindness. His sweetness toward a woman that he did not know. Perhaps his time in Rome had been lonely, and having her here allowed him to present his grand city to her. To spend time with a woman from his homeland who shared mutual friends.

"You're too kind." Molly opened her bedroom door, turning to face him. "I do not know how to thank you for having me here and being my escort. I shall tell Whitstone of your kindness. You can be certain of that."

Mr. Armstrong nodded, stepping back and placing space between them. His eyes met hers and held. Molly's heart sped up once more.

"No need for that. Your company will be thanks enough."

Warmth touched her cheeks, and Molly prayed he thought her flush was from her tour of Rome and not his sweet words or company. Which, of course, was exactly why it was.

CHAPTER 3

The following morning, Hugh sat at his breakfast table that overlooked the gardens and read his mail that Marcus had brought in to him. Another letter from Sarah told him of Henry's funeral and the outpouring of grief that the *ton* had managed to feign. He doubted anyone in society was honest and capable of any emotions other than greed and hate.

The sound of slippered feet caught his attention, and he looked up just as Miss Clare stepped up into the room, a small, welcoming smile on her pretty mouth.

"Mr. Armstrong. Good morning. What a beautiful day it looks to be." She sat to his side, looking over the abundance of food to choose from that sat before her.

He had taken to serving himself since living in Rome, and having the food on the table instead of a sideboard was much easier for both him and his servants.

"It is going to be lovely, and because that is so, I have an idea."

She glanced at him just as she placed a piece of bacon on her plate. "Even better. What is this idea?"

Her exuberance for life, for seeing the city he now called home, sent a kick through his blood. For years he had gone about with the same routine, rarely venturing out to socialize, keeping to himself and running his vineyard. To show off his home, his city to someone who did not know who he was, was liberating.

Made him feel like the young gentleman he once was in England that had his whole life ahead of him and little to worry about.

"You'll need your best walking boots, for I'm going to take you to visit the Colosseum. We'll return here in the early afternoon before it gets too hot." He wanted to take her to the Colosseum, show her the majestic building, and, if permitted, take her into the building's underground apartments where the gladiators waited to live or die.

Miss Clare's smile lit up the room, and he found himself grinning back at her. "Are you certain I'm not taking up too much of your time? I do not want to drag you away from your work."

He waved her concerns away, pouring her a cup of tea before finishing his own. "Not at all. I want to do this. Whitstone would never forgive me if I did not take care of you and show you about." Not that he needed the excuse of his friend to make him escort her around. Miss Clare was a sensible, intelligent woman. It was no chore being in her presence.

The walk to the historical site took only half an hour, the stroll through the winding cobbled and paved streets pleasant on a warm morning. Behind them, Marcus and Miss Clare's chaperone, Miss Sinclair, chatted and seemed to be getting along quite well.

The Colosseum had several arched doors to enter by, and Hugh pulled Molly through the first one they came across, walking into a large, curving tunnel, several degrees cooler than the air outside.

"What an amazing building this is." Miss Clare stood looking out over the Colosseum, her mouth agape at the sight that beheld her. It was a common reaction and one that Hugh himself had had when he first visited the place.

They climbed stairs heading up to the tiered seat section that overlooked the central orchestra and stage. "This was all once marble-veneered, but over the years, people have stripped it of its precious decorations, and the weather has not helped. What a sight it must have made. Can you just imagine?" he asked, watching her. Warmth seeped into his bones at the unguarded pleasure that blossomed on her face. She took every ounce, every nuance of the building, no doubt imagining it in its prime.

"To think gladiators fought and died in the arena below us. And you said we might be able to go beneath?"

"Of course. It is no problem." They walked along what was left of the seating areas that surveyed the central stage—the overwhelming magnitude of the place something he'd never forget. "I haven't been here for some years. I'm glad that I'm here with you today, Miss Clare. To reacquaint myself with the city that I now call home." And he was. She was a breath of fresh air into his life that had stagnated of late. He had his investments, his villa at Naples, and the vineyard, but no social life. Not when it came to attending balls and parties thrown by visitors from London to Rome. People who knew him and what he'd been accused of.

"To imagine the roars of the people barracking for their favorite gladiator echoes still through this old stone. I adore history if you have not noticed already. It was one of the reasons why I wanted to come here."

"What was the other reason?" he asked, enjoying himself more than he ought, especially for a man who had been notified of his brother's death only the day before. Not that Henry ever cared about anyone other than himself. Even so, as a brother, one ought to feel something. Regret, sadness. He felt numb. He'd lost all respect and affection for his sibling when he'd turned his back on him in London and let him face alone the savage wolves that were the *ton*.

"My friends." She smiled at him over her shoulder before leaning on the stone railing and studied what was left of the combat ring. "I love them, do not mistake me, but they're determined to see me wed. Married off and happily situated just as they all are."

"You do not wish to be married?" Today it would seem he was full of inappropriateness. He was talking to an unmarried maid of her love affairs. That was not to be borne. Even so, he was curious why someone would run thousands of miles away to evade marriage.

"If I fall in love and marry, that is all very well, but if I do not, that is all very well. I'm not a young woman, Mr. Armstrong. If you have not guessed already."

"You are not old either, Miss Clare. There would be many a gentleman who would offer for you, I would think."

She chuckled, shaking her head. The action caused a curl to fall loose from her motif and bounce upon her shoulder. His gaze dipped to the unblemished skin where the coil sat, a fine collarbone pulling the eye toward her sweet neck and ample bosom that her walking gown failed to conceal. Miss Clare was extremely appealing. The word lush floated through his mind, and he severed his inspection of her before she noticed.

"You would be wrong, Mr. Armstrong. I have not had one offer in all the years I have graced the London ballrooms. But I am happy for my friends, each of their husbands I adore and love like a brother. I shall never be lonely, do not fear, but I have come to accept that perhaps my time has passed, and so before my life does too, I must seize the day and see this wonderful world for myself."

"I admire your will, Miss Clare. I wish more women had such a strong constitution. My sister certainly does. You would like her, I think."

"You have a sister? Who is she? Maybe I have met her before?"

Hugh pointed to the stairs that led down into the bowels of the Colosseum, taking Miss Clare's hand and pulling her toward the entrance. "Sarah is her name, but she is some years younger than me and for years has refused to attend the Season. She spends most of her time in the country with her horses and dogs."

"I think then perhaps I shall like her very much."

He chuckled. The morning drifted by pleasantly. They took an hour-long tour of the underground of the Colosseum. It was an agreeable day and Hugh found himself laughing a lot more than he had in years. They returned to the villa, dusty and weary after their excursion, just as the sun reached the hottest time of the day.

Hugh pulled Miss Clare to a stop in the atrium, not willing to relinquish her hand. "Will you dine with me on the terrace this evening? I feel I do not wish for this day to end."

A light blush stole over her features, and the urge to reach out, touch her pretty face, was overwhelming. He had not thought to meet his house guest, nevertheless find her so sweet and charming. When the Duke of Whitstone had suggested that he help him in housing Miss Clare, he'd imagined a young, spoiled debutante. One who would simper and preen as they all did and drive his servants to distraction. He'd fled to Naples imagining such a visitor. How very opportune and fortunate he was that Miss Clare was nothing of the kind.

He liked her.

"That would be delightful, thank you, Mr. Armstrong. I shall rest for the afternoon and see you at dinner."

He bowed, watching as she went up the stairs, admiring the sway of her hips in her pretty dress. He turned, rubbing a hand over his jaw and striding to his tablinum in need of a stiff drink. He'd offered protection for her for the few weeks she was in Rome. He wasn't to molest her. Whitstone would beat him to a pulp should he seduce the chit, even so, sometimes, a good beating was worth it if the woman who warmed your bed was as delectable as Miss Clare certainly was.

With such thoughts, was it any wonder he was banished from England.

Dinner that evening was everything Molly missed from England. Mr. Armstrong's cook had outdone herself with a roast lamb, vegetables, and turtle soup. Dessert consisted of seasonal fruits along with jelly and cakes. Even so, no matter how delicious the fare, it did not make her one ounce homesick. She loved being here in Rome, visiting the ancient city and meeting its people.

She glanced at Mr. Armstrong, so very imposing, intelligent, and too good-looking to be unattached. Not that she knew much about his past, only that he was the Duke of Whitstone's friend, and therefore someone she could trust. There was probably a gaggle of women waiting about

Rome for him to call. For all that she knew, he may have a mistress who was missing him.

Molly shifted on her seat, taking a fortifying sip of her wine. She didn't want to think of him with anyone else. The idea of Mr. Armstrong in a passionate embrace with another woman made her want to cast up her accounts. An absurd reaction since she'd only known him a day.

But there was something about him she liked. He was kind and attentive and did not mock her many questions regarding life here or the treasures the city held. Their day at the Colosseum had been marvelous, and he'd been patient with her as she had taken it all in, no matter how long that took her.

Not all men would be so thoughtful.

"Shall we adjourn to the tablinum? I have two chairs that sit before a fire in that room. I know it is warm during the day, but I still like a little heat at night. I suppose you may take the Englishman out of England, but you cannot take England out of an Englishman."

"That would be lovely, yes."

Mr. Armstrong stood and came and helped her with her chair. "Bring your wine. We shall have after-dinner drinks together."

She did as he bade, before he reached out, placing her hand on his arm to escort her from the room. The moment her fingers touched his shirtsleeve, heat threaded up her arm and settled in her stomach. She swallowed, schooling her features, not wanting him to see just how much he discombobulated her. He would think her a fool for reacting so, especially when they hardly knew each other.

"You're very brave," he said, guiding her toward a part of the house she had not seen as yet. "Not many women would venture abroad with a companion and not much else. Whatever possessed you?"

"Do you reproach me for such a journey, Mr. Armstrong?" she asked, sitting in one of the leatherback chairs before the hearth. Mr. Armstrong walked over to a decanter and poured himself a whiskey.

"Not at all, but I am interested. Women do travel, of course, but they're either widowed or traveling with their husbands. I'm curious, that is all."

Molly thought back on her cousin Laura, how she had suffered through the birth of her son and subsequently paid for that birth with her life. The child only hours later following his mama to the grave.

"Many years ago, I was told never to wait for what I wanted. That if we laid all our hopes on those of others, we were destined for sadness. I promised myself I would not settle for anything other than love if I married, and if that did not eventuate that I would resolve myself to be fulfilled with only me for company. That I would not miss out on the world's gifts merely because I was unable to be someone's wife."

Mr. Armstrong took a sip of his amber liquid, watching her over the brim of his glass. "Your friend sounds a little jaded."

"She was and rightfully so. Although, I promised her that I would never be taken in by false promises and sweet words, and I haven't so far. Now at my age," Molly said, smiling a little. "It is becoming less likely each year."

Mr. Armstrong cocked one brow. Her stomach twisted at the wicked, amused glance he threw her. "From where I am sitting, Miss Clare, you are far from invulnerable." He finished his drink, setting it down with a clink. "Would you like to attend a party with me this evening? They are acquaintances, business associates I deal with in Rome. They're not titled or whom you're used to socializing with back in London, but they are good company and would welcome you if you attended."

Heat crept across her skin, and Molly took a sip of her wine, hoping her flush would not spread across her cheeks. She was not invulnerable? Whatever did he mean by such a statement? "I shall be safe enough. I have you to guard me. Have I not?" she said.

He chuckled, nodding. "Of course."

"Then I shall like to attend with you. If you're certain, it will be welcome." She studied him a moment, wondering about his past also. "You left London yourself. Why is it that you ended up in Rome?"

He frowned, sitting forward, his attention lost on the burning wood in the grate. "I disagreed with my family and could not stay. They granted funds to start my life here in Rome, and I accepted. I shall never return to London."

The thought that she would never see this man grace the floorboards of the great London homes left a pang of regret to lodge in her stomach. She didn't want to never see him again, and it was unlikely that she would ever return to Rome.

"I'm sorry to hear that, Mr. Armstrong. I'm not certain that I could be estranged from my family forever."

"Sometimes," he said, "estrangement is necessary for one's sanity. In any case, I have lived here for many years and love it as much as I loved my life before leaving London. I no longer miss it too much."

"May I ask one more question?" she asked, finishing her drink and placing it, too, on the table before them both. His gaze met hers, and she fought the urge to fan her face. He was so very intense. His attention fixed on hers with such fervor that one couldn't help but think he was reading her mind. No gentleman had ever paid so much attention to her or spent so much time.

"If you wish to?" He leaned back in his chair, waiting.

"What is your given name?" she asked.

All tension fled his features, and he chuckled, his smile just as devastating as the sound of his deep, rich voice that was suggestive as hell.

"Hugh. My name is Hugh, Miss Clare. And yours?" he queried.

"Molly," she said, feeling oddly embarrassed by their admissions. "May I ask one more question?" she continued, daring herself to be bold. To seek what she wanted. Not that asking for a man's name was so very scandalous, but women were taught not to be so forward. A lesson hard to unlearn.

"Yes," he said.

"May I call you Hugh instead of Mr. Armstrong when we're alone, such as we are now? Or when we're looking about Rome?"

"So I'm to accompany you about Rome more than once?"

"Well, I ah…" Molly wasn't certain what to say. There was no guarantee that Mr. Armstrong was even staying in Rome during her stay here. He may only be here a day and then traveling back to Naples.

He stood, coming over to her and pulling her from her seat. His hand was large and strong, his fingers entwining with hers. Heat licked at her core, her body unlike its steadfast, no-nonsense self it always was. He made her want things she'd never wanted before. He made her want him. She looked up at Hugh, unable to step back and give them the necessary space to be proper.

"It would be a pleasure to be here in Rome for the duration of your stay, to be your tour guide, and yes, you may call me Hugh, but only on one condition."

"Condition?" She cleared her throat. Why did she

sound so breathless? He would imagine her fascination with him in no time if she did not get a hold of her emotions. She was being a silly chit, and would start to sound like an adoring debutante soon if she did not guard her heart. She was not in Rome to lose her head to a man. She was here to tour the city. He was merely a polite host. A gentleman determined to make her stay here a happy one. A memory that would last a lifetime once she returned to England. "What condition is that?"

He lifted her hand to his lips, kissing her fingers. His lips were soft. So very smooth and warm, and her mind imagined where else those lips would feel so sweet. She bit her lip, fighting to stem her wayward thoughts.

"That I may call you Molly in turn."

She nodded, unable to form words right at that moment. If she were as bold as her friend Evie or Willow, she would close the space between them and take what she wanted. A kiss. Her first kiss. But she could not. She had never been bold, not in that way, at least. "I would like that," she said at length, taking a welcome breath as he nodded once and started for the door.

"We leave in an hour for the party. Are you able to be ready by then?" he asked, stopping at the threshold of the room.

"Of course," Molly said, watching him go and taking a moment to compose herself. Heavens forbid, she had almost swooned at his attention. What an intoxicating man he was, and a little mysterious. She had not heard of the Armstrong's in London, and it was interesting that he went to school with Whitstone and was of that social sphere and yet not titled. A mystery, and one she would untangle if she were able while she was here.

But tonight was reserved for dancing and fun. Experience what society was hundreds of miles away from the one she graced in England. And if she were lucky enough, perhaps Mr. Armstrong, Hugh as she would forever think of him, would offer his hand for a dance. A waltz in his arms sounded quite the perfect end to a most assuredly ideal day.

CHAPTER 4

The party was an opulent affair. The society in Rome was varied, and he was glad the social sphere he graced now knew nothing of his true identity or the family in which he came from.

Even so, their host's villa that sat overlooking Rome was grander and larger than his own. The family had made their wealth in wine and had houses all over Italy.

Tonight the atrium was the location of the entertainment, to the side in the tablinum sat an orchestra that played both modern and ancient tunes. Similar to his home, the atrium here was tiled in mosaic flooring, a central pond the main feature. This villa, however, being on a larger scale, the opening in the atrium was large enough that one could look up to the heavens and see the night sky in its full glory. Millions of stars framed just for them.

Servants carried around platters of drinks and supper, no need to stop the festivities to sit and eat like back in London. Hugh stood beside a Grecian statue, sipping his wine as he watched Molly speak with their hostess. Her laughter carried to where he stood, and he could tell that she was enjoying their conversation.

She was a beautiful woman, and the more time he spent with her, the more he looked forward to the next time they met. While getting dressed for this evening's reception, he'd thought of what they could do tomorrow, where to take her and what to see. He hoped that she would like his choice and continue to allow him to be her escort while in Rome.

For a moment, he allowed himself to imagine that he'd never left London, that he'd been able to meet Molly in society and court her as he liked. She certainly brought a calmness wherever she went, and he found himself wishing they had met before the scandal that sent him abroad broke.

His mother and brother conspiring for him to take the fall for his brother's indiscretion ensured he was no longer part of that family. It goaded his pride that he'd had to live on the funds his brother sent to ensure his survival for some years, but for the past eight, he'd not had to. Out of spite, perhaps, he still cashed those checks from London, but turned around and donated the funds to the women of Rome, who found themselves *enceinte* and without a protector or husband.

It was the least he could do to try to honor Laura in some way, make recompense to the woman his brother had ruined.

"Why are you not dancing, Mr. Armstrong? You look well enough that I do believe you will survive a turn about the dancefloor."

He chuckled, reveling in her bright eyes and smiling mouth that he had an overwhelming urge to lean down toward and kiss. To test his theory that her lips were as soft and willing as he suspected. Or at least hoped.

"We're back to Mr. Armstrong? I did hope you would call me by my given name as we agreed."

She shrugged, taking a glass of champagne from a passing servant before taking a sip. "We're not alone, which was part of the agreement. What if someone should hear?"

"No one shall hear with all the noise of this party." He wanted to hear his name on her lips. For all his fleeing of England had left a sour taste in his mouth, having Molly here, an English woman who was sweet and kind, to hear his name spoken by her did odd things to his soul. Warmed it after ten years of being chilled.

"Very well," she said, smiling at him, the loveliest blush speckling her cheeks. "I shall do as you ask, but should anyone step nearby or other guests join us, we must revert to our formal names."

"Agreed," he said, turning back to take in the guests lest someone spy his marked attention on the woman who was lodging under his roof. He ought to leave, go to a hotel and stay there for the duration of her stay, but he could not, and for reasons he'd not think too far upon at present. "You have not danced as much as I thought you would."

"Oh, I've danced plenty, and you very well know it. Why I just finished a dance with Lord Brandon, whom I know from London. Do you know him?"

Hugh schooled his features as a knot of anxiety lodged in his gut. Was Lord Brandon in Rome? How did he not know? His attention slipped over the crowd, and it did not take him long to spy the earl, who was mutual friends with Duke Whitstone. A peer who was fully cognizant of why he'd fled his homeland.

"How do you know the earl?" he asked.

"Through the Duke and Duchess of Whitstone."

Hugh kept surreptitiously checking to see where Lord

Brandon was situated. He was happy to see that within a few minutes of spying him, the gentleman and his handsome Italian wife were taking their leave of their hostess. He breathed deep, thankful his night had not ended with a confrontation between him and his lordship.

"Tell me how you came to know the Duchess of Whitstone? From the correspondence from His Grace? You're very close friends."

"We went to school with each other in France. Each of us was sent away from home for various reasons. I, because my parents feared that I would throw myself away on some rogue for reasons I shall not bore you with. Even so, we all met at Madame Dufour's Refining School for girls. Our friendship has never waned over the years, and although our lives do take us on different paths, we always are there for each other when needed."

Hugh wished he had such friends. He'd lost so many of his set when his brother had forced his scandal onto his shoulders. In hindsight, he should have made his brother clean up his own mess. Face the matrons of the *ton* looking down their noses at him for his ungentlemanly behavior. But they had not. Oh no, the future Duke Henry could not be besmirched by a woman of loose morals, even if that woman had been a childhood friend and neighbor.

"They sound like the best of people. You are lucky to have such friends."

She threw him a small smile, and the concern of him being outed to her for his brother's sin lessened. "I believe I am."

The strains of a waltz drifted across the warm night's air, and Hugh placed down his glass of wine, bowing before Molly. "May I have this dance, Miss Clare?"

Without hesitation, she placed her silk-gloved fingers

onto his palm, closing them tight about his hand. "I would like that very much, Mr. Armstrong."

Hugh led her out onto the dancefloor beside the central fountain. They took their places on the makeshift ballroom floor and waited for the music to begin.

His fingers closed about her waist, the tulle that sat over her emerald-green gown shimmered under the stars and hundreds of candles that the Costa family's servants had placed about the room. He pulled her close, not missing the moment her eyes flared at his action. As close as they now stood, it was not as close as he would like.

The gown was soft under his touch, her waist small and delicate. The music started, and he whirled her into the steps, spinning them before waltzing about the room. The scent of jasmine teased his senses, and he studied her hair a moment, wondering if that was why she smelled so damn good.

"You dance very well, Mr. Armstrong. I suspect you had dance lessons as a young man."

He'd had dance lessons for a lot longer than that. As a duke's son, no child of his father would be lacking in ballroom etiquette or grace. He'd known how to dance and dance well since he was in short coats. "I do try to ensure I never tread on any of my partner's toes. I hope not to disappoint you, Miss Clare."

She glanced up at him, their gazes clashed, and for the life of him, he could not look away. Her eyes, sharp and quick, watched him with utter conviction. He realized he never wanted to be looked upon any other way from Molly.

"Now, I only have to fear that I shall tread on yours. I do hope that is not the case," she said, laughing a little at her quip.

She was all womanly curves, tempting and a stark

reminder of all that he'd lost by fleeing to Rome all those years ago. Had he stayed in London, there was little doubt that he would have married by now. Settled down with a woman such as the one in his arms and had a handful of children. He'd always wanted a family, his father had been loving, and he wanted to be just like his sire.

Hugh sighed and concentrated on the dance, not wanting to dwell on the past. He wanted to enjoy himself and give Molly a pleasant evening that was just as enjoyable as her day was.

"You have proven yourself to be just as apt at dancing as me. Why these last two turns about the room, and you have not injured my feet once."

"I confess, I too have had many years of practice. I'm sure it will not surprise you to know that I'm not a woman in her first season. I'm eight and twenty. At that age, I do believe I could become a master of dancing and give instruction."

Hugh pulled her close as he guided them about a turn at one end of the room. The atrium ballroom was a crush, beeswax candles lay within the sconces on the wall, making the makeshift ballroom magical.

"You are not ancient at eight and twenty, Molly. If we're declaring our ages, I must advise you that I'm two and thirty. I hope you do not think that too old for a woman such as yourself." Hugh glanced over Molly's head, not wanting to see if she was shocked or delighted by his words. Words that he'd not thought to utter. He would need to be better behaved before he did say something that had her packing her bags and heading back to England.

"Isn't it always gentlemen who believe women of my age are too old to be of use to them? Men, it would seem, have the luxury of being any grand age to make an equally grand match. Women, on the other hand, if they are not married within a year or two of their coming out, are termed old maids and too long in the tooth to do anything but be shipped off to the country to be a caregiver for either their parents or their sibling's children."

The thought was not a pleasant one, but Molly was right. Society could be cruel and unfair to women. "Well, I shall not let anyone ship you off to the country, my dear. Not at least while you're here in Rome with me in any case. I shall keep you safe from purgatory."

She studied him a moment. Hugh met her gaze, and a punch in his nether region would have been less injuring. There was something about the woman in his arms that he relished. She made him think of things, of home and building a home, of children, while another part of her made him crave.

Made the rogue he'd once been when he'd had the freedom to do whatever he liked—before his brother's demand had made him vilified by his peers—want to slip out of the dance, hide somewhere in this Roman villa and kiss her until the sun came up.

"You're quite the gentleman, and I thank you. If I am to travel out in the country, I do hope you'll accompany me. I should imagine you have seen many wonderful things in this country that a tourist such as myself may not know about."

He could, he supposed, convey her down to Naples and show her his country estate. Hugh could picture her now standing on the balcony that housed the ancient city's views beyond, the warm Mediterranean sun and sea air teasing her unblemished skin and sweet figure.

"It would be my honor to show you a little more of Italy if that is your wish. Simply tell me when you would like to go, and I shall arrange it."

"Really?" she asked him, surprise blossoming on her

features and making her even more beautiful than she already was.

His hand flexed about her hip, and he wished he could steal her away now. He coveted that what he was feeling about the woman in his arms was reciprocated.

Hugh steeled himself to finish the dance less he make a fool of himself with a woman he'd only known a day. It was only because bedmates had been absent from his life of late. His life in London had also plagued him, memories of everything he'd given up by agreeing to his brother's demands taunting him of what he'd lost.

Now that he was the duke, he supposed he no longer had to hide away in Rome. He could return to London and take up his place in society. His mother had passed some years ago. His sister certainly would welcome him back, and he needed to be in England to support her.

But he could not. They had turned their back on him, and now he would never return home. Out of spite or pride he could not say, but England and the society he once graced could go to the devil. Which would mean that after Molly's four weeks in Rome, he would have to say goodbye to her as well.

The latter impending day did not sit well with him. It was a day not to be borne.

CHAPTER 5

They returned home from the ball in the early hours of the morning. The impending dawn glowed bright on the eastern horizon, some of Rome's buildings already turning from dusky gray to a warmer shade of sandstone.

They walked through the courtyard in silence, Mr. Armstrong's warm, large hand on the small of her back, leaving her breathless and flushed. He'd been so very attentive all evening, so very handsome and sweet.

A woman could fall for a gentleman like Hugh.

A smile quirked her lips as they stepped into the atrium, a lone, male servant asleep on the chair near the door. "May I escort you to your room, Molly?"

"Thank you," she said, starting up the stairs, the sound of her name on his lips warming her blood. Molly's skin prickled, all too aware of the tall, muscular figure walking beside her. She had not thought to meet any gentleman while in Rome. This was a holiday purely to enjoy the sights of Italy. It was indeed a fortunate turn of events that Mr. Armstrong had arrived in her life. Ava had mentioned very little about Hugh, she had never met the gentleman, and had assured Molly that he was away from the city for the duration of her stay.

How very fortunate she was that he'd come back and decided to stay. Her trip to Rome already in the day she'd spent with him had been tremendous, and she hoped just the start of many more to come.

They came up to the door to her room, and she paused, turning to face him, having to glance up due to his towering height. "Thank you for the wonderful night. I shall treasure it always. I cannot remember the last time I had so much fun."

His lips quirked into a grin, his eyes inviting and warm. "The pleasure was all mine, Molly." He leaned down, the brush of his lips against her cheek making her breath catch. Should she turn just the littlest bit, their lips would meet. The scent of sandalwood teased her senses, and unwittingly she reached out, clasping his upper arms. Strong, toned muscles met her fingers, and she had the overwhelming urge to squeeze his flesh, see if it was indeed as strong as it felt beneath her fingers.

He pulled back, watching her. Time stood still. Her stomach fluttered when he didn't move away. She could kiss him if she wished. Did she want to? Did he?

Oh yes, yes she did, very much. His gaze dipped to her mouth, and liquid heat pooled at her core. Her breath hitched, she fumbled for the door handle, pushing herself into her room, and away from temptation. "Thank you again, Hugh, for the pleasant evening. Goodnight," she said, not waiting for his reply before she closed the door.

She stood there a moment, forcing herself not to move, not to wrench open the door and jerk him into her arms, taking from him what he was so obviously offering.

The sound of retreating footsteps sounded in the hall outside, and she breathed out a relieved sigh. She couldn't throw herself at him. They were starting to be friends. He was going to be showing her about Rome some more and the surrounding countryside. She could not jeopardize any of that. She wouldn't. Her time here was so precious, to start a love affair with a man she would not marry would be the worst decision she could ever make.

Her cousin played that game of giving herself to someone before wedding vows were spoken and had paid for her error of judgment with her life. She would not be another silly chit to be fooled by a handsome face and sweet words.

No matter how alluring that may be.

THE FOLLOWING day Hugh was impatient for her to visit the Vatican, and by the time she had broken her fast in her room and come downstairs, a carriage was waiting for them to take them to their morning location.

If he missed her at breakfast, he did not say, and nor was she willing to give an excuse as to why she had not ventured down. After their almost-kiss last night, embarrassment had kept her upstairs.

Why she was acting like a blushing debutante, she did not know. From Hugh's easy manner and charming self, he seemed oblivious to what had transpired between them.

"I shall ride on the box if you do not mind, Miss Clare," her companion said, smiling up at Mr. Armstrong's manservant, Marcus, who had already sat on the driver's seat.

Molly took in the secret little smile between the two and wondered if her companion, too, was embarking on her own adventure, one of her heart. "Of course, if you wish."

"If you need anything, do let me know. I will have Marcus stop the carriage."

"Miss Clare," Hugh said, holding out his hand to help her climb up in the equipage.

Molly braced herself to feel his touch and fought to school her features when her body thrummed at his presence, his voice, and warmth.

"Thank you." She swallowed her nerves and climbed up into the carriage, settling back onto the squabs and waiting for Hugh to join her.

The carriage dipped as he climbed inside, he rapped on the roof, and the carriage lurched forward.

His usual affable self, he seemed pleased to be with her again, no hint as to what had transpired between them in the early hours of the morning clouding his opinion of her. It was as if all was forgotten or was only imagined in Molly's mind.

This was for the best, of course. Molly did not need him to think that there could be anything else between them other than friendship. Unless, of course, she fell in love with him and he offered for her hand. Then, and only then, would she be willing even to contemplate giving herself to the gentleman.

Dressed in tan, buckskin breeches and highly polished black hessian boots, he again looked like a gentleman ready to stroll about Hyde Park. His white shirt had a loose cravat tied in the barrel knot design and a tan jacket. No waistcoat. No hat. No gloves. Not overly formal, which seemed to suit him. Not that he needed much clothing to look the epitome of sophistication, she would gather he need wear nothing at all, and he'd be perfect in her opinion.

Heat brushed her cheeks, and she took an interest in the streets passing them by outside the window.

"You shall like the Sistine Chapel, Molly. The paintings on the ceiling are simply unforgettable."

Excitement thrummed through her veins, not only because of their destination but because they were alone. How fortunate it was that Miss Sinclair had taken a liking to Marcus, and if the manservant's sweet smile back at her companion was anything to go by, he liked her also.

"I cannot thank you enough for taking me about, Hugh. I shall tell Ava and Whitstone of your kindness to me while I was here."

He threw her a small smile, glancing out the window. "It is a shame that you're only here for such a short amount of time. I feel like I shall miss you when you return to England. It has been so very long that I've had a little part of home beneath my roof. The last time it was Whitstone himself who had come to visit, and you being a mutual friend of His Grace, I know that I can trust you with such declarations."

Molly reached out and took his gloveless hand, squeezing it a little. "I should imagine it is very hard to be so far away from your home. Do you think you shall ever return to England? I know I should look forward to seeing you again."

"I will never return, no." A muscle worked in his jaw, and he frowned, staring at something outside the carriage window. "Rome is my home now, and this is where I shall stay. But," he said, placing his hand over hers that she realized was still laying atop his, "you are always more than welcome to stay anytime you wish."

"If only I could, but my family could not afford to send me for too long. If it were not for my friends, I would not have been able to make my dream a reality. I could not impose on you for any more length of time than I plan on doing already."

"Nonsense. I would more than welcome you to stay, whenever and however long you like."

"We're already skirting on impropriety with me under your roof and you in residence. I do not think I wish to push my fortune too far, sir."

His hand lifted hers a little, and he started to play with her fingers, tracing them with his own through her kid-leather gloves. "You should take these off. It is too warm for gloves in Rome."

Without waiting for a response, he flicked open the two little buttons on her wrist, his bare fingers slipping under her glove to pull her hand free of the soft leather. Fresh air hit her flesh, and he was right, it was cooler not wearing them.

He turned her fingers over, inspecting them. "You have lovely hands."

Molly looked at her gloveless hand encased in his. It looked small and delicate against his large, tanned one. She'd never really paid much heed to her hands, but perhaps he was right. They were certainly not awful-looking.

"You have large, strong hands." The words slipped from her lips, and as much as she may wish to take them back, she could not. It was an absurd notion, but she'd already spent too much time thinking about his hands and what they would feel like caressing her flesh.

Nice, very nice indeed.

The carriage turned, and Hugh moved to the side of the equipage, taking stock of their location. "We're nearly there. Should we be fortunate, we may get a glimpse of a cardinal or the Pope himself. Would you like that?"

"Oh, very much, although I'm no longer so very religious, I still respect those who are. Are you catholic, Hugh?"

He grinned, shaking his head. "No, protestant, and you?"

"The same." She moved over to the window and, pulling the leather strap, lowered the glass. Molly leaned out of the carriage, looking straight ahead and gasped. An imposing, Renaissance building met her vision, complete with a large dome atop it, columns and ornamental statues adorned the building, giving it an air of grandeur she'd never seen before. The carriage rumbled up the long road, gaining ever closer to the circular square. The buildings that circled the Vatican City faced this large square, and people milled about in the area, taking in the magnificent sights.

"I feel that I'm going to enjoy our outing today," she said as the carriage rocked to a halt, and Marcus opened the carriage door.

Hugh jumped out, reaching back to take her hand to help her alight. "You will be amazed, I'm certain. So many people never get to see such gifts. This will truly be a day you will never forget."

Molly couldn't help but smile at Hugh's words. There was little doubt that the day already was one never to forget. Hugh placed her hand atop his arm, turning to face his driver and her companion. "Please come back to collect us here in St. Peters Square in a couple of hours."

"There are plenty of people about, Miss Sinclair. You may return to the villa." Her companion beamed at Marcus, and it solidified Molly's curiosity. There was most certainly something up between the two people.

The driver tipped his hat as Marcus climbed back onto the box. "Of course, Mr. Armstrong."

Molly didn't spare the carriage a second glance as it turned and rumbled down the gravel road. Instead, her attention was caught and held by the magnificent buildings before her. They started toward St. Peter's Basilica, it's large, imposing dome looking down on the populace below. From the abundance of people, it seemed to be the most popular structure to visit.

"We shall go to the Sistine Chapel through St. Peter's Basilica. I want you to see the nave."

Excitement thrummed through Molly. She was in Rome, at Vatican City, and with a gentleman she'd not thought to have met. He was a wonderful host and guide, and she could not thank Ava and Whitstone enough that they were friends with Mr. Armstrong.

They walked up a line of steps heading toward the entrance to the large church. They passed under six high columns before stepping into the portico and then the nave. The gold and ornate columns were unlike anything Molly had seen before. Marble, sculptures, and murals were a feast to one's eye. She could not take it all in, the size alone was tremendous, so many details and history that it would take a person years to view each and everything under the grand roof and view its beauty.

"This is overwhelming. I always thought Westminster and St. Pauls were beautiful, but this is another beast altogether."

Hugh chuckled, walking them leisurely up the middle of the nave, he too looking about the great space. "It's a feast for any historian or antiquities collector. You can understand why so many people come to admire this church."

"Oh yes," she said, squeezing his arm a little. "Take me to the Sistine Chapel. I cannot wait any longer."

He nodded slightly. "I'm at your service, Miss Clare." He pulled her back out into the portico and, turning left, they headed up some stairs before turning left again and climbing stairs that worked their way up one side of a building separate to St. Peter's Basilica.

"I had always thought the chapel was part of the church. From where you're taking me, this is not the case?" she asked, staring ahead to the door that loomed before them.

"It's a chapel off to the side and separate. I did not know this either until I visited for the first time. I'm glad I have a companion who appreciates history and beauty as much as I do."

She met his gaze as they made the top landing, and she beamed at him, her body thrumming with expectation. "I'm delighted you're here with me too. Had I done this alone or with Miss Sinclair, who dislikes travel and anything different to what she is used to, it would not have been the same. Thank you for escorting me, Mr. Armstrong. You're truly a good man."

"I wouldn't go that far, Miss Clare." His laugh held an edge of mocking, and she wondered at it. He was a good man and had been a wonderful friend to her these past days.

"I would," she disagreed as they walked through a small door into a rectangular room full of painted murals. Molly bit her lip, speechless by what she saw.

"Michelangelo, for all that he proclaimed to be a sculptor and not a painter, certainly had talent when he held a brush."

Gaping, Molly closed her mouth with a snap, arching her neck to look upon the roof that she'd read so many books on, but had never beheld in life. The famous making of Adam stared down upon them, grand and celebrated. She blinked back tears at finally being here, at seeing this treasure from a master of art.

"Beautiful, isn't it?" she said, swiping at her cheek and

yet not embarrassed by the fact she was emotional before Hugh. One could not look at such art and not be moved, to be indifferent to what adorned the walls could only mean the person had no soul.

"I quite agree," he whispered.

Molly glanced at Hugh and found him staring at her, his eyes heavy with an emotion she did not recognize. She tore her gaze away, calming her racing heart. This was not the place for her to throw herself at him. They were friends, he did not mean anything by his words, merely that the paintings were beautiful. Not that she was.

She stepped forward, taking in the images of the popes drawn on a higher level of the room, of the arched windows and floor that was some sort of mosaic of a circular pattern, seemingly more modern than the historical room and paintings that stood within.

They studied the paintings for some time, a guide coming over to them and telling them a little of the painting's meanings, of how long it took Michelangelo to paint the room.

Several hours passed before they exited St. Peter's Basilica, their carriage waiting patiently outside The Square. "Are you pleased that you traveled thousands of miles to see Rome and all of this?" Hugh asked, pulling her close to his side as they strode across The Square.

Molly breathed deep, feeling at home in this city, this country. Although she had friends that she adored and loved in England, they were all married now, on paths of their own. Her family no longer circulated in town, not after what happened to her cousin. Even though they never circulated in the sphere in which her friends now enjoyed, it still allowed Molly to have her family in London and not be isolated.

She was alone quite a lot now that Evie had married

and moved out of the townhouse they once shared with Willow.

Molly pulled Hugh to a stop. He glanced down at her, a small frown line between his brow marring his perfect visage. This close, she could admire his long obsidian eyelashes, the slight shadow of stubble across his cheeks and jaw. An ache thrummed deep in her belly, and for the first time in her life, she acted upon her feelings.

Her fingers slid up behind the lapels on his coat. She clasped them tight, pulling Hugh close before leaning up and kissing him in the middle of St. Peter's Square.

Molly ignored the gasps from those passing them by and viewing their public display of affection, but she did not stop. His lips were as soft as silk just as she imagined them to be. His arms wrapped about her waist, pulling her close, and he deepened the kiss. taking her mouth in a kiss like she'd never imagined before. His tongue slipped into her mouth, and she gasped, having not expected such intimacy when she'd started this foray into passion.

The sensation was unlike anything she'd ever experienced, but she liked it. Liked having him kiss her with abandon and without care of who saw them. They were in Rome, after all. The eternal city that had seen millions of love affairs just like the one she was embarking on.

Molly held on to his shoulders, mimicking him as much as she could. Her first kiss was all heat and deliciousness, and she couldn't get enough. She never wanted to stop kissing him.

He reached up, clasping her face with his hands. He tipped her head a little, and the world stopped spinning. At this angle, somehow, he made her open to him like a flower, blooming from his warmth. Before she knew what she was about, she slid her tongue against his, marveling at the friction.

Hugh moaned, his hands spiking into her hair as he wrenched her closer. His body, hard against hers, made her breath hitch, her most private of places ache. Their kiss turned desperate. Distantly, as if a million miles away, she could feel her hair unraveling under his onslaught. She cared little. All she heeded was this sweet, kind, virile, handsome man who was kissing her within an inch of her life.

The sound of a gentleman clearing his throat nearby impinged on their kiss, and Hugh pulled back, staring at her as if he didn't know who it was in his arms. Molly refused to glance about to see who was watching, judging them. They could all go to hades as far as she was concerned.

"That was..." he said, his words breathless against her lips.

"It was, wasn't it?" She grinned and stepped out of his hold. Molly took his hand and started toward the carriage. Her hair fell about her shoulders, and she didn't try to fix it before they made the carriage. There was little point. Half her pins were scattered about St. Peter's Square, after all.

Along with her reputation should anyone have recognized her.

HUGH HELPED Molly up into the carriage and followed her inside, slamming the door behind him to mask his shaking hands. Damn it all to hell. What had just happened? Never in his life had he ever acted in such a scandalous way. And in St. Peter's Square to boot. The Pope would disapprove should he have seen such a public kiss between two people not even married.

What had he been thinking?

As to that, not a lot. Nothing at all except how perfect

Molly felt in his arms. How her sweet, soft lips felt pressed up against his and how much he wanted to feel them again.

Right now.

He pulled the blinds down in the carriage, giving them privacy. "You kissed me, Molly. Does that mean you want to kiss me again?"

Her eyes flew wide with alarm, and he grinned, marveling at how she could kiss him with such sweet abandon and then be shocked when asked about it. How adorable was this woman and how much would he miss her when she left?

"I like you," she stated, matter-of-fact, her hands clasped tight in her lap. "I never kissed a man before, you see, and after the wonderful day we've just had, well..." She paused, glancing at something in her lap, those sweet lips she'd just kissed him with clasped tight between her teeth, driving him to distraction. He gripped the seat, forcing himself to remain where he was and not move. Not molest her again in the carriage this time when there was no one to stop them.

"Well," she continued. "I decided that I wanted it to be you whom I kissed. You're probably going to be the only man I ever kiss, and so I took what I wanted. I do apologize if I shocked or offended you."

Hugh chuckled, leaning back in the squabs. She met his gaze, and he hoped she could read in his eyes that he was far from offended. Aroused, intrigued...yes. But offended? Hell no.

"Let me tell you, Molly, that you have my permission to kiss me whenever you desire. I've not been with a woman for some time, and your company these last few days has been a sweet elixir to my soul. A stolen kiss or two will hurt no one, especially me."

Her cheeks bloomed into a pretty rose hue, and he shifted to sit beside her, reaching up to brush her hair back behind her ear. "I'm glad you kissed me because I've wanted to kiss you from the moment I saw you in my atrium, in your pretty blue gown and excited about seeing Rome for the first time."

"Really?" A smile blossomed on her lips, and he couldn't help but grin back. "So I can kiss you whenever I like?"

He nodded. "I wouldn't be a gentleman if I did not suggest that if we're to kiss again that it should be in private. Perhaps St. Peter's Square is not the best location, but a carriage with the blinds drawn, well, no one will see us here."

"That is true." Molly glanced about the coach, her inspection taking in the lowered blinds. "I want to kiss you again. Am I not scandalous?"

"A little," he teased. "But so am I, so we're a good match." Hugh didn't wait for her to initiate the kiss this time. Instead, he seized her sweet face and kissed her, deep and sure. Their tongues tangled, heat licking his skin, his cock aching for her touch. He'd not reacted to a woman in such a way ever in his life. He wanted to make her crave him as much as he feared he would covet her when she left.

Her arms tangled about his neck, her breasts, full and heavy, sat against his chest. His hands itched to clasp a handful of the voluptuous flesh. To tease and pinch her nipples, he was certain would be puckered little knobs inside her dress.

The thought of licking, kissing her there, sent a bolt of desire to his cock. "You're so sweet. I cannot get enough of you," he gasped against her lips.

She stared back at him, her eyes cloudy with desire, her lips swollen from his touch. "And I, you."

Hugh took her lips again, hoisting her up against his person. Her stomach sat against his engorged cock. He wasn't sure what she would think of him, or his reaction to her, but when she undulated against him, sliding her sweet body to tease his, the world's axis tipped.

It took all his self-control not to slide his hand down her back, clasp a nice handful of her ass and grind against her. She moved closer still, pushing him back against the window, her untutored kiss before becoming more proficient with each passing moment. Molly was a quick learner. If he weren't careful, she would undo him in the carriage like a green lad who'd never touched a woman before.

The carriage rocked to a halt, and with a jerk, he sat them up. "We're home." The word home reverberated about in his mind. The Roman villa was certainly his home, but he liked having Molly under its roof and being part of his life. To take someone about, a little slice of home that he vowed not to miss, soothed the beast that roared inside that hated what his family had done. Having Molly here reminded him of everything that he'd lost because of them. The possibility of a future. A wife as passionate and sweet as his houseguest was. Perhaps even Molly herself.

She sat up, adjusting her gown and addressing her hair as best as she could before the door opened, and Marcus set down the steps for them.

Hugh jumped down, turning about to help her alight. Her fingers enclosed within his and a bolt of awareness shot up his arm. He took a calming breath, pushing down the ache in his chest at the realization that she would be leaving in only a few short weeks. He wasn't so certain that he wanted her to leave at all.

If he could, he'd keep her for himself. Forever.

CHAPTER 6

The following day Molly toured the markets of Piazza Navona with Miss Sinclair, along with Hugh's manservant escorting her since Hugh had to address some missives from England that had arrived the day before when they were at the Vatican.

Molly picked up some flowers from one of the stalls and a collection of gifts that she would take back to England for her friends. One vendor was selling little porcelain statues of famous gladiators of ancient Rome. Hallie would love these, especially since she was so very fond of history.

They strolled the markets for some time, breaking their fast at a stall that sold bread and dried meats. Molly had never eaten in public like this before, and it was a marvel, a liberating feeling. She could get used to being a Roman citizen, especially if she were fortunate enough to return home to the villa and see Hugh each day.

The thought of him sent her stomach to catapult into a thousand circles. After their kiss in St. Peter's Square and then in the carriage on the way home, she had thought they would dine and spend time with each other for the evening, but Hugh had received a mountain of letters that even this morning was taking up his time. Stopping him from accompanying her today.

They made their way back to the carriage, Marcus carrying her parcels for her. Miss Sinclair had seemed to have a change of heart regarding the city and travel. She was all smiles and compliments on their outing. Marcus was a positive influence on her.

As she waited for the parcels to be hitched, her mind turned to Hugh. What was the business that was so very important that he'd been unavailable last evening and today? Perhaps he still had business dealings in London that needed taking care of. She had been monopolizing his time somewhat since he'd offered to take her about Rome. It was only expected that he would have to decline and stay home to complete his work some days.

Molly climbed up in the carriage, nodding to Miss Sinclair as she pulled off her bonnet, wiping her brow with her lace handkerchief. "What an enjoyable morning. However, I fear a megrim is settling in."

"If you're feeling poorly, I'll have Maria bring up a tisane for you. Will you be dining with the servants, or would you prefer to dine in your room?"

"I should not leave you alone with Mr. Armstrong as much as I have, Miss Clare. My duty is to keep you safe. It is already terribly scandalous that we're staying under his roof with him in residence. I just hope the news does not beat us back to London. Your reputation will be ruined."

Molly glanced out the window, grinning at Miss Sinclair's words. Her reputation was already ruined had anyone seen their kiss yesterday in the square and recognized them. She could not regret it, however. Her first kiss had been given freely to Mr. Armstrong, and from the moment he'd kissed her back, she knew that her bold actions had been the right thing to do.

"We know so very little about him, Miss Clare. I would hate to have your reputation ruined by not doing my duty as your chaperone."

"I'm eight and twenty, Miss Sinclair. No one cares what I do or how I go about. You forget what it was like for me in London. Other than my friends, no one cared about me at all. I was not titled nor rich, practically invisible."

"I do not think your parents would agree, Miss Clare. Think of your cousin. She was lured in by a pretty face and false promises. I do not want to see the same happen to you, and God knows, Mr. Armstrong has a face akin to wickedness. What a handsome man, and one who knows how to use such looks, I'm sure, when the need arises."

Molly chuckled, unable to disagree with her companion's summations. "A pretty face will not fool me, but even so, Mr. Armstrong is a gentleman and has been very kind to me. But I promise you, Miss Sinclair, that I shall not do anything that will harm my family or myself. I will not make the same mistake as Laura."

"He promised her marriage, Miss Clare. She thought herself in love."

"I know what Laura thought." Molly knew firsthand what her cousin had been promised, and the heartache her friend had gone through before her son's birth. The death of them both only a few days later had left the family scarred and cautious.

Lord Farley, the Duke of St. Albans's younger brother, was a fiend who did not deserve to breathe as far as Molly was concerned. If only she could tell the prig to his face that she hated him, that what he'd done had ruined her friend and her future.

Had caused irreparable damage to the family that they struggled to this day to live with.

Molly wasn't naïve enough not to know Laura too was at fault, she had allowed things to go too far between them before they were married, but still, when one falls in love, she could see how very difficult it would be to deny oneself what one desired.

Just as she now desired Mr. Armstrong above anyone else. He could be her downfall, the man who made her want to throw all caution aside and simply live, love, and play to her heart's content.

As much as she did not understand her cousin's emotions or what made her do the things she had done with Lord Farley, she could understand them now. After kissing Hugh, she could understand the desires of the heart were sometimes too great to resist.

The carriage rocked to a halt before the villa, and Miss Sinclair continued to look displeased with her. "He's taken a fancy to you. The staff can see it as plain as day, and so can I. He's a man, his risk is nothing to yours. Please keep your head about yourself when with him. That is all I ask."

Molly reached across the seat and clasped Miss Sinclair's hand. Her anxiety on Molly's behalf doing her character and position justice. "Mr. Armstrong's attentions will not injure me, I promise. He's an honorable man. I may be a little long in the tooth, but I think he's genuine. He'll not play with my heart unless he intends to keep it for himself. There is hope yet, Miss Sinclair that I may have found my match."

Molly smiled and turned to alight from the vehicle. The villa door stood ajar, and inside the home's walls stood Hugh, waiting for her in the afternoon sun. His shirt was free from his tan breeches, the arms rolled up about his elbows and showing off his golden-hue skin and muscular forearms.

Butterflies took flight in her stomach, and she stifled a sigh of delight at the sight of him. How could a man that she'd only known a few days be so consuming? Make her feel like a green girl experiencing her first Season and being courted by London's most handsome man.

She walked up to him, unable to stop the smile that formed on her lips. "Good afternoon, Mr. Armstrong. I hope you had a productive day as you'd hoped."

He guided her over to a part of the garden that housed a small marble alcove and bench. Vines grew above the seat, giving the occupants privacy. Molly sat, pulling her shawl about her shoulders as the temperature in the hidden niche was cooler than in the courtyard.

"I was able to finish what needed attending, but I could not concentrate."

"Really?" Molly frowned up at him. He sat beside her, the side of his leg touching hers. Her skin prickled in awareness, and she took a calming breath, needing to control herself and her reactions to him. He did not need to know that she liked him perhaps more than she ought to like a man she hardly knew. "Why could you not concentrate?"

He reached out, sliding his thumb across her bottom lip, and she leaned into him, wanting more of his touch. To have his thumb replaced with his lips. "I could not concentrate because I knew you were walking about Rome without me. I fear that you can never return to London as I'll miss you too much."

His sweet words made a pang of regret and panic take flight inside her. She could not stay, not unless he offered marriage, but she was unsure if he asked whether she could live so far away from her friends and family. Even with the intoxicating, consuming man that was slowly taking her heart and making it his.

"You tease," she said, making light of his words and not wanting to face just what they did mean, what they could imply for both of them.

He shook his head, closing the space between them. "No, I'm not. I've never been more honest."

The moment his lips touched hers, Molly was lost. She gave herself to his kiss that turned demanding and wicked, and unlike the other kisses they'd shared so far. This one took her breath away. His hand spiked into her hair, making her gasp. The moment she did, he took advantage and thrust his tongue against hers, pulling her into a world of desire, needs, and wants.

Her body ached for his touch. She clasped his side, anchoring herself lest she float away and never return to her body. Faintly, she was aware of his other hand, sliding up her waist. A moan burst free when it covered her breast, kneading the aching flesh. His thumb and forefinger found her nipple. He rolled it through the fabric of her dress, and she moaned.

She crossed her legs as she leaned against him, trying to appease the deep, thrumming ache between her legs. It did not help. She wanted him to touch her there as well. To tease and kiss her and bring that desire to heel.

"You're the sweetest woman. It is confirmed you must stay. Forget London and stay here with me."

Molly pulled back, hoping he was playing while a little of her wished she could be so brave. "You'll have to convince me harder than this, Hugh."

"Hmm," he said, grinning at her, his chiseled jaw and high cheekbones reminiscent of the many statues of gods that littered Rome. "Is that a challenge, Miss Clare?"

Molly stood, pulling him to stand before starting back

toward the villa. "It most certainly is. Change my mind, and we'll see."

"I will win, you know. I'm very persuasive."

She chuckled, not caring that Miss Sinclair stood on the balcony above and saw their interaction or the closeness of their friendship. She had not done anything so very wrong. A kiss was not the end of her reputation or the end of the world. And it was not like Miss Sinclair was not embarking on a love affair of her own. "We shall see, will we not?"

"We will," he said, kissing her hand and throwing her a wink.

CHAPTER 7

Late that evening, a knock sounded on her bedroom door and, having dismissed Miss Sinclair some hours before, Molly slid from atop her bed where she had been reading, placing the book down before seeing who was there.

She cracked the door but an inch and fought back the urge to grin like a silly nincompoop. "Mr. Armstrong. Is anything wrong?" she asked, opening the door farther and checking up and down the hall that there was no emergency he was waking her for.

"Not at all. I wanted to show you something in the villa that I have recently had restored. I think you shall enjoy it."

"Really?" Intrigued, Molly stepped out into the hall and shut her door. Hugh held out his arm, and she took it willingly, any excuse to touch him, and she would. When she returned to London, she would miss him dreadfully.

After they had dined together, her mind had raced all evening with what he could mean by trying to persuade her to stay. Did he intend to ask her to marry him? If he did, would she say yes? Molly glanced at him quickly, knowing full well the answer to her question. Oh yes, she would marry him without a second thought.

Even knowing him so little, he made her blood sing, her body yearn and no one, not in all the years she'd treaded the ballroom floors in London, had reacted so to a man.

They made their way through the villa through the atrium and out into the courtyard. Sconces burned against the villa's walls and lanterns lit the garden paths, lighting their way. They headed in the direction of a room that had an oiled wooden door leading into it. Many such rooms ran about the villa walls, and Molly was yet to see what was in those spaces, but this one's door looked repaired and varnished.

"It's inside here." He turned to watch her a moment, and before she knew what he was about, he stole a kiss. Molly tried to make it linger, but instead, he grinned, turned, and threw the door open.

Molly gasped, stepping into the warm, tiled room that had an arched ceiling. She could not believe what she was seeing. It was as if she were stepping back two millennia to Roman times. The room held two deep, tiled pools in the center of the space, sconces burned on each wall, and what looked to be steam coming up from one of the pools made the water inviting.

"Is this a bathhouse?" she queried, taking in the painted mosaics on the wall that although were new, were of scantily clad men and women enjoying baths such as the ones that sat before them.

"It is. Rome used to have hundreds of them as you would know, and this villa had a derelict, ruined one when I bought it. I've had it restored and have had the hypocaust under the floors cleaned out and rebuilt. The hot air that flows beneath the caldarium or hot bath is heated by coal and warms the floor and water. The frigidarium or cold bath I put in myself, the room did not have one. This bath was located in the room next door, but I needed space for servants' quarters and so placed it in here as well. But of course, there is no heating system beneath this bath."

He took her hand, pulling her toward the steaming-hot bath. "I thought you might like to bathe. Alone, of course," he said, grinning wickedly and making her body hum. "You may use the room whenever you like."

Molly didn't know a great deal about history and had learned much more from listening to Hallie and her many travels. However, one thing she did know about Roman baths was what happened to the person after they bathed. "You do not have a servant who rubs you down with oils after your bath, Mr. Armstrong?" Molly couldn't help but chuckle at her teasing. For a moment, Hugh looked a little shocked by her words.

"I do not. No." He moved over to a nearby daybed that sat in one corner, sitting on its edge. "I can arrange that for you, however, if that is what you wish."

Molly joined him, standing before him. He glanced up at her, his long locks mussed with a little curl. He looked vulnerable all of a sudden, and something in her chest ached. She reached out, running her hands over his unshaven jaw, reveling in the feel of his short whiskers. "Are you trying to tempt me to stay in Rome with this bath that I have at my disposal whenever I wish?"

He shrugged, a teasing grin upon his lips. "Is it working?"

Molly looked over her shoulder at the water. The bath looked deep and clean, and so appetizingly warm. It had been so very hot in Rome, and she would revel in bathing. She went over to the bath, looking over her shoulder and meeting Hugh's gaze. He was watching her, a hungry light in his eyes that made her stomach clench. She wanted him to look at her like he wanted to consume her and gorge on every piece of her body. The thought of him, kissing her the way he did in the carriage, of having him take her, left her aching.

Perhaps she ought to jump in the cool bath instead. All his deliciousness was making her discombobulated.

"Can you help me with my buttons?"

His eyes flashed with need, and without hesitation, he stood, striding toward her like a Roman warrior heading to war. Molly looked at the water, steeling herself for his touch on her back. And then it was there, the slip of his fingers upon her gown. He made short work of the buttons that ran down her back.

As the last button on her gown let go, Molly brought up her hands to clasp the front of her dress. Hugh did not stop there. His fingers slid down atop her bottom, the tug of the drawstrings on her corset making her wobble. She bit her lip and closed her eyes, forcing herself not to turn around. Should she do so, she would be lost, and she could not do that. For as much as she had come to realize that she wanted Hugh, wanted him to want her to stay, possibly marry her if that was where he thought their friendship was heading, she could not give herself unless the words were spoken.

At least she did not have the worry that he was merely a wealthy lord looking for a little entertainment while she was in Rome. His being untitled suited her, and she liked that he was a self-made man, had not inherited his fortune from his parents.

"What is it that you do here in Rome, Mr. Armstrong? You have not told me."

His fingers slipped between the laces, working their

way up her back. "I grow wine on my country estate here in Italy, and I dabble in the shipping of goods back and forth from India and England. I've been fortunate that I'm not beholden to anyone, and I live a comfortable life here in Rome."

"Your parents, are they still alive?" Not that she wanted to intrude or seem ungracious, but she was curious. For as much as she longed to turn about and crawl into his arms and stay there forever, they did not know much about each other's lives. If she were to stay in Rome, if he did happen to ask for her hand, they ought to know everything there was to know.

"No, unfortunately, my father passed some years ago and my mother more recently. I was not there for her passing, not that she would wish for me to be."

Molly frowned, a pang of sadness swamping her at the pain she heard in his voice. She turned, staring up at him and wishing she could make the memories of his parents happy ones, just as hers were for her own.

"You were not close? I'm sorry if you were not."

He sighed, running a hand over his jaw before striding toward the door. "I am not. My mother made it clear when I left England that I was not needed or wanted there. I thought it would be contradictory to both our true feelings should I try and be there when she passed. I was correct when she wrote to me, telling me she did not regret her decision of years before."

For all of Hugh's words, there was something within his eyes, a pain hidden from those around him. He was not as immune to this hurt as he stated. The tightness of his mouth told her that no matter what his mother had said, her child had wished it otherwise. He wanted his mother's love, just as all children do, whether they receive it or not.

"I'm sorry, Hugh. That could not have been easy."

He grinned, the wicked and teasing gentleman once more. "What is not easy, my dear, is leaving you alone in this bathhouse to bathe without me. If you think my soul is tortured, it is, but only because of you and not because of a parent who may have had two sons, but only required one."

HUGH SHUT the door on the bathhouse and forced his legs to move toward the villa. The sanctuary of his tablinum. He supposed Molly would be curious about his past, his life when he lived in England. He'd not been prepared to answer such questions, not when he didn't want her to know he was the infamous Lord Hugh Farley, who had ruined a young debutante's life before fleeing to the continent.

Or so everyone thought.

Now the Duke of St. Albans, he supposed he could return to London, lift his nose to anyone who would naysay him, but it wasn't to be borne. He would not give the rats the gloating rights to curse his name and give him the cut direct. Not that they would. Not as one of the highest-ranking and wealthiest peers in England.

With the death of his mother and brother now too, all ability to clear his name was lost. There would be no redemption for him back in England, no matter how much he would like to return. To take up his duties for his father's sake, if no one else's, but he could not. His brother had ensured his name was mud.

Hugh strode into his library, closed the door, and went to the settee that sat before the unlit hearth, sinking into its plush cushions. With Molly intent on returning to England he would have to make a choice. Ask her to stay, to marry him, but therein itself was a problem. He could not marry her under false pretenses. Should he do so, any heirs they produced would not inherit his title, which left him with one choice.

To tell Molly the truth of who he is and the real reason he lived in Italy.

Unless, he could sign the marriage register in his real name without Molly being aware… Even so, he would have to check the legality of the marriage before any children were born.

What a conundrum.

He rubbed a hand over his jaw, the thought of admitting his lineage, his shame, not the feigned one his brother and mother had heaped on his head, but the shame of letting them force him to take the fall left a sour taste in his mouth.

Should he tell Molly the truth, he wasn't certain he could face the horror, the hurt that would shadow her pretty visage. He never wanted her to look at him as if she did not know who he was. To imagine her think him a cad who ruined a young woman's life was a shame he could not bear to see from her.

Why, however, was uncertain. They had known each other for such a short time, but the fire and the chemistry that burned between them were undeniable. Molly was a woman who had friends in high places. There would be little doubt in his mind that she would've heard of Miss Laura Cox and the wicked Lord Farley's ruination of her.

Hugh clasped his hands before his face, leaning on his knees, staring at the blackened hearth in thought. He would be better off leaving her be. Stop all flirtation, all clandestine trips to the bathhouse such as the one tonight. Stop the stolen kisses in the carriage and merely become the host he was supposed to be. Or even better, leave Rome and return to his country estate near Naples. Remove himself from the temptation that was Molly.

He swore, throwing himself back into his chair. The idea of leaving Molly was no more palatable than telling her the truth and watching her leave for London. It was a hopeless case and one he would have to think upon more. Tonight he could not decide his course of action. What he could decide upon, however, was that he needed a stiff drink. Or perhaps, many.

CHAPTER 8

The following evening Molly once again stole down to the courtyard of the villa and snuck into the bathhouse. The room appeared prepared for use at any time, the sconces burned against the walls, the mosaic floor warm under her feet. Molly sighed, luxuriating in the most opulent space she'd ever experienced in her life.

Back in England at her family's small cottage, she had only ever bathed in a hip bath, and the one they had had not given her the ability to swim in warm, fragrant water. Whatever sweet flower oils they were putting in the water were delightful, and other than Hugh himself, she would miss this Roman bath more than anything else when she returned to England.

She had now been in Rome for almost a week, and so much had happened. Not only with her tours of the city, but here with Hugh. They had become friends instantly, and that attraction she felt for him had only grown with each moment she spent in his presence.

Today, however, he'd not been at the villa. The housekeeper had been at a loss as to his whereabouts.

Molly slipped off her robe and untied the small ribbon at the front of her shift, letting that too fall to the floor to pool at her feet. She sank into the water, careful not to slip on the steps before the warm bath engulfed her. Molly smiled, dipping under the water and swimming to the other end. She chuckled, knowing she was frolicking like some water nymph, and she was. Who would not when given such a gift of a Roman bath to use whenever they desired?

The door to the bathhouse opened, and she squealed, swimming to the side of the bath to stop Hugh from seeing her naked. He stumbled into the room and shut the door, seemingly oblivious to her being there.

"Hugh?" she asked. His head flicked up. His glassy eyes focused on her for the first time. Was he drunk?

"Molly," he panted. "I did not know you were in here. I thought everyone was abed."

"I was in bed," she started, watching as he moved over to a daybed, slumping down on the mattress. "But I grew hot and wanted to bathe. I thought it might help me sleep." She paused, watching him as he lay there, one arm slumped over his face, his legs off the side of the daybed as if he could not be bothered to lift them farther. "Are you well, Mr. Armstrong?"

"Do not call me Mr. Armstrong. Please."

He sounded tortured, ill even. Should she risk getting out and slipping on her clothes? He seemed to be only a minute or two away from sleeping. Her towel sat upon a nearby chair, but to clasp it, that too meant she would have to step out of the water completely to ensure her modesty was preserved.

Why had she not placed her towel closer to the bath?

"Are you well then, Hugh?" she asked again, moving along the side of the bath toward the steps.

"I am somewhat drunk, but not ill."

He seemed odd this evening. His words were hard and did not invite conversation. Was he angry at her? The reason for such a turn of character did not make sense. She had not seen him today and the last time they had spent time together, they had parted on good terms.

"What is it then?" she queried, wanting to know what ailed him.

"You."

"Me?" She stood on the bath floor, glancing at him over the side of the pool. He sat up, staring at her, and the desire that blazed in his ebony orbs fired her blood. It was dangerous for him to be in the room with her. She swallowed, her body tingling as his gaze dipped to her shoulders. Not that he could see beyond, but there was little doubt from his visage that he imagined what the rest of her looked like, naked and wet in the water.

"What have I done?" she queried when he didn't say anything further.

"You torment me."

Molly shut her mouth with a snap, unwilling to listen to such hogwash, and certainly unwilling to listen when he was foxed. She strode up the bath stairs, clasped her towel, and wrapped it about herself, ignoring the fact that her body burned. She could feel his attention upon her, scorching its way up and down her body as she covered herself with the soft linen.

Obscured enough to face him, she stalked over and stood a bare foot from his person. "I torment you. You sound like a petulant child. I have no more tormented you than you have me."

"Really?" He stood, towering over her. The breath in her lungs seized. His shirt was open, gaping far enough to see his chest and the scattering of hairs atop his skin.

Her mouth dried, her core ached.

"How do I torment you? Tell me."

His words, barely audible, were in themselves tormenting. His deep, throaty words made her yearn for more. Not just a stolen kiss, but a touch, caress, his hands pulling her against him so their bodies could take pleasure. There was little doubt in her mind that he could give her a lot of satisfaction. Her friends had been honest and open with her, telling her that she should not settle unless the gentleman who had taken her fancy made her burn.

She now understood those words, for burn she did. For him. She would not tell him how he made her feel. She would show him instead.

Her rules be damned.

HUGH WANTED MOLLY with a need that he'd not expected to feel. His body was not itself. He ached every hour of every day, craved with an urgency that made his stomach churn. He needed her touch and her sweet, untutored kisses. She was all he thought about. A novelty he'd not experienced ever. But he was torn. What would she think of him when she found out the truth of his departure from England? Of what he was accused of?

Even if those accusations were incorrect, it did not change the fact that everyone thought it as truth. Miss Laura Cox was from a wealthy family, circulated in his social sphere. Even if her father wasn't titled, they were rich enough to be included in the nobility's social calendar. His brother had gone about his life in London after ruining Laura without a blink of an eye. Only too happy to ooh and ahh over the rumors, commiserate with his friends of his brother's downfall and atrocious behavior. A downfall that Henry should have faced instead of Hugh.

How was he to tell Molly of his past? To expect her to believe that he was innocent of the crime? It was his fault. He should never have agreed to take the fall. Should have told the truth and let his brother face the wrath of their peers. Laura, a sweet woman who he remembered being full of life and promise, had not deserved what she was meted out. His brother, having played with her emotions, should have offered for her hand, especially when Henry took her innocence and got her with child.

Henry had not. Instead, his brother had shunned her, watched from afar as the light in her eyes dimmed to a deathly gray. Ignored her until she no longer attended events and eventually left for the country. Hugh remembered the day his mother had received the missive from Miss Cox, demanding the Duke of St. Albans make good on his promise to marry her. That she would tell her father of his conduct if he did not do the right thing.

His mother had been enraged toward Laura. A fit of misplaced anger, as it should have been directed at her eldest son. From that point on, Henry ceased all communication with Miss Cox and explained that they did not take well to threats. That there was no proof that he was the father or that she had not given out her body to other gentlemen of their set.

That was when Hugh was asked to be the gentleman who had ruined her. To be the one to take the blame, so the head of the family's reputation wouldn't be besmirched. He refused, of course, and so his mother and brother put into play the rumors, the slander that forced his hand.

To this day, that decision haunted him, and now, standing before Molly, he knew his truth would be the end of their newly forming friendship.

She would hate him for the fiend, the lying ass that he was. The bastard he'd been.

And so this morning, he had fled Rome. Had ridden out before dawn, determined to leave Molly and the temptation she brought to his life. The wants and needs to be a man she could love, admire, and marry. He had started toward Naples, removing himself from her life, leaving her to her holiday and tours, not being a distraction in her world.

He may be the Duke of St. Albans now, but his brother had gone to his grave, the respectable, noble god. Hugh was the degenerate, scandalous sibling who ruined innocent women and broke families apart.

True or not, it was what everyone believed.

"I want you. With each breath that I breathe, I want you more, and yet I cannot have you." With each inhalation, her towel lifted, giving him a small glimpse of her ample bosom. Her skin was fragrant, smelled of sweet flowers, and his mouth watered with the want that thrummed through him. He wanted to kiss, taste his way over her skin, gorge on her until he was satisfied.

Which, he was starting to believe, would never be the case.

Her tongue came out, licking her lips at his words, and his cock hardened. He was acting as bad as his brother, wanting to deflower an innocent woman just to quell his wicked appetites.

"Why can we not be together? If we both choose to be so?" Molly asked him, her eyes, fathomless pools of need he could happily drown in as she stared at him, waited for him to answer.

The answer was as complicated as his emotions toward the woman standing before him. Tangled and caught up about them. If she only knew the truth, the answer to her question would be simple. He would never even have the opportunity to court her, for she would never have given him a second glance. "You're a virgin, an unmarried maid. I will not ruin you," he said instead.

"I'm also eight and twenty. I think I am old enough to choose my path. To determine what I want and when I want it. I want you too, Hugh." She sighed, stepping closer to him, the linen of her towel teasing his chest. "I do not understand what is happening to me, but when I'm around you, all I can think about is your touch. I ache in places for you that I did not know existed before we met. I—"

He kissed her. Hard. Took her mouth in a searing kiss that startled him in its intensity. To stand there, hearing her words, was torture he could not endure. Her tongue tangled with his, her arms wrapping about his neck, her towel forgotten.

He reached behind her, pulling it free from her body. His hands snaked across her skin and clasped her ass, picking her up to straddle him. She gasped against his lips, but did not shy away, kissed him with an abandon that left him reeling for purpose.

A voice, a drum in his mind told him to stop. That this was wrong, he was acting like his brother, but he could not. He could no sooner deny her needs than he could deny himself air.

This is not what he'd thought would occur between them when he'd first met her, but having grown to know her over the past week, he realized that it was inevitable they would come together. The attraction, the sizzling air that always circulated about them when they were together, was proof enough that they would become one.

She undulated against his cock, moaning through their kiss, and he walked them over to the bath. He set her down, ripping his shirt over his head and throwing it away somewhere over his back. The touch of her hands on the buttons of his breeches made his stomach quake. She made short work of them, ripping his pants open and assisting him in pulling them down. She stood back, staring at him, a wicked glint and admiration in her eyes as she took her fill.

Hugh stood before her, quiet and willing for her to enjoy what was hers. For it was true. He was hers, forever after this night. He would never look at another woman, not after bedding such a sweet, beautiful being such as his Molly.

Molly took his hand, leading him into the water. The bath was hot, the fragrant scent of flowers permeating from the steam. Hugh stood to the side of the bath, leaning up against it as he watched her float about in the water before him. Hell, she was beautiful, made his heart ache.

"You're too far away." The words reverberated about in his mind, forcing him to take into account that she only had three weeks left with him before leaving for England. He could not let her go. To remain in Rome without her left a hollow, gaping wound deep in his chest.

He'd been content before, went about his days busy with his estates, with his winery in Naples, but to think of going back to the way his life was before Molly was no longer possible. He already knew he would pine for her, miss her, want her until it drove him mad, or pushed him back to England. A country that he would not return to, not after it turned against him without a second thought.

Her lips twisted into a teasing grin, and she swam up against him, straddling him. The breath in his lungs seized at the slippery, willing feel of her in his arms. He tamped down his rakish needs that wanted to seize, conquer, and take what she was so obviously willing to give.

He kissed her, starved of her since the last they were together. He could get used to having her just as they were. Alone and as if the world and its prejudices could not touch them, would not impinge on their decisions or life.

"Stay with me in Rome," he pleaded, holding her fast against him, biting back a groan when her naked self slipped against his cock.

"I will be honest with you, Hugh, because I don't want any secrets between us, but I cannot stay. Not because I do not want to, but because I will not be your mistress. I will not be anyone's mistress."

He frowned, tipping up her chin so she would look at him. "I do not want you to be my mistress. I want more from you than that." He wanted her to be his wife, but how could he ask her to be so when she didn't know anything about him, and when she did, she would likely scorn and run for the hills.

It was a risk he would have to take, for damn it all to hell, he didn't want to lose the woman in his arms. She was perfect for him in every way. For the first time in his life, he was where he wanted to be and with the woman who completed his circle of happiness.

"How much more?" she asked him, her eyes full of trepidation at what his next words would be.

"I know we have not known each other for long, hell, we hardly know each other, but for the first time in my existence, I know what I feel is right. It is what I want and what I want most of all is you. Will you marry me, Molly? Be mine?"

Molly stared at Hugh, her mind a kaleidoscope of thoughts over why she should not marry him. Why the answer to this question ought to be a no, they did not know each other, had met but a week before. Even so, the thought of saying no to the man who held her in his arms and watched her with something akin to fear lurking in the deep depths of his eyes, was impossible to fathom. She wanted to marry him, to be his and no one else's.

She also knew that never had she felt about anyone else how she felt about Hugh. Her body came alive when he was around. Today when she had explored the markets alone and without Hugh, only Miss Sinclair for company, she realized that a little spark that lit Rome to a glowing beacon was not there. Hugh made her travels about the city enjoyable, brought humor and knowledge, gave her a taste of this foreign, ancient city she would otherwise not have experienced.

She was falling in love with him as much as her mind had fallen in love with Rome.

Molly stared at him, so very thankful that she had found the man before her. A man who would be hers forever. All hers and no one else's, even if she had to travel halfway around the world to find him. "Yes. Yes, I will marry you."

He smiled before kissing her. His mouth was hot, insistent, and her body hummed for completion, to be taken and inflamed. Her skin was on fire, and she could not help but rub against him, seek the pleasure that she knew he could give her.

Hugh spun them about, pushing her up against the side of the bath. He hoisted her higher on his hip, his cock teasing her core. She groaned, laying her head against the bath's tiled side as he worked her aching flesh to an inferno. "Yes, take me. I want you so much." Molly didn't care she was begging, or that he had so much power over her at present. All she cared about was that he would make love to her. Give her what she wanted and had not known she'd been missing all these years.

"I can wait, Molly. We do not have to do this now. We can be married within a few days and then come together if you would prefer."

"No." She shook her head, not wanting to wait that long. A time that seemed as far away as the moon. "I want you now. Please, give me what I want." *You.* She didn't say the word, but her mind chanted it like a drum.

His clasp on her bottom tightened, and then she felt him, the hard, silky-smooth head of his manhood pressing against her core. He watched her as slowly, inch by delicious inch, he filled her. With the water's help and her need for him, Molly did not feel the stinging pain she expected. Surprisingly she did not feel anything but exquisite pleasure.

Molly reached up, clasping Hugh's jaw and bringing him to her for a kiss. She gasped as he thrust the last inch of himself into her. Her body urged him to move, and then he did. He thrust into her, joining them forever, and Molly knew what it was to feel loved.

His pumps were deep and constant. Each one hitting a special little place deep in her core. Need ran through her, hot and wild. She held on to him, pushing against him, taking everything he was giving. Her whole center shifted to where they joined, the need to reach whatever apex he was forcing her toward.

"Fuck, you make me burn." His hot breath rasped against her neck. He nipped her skin before laving the bite with his tongue. A shiver rocked through her, and she sighed. "So tight. Mine."

"So big," she retorted. He groaned, the sound a mixture of pleasure and pain. His hand closed over her breast, his thumb and forefinger pinching her nipple. A shot of awareness raced through her body, heightening her pleasure.

"Come for me, my darling."

His words whispered against her ear were her undoing. A feeling unlike one she'd ever experienced ricocheted from her sex and out to every part of her body. A delicious tremor of pleasure convulsed from her sex to the tips of her fingers. Molly screamed his name, but Hugh did not stop. His thrusts only heightened her pleasure, sending waves to convulse through her blood.

"Hugh," she gasped, letting him take her, fuck her as he said and stoke the fire he had ignited in her soul.

"Molly," he groaned, as he too found release, his seed rushing into her core as he followed her climax with his. Their breathing ragged, they stood locked together. She clasped him tight, holding him against her as she tried to calm her racing heart. Molly had never felt so satisfied in her life, so fulfilled and inflamed.

"When can we marry?" she asked, kissing him as he regained his breath.

He grinned, chuckling at her question. "Is tomorrow too soon?"

She grinned back. "Tomorrow sounds perfect."

CHAPTER 9

Tomorrow wasn't too soon. Molly stood beside Hugh in a quaint, Roman church just outside the city and took her vows to be his wife. Miss Sinclair and Marcus stood as their witnesses.

Molly glanced up at Hugh, not believing that she would soon be his wife. A partner to a man who had made a successful life for himself away from England. Her husband. Which would mean Rome would be her home from this day forward. She did not care that he was not titled, or that her marrying him may limit her time with her friends back in England. They would be happy for her because she had found the man she loved.

A man who loved her in return.

Heat rushed onto her cheeks at the thought of their wedding night. Tonight, they could sleep together in the villa. Not apart like they had to when they had returned from the bathhouse only a day before.

To imagine that time was only yesterday was beyond comprehension. It a matter of only a few hours they were uniting their two families. Had her skin not been holding her together, she was sure she would burst apart with excitement.

"I now pronounce you husband and wife," the priest declared, smiling down at them.

Hugh turned to her, the love shining back in his eyes, humbling her. He took her hand and kissed her gloved fingers, his intense, burning stare watching her as he bestowed the sweet gesture.

She wore a ballgown that she had made for last year's Season, a blue so light in the shade that at times it could almost appear white. Molly glanced at her new husband. The idea that she had traveled partway around the world and met a gentleman who made her body and mind not her own, and marry him was an idea so foreign to her she couldn't believe it was real. She'd never acted so rashly and made a decision that would affect the rest of her life so quickly.

Marcus and Miss Sinclair clapped at the celebration of their union, coming up to them before they signed the paperwork to officiate their day.

"Are you happy, my darling wife?" Hugh asked her as he helped her into his carriage, shutting the door behind them and enclosing them in a space all for themselves, away from servants and her companion.

"I'm so happy and a little dazed. I've never made such a huge decision like this before in my life and so quickly."

"You do not regret it, I hope." A shadow of fear lurked in his eyes, and Molly closed the space between them, coming to sit on his lap. She wrapped her arms about his neck, holding him close.

"I will never regret marrying you. I adore you. I hope you know that."

"I love you so very much, Molly."

His declaration sat between them, a knot that tied her

to him forever, for she had fallen headlong and absolutely in love with the man in her arms. He was her equal, the man who made her a better person. He filled her life with adventure and laughter. She snuck a quick kiss, running her hands through his hair and pushing it away from his face so she could see his gorgeous visage better.

"I love you too. You're a gift that Rome has bestowed on me that I had not thought to receive."

His hands wrenched her higher on his lap, her bottom snug between his legs. He kissed her. Hard. Molly threw herself into the kiss, showing him how much she cared and loved the man in her arms.

His tongue tangled with hers, sending a bolt of desire to her core. She ached for him, longed for his touch the moment they had parted ways the night before after their delightful bath together.

Now she never had to leave his side if she did not choose to. She could kiss and touch, play, and have him whenever she wanted. The idea was an elixir that she could get used to, and quickly, she mused.

His tongue tangled with hers, his hands slipping up her waist to clasp her breast. He wrenched the bodice down. Cool air kissed her breast before his hot, warm mouth brushed her skin. His lips worked her flesh, his tongue flicking out to tease her nipple. It beaded, and on a sigh, she closed her eyes, reveling in his touch.

"I want you. I cannot wait."

"Me, either." He lifted her off his lap, a feat had he not done it she would've thought impossible. She was a tall woman and with womanly curves, and yet, he lifted her as if she weighed no more than a piece of parchment.

Molly only stood before him a moment before he had her straddle his hips. His hands fumbled with her gown, dragging it up to pool about her waist. Her wet core met with his hardened manhood, and she understood what he was about. Expectation thrummed through her veins. He reached between them, flicked his front falls open with little finesse. She shivered, need riding her hard, and then he was there. Pushing into her wet heat, his thick, firm manhood filling her to completion.

The carriage rolled through the streets, the sounds and smells of Rome but a passing thought as he took her, hard and fast in their enclosed sanctuary. Molly held on to him for purpose, riding him as he instructed. The position gave her power over him she liked, a heady experience that Hugh seemed to savor as well.

She kissed him, lifting herself and using the carriage's rocking movement to her advantage.

"Yes, fuck me. God damn it, you're beautiful and mine. All mine."

"Yes," she gasped as the first tremors of pleasure started to thrum through her body. Molly wanted more of the same, greedy for the pleasure he could launch into her life. She slammed down on him, took her pleasure, rode his manhood, and pushed herself into the abyss of ecstasy.

Hugh kissed her scream into submission as their mouths and bodies fused. His own moan tangled with hers.

She slumped against him, half on his lap and the cushioned seat. "I do not think I shall ever view a carriage ride the same."

He grinned down at her, a small flush spreading across his cheeks and making him look like a green lad who'd just been extremely naughty with a woman. "I aim to please and show you all the magnificent heights of this city that you can have."

Molly chuckled, laying her head on his shoulder and looking out the window. "We did not even close the blinds. I hope no one was watching our carriage too closely."

He shrugged, one hand idly rubbing her arm just below her sleeve. "Let them talk should they have seen us. I was making love with my wife. There is no sin in that."

No, she mused. There was not.

HUGH WAS the veriest bastard under the sun, but he would repair his sin. He would make things right with Molly when he told her the truth. He just needed time. Now that she was not returning to England, he would explain to her the truth of his past, why he was in Rome, and face her wrath then.

When she could not run away from him. Not without a fight.

With Molly's humble family, it was a possibility that she'd never even heard of his family, of what he was charged with having done. His brother had not married, had merely carried on his wayward ways, except Hugh supposed he did learn a valuable lesson in not dallying with unmarried maids and kept his bed partners to widows or married women.

He was thankful that not all his friends had thought him a cad, had not believed the slur on his name. The Duke of Whitstone one of them. His Grace had been at his estate when his brother's missive had descended on him, demanding he take the fall.

Had Whitstone not been visiting his home when his brother's note arrived, his good friend too may have not have believed him. Hugh was far from a saint and had had his fair share of lovers, although he'd never dallied with virginal debutantes.

Stupid Henry had ruined so many things the day he wet his cock in a cunny that he should never have touched.

Molly, too was friends with Whitstone and trusted the duke. If he wrote to his friend, had him help him explain that was he was accused of was incorrect, there may be no impediment to their marriage working.

He could not lose her now. He loved her with an intensity that scared him and one he'd not thought to ever experience.

Hugh helped her alight from the carriage. He leaned down, picking her up before carrying her over the threshold of their villa, their home, and where he hoped they would start a family. Thanking the staff who lined up to congratulate them, they hastily made their way upstairs toward his suite of rooms. Their room from this night onward. He slammed the door closed, turning the lock and shutting the world away from their sanctuary.

Molly made short work of her gown, throwing her veil to the side and stepping out of her silk slippers as she watched him. Her luscious hair fell about her shoulders, her eyes glinting with expectation.

Hugh ripped his cravat free. His coat and waistcoat soon followed along with his breeches. "Get on the bed," he ordered, striding over to her with a casual air that was the opposite to how he felt.

Inside, his body quivered with need. Already he wanted her again. To lose himself in her hot, tight cunny. To make love to the woman who was a gift he'd not thought to ever receive.

"What are you going to do to me?" She did as he bade, sitting on the bed before scuttling back a little on the linen.

Hugh came to stand before her. He dropped to his knees. Her eyes widened, and she let out a little squeal when he clasped her ankles and pulled her to the edge of the mattress.

"Lay back," he ordered. Without question, she did as

he asked, her breathing ragged. He took in her beauty, her small stomach he hoped would bloom and stretch with their children in years to come. He pushed her legs apart, giving him a view of her cunny. She glistened in the afternoon light, and the musky, sweet scent of her teased his senses.

His mouth watered with the thought of tasting her, eating her until he was sated. His cock twitched, jutting out in front of him, primed and ready. He stoked it quickly, teasing himself. He wanted to come, to fuck her, but that could wait. Right now, he wanted to make her shatter on his lips. To hear her scream his name and grind herself against his face like he'd dreamed about this past week.

He cast a quick look up at Molly and found her watching him, her perfect, white teeth clamping her bottom lip in expectation. Hugh reached up, sliding his hand across her stomach to squeeze her breast. "You're going to love this, my love."

Hugh leaned forward, kissing his way up her leg, taking little love bites as he went. She squirmed under his assault, and he grinned, knowing there would be a lot more squirming by the end of the night.

He licked her skin, it smelled of spring flowers. Hell, she was sweet, so willing and reactive. He was a lucky man to have married such a woman. He licked his lips, rubbing his thumb over her nubbin, coating his finger in her juices. She moaned but didn't shy away from his touch, instead, she spread her legs wider, her wicked gaze begging him to do more.

Oh, he'd do more, so much more before they had finished their first night as a married couple. Unable to wait a moment longer, he slid his tongue along her cunny. He used slow, smooth strokes, the need to savor the taste of her on his lips stopping him from rushing. Her fingers clamped into his hair, holding him at her core, and he ate her sweet petal, licking and flicking her receptive nubbin until she was writhing with need.

He had imagined Molly just so, letting him bring her to climax. Hugh placed his hands beneath her bottom, pulling her closer to his mouth and kissed her there. Used his tongue to tease, to delve. With one finger, he slipped into her. Her body clamped down on him, and his cock twitched, beaded with his own seed.

So tight. So hot.

Patience, he reminded himself. This right now was all for his wife. To give her pleasure without having to receive any in return. Not physically, in any case. In truth, however, his cock stood erect, poised for release. To give pleasure was just as exciting as receiving in his estimation.

She rode him, lost all inhibitions, and let him love her. His mouth made love to her, his finger teasing and giving a glimpse of what was to come. His cock.

"Oh, Hugh. Yes. Ohhh," she said, her thrusts frenzied. *Almost there.* He grinned, flicking her nubbin one last time. She broke apart before him, arms outstretched above her head, her body riding his face without thought or care.

She was fucking marvelous.

CHAPTER 10

The day after their wedding, Hugh surprised Molly with a trip to his villa in Naples. The carriage journey took several days, but upon arriving at his villa, which overlooked the Bay of Naples, she realized the jarring of her bones and numbness of her bottom was well worth the discomfort.

Behind the villa were fields of grapevines, ideal growing in the rich volcanic soil. They were abundant and the deepest green she'd ever beheld, and already an abundance of grapes hung heavy on the vine.

Molly stood out the front of the villa on her first night, Naples lights tinkling in the early evening, the sunset a rich red and orange. Still visible in the distance was the majestic Mt. Vesuvius.

Hugh came up behind her, wrapping his arms about her waist. "Do you wish to see Pompei and Herculaneum? We can travel down there in a day or two if it pleases you."

Molly clasped his arms, holding him to her. It was surreal that she was here, married, and in love. So much had happened to her in such a short period of time that if her feet were not firmly on the ground, she might swoon.

"You're spoiling me. My friend Hallie will be terribly jealous when I tell her of all the places that I've been to."

"She enjoys travel as much as you?" His words tickled her ear, and she shivered in the warm, evening air.

"She lived in Egypt for some years. She's a historian, but is now married to the Viscount Duncannon."

"Arthur?" Hugh said.

Molly turned to him, meeting his gaze. "Do you know Lord Duncannon too? I did not know that you knew many other people in the *ton* other than the Duke of Whitstone."

"I, um, know a little of him, yes. Through Whitstone."

Molly wondered at his words before he pulled her into the room just off the balcony where his housekeeper here had served up cold meats, bread, and pasta for dinner. Molly sat and smiled as Hugh didn't move to the end of the table, but sat beside her, reaching out to pick up her hand and kiss it.

"I'm so very fortunate to have you as my wife. I want to spoil you most definitely, so tell me what you would like to do tomorrow. We may go and see if the gardeners at the Royal Palace of Caserta will allow us to walk the grounds. The building is as majestic as Versailles."

"Truly?" Molly had never heard of such a place, but having seen and adored Versailles, another such building of similar architectural beauty would be an excellent location to visit. "I would love that. May we also visit the sea? They say the water is aqua in color, and I want to know if that is true."

Hugh chuckled, placing a large portion of chicken and ham onto his plate, along with a good helping of pasta. "Your wish is my command, my love. Do you wish to go sea bathing? I can arrange that for you as well if you like."

Excitement thrummed through her veins, and Molly knew she was grinning like a spoiled child getting everything that she wished. "Will you join me if I do?"

The heated look he threw her sent her blood to pump hard in her veins, and she clasped her stomach to stop its fluttering. "Do you need ask?"

Molly bit her lip, spooning a mouthful of pasta into her mouth. "No, but I wanted to make certain just in case."

Their days in Naples were full of laughter and pleasure. Simply the two of them, exploring, learning, and always loving when they came together at night.

Pompeii and Herculaneum took some days to visit. Walking about the areas of Pompeii, especially, left Molly with a sense of the gravity of what had happened to the people there. The excavation of the buried city was in its infancy, from looking at what had been unearthed so far, so much more of the ancient city remained hidden.

They had walked the beach in the Bay of Naples, and sea bathed just as Hugh had promised. The weeks sped by, and before she knew it, they had been in Naples a month.

They returned to Rome tomorrow, and Molly had to admit she did not want to leave. This city, its beauty, the mountains, and fields full of fertile, rich crops had imbedded into her heart, much like the man sitting at his desk right at this moment.

Molly put down the knitting she had started while here and stood, walking over to his desk. She ran her hands over his shoulders, sliding them down over his arms and peeking at the many letters that sat scattered before him.

He leaned back in his chair, smiling up at her. "What are you up to, my darling wife?"

She chuckled, coming about and sitting herself down on his lap. He adjusted her, hugging her to him before kissing her soundly. Molly melted into his arms, knowing when they returned to Rome, she would count down the days until they were back here again, alone and in their own little cocoon.

She ran her hands through his hair, putting it on end. "Thank you for this wonderful holiday. I feel so very blessed to have found you."

"No, it is I who has been honored. I feel I shall never be able to pay Whitstone back for the tremendous deed he's done by sending you to me."

Molly chuckled. "I'm certain he could think of something. Probably involve buying a thoroughbred if I'm to guess correctly."

Hugh nodded, his gaze darkening with desire. "No doubt."

Hugh lifted Molly to sit on his desk. Her delectable rump in his lap drove him to distraction, and for the past hour of working on paperwork from his estate here in Naples, he'd not been able to concentrate.

The sight of his wife, biting her lip, and attempting to knit, which did not seem to be a skill she was very adept at had warmed his blood. When she'd finally come over to see what he was about, he knew he would not let her go again.

Papers scattered to the floor. He slid his hand along her leg, liking that his wife had disregarded her use of stockings in the Italian heat. Her soft skin tempted him like no other, and he squeezed her thigh, electing a sigh from her delectable lips.

He could not wait a moment longer, and kissed her, pulled her to the edge of the desk and stepped between her legs. She opened for him, lifting her leg to rest about his waist.

Hugh fumbled for his front falls, ripping them open and freeing his hard cock, and then he was in her. They gasped at the contact, each time they came together was like the first. Hugh wondered if it would always be like this with Molly—all-consuming and wild, as hot as the midday sun.

She moaned, laying back on the desk, and she was his to have. Seeing her before him, his for the taking, her breasts rocking with each thrust caused his balls to tighten, his cock to swell.

He ran his hand up her hip to her breast, squeezing the ample flesh just as she liked. Hugh leaned over her, thrusting deeper, harder, and he knew she was close.

She mewled beneath him, without fear or reserve. She sighed his name, her hands reaching behind her for the desk's edge for purchase.

Hugh brought his hand down to her cunny, wet and tight. He slid his thumb over her engorged nubbin, and she came apart beneath him. Her core convulsing and pulling his own release forward.

Hugh fucked her hard, let himself go over the edge before slumping beside her on his desk, heedless of the mess their lovemaking had caused.

Her chest rose and fell rapidly with exertion, and he laughed, feeling his own heart beat hard and loud in his chest.

"I do not think I shall ever get tired of such an activity. You've positively ruined me forever."

He sighed, pulling her into the crook of his arm. "I adore you too," he said, kissing her temple. "Shall we adjourn to the bathhouse? I know how much you love to bathe."

She grinned, her cheeks a light-pink shade that made

his heart miss a beat. "You know me so well, husband. Let us go."

A WEEK LATER, Molly woke in their bedroom in Rome, so very thankful that the world was a different place to where it was only a month before. She was a wife. Mrs Molly Armstrong. The thought could not make her happier.

She sighed, rolling over and smiling at the curtains that billowed in the morning breeze. Hugh was not beside her, but then he often was not in the morning. An early riser her husband seemed to be, and was the opposite of who Molly had always been. But then, her seeking him out in his office had become a bit of a game, and a most pleasurable one each day.

A knock sounded on her door, and she bade enter her new lady's maid, a young Italian woman who was the housekeeper's granddaughter. The young woman had wanted to rise above being a maid in the household and had come to Molly, asking if she may practice as her maid.

She had agreed straightaway, and Miss Sinclair seemed only too happy to go back to her ways of watching from afar, and reading each day and not having to be so very busy trying to keep a watch on Molly. Now that she was a wife, Miss Sinclair had agreed to stay for a few more weeks and then travel back to London. Although from the growing affection between her companion and Marcus, something told Molly that a second wedding may soon occur.

Cassia bobbed a quick curtsy, before holding up two gowns neatly pressed. "Good morning, *Signora* Molly. What dress would you prefer for the ball this evening?"

Ah yes, the Earl and Countess Brandon's ball that she

had been invited to. Hugh had been less pleased for Molly to attend, and it was odd that the invitation had only been addressed to her. Perhaps Lady Brandon had not heard of her marriage and still assumed she was visiting Rome alone with her companion.

"The red silk is very pretty. I shall wear that tonight."

"You shall look beautiful in the dress," Hugh's deep baritone said from the doorway. He leaned against the stone, a contemplative look on his handsome visage.

Butterflies took flight in Molly's stomach, and she jumped from the bed, dismissing her maid who scurried from the room. She pulled Hugh toward a seat that sat before their unlit hearth. "Sit," she ordered him. His eyes widened in question before he did as she bade.

"What are you doing?" he asked, a mischievous glint in his orbs.

Molly kneeled before him, running her hands along the top of his thighs, the buckskin breeches under her palms soft to touch, and yet the muscle beneath bunched and pulled tight.

"If I'm to look fetching in my gown, it is only because I've married the most handsome man in Italy, and he's my escort."

"About that," he said, running a hand over his jaw. "I cannot attend the ball this evening. Some estate business has arrived from England that I need to go over. I'm very sorry, my love. Will you forgive me?" He leaned forward, kissing her. His lips were soft, warm, and desire thrummed in her veins.

Would it always be like this for her with Hugh? Would she always crave him as much as she wanted him at this very moment?

"I can attend on my own. I'm sure I shall endure the ball very well without you, but I shall miss you." She smiled, wanting to put him at ease. "I am, after all, quite used to attending such events by myself."

Hugh frowned, reaching for her. "I do not want you to go on your own. Why not stay here with me and we shall attend to our own festivity? Just the two of us?"

Molly chuckled, a wicked idea coming to mind. She reached up to the clasps on his breeches, meeting Hugh's gaze as her fingers made light work of the buttons. A sinful glint entered Hugh's eyes, and he adjusted his seat to help assist her in pulling his breeches down.

His manhood sprung free, fully erect and all hers. This close and in the daylight, she could study him much better, play, and learn. Molly ran a finger along a large vein that ran from the base of his penis to the head. A small droplet of moisture beaded on the top, and she ran her finger over it, rubbing it between her thumb and forefinger. It was smooth, just like his manhood itself. Never before had anything felt so soft. A velvety skin over hard steel. An amazing thing really when one thought about it, and she was both fascinated and tempted to learn more about what she could do with it now that it was hers to savor.

Molly leaned forward and licked the tip of his penis. It was salty, dissimilar to anything she'd sampled before, but not disagreeable. Hugh's hands clamped the sides of his chair, grounding himself still. Molly cast him a swift look. His jaw clenched, a small muscle pulsated at his temple. Even so he did not attempt to stop her, or guide her in her journey.

She leaned forward, this time licking the full length of him, from base to tip. His intake of breath spurred her on, and she suckled the tip of his manhood before taking him fully in her mouth. Her tongue rasped against his member, and Hugh pumped his hips, guiding her with his hands tangled in her hair how he liked it.

Molly liked it too. Loved that she could tease him, love him in this way just as he'd similarly loved her. She had fallen quite in love with Hugh's kisses against her cunny and had wondered if it were possible for her to give the same pleasure in return.

It would seem that it was so.

"Yes, suck me like that," he gasped, pushing deep into her mouth. Molly reveled in the feel of his manhood in her mouth, hard and deep. She reached down, touching herself, aching for him to do the same, anything that would sate her need of him.

"Oh, no, you do not," he said, pulling her off him.

Before Molly knew what he was about, he'd stood, pushing her to lean against the chair he vacated. Cool morning air kissed the backs of her legs, and she glanced over her shoulder to see her shift lifted to reveal her bottom.

Molly held on to the chair, expectation thrumming through her as Hugh positioned himself behind, and then he filled her. Thrust into her aching self and took her, hard and fast. Molly muffled her moans in the chair's cushion. Hugh took her rough and hard, everything that she wanted.

"Oh, yes. Hugh," she moaned. He reached about her waist and teased her flesh, rubbing her with his fingers and taunting her until she did not know where she began, and he ended. It was too much. The pleasure, the need too strong. He would break her into a million pieces and she would never go back together again. She mumbled incoherently as he took her, his hard chest coming over her back, holding her close as thrust after thrust pumped into her core.

And she was lost.

. . .

Hugh fucked Molly with a need that scared him. He could not get enough of his new wife, not just in this way but also in every way. To be near her was to be content, happy. He'd not felt that for a very long time.

He held her as he pumped into her tight, wet heat. Damn it, she was perfect, reactive, and always surprising him with her needs and desires. He'd not come to her room this morning to receive such a gift, and he would not leave until she too had pleasure.

The scent of flowers wafted from her hair. He breathed deep, knowing he would never get enough of her. She pushed back on him, taking her pleasure as much as he was giving, and he felt the tightening, the convulsing of her core about his cock. She screamed his name into the cushions. Hugh fucked her, let himself be pulled into climax by her spasming heat. He came hard, spilled his seed deep, and reveled in the satisfaction that came over him at having Molly in his life.

Hell, he loved her. So much.

Hugh disengaged, and pulling her shift down, picked her up and carried her to their bed. Not the easiest feat as he'd only removed his breeches from one leg in his haste to have her. He kicked off his pants and climbed into bed next to her, pulling her into the crook of his arm.

"Are you happy?" He needed to know that she was. That their time together was nothing but a happy one for Molly. She was the most important person in his world now, and he would do everything to protect and love her as much as she deserved.

"I'm so happy." She grinned up at him, snuggling down against his side, one arm thrown lazily over his stomach.

Hugh closed his eyes and yawned, tired and satisfied.

"Are you certain you cannot come to the ball with me tonight? I want to show off my new husband."

Hugh would love to go, but he could not. Lord Brandon was recently in Rome from London, and he knew of his past. The accusations, no matter how false, would be revealed if he attended. Even using his mother's maiden name of Armstrong, Lord Brandon knew his face. Would out him to Molly.

He needed to tell her the truth himself, just not yet. He wasn't ready for that conversation right now.

If he could, he'd persuade Molly to stay home with him, enjoy more of their time together, such as they just did.

"You could always not go and stay at home with me, as I suggested before."

"But you said you had work to do. I would only be in your way, and in any case, I'm looking forward to seeing Lady Brandon. She will have news from home, and as much as I love being here with you, I do miss my friends."

Hugh pushed back a lock of hair from Molly's face, marveling at her beauty. "I know you do, my love. You should go and enjoy yourself." He paused, pulling the bedding up over them more. "And I promise you the next ball that is to take place in Rome, I shall attend."

She turned and kissed his chest, and a bolt of pleasure thrummed through his blood. His cocked twitched, ready and willing to go again. Having a wife had made him the most rakish being in Christendom.

"Very well. I'm satisfied with those terms. I hope you shall miss me tonight?"

Hugh rolled Molly onto her back, settling between her legs. His cock hard and primed to go again. Her eyes darkened with need, and she wiggled, placing him at her core. Desire licked at the base of his spine, and he pushed into her a little way, teasing them both.

"Oh, I shall miss you, and when you return home, you will know how much."

"Mmmm," she gasped, lifting her legs about his back and pulling him into her.

Hugh bit back a groan. His wife was a hellion, and he loved every moment of it. "Are you after something, wife?" he teased, holding her and his need at bay.

She pouted, squirming on him and making him see stars. "You know I am." Her words were breathless, an edge of annoyance to her tone. Hugh chuckled.

"Tell me what you want." He needed to hear it from her. Hear her ask for him.

"You," she gasped. "I want you."

Hugh thrust into her, pleasure rocked through him, strong and hard, and he was lost. Lost in the arms of his wife. A place that he never wanted to venture from. Not today, or ever.

CHAPTER 11

The ball at Lord and Lady Brandon's was a crush. Molly arrived a little late after her husband came to their room to wish her a good evening, and they had ended up toppled onto the bed, enjoying each other instead.

Molly came into the atrium of the villa, the introductions long past, and made her way over to her hosts for the evening. She dipped into a curtsy. Lady Brandon beamed at her arrival, pulling her into a quick embrace. "Molly, my dear. How wonderful to find you in Rome. When Ava said you had traveled here, I was so pleased. We must have you over for lunch when you're free."

"I would like that very much." Lady Brandon took Molly's arm, turning her away from the party.

"Let us take a turn about the room. I feel there is so much to discuss. How has your holiday been so far? I understand you were to only stay a month, but you just returned from Naples, no? Has something changed in your circumstances to keep you here in my incredible home country?"

Molly wondered if she should tell her friend of her

marriage. She had not written to her family as yet and would hate for the news of her nuptials to reach them from someone else other than herself. She would ensure that tonight she would write the necessary letters. "I was to return and join the Duchess of Whitstone, and Countess Duncannon in London for the new Season. That, however, will no longer occur. I'm going to be staying in Rome for some time."

"Why is that? Do you like the city so very much that you have decided to make it your permanent address?"

Molly nodded, unable to hold back the smile at the thought of Hugh in her life.

"I was married last month, my lady. It has been a whirlwind courtship, but one that I do not regret. I have found the man of my heart, and I shall make Rome my home since this is his home also."

"Oh, my darling friend, I cannot believe it." Lady Brandon blushed a little, before taking two glasses of champagne from a passing servant. "Not that I do not believe that anyone should not wish to marry you, but that you have accepted him. I always thought you were settled as a spinster—a woman who enjoyed her independence. A point proven I believe by the fact that you're in Rome and only with a companion for company. How is Miss Sinclair? Still complaining about doing what she is paid to do?"

Molly chuckled, sipping her fruity drink. "Not at all. I do believe my companion has fallen for a handsome servant of my husband. I think it is only a matter of time before they marry. I do not see her returning to England anytime soon."

"Well, that is delightful news." Her ladyship beamed at her, her eyes bright and eager for news. "Tell me of the gentleman who has won your heart? Is he someone we would know? Is he a Roman man? We all know how very lovely they can be," she said with a wink. "It would not surprise me that one has captured your heart, my dear."

All true, of course, but not in this case. "He's English, has lived abroad for several years now. Mr. Hugh Armstrong is his name. Have you heard of him?"

Lady Brandon pulled back a little, the color draining from her cheeks.

Molly reached out to her, taking her arm. "Are you well, Rose? You've become quite pale."

Her ladyship shook herself a little before continuing. "Do you mean to tell me that Lord Hugh Armstrong, Lord Farley when he left England and is now the Duke of St. Albans, is your husband?"

The name Farley bounced about in her mind. Molly shook her head, clearing it of the troublesome thought that she'd married a man who went by the same name as the gentleman who had ruined her cousin's life.

"Pardon?" she said, unable to voice more words. There were hundreds of Farleys, and in Italy, surely. A common name that wasn't always linked with nobility. That Lady Brandon had jumped to the conclusion Hugh was the man who had ruined all her cousin's hopes and dreams, had left her heartbroken before she died was unfathomable.

It could not be Hugh.

"I do not think Mr. Armstrong is who you mean. I thought Lord Farley had traveled to Spain, not Rome."

Lady Brandon glanced about them, checking that they were alone. "I may be mistaken, but did I not hear a rumor that your family has a distant association with the St. Albans? Your cousin, Miss Cox, was ruined by Lord Farley. Is that not correct?"

Molly frowned, panic clawing at her chest. "How do you know that? No one knows of the connection. My family was very careful to keep others from being tainted by Laura's social demise."

"Ah, well as to that. When I married Lord Brandon and returned to England with him from Italy, I hired a dressmaker. She happened to be the late Miss Cox's dressmaker, and I heard a time or two little tidbits of information. Your name was said along with Miss Cox's, and it wasn't hard to assume a blood connection. You do look very similar to Miss Cox. I was aware of her during her first Season."

Molly nodded, swallowing as bile rose in her throat. If Lady Brandon knew of Laura and her connection to Molly, how many other people in London did also? Was that why she had never had any offers to her hand? Did they think her, too, fallen from grace?

Heat rushed to her face, and she took a fortifying sip of her wine. Hugh could not be Lord Farley. And what was this about him being a duke?

"You mentioned Lord Farley is now the Duke St. Albans. What has happened to his older brother?"

Her ladyship pursed her lips, a displeased line to her mouth. "Racing his curricle and lost control of the vehicle. Killed both himself and his valet. Before we caught our ship to Rome, it was all London was talking of."

Lord Farley could not be her husband. He could not. She would not believe such a thing. "Mr. Armstrong is not whom you speak of. I'm certain of it."

"Armstrong was the surname of the late Duchess St. Albans. It was her maiden name. I think I'm correct in this, Molly. I think this is too much of a coincidence to be an error."

Molly glanced about the room. She breathed deep, needing air. Her gown was too tight, her skin too heated. The room spun, and she clasped her ladyship for purchase.

"May we go someplace else? I cannot think straight in this room."

"Of course," Lady Brandon bustled her out of the atrium and into a nearby sitting room that was thankfully empty. "Mr. Armstrong, your husband, is who I believe him to be, is he not?"

This could not be true. Hugh could not be the one and the same man whom she'd sworn to hate for all eternity. "I cannot believe it. It cannot be so."

"But I think it is so, my dear. Miss Laura Cox was your cousin, was she not? I'm not wrong in that."

"You are not wrong." Her answer came out but a whisper, and she could not believe the words. The life that she had hoped to live evaporated before her eyes. A little mocking voice taunted her that this is what happened when one married without knowing the other person for very long. That this was a sign that she was not meant for love or marriage. That she should have been content being alone and having herself for company.

"Whatever will I do?"

"Have you consummated the marriage? I know I should not ask such a personal question, but is there a chance of an annulment?" Lady Brandon asked, concern masking her voice.

"There is no chance of an annulment. Most definitely not a route that I can take to fix what I have unwillingly done."

Her ladyship sighed, reaching out to take her hand. "Then it would seem that you're the Duchess of St. Albans. Whatever will you do? Will you confront him with this?"

"I will face him, yes. He has lied to me most cruelly." The idea that she would unwittingly marry the very man who ruined her cousin's life was unfathomable. Of all the people she thought she would meet abroad, he was not one of them. For years, the duke's younger brother had been rumored to be living in Spain, content to stay there and live off the family fortune. Had he been in Italy all this time instead? It would seem that he had.

"I shall walk you to the door and have your carriage summoned if you wish."

"Thank you, yes." Molly couldn't imagine what she was going to say to Hugh. How would she face him knowing who he really was? A stranger she did not know, not really. The forthcoming confrontation left a hollow feeling in her chest and dread to pool in her stomach. How did one leave a marriage? The idea was too awful to contemplate.

MOLLY FOUND Hugh in his tablinum upon her return to the villa. She shut the door and poured herself a well-needed brandy before seating herself across from him. His eyes followed her, hungry and burning with appreciation.

Normally his heady intent would have her slipping onto his lap to let him do as he wished, but not tonight and possibly never again. The idea of not being with him, her Mr. Armstrong, her husband making love to her, and spending time and doing all the things they had planned made her want to scream at the universe.

"Good evening, wife. How did you enjoy the ball? You did not stay overly long. Is everything well?"

She downed her drink, slamming the crystal glass onto his desk. "I did not enjoy it at all, unfortunately."

He sat back in his chair, and the heat that was banked in his eyes a moment before was replaced with unease. "Why is that? Did something happen?"

Molly shook her head, the image of her cousin and her small child dead in their coffin rising up in her mind like a ghoul. How could he have treated them like that? As if they were not worthy of his name and protection. How could she have married the very man who had ruined her cousin's life and the lives of her relatives? They had been devastated by the death of their only daughter. To this day, her aunt's wailing screams when Laura passed from this world would haunt her for the rest of her days.

She bit back tears, schooling her features. "I'm curious, Hugh, just what I should call you. Mr. Armstrong, whom I married, Lord Farley after what I was told this evening, His Grace, the Duke of St. Albans? Perhaps Duke will suffice since we're on intimate terms."

"Hugh will be just fine." His voice held an edge of steel, and she wanted to bend that metal rod, twist it, so it was no longer so rigid and unforgivable.

"You're Lord Farley? Now the Duke of St. Albans. I do not understand."

"I am now." He nodded, raising his brow. "You've heard of my family?"

She scoffed, wishing she did not know of his family as well as she did, but that was never to be. The past had occurred, the horrors along with it, and there was no changing that. "Lord Hugh Farley fled England after he was accused of dallying with an heiress, getting a child onto her, and leaving her to face the *ton's* wrath. Alone."

He didn't say anything, merely watched her in silence, and the urge to throw something at him, break his calm visage, overwhelmed her. Molly clasped the handles of the chair, forcing herself to not move.

"Did you ruin Miss Laura Cox, Hugh?"

"Who told you that I did? Lady Brandon? She is no reliable source, and I would not believe everything that she has to say."

"I've known Rose for some years, and trust her word.

Stop hesitating. Are you the one who society cast out due to your actions toward Laura?"

A muscle worked in his jaw. His lips thinned. "I am the very man who was forced to leave England over the scandal. But not everything is as it seems, Molly. Allow me to explain, and you may think differently."

Molly slapped a hand over her mouth, having heard enough. "See things differently." She stood. "You must be jesting. I will never see anything of that situation other than what occurred. You slept with my cousin, ruined her, and then left her for dead. She did die by the way, during the birth of your son. Did you know that?"

He stared at her, his eyes wide, his face draining of color. "Laura was your cousin? But your last name was Clare. I knew Miss Cox in town, and not once did I see you with her."

"My uncle made his fortune importing and exporting goods from India, he married my father's sister. My father is a vicar. A modest life and income, and because I was a few years younger than Laura, when her fall from grace occurred, I was sent away to France to school. To remove me from the scandal and to keep my reputation safe."

"We were both sent away. I'm sorry for what happened to Laura, but let me explain my side of events. You will see that I'm innocent in all this."

Molly strode to the door. A chair scraped behind her, and before she could open the door but an inch, Hugh was behind her, slamming it shut. She turned, glaring at him. "I married the one man my family and I swore to curse for the rest of our days. How can I return home and tell my parents, aunt, and uncle, that I have slept with our enemy? The very man who ruined a woman's life. You left her to die. For days she suffered in childbirth, and not one word from you."

"You do not know what you speak," he said frowning. "I cared for Laura as a friend, but that is all. I did not do what you accuse me of."

"Really, then tell me, Your Grace, who did? Your elder brother, perhaps? You cannot think that I would believe that your mother would go about society as she did, sorrowful and apologetic for her younger son's actions. No mother would throw the blame on one child over the other, especially if they were innocent of the charge."

He scoffed, running a hand through his hair and leaving it on end. "You did not know my mother." The words were self-derogatory, and she hated that this was what was happening to them.

"You go by the name Mr. Armstrong?" she asked, needing clarification.

"It's my mother's maiden name and not commonly known. A vicar's daughter would not know the intimate details of a duke's marriage that took place years before, now would she?"

The words were cutting, and Molly felt the nick of his tongue's blade just as severe as if he'd cut her with the physical object himself. So, now she was not good enough for him? Not high enough on the social ladder to circulate and know the Duke of St. Albans intimate details?

"I will pack my things and be gone by the morning."

"The hell you will." He glared at her, his eyes narrowing in anger, and yet fear, not hate lurked in his dark depths. Not that it would change her mind. He could not keep her here, no matter what he said or thought. She would return to England and forget her few weeks in Italy.

Or at least try and forget her time here.

Her heart ached at the very thought of it.

"You cannot stop me, Hugh. I will leave you and be gone by morning. Nothing you say or do will change that fact." The thought of their farce marriage near crumbled her resolve to remain strong. "We're not even married. All this time I've been living in sin and with a man I do not even know."

"We are married. I signed the register St. Albans, not Armstrong."

"That does not make it legal," she seethed, blinking to stem her tears. "In a court of law, I highly doubt that would make our marriage legitimate."

A muscle worked in his jaw as he thought over her words. "We will marry again. Without the guise of Armstrong."

She shook her head. Who was this man? "I will not marry Lord Farley, not now or ever. I'm returning to England."

"And so that is all I deserve. You choose to believe I am capable of such a crime and do not believe me when I tell you otherwise."

Molly crossed her arms. She wanted to go to him, to soothe the hurt in his voice, the pain etched on his handsome visage. But she could not. Her cousin's image, cold in her coffin, her little child laying in her arms, put paid to that notion. "What is your side, then, Your Grace? Do, please, enlighten me."

He growled, stalked to the fire where he fisted his hands on the marble mantle. "I never touched Miss Cox. My brother courted her during her first Season, made her believe she was loved and his favorite. Henry had many favorites, your cousin was merely one of them."

Molly listened, not liking that he sounded like he truly believed the words coming out of his mouth. Had she married a madman? A liar? Society would certainly say she'd married a rogue who had ruined an innocent woman and left her to face the *ton's* wrath. Laura certainly had paid the ultimate price for giving her heart to a man.

"Henry got her with child, and when she demanded he do the right thing by her, he threw her aside. Laura threatened Henry in a letter to my mother. A mistake she would live to regret. No one tells the Duke of St. Albans what to do."

She narrowed her eyes, the arrogance of the man, of his family. "She was an heiress, more than suitable for your family. I'm sorry, Your Grace, but the notion behind your excuse is absurd. For years, you've been living abroad, people know it only to be you that was shunned out of society, not your brother. I do not believe you."

"I took the fall, Molly. That is all. I was forced to leave England for the sake of the family image. I prefer Rome in any case, and I've been happy here. But now, as a married man, I know that my life has been missing one important element. You."

"Well, you shall miss that element again, for I am not staying. I cannot believe the Duke of Whitstone is your friend. Once he finds out that Laura was my cousin, I doubt you'll have even him as your supporter."

"Did you hear a word that I said?"

"I did," she said, “and I do not believe it. No one would leave their homeland, take the fall for anyone, not even for their brother." She glanced about the room, the well-stocked shelves of books, the leather chairs before the fire, and mahogany desk. The opulence that she'd never noticed before. Of course, she knew he was not struggling, but she had not seen everything as clearly as she now did. "They paid you to leave. Guilty or not, you choose money over honor." She rushed for the door.

"Molly, wait." He clasped her arm, and she shook off his hold.

Molly held up her hand, trying to gather all the tidbits of information as she knew them. "Say your brother did dishonor my cousin, you still chose to leave England. To live abroad and in the same type of lifestyle that you enjoyed back home. Instead of forcing your brother to do the right thing, making him marry Laura, you ran away. Like a coward."

He swallowed, his skin a deathly gray. "I had no choice, Molly. Please believe me that I did try. I know you do not believe me, but I did fight for Laura. Henry would not be moved, and my mother even more so. Do not leave me. I cannot live without you."

Her eyes burned with unshed tears, and she sniffed, not wanting him to see her cry. "You did not try hard enough. I do not know who you are."

He clasped her arms, pinning her before him. His hands shook, and she willed herself to be strong. To not be swayed. "You do know who I am. More than anyone else. Do you believe I could act so callously toward a woman? For all your sweetness and how much I love you, you are not nobility. I did not have to marry you if I did not choose to. I love you, fell in love with you, and want to spend the rest of my life with you. No title, not even a ducal one, could stop me from having you forever, and it did not.

"When we took our vows, I said mine as the Duke of St. Albans. The registrar is signed with St. Albans, not Armstrong. Why would I have not married your cousin had I loved her? She was an heiress, some would say more suitable than you were for my rank. It was not me, Molly. I was not the man behind your cousin's downfall."

She pushed him away, having heard enough. "I do not know what I believe, but what I do know is that everyone believes it was you, even your mother. You ran away to

Italy and hid here for years like some sort of criminal. How am I to just dismiss all of that? I cannot."

"You're making a mistake."

She turned and reached for the door, wrenching it open. "Maybe I am, but know this, you allowed me to marry you when so much of your past was hidden. Like a thief in the night, you concealed why you left London and your true name. Even if my cousin was not involved, you seem to be so very comfortable living a lie that it sends shivers up my spine."

"I intended to tell you the truth. I just could not find the right time. I'm sorry that I did not."

Molly scoffed, glancing at him over the shoulder. "Hindsight is a wonderful thing, is it not? If only we could do things over again, perhaps we would've acted differently, but I suppose we shall never know now." She walked from the room, leaving Hugh behind. She would return to London tomorrow first thing, return to England, and figure out her life without her husband.

A man she had thought she knew, loved with all her heart. Worse, however, would be when she faced her family. When they found out who she had married, they would never forgive her. They, too, would shun her and demand she leave them be. The thought sent a pulse of revulsion to course through her body, and she ran the last few steps to her room, just making it and retching into her chamber pot. She slumped against the wall, spent and nauseated. No more fitting end to a wretched night could she have asked for. Perfect.

CHAPTER 12

London - One month later

Molly returned to London a few weeks into the new Season. Her trip made less arduous and long due to Lord Brandon allowing her the use of his ship to escort her back to London. A welcome reprieve due to her stomach ailing her the whole time she was at sea. Molly had put her infirmity down to her churning stomach. Her thoughts taunting and mocking that she was returning home without her husband. That Hugh had not attempted to stop her the morning she left was a hurt that ripped her in half and would never heal.

How could he have sat in his office, staring at his paperwork, not bothering to look up as she passed his door? Molly wasn't sure what hurt her the most. That he was a liar, a man who had fled England after ruining her cousin, or that he couldn't care one whit that she was leaving him. Did not a man who declared he was in love with her, not fight to keep her heart? How could he have been so cold and aloof when inside her chest, her heart broke into a million pieces?

She sat in the parlor in the house her good friend Marchioness Ryley owned. A home Willow used to share with Molly and Evie until they married and went on with their new lives. The Duke of Albans' man of business had called in on her only yesterday, offering her the ducal property on Grosvenor square. He stated the house was fully staffed and at her disposal should she wish to use it. She merely only need travel there.

She would not be going anywhere near the London home or the duke's country estate. Neither home held any interest to her. Although at times, she had found herself driving past the house in town and looking at it, marveling at the grand Georgian design, the pillars and house frontage that had its own carriage entrance off the square.

A silly little fool who needed to remember why she left her husband in the first place.

Guilt pricked her soul each time she thought of who she was now. No longer Miss Molly Clare, but the Duchess of St. Albans. A traitor to her family, to her cousin. Even though she had not been aware of her wrongdoing, it still did not make her current circumstances right.

A light knock on the door sounded, and her footman announced the Duchess of Carlisle.

"Evie!" Molly stood, all but running to her friend to pull her into a tight embrace. "I'm so very happy to see you. Please tell me you are now arrived in town and are here to stay."

Evie hugged her back, before pulling her over to a nearby settee. Before sitting, she rang for tea, and came and sat beside her. "We are here for the remainder of the Season. I was so eager to return to town when I heard you were back from Rome. I also heard quite a remarkable rumor that you need to explain to me before my curiosity drives me to bedlam."

Molly knew only too well what rumor had brought Evie around to her home. Still, she was curious just how inquisitive she was. "When did you arrive in London?"

"Only just now. I had the carriage drop me here. Finn continued on to our townhouse." Evie adjusted her seat, meeting her gaze. "You traveled to Rome for an adventure, and from what I hear, you had quite a significant one. How are you faring being a Duchess?"

Molly sighed, slumping into her chair. "Not very well at all. I've made the most dreadful mistake, and I do not know what I shall do."

Concern replaced Evie's amused visage. She frowned. "Why is marriage to the Duke of St. Albans so very bad? He's rumored to be immensely handsome, not to mention rich. You'll be beholden to no one, not even your family. That is a good thing, is it not?"

Molly knew all too well how handsome Hugh was, and loving. The many mornings waking up in his arms had been the most wonderful of her life. His wicked grins that still made her stomach flip, her blood to heat. Even knowing the truth of his past. Her heart broke while her mind screamed to stay strong, to not forgive.

"Do you remember hearing of Lord Farley and his expulsion from London society and England some years ago? He ruined Miss Laura Cox."

A puzzled look crossed Evie's brow before she said, "I believe so. He fled to Spain the last I heard. Why is this relevant to your marriage?"

A tear slipped down her cheek, and she swiped it away. Annoyed that after all these weeks without Hugh, she was still emotional about everything. His conduct. Her leaving. So many things left unsaid.

Lord Hugh Farley was the Duke of St. Albans' younger brother." Molly met Evie's eyes and watched as comprehension dawned on her features.

"What? No, it could not be. You married the scoundrel that ruined that poor girl? Even his family turned against him. She was an heiress, perfectly acceptable really to marry a duke's second son, but he refused. How is it that your paths even crossed?"

"He was not in Spain, and he never went by the name Farley in Rome, but Armstrong. His mother's name apparently. Worse is yet to be spoken, however, Evie. So much worse." Her stomach twisted, and she took a calming breath, relieved when a servant brought in the tea and some ginger biscuits.

"I will pour, thank you," the Duchess of Carlisle said, dismissing the footman.

Molly took the tea and sighed in delight as the sweet brew met her tongue. She picked up a ginger biscuit and nibbled.

"Tell me what could possibly be worse than marrying that man?" Evie asked.

Molly sipped again, steeling herself to say the words that haunted her conscience. "Miss Laura Cox, the heiress whom my husband ruined all those years ago, is my cousin. My father and her mother are siblings. They were well-to-do. My uncle was business savvy and earned his fortune and climbed up into the society in which he wished Laura to marry. My father is a vicar, and so we circulated in different circles. When Laura fell from grace, I was packed off to France, where I would be safe from such rakehells."

"Oh, my dear Molly. I do not know what to say. That is, I have a lot to say, but I cannot believe how unfortunate this all is. What did His Grace say about Laura? How did he explain his actions toward her?"

"He said it wasn't him that ruined her, but in fact his brother, he merely took the fall. I do not believe him, of course. Now that his brother is dead, there is no one to naysay him."

"True," Evie said, biting her lip in thought. "But what if it is true? Is there a chance that he may be innocent?"

"I do not think so. His mother, the duchess even pulled away from him over his actions. No mother would turn away from her child, surely. You defend your children, love them and guide them as best you can."

"Not all mothers are created equal. From what I remember of the Duchess of St. Albans she was a taxing, haranguing woman who enjoyed belittling people she did not like. I do not think she would have been the most loving parent."

"Perhaps not, but it does not change what her son is accused of. Hugh told me himself that he knew Laura, he said that he'd tried to convince his brother to marry her, but was unsuccessful."

"So not entirely terrible, if he's telling the truth, that is," Evie said, her tone placating.

"Even if he's innocent of the crime, he allowed his family to let him take the fall. He was sent abroad, with all life's little luxuries that were not afforded to Laura. He's lived a full and happy life in Rome. Laura was buried at only twenty years of age."

"Oh, Molly, that is very sad. Whatever will you do?"

Molly stood, going to a nearby decanter and pouring herself a good serving of brandy. She downed it quickly, before pouring another. "I do not know. I married a Mr. Armstrong, not the Duke of St. Albans. I'm not even certain our marriage is legitimate, even though Hugh said he signed the register St. Albans."

Evie stared at her, eyes wide in shock. "So you may not even be married?"

Molly chewed her lip, frowning. "Possibly not." She paused. "To society we appear married, there is a register of our marriage, it was only the vows that were misspoken. I cannot let anyone know the truth. If they were to find out that our marriage may not have been legitimate, I will have ruined myself and brought more shame onto my family than I can bear."

"I agree. It is best that no one is told of your unusual wedding." Evie placed her teacup and saucer down, studying her a moment. "Where is St. Albans? Has he returned to England?"

"No," Molly said, hating that her heart panged at the thought of him being so very far away. "Hugh is still in Rome. It is unlikely he will return given our parting."

"And the ginger biscuits? How do they factor into all of this? Is there yet another secret you are keeping?" Evie asked, meeting her gaze.

Molly instinctively reached to cradle her stomach and the new little life that she grew there. A child made with love who would now grow up never knowing his or her father. Molly could only pray that it was a girl. To deliver an heir to the St. Albans line before she was certain their marriage was legitimate would be a disaster. After their cold parting, his declarations of love and affection toward her must not have been as sincere as she thought. There would be no second marriage to legitimize their union, even if she had wanted one, which she did not.

"The doctor has told me I'm *enceinte*. There are only a few weeks left of the Season, and I'm not showing a great deal. I do not think anyone will notice." Molly glanced down at her stomach, the small little bump hidden mostly from the material of her gown.

"Now that I know, I can tell, but the biscuits gave you away, my dear. Even so, you were married, and there is no shame in you having a baby by the duke. You must take up your position in the St. Albans townhouse with the belief that the marriage is legitimate. Your child will need to grow up in the homes he or she will inherit."

"I cannot go there. I would feel like a hypocrite. My family would never speak to me again should I take up residence there. In the home that has caused my family so much pain." Another tear slid free, and she dabbed at it with the back of her hand, annoyed she found herself in such a position. Her trip to Rome had been going so well, she had adored every minute exploring the country. For all of it to come to a dreadful end wasn't to be borne. The blow of leaving Rome was bad enough, nevertheless having to face the fact the man that she loved with all her heart had ripped hers from her chest and seemed perfectly content to let her leave without a by your leave.

How could he have let her go so easily?

"You must and soon." Evie paused, pursing her lips. "Has there been any communication from the duke or his steward regarding your position in society now?"

"His steward came here only a few days ago, notifying me that I may move into the St. Albans townhouse whenever I wish. No news from Hugh, however, but that does not surprise me."

"Why ever not? If you were my wife, I would move heaven and earth to be by your side. To try to win you back."

Molly lifted her lips into a semblance of a smile at her dear friend's words. She sat next to her again, reaching over to take her hand. "I know you would, but you love me as much as I love you. Hugh obviously does not love me as much as I thought he did."

"How could he not? You're the most perfect person I know."

Molly nodded, wishing that were true. If she had been more perfect, she would not have married the enemy. Or taken part in a fictional marriage either. What a fool she was. "There are too many things between us to make our union work, no matter how much I enjoyed his company."

"You enjoyed more than his company. I can see it in your eyes that you were in love with him. You miss him, do you not?"

Evie had always been able to read Molly better than any of their other friends. Molly was closest to Evie within their friendship group, but she did wish she could not pick up on such nuances. The thought of not seeing Hugh again left a crater in her chest where her heart once beat.

For the small amount of time that they were together, she'd fallen in love with her husband. Had given in to his every wish, his every whim. One look from his piercing gaze, banked with a fire and need made her biddable and willing.

For the rest of her life, she would be without him, unable to hear his voice or his touch. She swallowed the bile that rose in her throat. There was a reason why, of course, that she had to remove herself from his life. He was a seducer of innocent women. A man who ruined the life of her cousin. She could not simply sweep the past away that had affected so much of her upbringing, simply because she loved him. She loved the man she thought he was, not the man who he actually was. Had she known he was the Duke of St. Albans' younger brother, she would never have stayed at his Roman villa. Never have given him the time to get to know her.

"When is Ava coming to town? I need to speak to her. She cannot possibly know that the villa they offered to me while in Rome was Lord Farley's. Surely the duke would not have thrown me into the path of a man shadowed by a terrible scandal."

"Ava and Tate are not due in town for another week. They're holding a ball Thursday next. You should have to wait until then to speak to her, I should imagine."

Molly chewed her lip, thinking. "I suppose I should have to, but it does seem odd, does it not? I'm one of their closest friends. Surely they would not put me in such a difficult position."

"Did they know Miss Cox was your cousin?" Evie asked.

"No," she admitted. "No one knows that we were related, but they must have known that Hugh was involved. Unless they, too, do not believe the duke's brother and mother who accused him of the crime. They would not be so foolhardy, do you think?"

Evie picked up her tea and took a sip. "We shall not know the truth until they return, and I do not want you fussing over the answer to that question until you know the truth. Ava would never intentionally hurt you. I believe there is a simple explanation to your dilemma."

Molly hoped it was so. She slumped back into the settee's soft velvet, not quite believing that her life which had been going so perfectly well was now a complete mess.

"I shall talk to her at the ball, you're right. Until then, I will try to forget about everything."

"I think that is best, my dear. Now, tell me of the sights of Rome and the continent. I want to know everything."

CHAPTER 13

Molly had kept busy over the days leading up to the Duke and Duchess of Whitstone's ball by ordering a new gown and writing letters to her parents, aunt, and uncle, inviting them to London to stay with her.

If anyone had information regarding Laura and what happened that fateful Season, it was her aunt Jossalin. Surely they knew the truth or at least could help her in finding out what had occurred instead of hearsay.

She was not looking forward to explaining her actions, of how her marriage to the Duke of St. Albans had come about or how much she'd loved him. Molly could well understand how her cousin had fallen for such sweet words and exquisite touches that Hugh could bestow for she had crumbled like a biscuit under his touch. Blotting the missive, she stared down at the parchment and prayed that her family would understand she had been blind to his past. That they would forgive her.

It never occurred to Molly that the one man who made her blood sing would be the very one they had cursed to the devil years ago. The very thought of confronting her aunt with her mistake made her stomach churn.

LATER THAT EVENING was her first foray into London society. Evie and her husband, the Duke of Carlisle, had picked her up in their carriage, and it had taken minutes only to pull up before the Duke and Duchess of Whitstone's grand London townhouse.

The moment her name was announced, the room abuzz with conversation, music, and laughter noticeably quietened. Molly clasped her fan tighter, cooling her skin to stem from the never-ending sickness that ailed her. She raised her chin, not willing for any of them to look down at her or judge her choice.

Molly reminded herself they did not know that she was Laura's cousin, that the connection had thankfully never been made. It was only by chance that Lady Brandon had found out. She was certain no one else would know.

To imagine what they would think and say should they know the duke had married the cousin of the woman he ruined all those years ago sent a shudder of revulsion down her spine. The *ton* would then roar with ridicule, mock and criticize. She was not sure she could weather that storm as well.

"My darling, there is something that I need to speak to you about," Willow whispered to her as she joined them, pulling her toward where Hallie and Ava stood with their respective husbands.

Molly shot a look at Willow, not liking her taut tone. "What is it that you need to say? Is there something the matter?"

"There is news that you must know."

They came to stand before Ava and Hallie. She kissed them both in turn, greeting the dukes standing at their wives' backs, before turning toward the gathered throng. Willow worked her hands before her, glancing at the door. Hallie pulled her aside, and dread pooled in her stomach. "Willow, what is wrong?"

The hair on the back of her nape rose as the muttering of voices dimmed. The music fell as conversation quietened. Molly forgot her question to her friend and looked to see what had everyone so fascinated.

The booming voice of the major-domo bellowed out the name of the latest guest. "His Grace, the Duke of St. Albans."

Molly stilled, her body seized with panic. Hugh was in London. Willow clasped her hand, squeezing it a little. Molly searched him out in the crowded room, but she could not see him. Was it really Hugh? Was he back in London?

A small part of her mind screamed it was because he was here for her. That he'd come to repair their broken marriage, but there was little he could do. The past, no matter how many apologies one gave out, could not change what had occurred.

Unless he is innocent of the crime.

Molly pushed the unhelpful thought aside. He was guilty, had fled London to escape the *ton's* censure. No one innocent acted in such a way.

"That is what I wanted to tell you. Your husband has arrived in London, and from what I heard from Abe, he was at Whites Gentleman's club today with the Duke of Whitstone. His Grace was overheard telling Whitstone he was in town to win back his wife."

Oh, dear Lord. Did that mean all of society knew that they had a falling out? It was no secret what his scandalous past incurred, and now they knew she had scurried back to England from Rome. She could only imagine what the *ton* was saying about them both behind closed doors.

Heat rose on her neck.

"You've gone very pale, my dear. Are you well?" Ava took her hand, patting it a little.

Thoughts of what the Duke of St. Albans and his family did to hers rushed back into her mind and made the room spin. Of her cousin who had been courted and promised things during her coming-out by Hugh. How all of those things had come to nothing, not after receiving what he wanted all along. Her innocence and nothing else.

"Ava, did you know Mr. Armstrong was Lord Farley when you saw me off to Rome?"

Her friend's brow furrowed, a grim look on her face. "I did not, no, my dear. Tate has explained his absence to me since your return, and I know my husband, Molly, he would not lie nor support a liar. He believes St. Albans to be telling the truth."

"Did he see Hugh's brother demand he take the fall for him?" To have been a witness would at least clear Hugh of that offense.

Ava shook her head. "No, he read the missive that was sent to Lord Farley from his family."

Hope bloomed in her heart that perhaps Hugh could prove his innocence after all. "Well then, Hugh just needs to show me that letter so I can see for myself what was asked of him. Not that it changes the fact he went along with such a heartbreaking ruse."

"I'm sorry, Molly, but you cannot. So enraged was Hugh by the demand, the letter was burned that very night. You will not be able to read it, my dear. I'm so sorry." Ava stepped back, joining her husband, who looked sheepish at best.

She swallowed her nerves at facing Hugh again. There was nothing he could say that could change what she thought of his conduct. But blast it all to hades, he looked dashing.

She watched, along with every other woman in the room, as the Roman god of sin strode across the ballroom floor. Gone were his tan breeches and cravet-less shirt that he often wore in Rome, and in its place was a man made for ogling. For pleasure and all wicked, delicious things. His eyes bored into her, never diverting to anyone else, and for the life of her, she could not look away. She ought to run, her mind certainly screamed to flee, but she could not. A small part of her wanted to hear what he had to say. How he would explain away his actions. He'd tried in Rome, and he had failed. He would fail again here.

"I'm so sorry, Molly. I can only imagine what you are feeling." Evie clasped her hand, standing beside her and facing down the duke like a knight going into battle.

"Oh dear," Evie whispered, the words rushing from her the closer he came. "He is a marvelous specimen."

Molly's breath hitched, and a sheen of sweat broke out on her brow. She took a calming breath, needing to compose herself for the inevitable confrontation. She had not thought to see him again. Had thought he would stay in Rome as he said he would.

The Duke of Whitstone and Carlisle stepped in front of Molly and came to greet Hugh. Molly watched them, the genuine accord and friendship shone through all of their eyes. Betrayal coursed through her blood. How could they be friends with a man who had caused her family so much harm? Molly reminded herself that they did not know Laura was her cousin. A fact she would soon amend.

Worse still, how could she still love that very man?

Molly blinked back the burn of tears. She no longer

loved him, to do so would be the veriest perfidy. The three dukes, the highest nobles of the realm before royalty, stood together, laughing and talking as if they had not spent the past ten years apart. All the while, Molly felt the scorch of Hugh's eyes on her. His gaze slid across her person, from her head to her toes and back again like a physical caress.

Her breasts felt heavy and large in her gown. With every breath, her bodice's silk rippled across her nipples that were already sensitive from the child she carried in her womb. She supposed she would have to tell him that she was *enceinte*. So many things they needed to discuss, to plan on how they would continue this marriage apart.

A shadow fell before her, and she took her attention off the dancers and met Hugh's stare head on. He picked up her gloved hand, never averting his attention before kissing her. "Duchess." The title slipped from his lips like a caress, a declaration of fact, and one from the measured tone of his voice he intended to keep as truth.

"Your Grace," she answered, glad that her voice didn't wobble like her knees beneath her gown. She dipped into a curtsy, allowing him to keep her hand in his as he came to stand beside her. Had he stopped her from leaving Rome, they could have had this conversation there, worked out the particulars of their union. But no, he had to choose the very first ball that she attended in London to have it out with her.

"I've missed you." The whisper of his words tickled her ear, and she fought not to shiver. How could she be tempted by such a man? A seducer of women, and one who would let them suffer the consequences of those erotic actions. "We need to talk." His hand shifted to wrap about her waist, his fingers taking a long time to settle on her hip.

"What if I do not want to talk to you?" Molly did not dare glance at him. To stare at such beauty would only end with her being blind to his actions. She needed more time to compose herself and prepare for their confrontation. They could not have it here, at the Whitstone's ball. That would never do.

The sounds of a waltz started to play, and couples hurried out onto the dancefloor. The duke clasped her hand, pulling her along with them. Molly followed, not wanting to make a scene. She smiled, looking to all the world as a woman who was gleefully happy her husband was going to dance with her. The truth could not be more opposed.

He swung her into his arms, too close for her comfort. Molly tried to step away, put a little space between them, but she may have been trying to shift a limb of a tree for all the good her actions did. "You're holding me too tight, Duke."

His wicked grin made her countenance slip, and she narrowed her eyes. He chuckled. "So much fire in your veins. I have missed you, my darling love."

Her heart gave a thump at his words. Damn him and his sweet endearments. His playing with her was cruel and unkind. "You can no longer call me your darling love. I am not."

One brow rose with a disbelieving air. "Are you certain, my darling love? I know that my feelings have not changed from the moment you abandoned me in Rome."

"I did not abandon you, I left you perfectly capable of looking after yourself with your staff. Has your memory failed you so miserably that you cannot remember why I left in the first place?"

"Oh, I remember, and I'm in London to ensure you believe the truth, if not from my lips, then from those who know what really happened."

Molly shot a look at Hugh, a little glimmer of hope

taking light inside her that there may be someone who knew what really happened. As much as she wished she could believe him, her family had thought Laura's lover was Hugh. Why would anyone lie about such a thing? Her aunt and uncle would never have made up such a falsehood.

The dance pulled them into a couple of tight turns, and his clutch increased, keeping her locked against his person. Her body purred in response as if it remembered what he made her feel, wanting more of the same. She could not give in to his seductive charms. Not without knowing the truth behind his banishment. What she needed to do was speak to her aunt and uncle.

"I have ordered your staff to pack your things to move into St. Albans London house. Your place is with me."

She huffed out a breath—the audacity of the man. "I will not be going anywhere with you. As far as I still understand, you ruined my cousin and left without a backward glance. Agreed to funds over honor. I'm surprised that you're here in London at all. When I left Rome, I had the distinct feeling that I knew what my cousin went through when you let her go without a fight."

"I never ruined your cousin. Why will you not believe me?" She swallowed, sensing his visage of an aloof, sanguine gentleman was slipping. "It was not me who laid one finger on your cousin. It was my brother." A muscle worked in his jaw, and he stared at her, hard. Frustration burned in his stormy gaze.

Molly wished she could believe him, wished she had not lived for years, knowing another tale. Somewhere between the start of their dance and their conversation, they had stopped dancing. Out of her peripheral vision, she could see other couples continued to waltz about them. "I'm sorry, Hugh, but I do not know whom to believe."

"If we're to stay as we were in Rome, I need you to trust me."

"Trust you? You did not even marry me using your real name. How can I trust you? If you were not trying to hide your identity, why did you not tell me the truth? All of it, the weeks we spent together look like a falsehood now. How can I trust you ever again?"

"First, I signed the marriage register with St. Albans, you just did not notice it. Second, I would not be in London, having the *ton* gossip and sneer behind my back unless what I said was the truth. Unless I knew they were wrong, and I was right. My friends, the Duke of Whitstone and Duncannon believe me, but you do not. I do not understand it. I thought you loved me. Was that a misunderstanding on my behalf?"

The music faded to a stop, and she pulled out of his hold and strode for the entrance hall. She needed to leave. How could he ask her such a question? He knew as well as herself how much she adored and loved him. To be angry with her made no sense. It was not she who had done the wrong thing. He had. A youth at the time or not, did not excuse his actions.

He caught up to her in the foyer as a footman was handing her her pelisse. Hugh clasped her hand, calling for his carriage.

"I can have a Hackney cab called. I do not need you to return me to my home."

"The hell I'll allow my duchess to travel in a hackney." The black, highly polished carriage rolled to a halt before the townhouse's front steps. Hugh held out his hand to assist her into the vehicle, and she ignored his proffered hand, climbing up herself.

He followed, calling for St. Albans house. She scowled at him across the shadowy space that separated them.

"I'm not staying at Grosvenor Square. You cannot make me."

"I can, and you will. Whether you love me anymore, trust, or believe me, St. Albans House is where its duchess resides. You will be safe there, be well cared for when I return to Rome."

She could not look at him when he mentioned such things. So he intended to leave her? Of course, he would, if she could not believe or love him as she had in Rome, what was left for him in London? Her heart ached at the very idea of Hugh living so very far away from her. If her aunt confirmed Hugh as the one who had ruined Laura, what was she to do? The man she fell in love with in Italy was honorable, sweet, and kind. So very loving to her, at least.

Her cousin had been played the fool, so how could she forgive such treatment to soothe her own selfish wants and needs from the same man? An older, more mature Hugh than Laura obviously knew. An impossible choice.

"Very well, I shall stay at St. Albans House, but until I know who is telling me the truth and who is not, I do not wish to live as husband and wife. Please do not expect me to open my apartment doors to you. I will not."

His eyes flashed with annoyance, and for the life of her she could not look away. To stay away from her husband would be a chore, Molly had no doubt about that. Her body yearned for his touch, his lips on her flesh, what his clever hands and mouth could do that sent her pulse to race. Her core ached at the memory of their last coming together, and she crossed her arms over her chest.

"When you learn the truth, my love, and you will, I expect recompense for the time that I've had to live without you."

She scoffed at him. "And if you are proven to be the

ruiner of young, unmarried women, what do I get? Oh, let me tell you. A farcical marriage to a man who will live hundreds of miles away from me and I stuck with society forever laughing at me that I had been fool enough to marry the man who ruined my cousin."

"They do not know Miss Cox was your cousin. And anyway, I am right, and you are wrong, so it will all work out in the end."

"It will only be a matter of time before they do know Laura was a relation." She shook her head. "You're so very sure you'll be proven innocent."

He leaned forward, his beautiful features coming more into focus as they rumbled through the London streets. "Do you not wish to see me proven innocent? You seem determined to believe everyone else except me."

Molly wanted to reach out, soothe the hurt she could read in his eyes, but she did not. Instead, she slumped back onto the squabs and watched the passing houses in Mayfair go by. "I have invited my aunt and uncle to stay. If anyone knows the truth it is them, and then I shall know how to act."

CHAPTER 14

The following weeks in the St. Albans house were not a comfortable existence, certainly not for Hugh. His wife went about her days, paying calls, visiting her close friends, and hosting them in return. Outwardly, the *ton* believed that they were a happily married couple. That Miss Molly Clare had tamed the rogue Lord Hugh Farley, now Duke of St. Albans, but they would be wrong.

Their close friends knew the truth of the situation. That when they were home, Molly barely spoke to him, spent her days in the warm, sunny parlor at the back of the house while he whiled away his hours in the library at the front.

He hated their separation and would do anything to correct the wrong. Molly had come to him and told him that next week her aunt and uncle would be traveling to town to see her. To discuss what they knew.

Molly's family had not taken the news of their marriage well, and her parents had refused to attend, to come along with her aunt and uncle. Hugh knew the slight hurt Molly. She had been close with her parents. To have them turn their backs on her now, left a rage to simmer in his blood.

No one gave the cut direct to the Duchess of St. Albans and got away with it.

Hugh leaned back in the leather-bound chair behind his desk, his mind frantic on how he could prove to her his innocence. He had hoped to speak to his late brother's valet, who was privy to all the duke's whereabouts and had known of his liaison with Miss Cox, but returning to London, he'd found out that he'd been killed along with his brother in the carriage accident.

And now he was fucked. How was he going to prove that it hadn't been him, he was merely the brother, the spare who had taken the blame? The letter his mother had sent too was no use, for the fool that he was, he'd burned the blasted thing in a fit of rage.

Over the last two weeks, he'd watched his wife with a longing that both frustrated and vexed him. He'd never been a man who could not live without a woman. His life up to meeting Molly had been full, entertaining, and had its shares of liaisons too, but it was different now. He wanted her trust, her love. To have her back in his arms where he knew true happiness and contentment.

The ducal bed was vast and cold as it now lay. He wanted her back in it, to be with him.

"Your Grace, the duchess," a servant puffed, sliding into the library on the polished parquetry floor, his breathing ragged from running. "She has collapsed in the back parlor."

Hugh shot to his feet, running past the pale and wide-eyed servant as he raced to the parlor Molly liked to use. He charged into the room, seeing a maid trying to rouse the duchess. Hugh slid down next to her, leaning close to her to hear if she was breathing. A small flutter of breath touched his cheek, and relief washed through him like a balm. She was alive. As long as that were so, all else would be well. "What happened? Was she feeling ill this morning?" he questioned the maid.

She shook her head, frowning. "Her Grace was well when I brought in the tea just now. As I stoked the fire for her, she complained of dizziness and dropped the teacup she was holding. She must have been leaning forward on the chair a little, for she slumped onto the floor."

"Send for a doctor and hurry. I will carry Her Grace to her room."

"Yes, Your Grace," the maid said, dipping into a curtsy.

Hugh reached under Molly and scooped her up in his arms. He carried her to her room, a maid hurrying before him to open her door and pull back the bedding.

Just as he laid her down on the cool linens, she stirred, confusion clouding her features. "What happened?" she asked, looking about her room. "How did I get back into my bedchamber?"

"You swooned in the parlor. I have sent for the doctor. How are you feeling?" He reached out, touching her forehead. She was not warm, it did not seem like there was anything wrong with her outwardly.

"Not again," she mumbled.

Hugh frowned. She'd fainted before today? "This is not the first time you've collapsed?"

"No," she sighed, rubbing her brow. "I found myself on the floor in my room last week, but I'm, well, merely pregnant, Hugh."

Hugh stared at her, slack-jawed. "What?" He stumbled back, running a hand through his hair. He took in his wife, and for the first time, noticed that her stomach was a little bigger than when in Rome. Her breasts too strained against her day gown, and her complexion was pale.

"You're what?" Emotion welled up inside him, and he blinked back the burn of tears. He was going to be a father?

She stared at him, patent and calm, a little quirk to her lips. His heart gave a thump. She had not smiled at him at all since his return. "We're having a baby, Hugh. I became ill on the boat back from Rome, and when that illness did not abate, and my courses did not arrive, I knew that I was carrying your child."

"Why did you not send for me?" Pain sliced through him that she would keep such news from him. Did she loathe him so very much that she would deny him the chance to be a father? To teach his child right from wrong. Guide his daughter how to be kind and resourceful and his son, honorable and strong. All the things that his parents failed when it came to his elder brother. His sister Sarah was kind and resourceful, a woman not to be crossed, and he loved her for it, but it had been his father who had taught them what was good in life and how to treat people. His mother had spoiled their older brother and ruined him, made him the man who was now causing all the problems he faced within his marriage.

"I wanted to be sure first, and then the fear that you would not come, would not care to return stopped me. We did not part on the best of terms."

He came over to where she lay and sat. He picked up her hands. They were cold to the touch, and he rubbed them, trying to bring warmth back into her veins. "I know you do not believe me, not many do, my elder brother was a masterful liar and swindler. It was probably why your cousin fell for his false charms so easily. With all that is between us and still to be solved, I will always be here for you, whether you wish me to be or not. I love you, Molly, and I'm going to fight for you until the truth is known."

She squeezed his hand a little, and hope bloomed in his chest. Somehow he'd find someone who knew the truth and clear his name. He would not lose the woman he loved, adored with all his heart over a brother who had brought nothing but pain and cruelty wherever he went. He would not take the one good thing in his life.

His wife.

CHAPTER 15

A week later, Molly sat in her favorite parlor that was for her own personal use and poured her aunt and uncle tea. They had traveled up from the country the day before, opting to stay at a hotel rather than here with her or at their London home where Laura had passed. Her hands shook as she poured the tea, and she hoped they did not notice. She had woken up more ill than normal, her stomach roiling with dread at having to face her family and explain her actions. Try to get them to understand that she had not known that Mr. Armstrong was one and the same as Laura's lover.

If that were the case, after all.

She handed them both a cup of tea and sat, steeling herself for the forthcoming conversation. "Thank you for coming today to see me. I know it's not under the best of circumstances."

Her aunt refused to look at her, and as for her uncle, he stared, a look of contempt shadowing his normally jovial countenance. "We were shocked and saddened to hear of your wedding. Not a statement I thought to utter, but Molly, what were you thinking marrying this bounder?"

Molly swallowed, eschewing that anyone would talk of Hugh in such a way and hating that they may be right. "I married a Mr. Armstrong, not Lord Farley. I did not know Hugh was in any way related to Lord Farley or St. Albans."

"How could you have done this to us? After everything that man did to our family?"

Molly adjusted her seat, her hope that Hugh would be vindicated in his claims to innocence slipping away like the seconds of time. "I did not know, and the marriage was consummated before I found out the truth. I cannot change what is done, but my future happiness relies on what you tell me today. Are you certain that it was the Duke of St. Albans' younger brother that seduced Laura?"

"Why our darling Laura never told us exactly who it was that ruined her, we did find in her bedroom dressing table a small likeness." Her aunt searched through her reticule and pulled out a miniature frame and picture. "Here, this is the likeness with the initials H St. Albans on the back."

Molly took the small painting and immediately viewed a man who very much looked like Hugh, although there were some differences, this gentleman seemed to have more of an aquiline slant to his nose than to Hugh's straight one. His eyes also were smaller, less almond-shaped to Hugh's, beadier. "While they are similar, the H could also stand for Henry, my husband's elder brother."

Her aunt's mouth pinched into a disapproving line. "While we may like to think a duke took an interest in our Laura and courted her, I have little doubt that it was the younger brother who suited her better. A second son could marry an heiress such as Laura, not the heir. And I saw Lord Hugh Farley with Laura at balls and parties, sometimes with their heads together as if they were plotting and planning their futures."

Molly sat back in her chair, taken aback by the idea that Hugh had been close with her cousin, had been, in fact, her lover in truth. Within her own mind, she had decided to find the truth before believing anything else. The idea made her want to cast up her accounts for the second time this morning.

"Could he have been acting on behalf of the duke? Or trying to persuade Laura to look to someone else than his brother? Warn her off, perhaps?" If the duke was anything like Hugh had explained him to Molly, his brother was the worst of people. The other alternative that Hugh had been lying to her, had in fact been Laura's lover was unthinkable.

"May I keep this likeness? I wish to show it to Hugh and ask him if he or his brother is in the image."

"Laura's lover was not the duke," her uncle said, pointing to the small painting in her hands. "Never once did we see the duke with Laura at any balls or assemblies. When Laura confronted the Duchess of St. Albans about her son's actions and the consequences Laura then faced, she promised retribution against her son."

Her aunt dabbed at her cheeks, her eyes welling with tears. "Laura did not confide in us at first, took all this trouble on herself without help. By the time the scandal broke in London, Lord Hugh was banished from England and Laura heavy with his baby. She took his leaving hard, and by the time she had her son, she no longer had the will to live."

"Your husband killed our daughter." Her uncle glowered, his voice wobbly with emotion.

Molly stared at her aunt and uncle, the pain echoing off them still after all these years. That they lost not only

Laura but also the babe made her departure from this realm even more devastating.

"Laura was an heiress, why did the Duchess of St. Albans not make Hugh marry her? Why force Laura to hide in the country, and send her son away abroad to live out his days? It makes no sense."

"The duchess was a proud woman, a daughter of a duke herself. She did not believe in the different classes marrying. Not even her younger son would she allow to marry a woman whose inheritance came from trade. Her sons would marry women equal to their birth or no one at all."

For a moment, Molly thought about what the duchess would think of her marriage to Hugh. A vicar's daughter without an ounce of money to her name. A weight settled on her chest, and she took a calming breath. She had loved her cousin. Outside her family, she had been like an older sister, wise and beautiful and always kind. To think that her Hugh had left her to die with a broken heart, in turn, crumbled Molly's heart in her chest.

"Did Laura leave a diary at all? Anything that can, without doubt, prove who the father of her child was?" As small as it was, Molly hung on to any tidbit of chance that Hugh was innocent as he claimed. He had to be. She loved him, was having his child. If she did not find out the truth, forever there would be this divide, a shadow that hung over their union. She could not live like that. She would rather never see him again if that were the case.

"We have not been able to find it. We've searched her room, everywhere where we thought she would leave such an item, and we knew she had for we gave her a diary the year she came out in London. We wanted her to be able to look back, read about her first Season. What a terrible memory that year ended up being for her."

Her aunt fumbled in her reticule and pulled out a handkerchief, dabbing at her eyes and nose. "She had been so happy, Molly. So full of promise and dreams. The day she died was a relief in the end, for her eyes had long stared at us as if in death. Her heart was broken and would never heal."

"And by your husband." Her uncle stood, helping his wife to stand. "You are welcome to search our London house for a diary if you think it'll help you ease your guilt."

Molly stood, ignoring the barb that embedded deep into her heart. She had hurt her family, and if what they had just stated was true, her husband had been Laura's lover. Despair washed over her, and she fought not to let the emotion make her panic. She walked her aunt and uncle to the front door.

"We are headed home today, we do not wish to stay in London a moment longer than necessary. Laura birthed her child in our London home. If the diary is to be found anywhere, it will be in that home. You are welcome to go there and search. We have a housekeeper, and two maids who live there, and you may ask them for entrance."

Molly nodded, handing her aunt her pelisse. "I am so very sorry to hurt you in this way. I fell in love, I did not know the truth of whom I fell in love with."

Her aunt reached out, clasping her cheek with her gloved hand. Molly reached up, holding her aunt's hand to her face. "We love you, our dearest Molly, and therefore we hope that you find a different answer to the one we've given you today, but when the truth does come out, and you feel you have nowhere to turn, please know you always have us. We shall never turn you away, no matter what you have done."

"Thank you," she said, a lump wedged in her throat. She stood at the door as they walked down the few steps to enter their carriage. Molly watched them go, thinking over what she would do. If Laura's diary held Hugh's name, her marriage would be over. Her future forever changed to the one she thought she would have when she'd said her vows. She closed the door, turning for the stairs, weary and in need of rest. Tomorrow she would face the answer she sought. Today had already been trying enough.

HUGH WATCHED from the library door as Molly farewelled her aunt and uncle before returning upstairs to her room. He hated to see her so conflicted, sad, and lonely with the choice that she had to make. Desperate that he was, he'd spent the past hour listening in on her discussion with her family. The truth of his conduct was out there, he just needed to find it.

One glimmer of hope that had shone through was the mention of a diary. He could only hope that when Molly found the journal and God save him, he hoped she did, that he would be vindicated and proved innocent in this whole mess.

He knew he could not push her with her choice, make her believe him, he'd tried that enough already and had come up against a brick wall each time. She had to know the truth for them to have any chance of a future together. Any chance of getting her down the aisle a second time to ensure their marriage was legitimate.

Hugh shut the door and walked over to the fire, leaning against the marble mantle. He glanced about the room, his brother's office, not that he'd been taking care of the estates very well since Hugh had lived in Rome. His brother had turned to gambling if the many IOUs in his desk drawer were any indication.

Within a few days of being back in London, Hugh had settled his brother's debts and paid off any accounts he had outstanding around town. Had his brother been trying to ruin the family? That he could never know, but it certainly seemed fiscally that way.

He slumped into a nearby chair and rested his head in his hands. If Laura's diary was never found, Hugh would have to set out to win Molly's trust and love. He could not live without her. To not see her smiling face at him every morning on the pillow next to him. Watch as her cheeks blossomed into a delightful, rosy hue whenever he said anything inappropriate. He couldn't live separately from the one person that was the sole reason his heart kept beating.

And soon they would have a child. A son or daughter that was part of both of them. He did not want to raise the child without her, nor did he wish to only see the child when Molly bade him access. To be a family meant he needed her here with him, sharing their lives and everything else that came their way.

His stomach roiled with the idea that she would come up empty-handed when she searched her aunt and uncle's home. If Laura had burned her diary before she passed, there was no one left to know the truth.

A chill ran down his spine at the possibility that they could be severed from each other forever for a crime he had not committed. But would she trust him even if there was no one to tell her different to what she believed? If she loved him, she would trust his word, for God knows, he was not a liar. He would swear even on his own child's life, that it was not him who had ruined Miss Laura Cox, but his brother, St. Albans.

CHAPTER 16

Molly slumped back on her heels, staring at her cousin's bedroom, the bedding pulled off, scattered about the floor, and thoroughly searched. The few loose floorboards that she had found had been lifted, and with nothing to show for her efforts beneath them. She glanced down at her arm, blackened from the soot that had tarnished her clothing as she reached up and searched the chimney. With the assistance of a maid, Molly had moved furniture, emptied drawers, and padded the garments still occupying those cupboards, and nothing. Not a trace of this supposed diary.

It was not here, at least not in this room. Laura's chance to tell the truth, to declare once and for all who had wronged her, was not to be found. Perhaps she had burned it, for reasons only Laura herself could fathom. Molly did not blame her. To read the pages of a diary, one that would have initially been filled with love and adoration, of secrets and trysts would be a cause of despair if those moments of affection were no longer hers to have.

Molly would have burned her memories as well.

A little flutter caught her by surprise, and she reached for her stomach, her breath catching. She waited with bated breath to feel the movement again. She lent a half-laugh, half-sob when the little fluttering happened again.

Her baby. Their baby. The love of her life's child and the very man over whom she had to make a choice.

To trust and love him, or leave.

Molly pulled herself up and started for the door. She could not make a choice here, in her cousin's bedroom and where she passed. She needed to go to the one place she had always felt safe at home and at peace.

Within an hour, she was sitting in her best friend's drawing room, waiting for Evie to make an appearance. Her friend bustled into the room, her hair haphazardly pinned atop her head, as if she'd just risen from her bed.

Molly kissed her cheek, pushing down the pang of jealously of no longer having such afternoons abed with her husband. Of scurrying away to make love for as long as they wished. "I do apologize, Evie. I hope I have not imposed."

"Never, my darling." Evie rang for tea and sat across from her, taking in her rumpled gown and fixing the fishcu. "I was merely upstairs with Finn."

Heat bloomed on Evie's cheeks just as a footman knocked on the door, entering with the silver tea tray. Molly bit back her grin as she pulled off her gloves, setting them aside. "I do not know what to do, and I need your guidance."

"Anything, dearest."

"I saw my aunt and uncle, and they have confirmed what I imagined the worst. They do indeed believe the gentleman who seduced my cousin to her downfall was Hugh. He, of course, is adamant that he was not to blame. I do not know whom to believe."

"Does knowing that perhaps Hugh made a mistake in his youth change the way you feel about him? I know what he is accused of is very bad, the *ton* talk of nothing but his downfall and flee from England, but that will be nothing if you love him."

Evie's face swam as the tears Molly had been so stoically holding at bay, burst free. She sniffed. "I love him still. So much that it hurts to think of not being with him, but Laura was my cousin. I was sent away to France because of my family's fear of future rogues taking advantage of me, as poor as I was."

"You are very beautiful, Molly. I can understand your family being worried after such an event."

"I want Hugh, but to love him, despite what he has done means I lose my family. It would mean that all I've ever thought about the situation, my ideals and morals are worthless because I have chosen the very man who created the whole mess." An impossible choice and one she did not wish to make. "I know that Laura was not innocent in all this, she chose to give herself to him, but he could have married her, instead of taking the easy way out and fleeing the country. Hugh could have shouted from the rooftops that his brother had wronged an innocent young woman and be damned the consequences."

Evie stared at her, her eyes full of pity and concern. "I think you just made your decision, my dear," she said, clasping her hand. "But before you do, remember that Hugh was young, a boy of twenty. To go up against one's family, his brother a duke no less, would indeed be very hard. He fled, but that may have been because there was little left for him to do. No other option given to him."

Molly stared at her friend for a long moment, thinking over her words. His choice had he been innocent of the crime would not have been easy, that was true. But if Hugh was the gentleman who had ruined Laura, there was no forgiving of that fact. She would be lying to herself, going against everything she ever believed if she forgave such a sin.

The lump in her throat burned, and as much as she tried to swallow past it, it would not shift. However, was she to leave the man she loved behind? Commence a life where it was only ever half-lived?

"Remember, we're always here for you, my dear."

Molly nodded. She would need her friends more than ever in the coming months. Oh, who was she fooling? Years to come.

HUGH LOOKED up from his desk, the many letters to staff at St. Albans Abby before his brother's death scattered before him. He would chase down every last servant in England who worked here and the many estates he owned if it meant that he could find a single one of them who knew of his brother's liaison with Miss Cox. His life, his ability to keep his wife, depended on it. He could not fail her in this as well.

He'd failed her once before, he would not do it again.

Molly knocked on his door, waiting at the threshold before coming into the room. Hugh stood, striding over to her and pulling her inside. "You're very pale. What is wrong? Is the baby well?"

She didn't say a word, allowed him to place her onto the settee in front of the fire before he went back and shut the door, giving them privacy.

"I was unable to find Laura's diary, as I had hoped. If she had it with her in London during the time of her child's birth, it is no longer there." She shrugged. "Perhaps it never was."

He sat beside her, the pit of his stomach in knots. Would Molly believe him, or continue to think ill of him? How could she not trust him to be telling the truth? The notion she did not know him well enough to believe him ate at the organ beating in his chest.

"Not finding this diary, what does that mean for us, Molly?" Her answer meant everything to him. If she chose to believe him, trust him, and love him, his life would be fulfilled. After his father had died, the love he'd once known as a child became obsolete. He needed his wife to love him, to understand what he was saying as fact, for it was.

"I'm sorry, Hugh. I cannot stay here."

Hugh stood, distancing himself from her. He needed a moment to think, to take in what she was saying. His stomach roiled at the thought of losing her, and for a moment, he thought he may cast up his accounts. "You do not believe me still. I did not do what you accuse me of, damn it, Molly. I hardly knew Laura, and that is the God's honest truth. If you choose to believe my lying mother, my bastard of a brother over me, then I suppose perhaps you should leave."

"What are you saying?" She looked up at him, her eyes filled with tears, and he wanted to go to her, beg her to change her mind. To not look at him with eyes that were a mirror image of his.

Heartbroken.

"You may have use of St. Albans Abby in Kent. I will visit prior to the child's birth and we will marry to ensure its legitimacy. I will be a good father to him or her, but I will not be staying in England forever. I want to return to

Rome and expect my son or daughter to learn of his or her life there."

"I did not want this for us. You understand that, do you not?"

He dismissed her words, hurt, and disappointment riding hard on his heels. "What difference does it make now? You have made your choice, and you choose to believe gossip and falsehoods over the man you're supposed to love. I suppose the few weeks that we spent together in Rome meant more to me than they did you."

She stood, coming over to stand before him. "You cannot think that to be true. I loved and adored you."

A bark of laughter escaped at her words. She flinched at the sound. "Loved and adored. All past tense and precisely what our marriage has become. Past tense." He strode for the door, wrenching it open so forcefully that it slammed against the wall with a resounding thwack. "I shall order your belongings to be packed and loaded onto a carriage first thing tomorrow morning. Good day to you, Duchess."

Hugh beat a path toward the front door, ignoring the fact that his vision swam in unshed tears. How could she not judge him justly? Had someone accused her of such crimes, he certainly would have stood by her, not allowed anything to tarnish her name.

He blindly strode across Grosvenor Square, ignoring any who greeted him. He needed a drink. That's what he'd do. He'd go to Whites and get blind drunk, and maybe a night of gambling would soothe his hurt.

The notion was almost as absurd as the idea that Molly would change her mind. That he'd return home later this evening and find her warm in his bed. There was no future here. Not anymore. He had hoped that their life could be both in England and Italy, but it would seem that it was not to be.

For years he'd been known as the villainous younger brother of the Duke of St. Albans. Well, now they could keep him that way. The fight to clear his name fled, and his shoulders slumped. Let the *ton* and his wife believe what they wanted. They could all bloody well damn go to the devil.

CHAPTER 17

St. Albans Abby – Kent

The Season ended in town, and fall turned the leaves orange and brown across the land. Soon winter would be upon them, and so too would her time to have her child. Their child.

Molly had moved down to the ducal country estate in Kent after her inability to find the diary of her cousin and read in Laura's own words what had really happened that Season all those years ago.

The days stretched endlessly without Hugh, and Molly found herself thinking more and more about what her husband was doing why she was rusticating in the country. She read, of course, did needlepoint, walked about the estate, learning the lay of the lands, and the tenant farmers who worked for Hugh, but it was not the same.

She missed him.

Dreadfully so, and a little part of her mind would not let go of the hurt, the devastation she had read in his eyes the day she parted from him in London. An awful gnawing feeling kept her awake at night, telling her that she'd made a mistake. That it was his elder brother and not Hugh who had done her cousin wrong.

That she should have believed him above everyone else.

The more she spoke to the staff here at the Abby, the more she doubted what society and her family had come to accept. The late duke was not missed. In fact, he was tantamount to a bully if Hugh's sister, who returned last week from Bath, explained him to be.

Since her return, Sarah had been a godsend, keeping her company and helping her to know of the family dynamics that Hugh had grown up with. All of those things, including Hugh's adamant statement that he was innocent, culminated in her change of mind.

Which left another problem for her to face.

However, was she to stand before Hugh and ask for forgiveness? Ask him to forgive her for allowing what others believed to sway her opinion of him? She had left him. Her husband. The man she loved more than anyone or anything in this world, save for the child that grew in her womb.

He would never forgive her.

"Is that a carriage?"

Molly looked up from the Belle Assemble she was staring at and not the least interested in what lay in her lap and glanced toward the front drive. They were seated in the parlor that sat just off the entrance hall, the room giving its occupants full view of anyone who visited the estate.

The carriage was traveling faster than it ought, and Molly stood, going to the window to see who it was that had come. Sarah joined her, her brow furrowed as a woman all but bolted from the vehicle before it even stopped.

"I've never seen the lady before. Do you know her?" Sarah asked, turning toward her.

Molly was already moving toward the front foyer just as her aunt stepped into the room. Her attention immediately snapped to the cloth parcel she held in her hands, held closed by a frayed pink ribbon.

"Aunt, whatever are you doing here?" Molly kissed her cheek, hope blooming in her soul that her aunt's arrival could mean something in regards to Laura and her diary.

She was not wrong. "I found it. I found Laura's diary. Here," she said, handing it to her. "Read it."

Molly took the parcel. She pulled the ribbon, untying the knot, and glanced at what lay inside. Pages upon pages of letters, love notes, and in Laura's own hand, her own thoughts and dreams.

"I thought this lost forever. However, did you find it?"

Molly started toward the parlor, her mind scrambling to find a letter from the gentleman whom Laura had loved. The word Henry stood out like a blemish on a nose. Her eyes scanned the notes, the adulations, the longing, the sweet words between the two. Laura's sincere and Henry's, the late Duke of St. Albans a means and ways toward getting what he wanted. Laura in his bed.

"You could have kept this from me. To show me this does not put Laura into the best light, along with the duke. Even so, I cannot tell you how very happy I am to see these letters."

Sarah sat beside Molly, reaching out to clasp her about the shoulders. "I told you Hugh was innocent. Henry was a cad, a troublesome boy who grew up to be a selfish, arrogant man. I like to think that Hugh and I are like our father, kind, honest, and honorable. Henry took after Mama in all his wayward traits."

Molly's aunt studied Sarah a moment as if only just

noticing her presence. "Aunt Jossalin, this is Lady Sarah Farley, Hugh's younger sister. Sarah, this is my aunt Jossalin Cox, Laura's mama."

Sarah inclined her head a little. "I am happy to meet you, Mrs. Cox, and I'm sorry for all that you've suffered at my family's hand."

"It was not your doing, my dear." Her aunt's lips lifted into a semblance of a smile, but pain lurked in her blue orbs—pain left by the late duke's treatment of her daughter and what ultimately happened to Molly's cousin.

"Where did you find it?" Molly asked, skimming through pages and pages of notes. Henry was certainly a gentleman who knew how to play to a woman's heart-strings. The sweet gestures, his appreciation of her gowns at balls, and how her cousin comported herself within society would make anyone think that an offer of marriage would be forthcoming.

"A maid had packed it away with some of Laura's things upon her passing. The trunk was forgotten in the attic. On a whim, I decided to look through her old things, reminisce I suppose. See if I could still smell her." Tears welled in her aunt's eyes, and she dabbed at her face with her hand. "It was sitting atop of all her gowns and shawls. I was so lost in my grief when we were in London. I did not think of her things that were left to pack away at our country house. The staff took the initiative and did that for us, and I never sought to check on that myself. I wish I had, for had I done so, these many weeks you've been living estranged from His Grace would not have happened."

Molly reached out, clasping her aunt's hand. "What I do not understand is why Laura did not name her lover. The man who ruined her. Why protect the late duke when he'd treated her so poorly?"

"This letter may explain that, my dear." Her aunt handed her a missive that she carried on her person.

Molly unfolded the note, discolored by time. She gasped, unable to accept what she was reading. "He promised her that although he could not marry her, he would take care of her after the birth of their child. Send her away to one of his country estates and gift her a house on his land, including a maid and cook. Do you think he would have done this, Aunt?"

"I do not know, but if you read farther, he states that should she tell anyone of their affair, name him as the father of her child and not Hugh, he would leave her to rot."

"Sounds like Henry," Sarah said, her mouth pinched in a displeased line.

Molly looked back at her aunt. "So how did it come about that Hugh was cited as the villain?"

"That, my dear, is your uncle's cross to bear. We knew someone had meddled with our Laura. After all, she was pregnant, terribly discouraged and lonely, leading up to the birth of her son. We had not been blind in society, we had seen Laura about the St. Albans brothers, but then one evening, your uncle remembered seeing the then Lord Hugh Farley talking to Laura, and he believed what the duchess was saying.

"By the time this occurred, Lord Farley was already bundled into a carriage and headed for the continent. Spain supposedly, but that was what society was tittering. They refused to help Laura, the duchess would not allow either of her sons to marry a woman whose inheritance came from trade. That was not good enough for the St. Albans."

Molly placed the missive in with the rest of the letters and closed the parcel, placing it on the small table before them. "I know what that conversation had been about. Hugh told me himself. He told Laura to keep away from Henry. Tried to warn her of his brother's fickleness, his using nature when it came to women. I'm ashamed I did not believe Hugh any more than Laura had."

"You can, however, my dear, repair the damage the late duke and his mother have caused. You can mend the rift between you and His Grace. My Laura did not have the chance to fix her mistake, but you do. I suggest you return to town post-haste."

"You're right," Molly said, standing and striding toward the door. She wrenched it open, yelling for Thomas the butler.

The butler appeared from somewhere behind the stairs, bowing. "Your Grace?"

"I'll be leaving today for London. Have my maid pack my things and prepare a carriage. We need to leave within the hour."

The old household retainer started at her demand, before bowing and moving off to do her bidding. She turned, facing her aunt and sister-in-law. "Thank you, Aunt Jossalin for bringing me this news. I know it could not have been easy."

"Laura loved you like a sister, and would not want you to suffer because of her love for the duke's brother. Had she been of the right mind and known that your husband had been deemed the gentleman responsible for her downfall, she would not have allowed that."

"Go and change, Molly. You have a husband to claim and make yours. I shall see you soon when you return to Kent."

Molly nodded, her stomach knotted in nerves. What would Hugh say to her when she confronted him? Would he forgive her for thinking the worst? For not trusting and believing him, the man she loved above all others.

She ran up the stairs, determination riding hard on her heels. She would not let him push her aside. Not allow this mistake made by others to sever the love they had. That she still had for him.

If it were the last thing she did on this earth, she would win him back. There was no alternative to be had and no time to waste.

CHAPTER 18

Hugh tried to not feel sorry for himself or lose himself in the decanter of whiskey that he'd almost downed since the previous day. He lay in his bed, staring up at the ceiling. His eyes refused to focus on the mural, and so what he knew to be women floating in clouds, their roman togas and long flowing hair about their shoulders was nothing but a blur. Shadows that were oddly familiar to his life at present.

However had he allowed her to leave? Whyever had he done so? He'd done nothing wrong. He should have demanded she believe him. Told her as her husband that she would stand by his side or, or…

He sighed, groaning as the room spun. Who was he fooling? He could no more control his wife than he could control the ocean.

The sound of quickened footsteps echoed in the hall outside his room, and he sat up, leaning on his arms. Who was that running through the house in the middle of the night?

His bedroom door flew open, and his mouth dried at

the sight of his wife, hair askew, her afternoon gown rumpled from a day and well into the evening travel. She ripped off her gloves and dropped them at her feet, reaching behind her and shutting the door with a decided bang.

His speech seemed to have evaded his ability. His body tightened as it always did when Molly was about. He tensed, longed, and ached to hear her voice, to feel her touch.

When had he fallen so very hard for his wife?

A small smile lifted his lips, knowing the answer to that question. The moment she had seen Rome from his upstairs balcony the first time. The memory of it now sent a pang of longing to ripple through him so hard he had to force himself to breathe. Her long, silken locks flowing over her finely boned shoulders, her mouth open in awe of the city beneath her. He'd fought the urge to kiss her plump lips then and there and should have known she would mean change was coming to his life.

A change well overdue and most welcome.

"Hugh." His name was a rushed whisper as if she were relieved to find him here. He devoured the sight of her, the rounded belly of his child that grew in her womb. Her long legs and heaving breasts from her sprint upstairs. Hell, he'd missed her. He should have dragged her back to London and told everyone to go to the devil with their rumor-mongering. He loved his wife, and she ought to be with him.

And now she was here. But why?

"What are you doing in London?" The question came out as a croak, and he cleared his throat, watching as she took the steps that separated them, coming to stand beside the bed. Unable to help himself, he sat up, twisting to perch at the edge of the bed. She was so close, under an arm's touch from him. Hugh reached out and cradled her stomach, hating that he'd missed even a month of being with her.

She stared down at him, her eyes round with concern. Her hands shook at her sides, and he clasped them in his. "Tell me, my love?"

Molly slumped at his words, sitting beside him and pulling him into an embrace. She held him tight as if she never wished to let him go. He would never allow her to go anywhere from him again, that was for certain, if she let him.

"I was wrong. I judged you unfairly, and I'm so sorry, Hugh. My aunt found Laura's diary, and as you said, Henry was her lover, the father of her child."

This was no news to Hugh. Of course Henry was the father, proving that point was difficult, however, when there was no proof and his family had lied to persuade others that he was guilty of the crime. "Of course, he was, my love, but I am glad that you're finally on my side on the matter."

She pulled back, her lashes wet with tears, and his heart lurched in his chest. He wiped her cheeks, hating to see her upset. "I do not blame you, Molly. No one believes me, nor will they unless your cousin's diary is published, and I would never do that to your family."

"However will we clear your name in the eyes of society? They need to know the truth. Blame your brother, not you. It is unfair for them to treat you as they will, as I have. I'm so sorry, Hugh. I understand if you can never forgive me. I cannot forgive myself."

He pushed her wayward locks from her face, needing to see her clearly. "I was angry and upset, but I could also understand, my love. Laura was your cousin, and you thought her tarnished by my hand. Without proof, even I would struggle to believe you should you have been the villain."

She sniffed, meeting his gaze. "No, you would not. You said yourself that you would believe me before anyone else, and I did not offer you the same trust."

He shrugged, knowing it would be harder for a woman to believe a man than a man to believe a woman. "It does not matter now, my love. That you're here is all I want."

"I love you, Hugh. I should have believed you and no one else. I'm sorry that I did not come sooner. Not until I knew the truth."

He frowned, reaching behind her and playing with the ties of her dress. "Were you thinking of coming back to me? Before you knew the truth?"

She nodded, her hands untying his cravat. "I was. I missed you so very much. Even with the company of your sister, I was lonely. What you were accused of, I could not get out of my mind, and the more I thought upon it, the more I realized it was not true. That I trusted you enough to believe your word over that of others. People that I did not even know. I had all but decided to return to town when my aunt arrived."

He would kiss Molly's aunt the next time he saw the woman. Thank her profusely that she'd continued her search for the elusive diary. "Whether you came to your decision on your own merit or because of your aunt's visit, know that I'm happy that you're here. I've missed you so much."

Hugh could wait no longer, and he kissed her, clasped her cheeks, and drank deep from her lips. Her mouth opened, their tongues melding. His heart beat hard in his chest, a resounding drum he was sure she could hear.

"You taste of spirits." Molly pulled his shirt free from his breeches before ripping it off over his head, throwing it aside. "You're not a little foxed by any chance, are you, Your Grace?"

"I'm drunk with happiness." He grinned, groaning as her hand slipped against his falls, and she popped his buttons free. Hugh closed his eyes, sucking in a breath as her touch clasped his cock, stroking him with an expertise that left him aching.

"I've missed you so much. All of you." She kissed him, pushing him to lie back on his bed before straddling his hips.

"Your clothes. Remove them."

She shuffled off his lap, and he took the opportunity to move farther onto the bed. He lay back, his arms behind his head, watching her through hooded eyes as she slipped the gown off her shoulders to pool at her slippered feet. Her shift was all but translucent, and his cock hardened further at the sight of her. In the moonlight, her eyes blazed with need, and he took a calming breath, wanting to pleasure her before seeking his own release.

With a wicked smirk, she slowly untied the laces at the front of her shift. The material gaped, giving him a delightful view of her ample breasts. She pushed the shift off her shoulders, and it too landed with a swoosh on the floor.

She kneeled on the bed, crawling over to straddle his groin. "I want you so much." The siren that his wife was turning into... She slid against his cock, her heat, the wetness that coated him told him she needed him as much as he wanted her.

So deliciously hot. He wanted to roll her over, fuck her until he no longer knew where he started and she ended, but he could not. After the child was born, there would be plenty of time for that. Tonight would be different. He'd allow her to take him, use him to find release and then, and only then, would he come.

Hugh reached up, circling her breasts with his hands. She sighed, her nipples pebbling into tight knots. He sat up, pulling her against him and covered one nipple with his mouth. He flicked the beaded flesh with his tongue, giving it a love bite or two before soothing it yet again with his mouth.

Her breathing ragged, she reached between them, taking him in hand. His cock twitched at the feel of her hot, welcoming core. She lowered herself onto him, wrapping her arms about his neck as she embedded herself fully.

"Oh, yes," she sighed.

The urge to take her and make her his again rode hard within him, but he breathed deep, let his beautiful wife set her own pace, and find her pleasure and release. He held her tight against him, helping her undulate upon him. She was such a perfect fit, breathy moans, and sighs all the stimulation he needed to remain patient and wait.

His turn would come.

MOLLY PUSHED Hugh back onto the bedding, holding his shoulders as she rocked up and down on his cock. So hard and fulfilling. Teasing that special little place within her that craved and mourned the loss of him all these weeks.

Her body did not feel like her own. Everything was more sensitive, her breasts, her cunny, everything ached and wept more than before. It only added to the pleasure, to the need that rode hard within her.

She took all of him, rocked against him until the pleasure, the sensations thrumming through her veins were too much. A pulsing started at her core, exploding throughout her body. Molly moaned his name, took him until her body no longer convulsed around his manhood.

"Make me come," he demanded, not forcing anything upon her, willing to be at her mercy.

His command was like an elixir, and she continued, riding him with vigor. His manhood swelled inside her. His fingers dug into her hips, slamming her down upon him before he gasped, moaned her name, and spent himself long and sure inside her.

She kissed his words from his lips, taking his mouth in a searing kiss before slumping at his side, her leg carelessly laying over his waist.

He shifted, reaching down to pull the bedding over them both, before pulling her into the crook of his arm. His lips brushed her temple, his hand idly running along her spine.

"Does this mean you'll be staying here in London or at least staying with me?"

She looked up at him, and their eyes met. Her heart thumped hard in her chest over what she felt for this man. A man she'd allowed what others believed in him to cloud her own thoughts and beliefs. Never again would she doubt him, not for anyone.

"Can we return to St. Albans Abby in Kent? The Season is over, and I want to prepare for the baby. Make your childhood home, our home, our child's home."

He kissed her again, seemingly unable to get enough of her. Not that she minded, she loved being in his arms. This, right now, was what felt true. To be here again with her husband, her lover, and friend was all she needed.

"On one condition," he said, pulling back.

She glanced at him, wondering what he meant. "I will do anything. I hope you know that now."

His wicked grin sent her blood to pump. "We shall leave in the morning, but only if you marry me."

Tears blurred her vision, but she nodded. "Yes, of course I will marry you. Again."

He kissed her with such tenderness that she knew her heart would never beat for anyone else. After a time, she snuggled into his side, allowed the constant drum of his heartbeat to lull her to sleep. She had missed this, just the two of them, alone together. She pulled him tighter into her hold, silently promising to love him always.

And forever.

EPILOGUE

Early December 1829- St Albans Abby, Kent

Their baby boy, Lord Oliver Hugh Farley, Marquess Brentwood, future Duke of St. Albans lay snuggled in Hugh's arms, both father and son asleep before the roaring fire in the duke's study at the Abby. The room had become a sanctuary for the family. Lady Sarah, also retired here most evenings as the house was in an uproar with the forthcoming Christmas House party they were hosting.

Molly sat before the fire on the floor, going over all the acceptances they had received. So many people seemed only too pleased to believe the new Duke of St. Albans of his innocence in his brother's dealing with Miss Cox. With the help of the Duke of Whitstone, other friends, and that of her aunt who had made an appearance at a London ball, had gifted Hugh his absolution of doing anything wrong. Had placed the blame solely on who it was who had done the unforgivable damage, Henry, his brother.

"There are so many people coming. You have twenty acceptances here alone. Are there many more who will be in attendance?" Sarah asked, sitting on the settee and staring down at the letters scattered about the floor.

"No, this is all of them now. I did not think that so many people would agree to attend. It is winter, after all. Terribly cold time to travel." Molly chuckled, marking off the names on her list. "I suppose it is only fortunate that your home is so very large. We shall at least be able to give everyone a room to themselves."

"Our home," Hugh said, meeting her gaze, his eyes heavy with sleep.

She sighed, adoring him more and more with every passing day they were here. "Our home," she corrected herself. She turned back to Sarah, raising her brow. "You did not want anyone to attend? It is not too late to invite someone if you wish."

"No, there is no one I would suggest. As far as I'm concerned, society can go hang after what they did to Hugh for all those years. In turn, made me have to live here in England with Mama and Henry. It was not to be borne."

Hugh chuckled, the baby fussing in his arms at the sound of his words. "Had I known it was so very bad for you here, Sarah, I would have come home and taken you back to Rome with me."

She shrugged, giving her brother a small smile. "I do not blame you, Hugh, but I am holding you to your promise to take me to Italy after winter. I'm so in need of an adventure. I want to see where you have made your second home and see Rome and its history."

"It is a marvelous place that will forever hold a special place in my heart." Molly glanced at Hugh, the love burning hot in his eyes stealing her breath.

"And I, my love." Their son started to cry, and Hugh's soothing voice calmed him. He lay him over his shoulder, patting his back, and within a moment, the baby was settled once again.

"How many weeks are we to endure these guests?"

Molly chuckled at Sarah's question. "Only four, which is not too many, I think. And you will love my friends, Sarah, just as much as they will love you."

"I'm sure I will, and they will be the only ones, but mark my words that if anyone should even mumble anything about Hugh and the scandal that followed him about for all those years, I shall not be held responsible for my outburst. Nor will I take well to having a set down from my brother concerning my sticking up for you either."

Hugh nodded, kissing their son on his little bald head. "I promise not to chastise you should you say something in my defense."

"You needn't worry about that, however." Molly stood, placing the replies on Hugh's desk before coming back and sitting next to her husband. "I did not invite anyone whom we're not on close terms with. Everyone coming will be jolly and happy to be here to celebrate the Christmas period, and Hugh's return to England after all these years."

Sarah sighed, smiling at them both. "I am happy for you, Hugh and Molly. You deserve happiness after all that you endured. I promise to be on my best behavior."

Molly smiled. Hugh chuckled, a disbelieving tone to his laugh. "I shall believe that when I see it, sister dear. If what I remember of you and your antics, you were always a little rascal."

Sarah raised her chin in defiance. "I have never been a rascal, merely a woman of independent thought. Like your wife."

Molly met Hugh's eyes, reveling in the love that she saw staring back at her. "If that is the case, then, my dear sister, just as I've said to my beautiful, smart, and kind wife, please do not ever change."

Had she been standing, her legs would have wobbled at the sweet declaration. She closed the small space between them and kissed him, oblivious of their company. "I love you too," she whispered for only him to hear, her heart full and incandescently happy.

The sound of Sarah mumbling about kissing before her faded as she left the room. Molly chuckled, reaching up to play with the little fluff of hair on their son's head.

"Happy?" Hugh asked her, meeting her eyes.

She swallowed the lump in her throat, unable to voice just how much she was. "Very much so."

His wicked grin made her stomach somersault. "Me too."

They smiled at each other a moment before she laid her head on his spare shoulder, watching their boy. Their little family. A piece of paradise not in Rome, but snowy, country Kent.

It warmed her heart as hot as the Mediterranean sun had her life.

THE MARQUESS IS MINE

League of Unweddable Gentlemen, Book 6

She'll never let anyone break her heart. Not again, anyway…

Lady Sarah Farley has learned many of life's lessons the hard way. She now knows the ton will viciously turn on anyone, anytime. And love? That only brings devastation. But when a particularly handsome ghost from her past re-emerges, she can't help but wonder if life is about to teach her poor wounded heart yet another painful, unwanted lesson.

Lord Giles Longe, Marques Gordan, never wanted to hurt Sarah. But he couldn't have married her back then. His father wouldn't have allowed it. Everything is different now, though. He will make amends. And if it's the last thing he ever does, he will make her remember the friendship—and pleasure—they once shared.

. . .

Is a Christmas ball at St. Albans Abbey the perfect setting for Sarah to regain her trust in love—and in Giles? Or is their second chance at happily ever after doomed to end as badly as their first?

PROLOGUE

St. Albans Abbey, Kent
1815, Summer

"Get off her, you tyrant!"

Young women of a particular age were wont to become romantic. It was no different for Lady Sarah Farley, youngest child of the late Duke of St. Albans, at the impressionable age of fourteen. With those words uttered to her eldest brother, Henry, by her younger brother's best friend, it was the exact moment that she fell in love with the boy.

Lord Giles Longe, Marquess Gordan. Her hero.

Henry stepped back from trying to take Sarah's self-portrait she was finishing. A sketch her father had started and one of the last things he had done with her before he passed the previous year. "This is my house, Gordan, and I can do whatever I want. I'm the duke. You're nothing but a child who should know when to speak to his betters."

Her hero scoffed, pulling Sarah to stand behind him.

"I'll try to remember my manners the next time I'm before one."

Sarah looked between Lord Gordan and Henry and didn't miss the hatred they felt. It was so palatable that she could almost taste it. Lord Gordan, Giles to his friends, was two years younger than her elder brother, the duke, and already at nose level. Her brother's eyes were narrow and unkind, Giles was the opposite, wide and clear and filled with a compassionate light.

Her favorite brother, Hugh, had invited Giles to spend the summer with them, and he had arrived only yesterday. Sarah could not remember having been more excited about having house guests. With her father's passing, they had been in mourning a year, but this summer, her mama had allowed Hugh to invite his school friend. The moment she had spied the devilishly handsome gentleman alighting from his carriage from the attic window, her heart had moved.

For a boy of eighteen years, the same as Hugh, he moved with grace and ability. He was tall but did not look awkward in his frame. Oh no, already his shoulders were wide, strong, and gave a hint to a rakehell in the making.

Every gentleman Sarah thought handsome was destined to turn into a rake. She sighed, glancing down at his hand that remained on her wrist, holding her away from Henry. Such lovely, strong hands too. Perfectly shaped for holding one against one's heart.

In only a few short years, she would be off to London, to have her first Season, and then men like Lord Gordan would court her, flirt, and wish to marry her. As a duke's daughter, she would have ample to choose from. Not that she needed to accept any who bowed before her, for her heart had been moved by Giles and would forever belong to him.

"Are you unharmed?" he asked, leaning down to be closer to her shorter height. Henry told her a duke's daughter did not need a self-portrait. That as duke's daughter, they could hire a painter for such menial work. No sister to a duke should be sketching so.

Henry was a fool.

Sarah was well aware of what was expected of her in society when her time came to enter it. Until then, she would not allow him to take the things that meant more to her than life itself. The drawing her father started being one. Her father would never have allowed Henry to treat her with such disrespect, and neither would Hugh, who stood behind her, glaring at their elder sibling.

"Leave her alone, Henry, or I'll bloody your nose like I did last week."

Henry sneered at the three of them. "I'll cut you off, you two, you'll be left with nothing if you do not do as I say. Now get outside and play like children if that is how you're going to behave, with your stupid sketches and silly school friends who come to stay."

"Gladly," Hugh said, gesturing for Sarah and Giles to join him. "Come on, we'll do as the duke says. Let him have his lofty ideals and solitude, we can have better fun outdoors anyway."

Sarah followed, but not before Henry took one last swipe for her drawing. This time he clutched it, and laughing, ran over to the roaring fire, and threw it onto the flames. Sarah screamed, reaching for the parchment, but Giles grabbed her, hoisting her back from the flames that wrapped about the image and consumed it.

"Sarah, no, you'll hurt yourself."

A sob wrenched up from somewhere deep inside, and she lent a scream. Tears streamed down her cheeks as her sketch darkened and burned before her eyes.

"You bastard." The sound of a fist hitting flesh rent the air, and Sarah turned to see Henry's legs go flying over the settee, his own cries of pain muffling the sound of her sobs. "How could you do that to Sarah?"

Henry stood, his footing a little unsteady as he pinched his bloody nose, trying to stem the bleeding. "Easily, she's a baby and needs to grow up, and mark my words, Hugh, should you hit me again it'll be the last time."

"Touch anything of Sarah's again or her, and it'll be your last day on earth," Hugh said, pulling her into his arms and helping her from the room. Sarah sobbed against her brother's chest, and no matter how they tried to make her happy, distract her with ideas of finishing the fort her father had started to build last year, fishing or swimming, she would not be moved.

Today she needed time to mourn her loss. Her father's drawing. Their drawing. "I think I shall go upstairs to my room. I do not feel like going outdoors just now."

Her brother and Giles walked her to her door and waited as she stepped into her suite, her sanctuary. Hugh walked off, but Giles watched her as she turned to shut and lock the world away.

"I'm so sorry, Sarah."

She shrugged, wiping away more tears as they fell. "Henry has always been a selfish beast. Today he merely proved it before someone outside our family."

Giles reached out, lifting her chin to meet her eye. His thumb slid across her cheek, wiping away the tears that fell unheeded. She hiccupped, the lump in her throat hard to swallow past.

"I do not like to see you cry."

His dark, stormy eyes were filled with concern, and she reached up, touching his hand. "I will be well again, my lord."

Lord Gordan did not look convinced, and yet at her brother's command to join him, he reluctantly stepped back. "When you're ready, join us outdoors. Although the summer has not started off well for you, Hugh and I will make it fun and one to remember."

She nodded, not quite convinced that would be the case, but willing to try. "Of course." She rallied a smile, wanting him to believe she was well again, even if her heart ached for her loss.

"While I'm here, His Grace will not touch you or anything you own."

Her heart gave a decided flip at his words. Hugh's friend was not only handsome, but he was also honorable. He strode off down the hall, and she watched him go, bedazzled a little by his sweetness.

Sarah could not wait to have her first Season. What a pity she had four more years to wait. The thought discouraged her all over again.

CHAPTER 1

St. Albans Abbey
December 20, 1829

There were two things in life that Lady Sarah Farley, sister to the duke of St. Albans disliked more than anything else in the world. Entertaining Marquess Gordan, or Giles as she'd once called him, and seeing Marquess Gordan in her home.

When they had been friends.

The sight of the beast across the ballroom floor where the Christmas house party her brother Hugh and his new wife, Molly, were hosting was not to be borne. Or the fact that he hadn't even gazed in her direction for the past hour.

Beast.

Was she still as invisible as she'd always been with this man? Romantically at least. It hadn't always been so between them, they had been friends once. A long time ago, but no longer. *Ass*, not man, she corrected, sipping her champagne and glaring at him over the rim of her glass.

Why her brother Hugh had invited him in the first place confounded her. She'd begged him not to, had told Molly the reasons why the marquess should not attend. Well, at least the ones she could admit to publicly, and yet, the fiend had arrived and was strutting about the room as if he owned it.

Peacock.

"Please do not be angry with Hugh, my dear. Lord Gordan was an old friend and one he has missed. Having him here will help in clearing your brother's name in the eyes of the *ton*."

"People already know the truth, no point in bringing back the old guard simply to please them more. Hugh has other friends. Lord Gordan does not need to be reimagined into the fold." Sarah wasn't sure she could stomach much more of these so-called friends returning into her brother's life after distancing themselves from him when he needed their support most.

She had never believed her elder brother Henry's claims, or that of her late mother that Hugh had been the one to ruin Miss Laura Cox, an heiress, several years before. Henry had always been selfish, a well-seasoned liar, and someone who could not be trusted. The favored son, eldest and the Duke of St. Albans, it was not surprising that their younger brother was asked to take the fall, the shame that Henry could not face himself.

"You really do not like Lord Gordan do you, my dear? Is there something you wish to tell me? Other than your more benign reasons you have already noted as to why he should not be here?" Molly asked her, taking her hand to make her look at her sister-in-law.

Sarah shook her head, not wishing for anyone to know her shame. Her regret. "No, I merely do not agree with some of these men showing up here and pretending that they are long-lost friends. That Hugh's displacement half a world away was not of their doing. They may have forgotten, but I have not. I missed years of being with Hugh because of this catty society. I will not forgive them."

Molly leaned over and kissed her cheek. "Hugh loves you so very much, and so do I. We do not want you to be unhappy. It is Christmas, after all. Forget about those gentlemen who now scramble about Hugh's feet and look to others for amusement and flirtation. Focus on ones who did not turn their back on your brother. There are many eligible men here for the month-long house party. Surely there are others who may take your fancy."

Sarah sighed, wishing that were the case. It was not. There had only ever been one man whom she'd longed for. Had wanted with such rebellious disregard that she'd acted on that impulse many years before and lived to regret her actions.

How dare the cad even show up here. He ought to be horsewhipped, and by her. This idea was tempting, and if she put on a warm enough cloak, she could fetch a whip from the stables and do exactly what she envisioned.

How had she been so stupid and irresponsible all those years ago? After her brother's banishment from England, one would think one would learn to be careful. To follow the rules society placed upon their young heads and not step out of line.

Not Sarah. She had thrown herself at his lordship during her first Season. As the wealthy daughter of a duke and now a sister to one, she had thought herself invincible. A woman whom any man would gladly fall at her feet and then sweep her off those said feet and marry her.

Lord Gordan had not, and it was not until she had kissed him on the darkened terrace, practically threw herself against him, pushing him up against the ivy trellis that she realized her mistake.

He'd not kissed her back.

In fact, he'd set her from him, gave her a proper verbal scolding that even to this day made her ears burn, and had stormed back indoors to her elder brother's ball and had barely spoken to her since.

Not that she cared if she ever spoke to the man again. He did not deserve her regard or friendship, even if their icy exchanges were solely due to Sarah's lack of manners.

"I will forget about Lord Gordan and enjoy the house party. I promise I shall enjoy our Christmas together." Sarah smiled as Molly thanked her before rejoining her husband, Hugh. When his wife was close enough, Hugh wrapped an arm about her side and pulled her against him, keeping her close.

Sarah's heart twisted a little in her chest. How lucky Molly was to be loved and adored as much as her brother loved and cherished her. Their love and Molly's trust in Hugh gave her hope that she would one day find a grand love that would make her skin prickle and her body thrum.

Well, she had found that love until he up and proposed to someone else. She spied Lord Gordan coming toward her with determined steps, and she steeled herself for the forthcoming confrontation.

"Lady Sarah, how very festive you look this evening in your red-and-green gown. Anyone would think it was Christmas." His deep baritone made goose bumps rise on her skin, and she cursed his ability to make her not herself, even after all these years, and the time they'd been enemies and not friends.

Sarah bit back a scathing retort, mentioning that his sarcasm and lack of praise on her gown were not missed. But, because she promised her sister-in-law not minutes before to behave, Sarah smiled up at Lord Gordan and threw him a halfhearted smile. "How very astute you are, my lord. That schooling you partook in at Cambridge really has paid off that you're able to understand my color choices at this time of year."

He raised one brow, his lips thinning into a straight line. Lips that she knew to this day were as soft as butter, and made her feet curl up in her silk slippers. She licked her lips, wondering if hers had been as supple. Possibly not, she was forever chewing them, and she rode her horse a great deal. The air and sunlight did little good for one's skin, when one had too much of them.

"My parents were most proud of my academic record," he quipped, coming to stand at her side. "I have not seen you in town these past few seasons. Have you grown bored with London society? I do miss your impulsive kisses very much," he whispered, leaning down to ensure privacy.

Sarah gaped at his lordship. How dare he bring up her oversight? "It is not the act of a gentleman to bring up the foolish mistakes that a lady may have made in her youth. I have little doubt that my actions that night were brought on by my champagne sampling for the first time."

"Really?" he asked, cocking one brow. "And here I was thinking that your molesting of me was solely due to my charm and good looks. How very disheartening to know the truth."

Sarah ground her teeth, little amused by his teasing of her. "My memory, if correct, was that you did not like my kisses and told me so very abruptly to my face. I see no point in our conversing now." There, that ought to do it. He would leave now, and she could go on brooding, glaring at everyone who now thought her brother a respectable duke when only a year or so ago would not mention his name in polite society.

"We do not have to converse." He threw her a wicked grin, and once more she was lost for words.

Was he flirting with her?

The rogue!

He ought not. It would not get him anywhere. She had long given up any hope she may have had with his lordship. Sarah made a point of trying to find someone in the crowd. "I believe Lady Rackliffe is here this evening. Are you sure you do not wish to commence your love affair with her again? She's a widow now. Maybe this time she'll turn up for your wedding." Sarah chuckled, sipping her mulled wine and enjoying the fact that her words had shut the cocky marquess up.

He took a sip of his whiskey, staring out at the dancers before them. For a country Christmas party, Molly had invited many of their friends. Her closest four friends now congregated about Molly, and they laughed and talked as if they had not seen each other in years and not merely weeks.

Sarah wished she had friends like Molly. She'd been neglected as much as Hugh had been by their mother. However, her father had always been loving, but unfortunately, he passed when she was young. She was so thankful that Hugh was now home in England, although they would be returning to Rome sometime next year. They planned on traveling between their two houses, and Sarah had promised to go with them next year to see Rome and Naples.

"By my calculations, you are eight and twenty, my lady. I thought by now that you would have been married. Why ever have you not? No lord in London good enough for Lady Sarah Farley?"

She glanced at him. How dare he mention her name or turn the question back onto her?

"Spying on me, Lord Gordan? I did not know you were so very observant to my every move."

He scoffed beside her, sipping his whiskey. "You do hold yourself in high esteem. I was merely keeping watch on my friend's sibling while he was out of the country."

"Of course you were, my lord."

A shadow flickered in his eyes before he blinked, and it was gone. Did he remember how very close they once were? That he had been one of her best friends in the world? Or so she understood. All lies, of course. He'd not cared about her at all. Had only ever seen her as Hugh's younger sister and someone to protect, but never love.

Those summers seemed so long ago now. So much had happened between them that there was no way they would ever get back the friendship they lost.

"I hope that I did not teach you to be so cold and aloof as you are. Why, before I came over here to speak to you, you were busy scowling at everyone." He reached out with his thumb and smoothed the frown line between her brows. “What has you so out of sorts, Lady Sarah?”

The moment his skin touched hers, the breath in her lungs hitched. She slapped away his hand, but not before reading the awareness that flared in his eyes. He'd felt it too, the reaction they had always had to each other. Their first kiss was proof of that, no matter what Lord Gordan professed otherwise. She was certain it had affected him as much as her, no matter his anger over the embrace may have said otherwise.

A question lingered in her mind over what would happen should they act upon those feelings now. Would things progress differently between them? She could have sworn when she'd kissed him all those years ago, for a moment, he'd kissed her back. Having never kissed anyone before, she had never been certain if she had imagined his reaction or not, fleeting as it was.

Her body ached with want for him, for his lips to touch hers. From the age of eighteen, she knew her infatuation with Lord Gordan was more than just a young girl's fancy. She'd wanted him to be hers, and he did not want the same.

He had wanted Lady Rackliffe, Lady Edith Beadle then, an earl's daughter and sweet on Lord Gordan. Or so he believed.

Fool that he was, that had turned out not to be the case.

"Do not touch me, Lord Gordan. You forget yourself."

He bowed, seemingly sorry for his lapse in manners. "Apologies." He looked contrite, as if he had indeed lost his faculties for a moment. "It shall not happen again."

"I should hope not." She sipped her wine, noting that he didn't move away, but kept beside her, quiet and still. "Was there anything else that you wanted from me, my lord?"

A muscle worked in his jaw before he said, "You did not answer my question. Why are you so incensed this evening?"

She ground her teeth, hating that the one man she did not want to know her secret would ask such a question. Truth be told, he made her angry. His denial of her. His pushing her away. His severing their friendship the moment Hugh had left England.

"I'm not angry, my lord, merely weary of a gentleman like you who believes a woman should always look happy and jovial. I do not need to smile and simper just to please those about me. I'm a daughter of a duke, a sister to one, and have my own inheritance. If I wish to stand at the side of a ballroom and glare at those I do not think worthy of my family's hospitality, I shall do so."

His eyes widened before he glanced back at the dancers. "Are you saying that I'm not welcome here, my lady?"

She shrugged, feigning nonchalance when in truth, her heart beat loud in her chest. Giles had always been welcome at the Abbey, and most of all, by her. To say otherwise now would hurt him, but the slighted, angry debutante inside her growled at his denial of her. The injury he'd caused her heart that had never truly healed. "Hugh is happy for your company, that is enough, is it not?"

He scoffed. "I suppose it will have to do."

Sarah watched him stalk off, anger thrumming across his wide shoulders. A little piece of pleasure rolled through her that she'd hurt his feelings while, in turn, her heart ached at his leaving.

Her eyes met those of her brother across the room, and she smiled, feigning pleasure. He threw her a dubious look that spoke of a future conversation between them over her antics with Lord Gordan. She sighed. A month more of this would be a chore.

CHAPTER 2

Giles stormed from the ballroom and ran directly into the path of Lady Rackliffe. He inwardly groaned at his apparent good luck this evening. First, his run-in with Sarah and now Edith, his ex-betrothed. She stared up at him, all innocent as if butter would not melt in her mouth. A marvel, really, considering she had failed to arrive at church on their wedding day, preferring another over him.

The blonde goddess, Lady Rackliffe, was indeed a muse for men's fantasies. Large, voluptuous breasts, long, golden locks, and cool, blue eyes that slanted a little and gave her a wicked, enticing appearance that had once drawn him like a moth to a candle flame.

Not anymore. Now he looked upon her with the knowledge of what a spiteful, using minx she was.

Sarah floated through his mind, she too had long, blonde locks, but of a warmer hue, as if the sun had kissed her curls. Her eyes were a dark shade of green that he'd often thought the Scottish Highlands would be jealous of.

His body clenched, and he repudiated the idea that Sarah hated him. He deserved her wrath, just like the woman before him deserved his after she had jilted him, thrown him over for a much older, richer peer.

An ancient relic who had conveniently died within twelve months of their marriage, leaving her an heiress.

"Giles, darling. How wonderful to see you again. We should talk while we're at the house party. It has been too long."

He picked up her hands as they snaked their way up the folds of his jacket to wrap about his neck. He did not want her touching him any more than she had wanted to marry him.

"I would like that, Lady Rackliffe, but tomorrow perhaps. I seek my rest this evening. A long day of travel has wearied me." Not to mention the fact that Sarah's dislike of his attendance here hurt more than he cared to know. He wanted to be friends with her again. To be as close as they once were. Her hurried and spontaneous kissing of him during her first Season seemed to have put paid to their association. He cringed, hating himself for telling her off like a spoiled child.

She had not deserved his retort. He ought to tell her why he'd reacted so. Why he'd pushed her away and told her in no uncertain terms how inappropriate her kiss had been.

"Shall we meet somewhere, Giles? St. Albans Abbey has a beautiful, secluded conservatory, I understand. We may catch up there if you wish. After luncheon?"

He nodded, distracted, and having forgotten Lady Rackliffe was before him. "Of course. Tomorrow. Good evening, my lady."

Giles went to start up the stairs, but she halted him, clutching the lapels of his jacket with more force than he thought her capable of. "Are you not going to kiss me goodbye? Surely we're past such formal goodbyes, are we not?"

Giles recoiled at the idea of kissing her, but leaned down, kissing each of her cheeks.

A clearing of one's throat sounded behind him. He whirled about to see Sarah passing him by, starting up the stairs. She made a *tsk tsk tsk* sound. "Behave, dear guests. There is no mistletoe above you to excuse away your display of affection for one another."

Sarah's words were said lightly, playfully even, but Giles could see the anger and disgust that stared at him through her eyes. Lady Rackliffe appeared immune to Sarah's veiled criticism of their goodnight kiss.

She tittered before him, smiling up at Sarah. "Lady Sarah, so good to see you again. Where have you been for the last few years? We had thought that you ran off to the continent to live with your brother, so long have we not seen you."

Sarah halted halfway up the stairs, turning to meet Edith's amused visage. "If only, my lady. If only," she said, before continuing on and disappearing along the corridor upstairs.

Edith's smile slipped, and Giles bowed, seeing his moment to escape. "If you'll excuse me, Lady Rackliffe. I really must obtain some sleep."

Distantly he heard Sarah's slippered footsteps upstairs. His need to talk to her again paramount. He did not want her thinking there was anything between himself and Lady Rackliffe, as there was not.

"Of course, goodnight, my lord."

"Goodnight." Giles took the stairs two at a time and made his way toward the family apartments in the Abbey. The building was old, a medieval-like structure more than a modern Georgian home. Still, the Duchess of St. Albans had done a lot to it in the short time she had been married to Hugh, and the house was warm, homey, and once again had a feeling of peace and tranquility he had only ever known it to have when Hugh and Sarah's father was alive.

He turned the corner and spied Sarah almost at her bedroom door. Increasing his pace, he reached her room, just as she went to open it. He clasped the handle, slamming it shut. She spun about, the action placing him hard against her, his breathing ragged.

He swallowed the pleasant feel of her against his chest, her bright-green eyes staring up at him with shock. She blinked, and the contempt was there again, mocking and hating him as it had for years.

"Are you quite done rubbing up against me, Lord Gordan? I should not have to tell you twice in one night to remember who I am."

He stepped back, missing the feel of her the moment he did so. "I needed to explain that what you saw just before was not what it appeared."

Sarah raised her brow. Again, her derisive laugh grated on his nerves. "Really? You do realize, Lord Gordan that I'm eight and twenty and have long learned that when I see gentleman kissing ex-lovers, that one can only assume the ex should be excluded."

"I'm not sleeping with Lady Rackliffe."

She shrugged, her hand reaching behind her to open the door. "I couldn't care less about what you do."

He slammed the door closed again, pressing against her. Of course, he should not, but damn it, she spiked his anger and patience. "Is that true?" He leaned down, taking in the sweet scent of her hair, floral with a hint of rose. Damn, she smelled as good as she felt in his arms. Her hands fluttered to his chest, the pressure to push him away there, but not forceful.

"Has been for a very long time, my lord. Are you so dense you need me to remind you?"

He flinched, grinding his teeth. A smug look passed over her face, and rage tumbled through his blood. She did not care what he did? Well, he'd test that theory.

Seizing her face in his hands, he leaned down and kissed her.

And he was lost.

CHAPTER 3

The moment Giles's lips touched hers, Sarah knew the horrendous, catastrophic error it was. Not that she did not like having one of the most eligible, attractive, and rich men in all of England kissing her as if his life depended on it, but because a small, traitorous part of her loved it.

Damn him and his mouth that moved over hers, coaxed and teased her senses until her wits were scattered.

For appearance's sake, Sarah pushed at his chest. It was no use. He was steadfast in his preposterous notion of taking her lips and proving his asinine point. Even so, when his tongue slipped across her lips, she sighed, opening to him without realizing the devastation her acquiescence would mean.

He deepened the kiss, and no more was it delicate and beckoning, but hard, demanding. Made that special place between her thighs ache and clench. She pushed her legs together, trying to sate her need. Her hands ran along the lapels of his coat, his breathing ragged, she could feel each breath, the air going into his strong lungs, his chest firm and corded.

He would look so delicious without his clothing. Women had tittered about seeing him just so—the ones who had been fortunate enough to warm his bed. The idea of anyone seeing Giles unclothed so had sent such a shot of jealousy through her that she'd avoided society and all news of him for years, practically becoming a recluse.

That had to change now. With her brother back, the man kissing her to a jelly pool at his feet would be about her often, whether at St. Albans Abbey or town.

Their kiss was madness. Anyone could happen upon them, her family, a servant, her brother! The idea of being forced to marry Lord Gordan was like a cold bucket of water poured over her muddled head, and with all the strength she possessed, Sarah pushed him away.

"Enough," she said, her heart beating fast in her chest. He stumbled back, his eyes heavy and dilated, and she'd seen that look before. He'd looked at Lady Rackliffe so before their engagement.

She ground her teeth, hating that men could be so changeable. "You should not have done that, my lord."

"I have done many things that I regret, but that kiss, Lady Sarah is not one of them."

His words sent heat spearing across her face, and she took a calming breath, hating the fact that after all these years apart, he could still make her blush.

"If you wish to enjoy your time here in Kent, may I suggest that your attention be better spent elsewhere? I am not looking for a husband, nor do I like men who kiss me only minutes after being caught kissing someone else."

He flinched, a muscle working at his temple. "Do be serious. You cannot mean my kiss with Lady Rackliffe."

Sarah raised her brow, staring at him. He shuffled on

his feet, glaring at her. "I kissed her cheeks, not her lips, Sarah. If you had seen me," he said, stepping close again, "with my tongue down her throat, there may be a point to your concern." His breath was hot against her ear and she shivered, closing her eyes so as not to see his delectable self.

"It was you that I kissed without heed or caution. I want to kiss you again." His eyes met hers, and she read the longing in them. Her body ached for fulfillment. She was eight and twenty, after all. Like all people, she had needs, and those needs were becoming more and more powerful. Harder to ignore with each year that passed.

Having Lord Gordan tempt her in such a way was unfair, and she knew that she would not get an ounce of sleep tonight.

"Let me kiss you again," he pleaded, his lips brushing hers, but not demanding anything more. "You savored it. Admit it."

"Goodnight, my lord," she said, opening her door and all but throwing herself into her room lest she do exactly as he begged. Her eyes met his as she shut the door, and what she saw there sent heat and expectation down her spine.

Determination on Lord Gordan's visage would be hard to deny. It was any wonder he was a renowned rakehell for who could refuse sin when offered to you in a rich, titled, handsome marquess package that was his lordship?

One could not.

THE FOLLOWING morning Sarah broke her fast in her room, preferring not to dine with all the other guests. No doubt, Hugh and Molly would ask her about her absence later, but she could not sit across the table and see him.

Giles...

She may never be able to meet his gaze again after

allowing him liberties last evening that she should not. Sarah sat before her dressing table, her maid pinning up the last of her curls, and she stared at her features, her lips that had been kissed most ardently, even now they tingled in remembrance. The shadows beneath her eyes told her the effect Lord Gordan had on her. Her sleep had been restless, her body not able to settle and rest.

She pursed her lips. Lord Gordan had done that to her, and he probably damn well knew he would. All she could hope was that he, too, had a sleepless night and resembled hell also.

He did not.

Sarah ran into his lordship, striding in from the back of the house a little after leaving her room. His boots were wet with melting snow, some of which was still sticking to his shoes. His tan breeches hugged his athletic thighs, and her mouth dried at the sight. Her eyes devoured his every article of clothing, the perfectly tied Napoleon cravat, and his top hat held loosely in one hand. His tan coat and white waistcoat giving him the air of a country gentleman, innocent and able. He may be able, but innocent was the opposite of what Giles was.

He glanced up, skidding to a stop. He met her inspection, and something inside her crumbled just as it had when she was fifteen.

Sarah had a name for the emotion that coursed through her blood back then. It had been love, innocent and adoring, but now it was laced with so many more conflicting sentiments—desire one of them. Anger, most definitely, but passion above all.

This month-long house party just became a whole lot longer.

CHAPTER 4

Giles skidded to a stop, seeing Sarah watching him. He'd missed her at breakfast, having observed that she was not at the table, he'd eaten quickly and gone for a ride before the mid-morning breeze picked up and made it too bitter to go outside.

He'd needed a good, brisk ride this morning, if only to wake himself up. After his kiss with Sarah, his sleep had been deprived most severely.

He'd tossed and turned and thought about taking himself in hand to alleviate the need that coursed through his blood.

The idea of Sarah in his bed would not abate, and it was a problem he needed to face.

He was a friend to her brother, but also one of town's most notorious rakes. All thanks to Lady Rackliffe, but the idea of taking Edith or anyone else to his bed left a sour taste in his mouth.

The only woman he wanted beneath him, on top of him, before him and every way else he could think of was Sarah.

It was a damnable, vexing notion since he'd only kissed her last night to prove that she did, in fact, care what he did, a mistake he realized the moment their lips touched. He'd most certainly proved a point, however, one that he was a fool. He would long for her until he kissed her again if she would allow him to.

"Lord Gordan, good morning. I hope you had a pleasant ride."

Her benign chatter did not mislead him, and he crossed his arms, taking in her pretty, plum gown with a gold thread about the seams. His eyes dipped to her abundant cleavage, and he wrenched his gaze upward before she caught him ogling. "I did, thank you for asking, Lady Sarah. Pray, tell me, how did you sleep last night? I hope it was to your satisfaction?"

Two could play this game of mundane conversation, and he would win. He rarely lost with anything—innocuous chatter with women he wanted in his bed no different.

She pursed her lips, and he knew she saw through his question. "I slept very well, thank you."

He raised his brow. "Actually, I lie. I managed very little rest at all. Do you have any idea as to why that could be so?"

Her inspection of him was thorough, her gaze skimming from his neck to his shoulders, taking in his crossed arms, to his abdomen and beyond.

What on earth was she looking at?

He glanced at himself, and seeing nothing untoward, frowned. "Is there something the matter with my clothing, my lady?"

She seemed to shake herself from her musings. "Not at all, my lord."

"So you're just admiring the view then?" he teased,

catching her eye that dipped once again to his cravat. Her cheeks bloomed a pretty pink, and she moved past him, heading toward the back of the house.

He followed, the reasons as to why foreign to him. All he did know was that he didn't want their conversation to end and nor did he like that she could dismiss him so easily after their kiss the night before.

To Giles, that kiss had meant everything, changed everything in his life, and what he wanted.

Sarah, to be exact.

She used to care for him a lot. There had been a time when they would partake in many outings and adventures at this very estate.

Sarah entered a music room, a grand piano and harp occupying a corner each. Chairs sat about the instruments. Giles paused at the room's threshold, having not been in here for many years, not since Sarah's father had played for them all one Christmas a lifetime ago.

Sarah moved between the two instruments and sat on a padded window seat that overlooked the now-frozen-over lake, the snow falling heavily outdoors.

"You'll catch your chill sitting there."

She glanced at him as if she'd forgotten his presence. He ground his teeth. How could she be immune to him? Women never were, and once she had not been either. She had thrown herself at him, had, from what he could presume, wished for marriage.

Of course, he did not expect her to be pining for him all these years later, but they could surely be friends. From that footing, love could grow, he was sure of it.

Giles strode over, coming to a stop before her. He waited for her to look up, needed to see her clear, green eyes and make her understand that he was in earnest. That she was different from his past lovers. That with Sarah, he wanted a future as well as a past.

"I apologize for kissing you last evening without your consent. I'm sorry that I did not kiss you back when we kissed all those years ago, but surely, with all that our lives have been intertwined, we can be friends. I want to be in your life, Sarah. Not as a lover, or childhood friend, but as a man you can come to, one who'll support your opinions and ideas just as I used to. When you told me of them, that is." He took her hand, squeezing it a little. "Please tell me we can be so again. I have missed you."

SARAH REGARDED GILES. She pushed down the hope that bloomed in her soul at his words. He wished to be friends. Then where had he been all these years? She'd certainly been right here at St. Albans Abbey. He was the one who had not visited, not reached out to see if she was well.

Which she had not been.

Not with a brother like Henry whom she had been left with after Hugh fled England. Her brother had been dismissive, short-tempered, and scandalous.

Whenever he'd held house parties, she had to retreat to the dowager house if only to protect herself from his wayward, bastard friends. Not that she'd always been safe even there.

She shuddered at the memory of Lord Fairchild and his pursuit of her, his inappropriate words, and eventually his insistence that she allow him to kiss her. Sarah had fled to Bath without a backward glance and had not seen Henry until the day she laid him to rest. A carriage accident brought on by more reckless behavior.

"A little late now, do you not think, to take an interest in my life. Where have you been the last ten years, my lord?" Sarah reached over to a nearby chair and picked up a shawl left there for her use. "When Henry had thrown house parties, I always hoped that you would attend so that we may move on from my inappropriate kiss, but you never did. You never called in on your way home to Willowood Hall. Nor did you write. I think you're a hypocrite, so why would I want to be your friend?"

Giles flinched at her words, but what did he expect? Turning up at a Christmas house party held by her brother did not mean all was forgiven. Not by her at least. She could not excuse his actions at leaving her alone.

"You gave me the cut direct the remainder of the 1819 Season," he accused.

"You scolded me at the beginning of that Season after I kissed you. Why would I follow you about like a little lost puppy looking for attention? I may have been young and naive, Lord Gordan, but I'm not a fool. I know when I'm not wanted."

"I did want you. You were all that I did want," he admitted.

Sarah shook her head, not believing his words, not wanting to see the yearning on Giles's face. Denying him what her own torturous body craved was almost impossible with him looking at her so. To believe the truth to his words would only cause heartache for her in the future. There was nothing between them, had not been for an eon. It was time they stopped this silly game they were playing. The Christmas festivities had addled both their minds and was teasing them with impossible dreams.

Giles sat beside her, and she shuffled over a little. "No you did not. You would have kissed me back, married me instead of offering to Lady Rackliffe. You may have missed our friendship, but you were merely missing a woman you saw more like your sister than anything of a deeper, emotional level."

"I never saw you as a sister, and I do want you. It may have taken me ten years to say the words, but I'm saying them now."

"You need to halt your silly declaration." Sarah went to stand, and he pulled her back down on the window seat beside him.

"It's not trivial, it's true. Our kiss last evening was proof of how much I want you, surely you felt what can be between us. Give me a chance."

Sarah swallowed, her heart and mind a firestorm of debate. Of course, she felt what they could have, from the tips of her ears to the ends of her toes she'd felt the fire that had coursed through her blood at his touch. If she gave him a chance to court her, what did that mean? Would it lead anywhere? She had thought him truthful and honorable during her first Season, and how wrong she had been then. There was just as much chance now that he was fooling her yet again, playing her like the instruments that sat about them.

Even so, the flash of determination in his eyes gave her pause. Perhaps Giles was sincere, and this Christmas, she may get what her heart truly longed for.

Was she brave enough to risk her heart a second time? "Very well," she said, pulling her hand free from his. "I will give you a chance to prove you are sincere, Lord Gordan, but mark my words, this is your final time. I will not be gifting another."

His wicked smile somersaulted butterflies in her stomach, and she had a moment of panic at what she'd unleashed. "I will not need any more chances, Sarah. I will not make the same mistake twice."

CHAPTER 5

The following day Sarah's attention was fixated on Giles as he spoke with her sister-in-law, Molly before the hearth in the front parlor. The snow had continued to fall, forcing Molly, as the hostess, to come up with varied and fun ways to pass the time inside.

They played card games, billiards, charades, and danced. Even so, how Giles would woo her to his favor was something Sarah was looking forward to.

No matter what she had said to his face, she had missed her old friend, and the fun they used to have. She looked forward to seeing this other side that only the privileged few managed to observe—his seductive, courting side.

Whatever would he do to convince her his heart was hers to steer?

"You're grinning like a fool. What are you up to, Sarah?"

She started at the sound of her brother's voice, jumping back a little to stop spilling her mulled wine on her light-green gown. "Nothing at all. Why would I be up to anything?"

"Because you are, and I know it."

Sarah chuckled, not wanting anyone, least of all her brother, to know that she was getting reacquainted with Giles. The last thing she needed was to become the latest tidbit of gossip for London's *ton*. They had used their family enough for that.

"It is Christmas, Hugh. Everyone is more jovial at this time of year," she said, leaning up and kissing his cheek. How different it was to last year's Christmas where she had spent it alone here at the Abbey. Henry having decided to stay in town instead of returning home. He should have come home, had he done so he may not have died only a few weeks into the new year.

Her Christmas luncheon had been a sad affair, with only herself at the table, the memory of chewing her food while tears streamed down her face was not one recollection she wished to keep.

"Sarah?" Hugh said, taking her hand and pulling her close. "What happened to your smile?"

She rallied, squeezing his hand, and smiling for good effect. Her isolation was not Hugh's fault, and he did not need the guilt plaguing him over her sad life up to the point of his return.

He was here now, she was happy, and as much as she did not wish to be bombarded with Londoners for the Christmas season, she was glad the house was at least full, with lots of laughter and fun. No worries of the guests behaving inappropriately or trying to persuade her to a rendezvous.

Of course, except for Giles, but a stolen kiss or two between two people who were courting wasn't so very bad.

"All is well, brother. I'm just so very happy you're home. I have missed you at this time of year."

He leaned over and kissed her cheek. "I missed you too.

Promise me we shall never spend another Christmas apart."

"I can promise you that," she said, smiling. Her brother was called to another group of guests, and Sarah let him go. This afternoon Molly had organized a snowman competition, if the snow stopped falling that was. Sarah was looking forward to winning and going outside. They had spent too many days indoors as it was.

A tinkling sounded, and Sarah turned to see Molly calling everyone's attention with a small, golden bell.

"The snow has eased, and so I think that if we're to have this snowman building competition, we should do so now. So please, everyone, go and change into your warmest coats and boots and meet me and His Grace on the terrace where we shall notify you of your teammate."

Sarah did as she was bade, and within the hour, everyone assembled before the terrace doors. Over her green morning gown she had thrown on a fur jacket and scarf, and kid-leather gloves. Sturdy leather boots and a hat finished off her outfit.

"There will be a prize, of course," Molly continued. "Ten pounds and the honor of opening the Christmas ball with a waltz with a partner of your choice. As to whom you will be building your snowman with, the following guests, please team up."

Sarah listened as Molly named the guests. Those who were married were kept together while those unattached were paired.

"Lady Sarah Farley and Lord Gordan, please pair up."

Sarah shivered at the thought of being near him again and turned to seek him out. A hand slid across her back and down her arm. His fingers clasped hers, placing her hand on his arm.

She shot him a glance, having not known he was so near.

"Your muff is most complimentary."

Heat suffused her cheeks, and she stared at him, nonplussed. "From the tone of your voice, I cannot help but think you're saying something inappropriate, my lord."

His wicked grin undid her stoic sensibilities and proved her point. "That's because I am being immodest."

Sarah shook her head, turned back to her sister-in-law, and listened to the other guests still being paired. At the announcement that Lady Rackliffe was matched with the eligible earl, Lord Ambrose, Sarah took in her reaction. The earl had entered society the same year as them. He was a handsome gentleman and kind, and his pleasure at being paired with Lady Rackliffe was obvious.

Her displeasure, too, was most evident.

"We only have a limited time, a half hour at most before we need to return indoors, so I wish you well and good luck on your snowmen."

Two footmen opened the terrace doors and let the guests file outside. Sarah waited for the rush to subside before stepping outdoors. Chilly air made her catch her breath, and she pulled her scarf higher about her neck to stop the chill. Giles was beside her, his long greatcoat and highly polished riding boots made him appear taller than normal, wider across the shoulders and altogether too handsome in his beaver hat and leather gloves.

Sarah rallied her thoughts away from his handsome self and concentrated on the task at hand. "We must win this," she said, piling snow together into a ball. "I will not lose this competition, especially at my own home."

"And I shall not let you lose, Lady Sarah."

They worked together, piling snow up and up, rounding off the snowman's belly before moving on to his head. Some of the guests had already finished, their smaller men in no way grand enough to win, while others seemed too keen to rush and not compact the snow well enough, leaving it to crumble when the head was positioned.

Not theirs, however. Their snowman was strong, almost half Sarah's height and better than anyone else's she was sure.

"You will have to make yours bigger, Lady Sarah, if you wish to beat me," Lady Rackliffe shouted, laughing at her own words.

Sarah growled at the sight of her ladyship's tall snowman, compact and just as good as theirs. "Go and fetch some sticks for his arms and nose. I'll collect the stones for his eyes and mouth."

Giles nodded, running off to do her bidding. For a moment, she lost herself watching him trudge through the snow. Was the man destined to look perfect in any life situation he found himself? He was taller than most men she knew, and always, in her opinion, the most handsome. The thought that he wanted her above anyone else left her breathless, her heart pounding like it had the night she kissed him. With his golden locks, and devilish, wicked mouth he'd intoxicated her from the moment she'd first set eyes on him at the susceptible age of fourteen.

A snowball flew past, and the resulting scream when the snowball found its mark reminded her of her task. She ran over to a nearby garden, searched as best she could under the dormant rose bushes for small rocks. Finding only a few small pebbles, she ran back to the snowman, placing them on his mouth and face. Molly called out that they only had ten minutes left, and Sarah took stock of the other entrants they were up against.

Lord Ambrose took off his scarf and wrapped it about

the snowman, and Sarah frowned. They would have to do something similar if they wanted to win. Giles returned with his sticks, thin ones that suited the arms and nose well.

Sarah stepped up next to Giles and slid the scarf from his neck. A lazy, tempting smile tweaked his lips as he stood there, allowing her to de-clothe him. Her skin prickled in awareness before she rose on her toes and, holding his shoulders for support, slipped his hat off as well.

"You're awfully close, my lady. Are you trying to tempt me out here in the freezing air? Because it's warming my blood to no end."

Unable not to, she chuckled, shaking her head at his words. It wasn't any wonder women fell at this rogue's feet. He was amusing and wicked and reminded her of the fun-loving young man who had enchanted her all those years ago.

"If you kissed me out here before everyone, you would have to marry me."

He wiggled his brows, and she smiled. "Is that so very bad? I could think of worse fates."

Lady Rackliffe caught her attention by taking the jacket off Lord Ambrose as well, telling him without question that it must be so for them to win.

Giles heard her ladyship's words and cringed. "Please tell me I'm not going to have to part with my coat as well, my lady. I do believe winning at that cost is too high."

He turned back, and she sighed, agreeing with his lordship even though she would have taken his jacket should he have offered.

"Very well, I will not disrobe you entirely."

Giles watched her for a moment, his eyes full of mirth. He was so very good-looking. How fortunate he was to be blessed with such angelic features that left a woman's heart to flutter.

Molly called time, and her sister-in-law and brother walked about the group of snowmen before declaring Lady Rackliffe the winner.

Her ladyship jumped in glee, clapping her hands and laughing at the announcement before coming over to Sarah and Giles. Sarah took in the sway of her ladyship's hips, her overly bright smile, and knew it for what it was. She was determined to make Lord Gordan hers once more. The heavy-lidded gaze that promised whatever Giles wanted was clear for all to see.

"Lord Gordan, I must ask if you would be willing to open the Christmas ball with me. It has been so very long since we waltzed together. Too long," she whispered for only Giles to hear. Sarah heard her words too, the idea of anyone in Giles's arms but herself making her temper soar.

Giles looked about those who strolled past, heading back indoors before meeting Sarah's eyes. He stuttered his answer, and Sarah took pity on him. "I'm sure Lord Gordan would be honored, my lady. Shall we return inside? It is starting to get quite brisk outdoors."

Sarah turned without seeing if they followed, but she could hear the crunch of their shoes in the snow that told her they did. Sarah ground her teeth, having wanted to dance the waltz with Giles herself.

She continued through the drawing room, determined to find their butler, who would be acting as the major-domo for the ball. This year, the St. Albans Christmas ball would have two waltzes, not one.

CHAPTER 6

Giles escaped the house party later that afternoon. He stepped out the servant's back door, pulling his greatcoat closed, the brisk, afternoon air as cold as an arctic blast. He started toward the stables with quickened steps, noting the stable doors were closed. He let himself inside via a smaller side door, grateful to be out of the inclement weather.

The air inside the stables was a lot warmer, the building so well made that not a cold draft or freezing drop of rain penetrated the space.

A cooing and light, feminine chatter caught his attention, and frowning, he moved forward along the stalls, looking into each one to see who was there. Warmth speared through his blood at the sight of Sarah brushing her mount, her hands running along the flank of the sixteen-hand chestnut after each stroke of her brush.

The sight of her hands stroking the animal's flesh should not tempt him, but it did. From the moment she'd kissed him in London all those years ago, he'd thought of little else. Every woman he'd ever bedded, flirted with at entertainments, sated his lust with, all bore a striking resemblance to Sarah, and he knew the reason why.

He'd wanted her above everyone else from the moment their lips had touched.

His father, a proud and strict gentleman, would not allow his courtship of her due to her being Lord Hugh Farley's sibling. He'd been told in terms that brooked little argument that Lady Sarah was not suitable for the Gordan family, no matter her rank, and for him to look elsewhere unless he wanted to live life penniless.

He should have called his father's bluff, tested him on his words, and offered to Sarah anyway. He may have become poor as a result, but there was one thing his father could not take from him, and that was the title he would eventually inherit. Sarah herself was not without funds. They would have survived. A foolish mistake and one he would regret always.

Giles leaned over the stable door, content to watch her coo to her horse and enjoy her solitary time away. He wished he'd stood up to his father and told him that the rumors against Hugh were unfounded and possibly untrue, which they were proven to be in the end. That Lady Sarah was innocent of any slight.

That his sire had persuaded him to offer to Edith, now Lady Rackliffe, and he had, was an action that even he would find hard to excuse.

When Sarah had kissed him, but a day after his betrothal, he'd been so livid, not at Sarah, but himself for choosing the wrong woman. He'd lashed out, punished Sarah with words that had been untrue. Hurt the one woman he had wanted simply because he could not change the error of his ways.

He did not deserve her now, not after making her wait all this time, but he could not leave her be. A fire burned in his soul, and it was only Sarah who could extinguish it.

He wanted her.

Giles cleared his throat. "We missed you after luncheon. I did not know that you were hiding out here in the stables, or I would have joined you sooner."

Sarah walked about the back of her horse, pushing the mare across a little so she could brush the opposite side. "You should know that I often escape out here. The staff has been allowed the day to join their families for the festive season, and so I'm checking on the horses instead. They'll be back later this evening, but I needed to brush Opie in any case."

Giles watched her work the brush over the horse's back, the mare calm, her head lowered and her eyes barely open. "You're putting your horse to sleep."

Sarah chuckled, and the sound did odd things to him. He wanted to hear her laugh, her jovial voice, for the rest of his life. If he could persuade her to love him as he hoped she once had, their lives could be perfect.

"She relishes a good brush." Sarah slipped under the horse's neck, coming to stand before him. "What are you doing out here, my lord? I thought you would be too busy with Lady Rackliffe following you about every minute of every day to escape to the stables."

Was that jealousy he heard in her tone? He narrowed his eyes, shrugging. "Lady Rackliffe is happily situated indoors. I wanted to find you."

Sarah reached over the wooden door, sliding the lock across to let herself out. "Her ladyship will be most unhappy to have lost the company of her preferred."

"I'm not her preferred."

She laughed again. This time, he did not miss her mocking tone. "Oh, yes, you are. She's quite determined to secure you. However will you evade her charms? From what I remember, you were quite taken with them once before."

Giles helped her shut the stable door before bolting it closed. "That was a long time ago. She's not whom I want."

A light blush stole across her cheeks before she stepped around him, evading his eyes and his company. Giles followed her to the back of the stables to where a large pile of hay was stacked and strewn over the floor.

She turned, lifting her chin and once again was a duke's daughter, proud and confident. "What are you doing out in the stables, my lord? Are you going to help me give the horses some feed, or did you come out to go for a ride? I do not want to hold you up in any way."

He had intended going for a ride, but the idea was no longer so tempting. Not with Sarah keeping him company. "I will help, most gladly." Giles helped her load biscuits of hay for each horse, check their water and stalls for any steaming piles. After filling the last of the horse's water, he turned to find Sarah sitting on the hay, watching him, her eyes bright with amusement.

"You're laughing at me, why is that?" he asked, washing his hands in a small bowl, before striding over to her.

She grinned. "No reason. I just like seeing you like this. It reminds me of how we used to be when doing things together. Do you remember?"

"I do." He flopped down next to her, leaning back to look up at the wooden rafters above them, the hay acting as a barrier against the cold. Giles had to admit that right at this moment, his blood was heated. No doubt due to the fact he was with Sarah and quite alone at that. "There was nothing better than to explore the wilderness about the estate. I keep meaning to visit the fort out in the woods."

"It's still there." She leaned back next to him, her attention also on the roof.

Giles took the opportunity to watch her, taking in the pretty sweep of her nose, full lips, and faultless skin. He'd dreamed about her so often, but having her near, hearing her voice was so much better than any fantasy.

"I believe the sword you and Hugh carved is also. In the summer, I still use the fort. It's a wonderful place to read and not be disturbed."

"Your father was a clever man. I never doubted that it was not still standing."

She smiled at him, and his stomach clenched. She was so very close. He wanted to lean across the small space that separated them and kiss her. To do so would be dangerous, considering their current status, but even so, the pull to have her in his arms was overwhelming.

He clenched his fists into the straw at his sides, forcing himself to court her slowly and not keep molesting her with every chance offered.

"He was, wasn't he?" She turned, studying him a moment. "How long are we going to lie here, my lord?"

Giles frowned, meeting her gaze. "Stay here? Did you wish to return to the house? We can, if that is your wish."

"No," she said, chuckling. "I meant to say, how long are we going to lie here before you kiss me, Giles? That is what I'd like to know."

CHAPTER 7

Sarah was well aware she was playing with fire. Lord Gordan was a reputed rake. A man made for pleasure and fun. Not a gentleman easily brought to heel.

Not that she wished to control him, but she could not bear to hear of any liaisons he had should they continue along this path of courtship. His absence from her life had been severing. To be married and know that one's husband was unfaithful would be unbearable.

Even so, lying beside him in the hay, watching as his eyes darkened with wicked intent, she couldn't help but throw herself into the wild. For so many years, she'd not lived as she ought to have, no more would she wither away, secluded in Kent or Bath.

With an elder brother who hosted scandalous parties and cared little for restraint and her other sibling abroad under a shadow of scandal, she had hidden away, not wanting to be any further embarrassment or fodder for town gossip.

Sarah had managed and accepted her lot in life as well as anyone could in her position. But having Giles's dark-blue eyes all but devour her person as he closed the space between them, she knew to her very core that she was in trouble.

That allowing him such liberties would forever change her and her steadfast denial of her feelings for him that she had long bottled away, corked, and shelved.

His lips brushed hers, warm and soft, and a frisson of need coursed through her blood. He lifted his hand, pushing a lock of her hair behind her ear. "You're so beautiful. You may not believe me, but I've wanted you for so long. I attended each Season in town only to be disappointed when I heard you were not attending."

Sarah clasped his nape, sliding her hand up into his soft, golden locks. She steeled herself not to be carried away by his words. Their friendship had been distant for so long. It would take time for her to adjust to his enlightenment of what they could have. To trust him as she once had.

"Why did you never attend one of Henry's house parties then, or call at the Abbey? You knew I was here. You knew I was alone."

Pain crossed his features as she waited for his answer. "I wanted to come and see you. So much, Sarah, but my father kept me busy elsewhere and always demanded I attend the Season and stay in town."

"Had you been able to see me, what would you have said?" *Or done?* The question hovered on her lips and between them. She wanted to know would he have acted sooner. Defied his father for her had he seen her face-to-face. It was a lot harder to deny one's feelings when standing before the person one cared for.

"I should have done what I've wanted to for so long." He kissed her again, urging her to lie on the straw. She adjusted her position as little prickly stalks jabbed through the jacket over her gown. The feel of his tongue begging entry made her gasp, and he delved into her mouth. Warmth settled between her thighs, and she squeezed her legs a little, trying to stem her need. How was it that this man, an enemy only a week before, could make her so willing in his arms?

The kiss turned heated, his demands raw and hard, and unlike anything she'd ever experienced before. Her senses reeled, her breath hitched. She relished Giles like this. A little wild and without restraint. Sarah clasped the lapels of his jacket, holding him against her. His hand slid down her waist, his clever fingers sliding across to tease the undersides of her breasts, but no farther. Frustration made her whimper, and she pushed against him, wanting his hand to move, to kneed her aching flesh.

With each breath she took, her gown scraped against her nipples, spiking pleasure and want. She craved the feel of his hands upon her person. It didn't matter as to where so long as he gave her what she wanted.

His manhood settled against her core, and she whimpered, a spike of pleasure making her wet. Even with the abundance of skirts and multiple petticoats and two layers of stockings, Sarah could feel the substantial size of him. His hardness tempted her to squirm and rub up against him like a house cat looking for a good scratch.

She gasped, breaking the kiss, needing to calm her racing heart. Giles did not stop his assault. Oh no, he kissed his way down her neck, his tongue and teeth teasing her earlobe. The heavenly sensation wrought her senses to flee, and she lay back, welcoming him to do more, to take her if he wished, just so long as the delicious sensations coursing across her body right at that moment never ended.

. . .

"You're so beautiful, Sarah." Giles breathed in the sweet-smelling scent of roses her skin always held. He would forever love the pretty, petaled flower for the reminder of her.

His body roared with need, his cock hard and primed. Sarah's legs wrapped tightly about his waist as he rocked into her, sliding his cock against her cunny. Oh god, it felt good. Too good to stop even though they could be walked in on at any moment.

He was a rutting bastard to tease her, in a stable no less, but he could not halt. Did not want to pause the delicious heat that coursed down his spine and threaded into his groin. His balls tightened, release all but imminent.

Her fingers scored down his back through his greatcoat. Her little mewls of need told him he could make her come this way. The light flush on her cheeks and eyes heavy-lidded with passion were all he needed to know she was at the point of no return.

Giles slowed his undulation against her, needing to drag out their interlude. She moaned, closing her eyes, and the sight of her enjoyment almost undid his control.

"You approve, my darling?" he whispered against her ear, licking it for good measure and eliciting a gasp from her kissable lips.

"Yes," she sighed, pushing against him and meeting his every stroke.

He bit down on the inside of his mouth, stemming his release. He could not continue to tease for much longer, not unless he wanted to walk back into the house with a stain at the front of his pants.

"You make me want so much, Sarah."

"You make me need too," she said, her words a whispered sigh of delight.

Giles reached down, lifting her leg higher on his hip.

The urge to hoist up her gown, rip open his falls and fuck her, here in the stable, overwhelmed his senses. His control strained to a snapping point.

The sound of men's voices sounded outside the stable walls. The thought of being caught in such a situation doused his desire like sand on hot coals, and Giles wrenched up off Sarah, pulling her to stand as he did so.

Confusion clouded her sweet face, and he quickly checked her gown, removing the pieces of hay that he could see were stuck in her hair. She didn't help, merely stared at him, her eyes wide and heavy-lidded with unsated desire. He grinned, knowing he'd discombobulated her to the point of silence.

Giles dragged them before one of the horse's stalls, putting space between them. He leaned over the door, making it seem as if they were discussing the horse stabled inside. The stable doors slid open and in walked three men, one of whom Giles recognized as the head stableman.

"Good afternoon, my lord, Lady Sarah," Bruce, the eldest and most superior of the three, said, tipping his hat.

"Good afternoon," Sarah said, stepping away from Giles and heading for the door. "I hope you enjoyed your afternoon with your families. Did they savor the hams we sent over?"

Bruce pulled his cap off his head, holding it before him, a wide, genuine smile playing about his mouth. "It was most extravagant, my lady. We thank you and His Grace for your kindness."

Giles watched as Sarah reached out, clasping the older man's arm in affection. "You are most welcome, and it was our pleasure."

She left them then, and Giles remembered that he had come out for a ride, but no longer wanted to. Watching

Lady Sarah saunter out of sight, he could not think of anyone he'd prefer to ride at this very moment other than her.

He bid the workers a good afternoon and set out after her, determined to finish what they had started.

CHAPTER 8

Sarah did not make it very far into the house when she was dragged into the drawing room to have her likeness sketched by Lady Sebastian, who was renowned for her lifelike drawings of people using crayons.

Molly came to sit beside her, chattering of the house party and their plans over the coming days. Her closest friends were seated about them, watching as Sarah had her likeness drawn, they too busy with ideas for the new duchess.

Sarah absently listened as they gossiped and laughed about the past Season and the new one to come. What milestones their children had achieved and the Christmas Ball here at the Abbey, which was coming up.

None of the conversation points drew Sarah in. Nothing would, she was sure. After what she had experienced in the stables with Giles, she doubted she would ever be so again.

Who knew that a man could create a riot of sensations throughout her body, make her want to throw away her well-behaved self and see what else Giles could make her feel?

He was utterly a master at seduction, and she'd been only too ready for a tryst in the hay like some housemaid too free with her favors.

Sarah glanced up and met the eyes of the Duchess of Carlisle. She schooled her features, not liking the knowing tilt of the duchess's lips. Heat suffused her face. Why was Her Grace looking at her so? Did she know something about her venture with Giles only a short time ago?

Impossible, and yet, something told Sarah Her Grace was more perceptive than the others and saw something different in her.

"Oh my, Lady Sarah, the sketch is positively breathtaking. You look most beautiful and natural in this image," Marchioness Ryley said, standing behind Lady Sebastian as she continued to draw.

Molly walked about the easel and took in the image, her attention snapping to Sarah, a contemplative look in her eye. Oh no, not her sister-in-law too!

"Very interesting indeed. I think you shall like the likeness, Sarah," Molly said, smiling at her.

Lady Sebastian set down the crayon she was using and surveyed her drawing with pride. "I think it captures Lady Sarah honestly." Her ladyship picked up the parchment, handing it to Sarah. "Here you are, my dear, you may do with this drawing as you wish."

Sarah took the sketch and studied it, a croak of distress lodging in her throat at what she saw. Did she truly look to others as Lady Sebastian had expressed her?

Her cheeks were flush with color, her hair not as pristine as some of the other ladies present, and why would it be after a romp in the hay? Her lips were a deep shade of pink, and swollen. She bit her lip, her body remembering the passionate embrace and wanting more. Her eyes held a faraway expression as if she were still in Lord Gordan's arms.

Where she belonged...

Sarah lifted her hand to her cheek, feeling the heat from her blush on her fingers. Oh, dear Lord. Did Molly suspect? Duchess Carlisle certainly did, she feared.

"Thank you," she said, standing and starting for the door. "I'm most grateful and will cherish it always."

Sarah fled the room, not bothering with an explanation as to why. She smiled in welcome to the few gentlemen who milled about the foyer, some of them heading toward the drawing room. No doubt, they had been playing billiards or taking part in the gaming room that Hugh had set up for the duration of the house party.

Her room's safety beckoned, a place where she could hide the drawing from anyone else having to see. What would they think if they knew the truth? That Lady Sebastian had captured her every thought, her every desire, and crushing need that coursed through her blood still, after being with Giles in the stable.

She was almost to her room when a gentleman who came out of the servants' stairs stopped her dead in her tracks. Giles moved into the passage, unaware of her rushing to her room. He glanced up, pleasure filling his features and leaving her breathless once again.

"Sarah." He came up to her and, checking they were alone, lifted a sprig of mistletoe above her head. He leaned down and stole a kiss. "I missed you now."

He stood back, his gaze latching on to the drawing. "May I see it?" he asked.

Sarah swallowed the nerves that tumbled about her

belly at having this attractive, eligible lord, hers to do with as she pleased, before her again. "It's a silly sketch, nothing to mind." Sarah did not want him to see it, or anyone else. If Giles saw the expression on her face, reminiscing about her escapades with his lordship, he would know her secret.

That no matter what she said otherwise, no matter how much of a wall she built up around herself when it came to the man before her, he merely needed to clap his hands, and she came to attention.

Silly little fool that she was, she could not help herself. She wanted him. Had wanted Giles for years and wished that he'd been her knight in shining armor, the man who rode to St. Albans Abbey and saved her from her self-isolated fate.

He had not. No one had. Her brother Henry had made sure of that with his scandalous escapades in town after Hugh left.

He tipped his head to the side. "Let me see it, Sarah. I will not show anyone." He reached for the drawing, and she jerked it away.

"Did you draw it yourself?" he asked after a moment.

"No." She shook her head, her cheeks flaming. "I need to freshen up."

He grinned, knowing full well why she needed to bathe and dress for dinner. "Please let me see?"

He spoke in a soothing, cajoling voice, and she sighed, holding the sketch out to him. Not able to deny him anything, it would seem, for very long. "Very well, but do not say a word about it. I need no commentary on the likeness."

GILES TOOK THE PARCHMENT, holding up the sketch to take in the image. His mouth dried at the sight of Sarah, the distant light in her eyes, the knowing, wicked grin on her swollen lips.

He cleared his throat. "When was this drawn?"

Sarah crossed her arms over her chest. "Lady Sebastian was doing them in the drawing room just now."

The image of Sarah made his gut clench. Never had he thought an artist could capture a moment in someone's life so well, but Lady Sebastian certainly had. Sarah looked every bit a woman who had been thoroughly ravished. A woman who also enjoyed every lascivious, sinful moment of it.

He licked his lips, remembering their tryst in the stable. "May I keep it?" He would treasure it until the time came that he could have another one done of Sarah when she was his wife, and he was beside her.

"You cannot." She snatched it out of his hand, placing it behind her back. "What if someone sees you with it? They will ask questions."

He shrugged, nonplussed. "So what if they do?"

Sarah checked the passage for guests before rounding on him. "People will suspect if you have the drawing that there is something between us."

"There is something between us," he said, leaning down and whispering against her lips. He met her startled eyes, winking. "I want there to be something between us, Sarah. After what happened in the stables, I thought you would understand that more than any other."

"Ho, Gordan, I have been looking for you."

Sarah gasped, stepping back as if she were threatened by hot coals, her back coming up hard against the door.

Giles turned, smiling at Hugh, who strode toward them. "Albans, I too was just coming to find you," he lied, having had no intention. Truth be told, he was about to prove that he wanted Sarah in his life in every possible way that he could.

In his room. Alone, if she were willing.

"Come, man, we're about to start a game of billiards, and I need you to make up the numbers. All the other fellows are too busy cozying up to the ladies in the drawing room."

Giles nodded. "Of course," he said, bowing quickly to Sarah, before starting down the hall.

Hugh lingered, looking at the drawing that Sarah clutched behind her back. "I see you had your likeness sketched, Sarah. May I see it?" Hugh held out his hand, and Giles watched as Sarah stared at his appendage as if it were some crazed body part.

"No, I'm sorry. I will see you at dinner," she said, rushing into her room and shutting the door with a decided slam.

Hugh turned to stare at Giles, a frown between his brow. "Whatever is wrong with her, do you suppose?" Hugh approached Giles as he moved toward the stairs, knowing it was better to answer this question than Sarah, who seemed to be struggling with whatever was happening between them.

Affection. Enjoyment. Pleasure...

"I believe she is tired. I ran into her earlier at the stables. Maybe she needs a rest before dinner this evening."

"Yes, perhaps you're right." Hugh sighed. "Sisters, I will have to get used to having one again after all this time. Even so, I shall check in on her tonight to ensure she is well."

Giles didn't reply, not wanting to give Hugh any reason to suspect him of anything. Not yet, at least. He needed to win over Sarah before he won over his friend. "Tell me, who are we playing against?"

"Ah, Whitstone, and Duncannon. Both of whom believe we require a good trouncing."

Giles scoffed. "We shall see about that." He never liked to lose, not in a game of billiards or life. By the end of the Christmas house party, he too would win Sarah's heart.

Just as he had it ten years before.

CHAPTER 9

The following evening Sarah stood before the roaring hearth in the ballroom where some spontaneous dancing had been organized. The ladies took turns in playing the pianoforte for those who wished to dance while others had a turn about the room.

The room smelled of pine, one of the three Christmas trees at St. Albans Abbey stood in the corner of the room without decoration, the tradition of decorating the tree to happen Christmas eve.

A portion of the yule log burned in the grate. Sarah took in the many merry guests, conceding that it wasn't so bad to have all the guests stay at the estate. Over the few days that they had been here, they had been both kind and welcoming, not bringing up her time away or the reasons that occurred.

Hugh and Molly seemed to be enjoying themselves as well, and she couldn't help but wonder if they would return to Rome as much as they had stated they would. Certainly, they seemed very well placed here in Kent, with their new baby and marriage.

Sarah sipped her milk punch, her attention snapping to the door when Giles entered, Lady Rackliffe beside him, looking as pleased as she always did when around his lordship.

A prickle of annoyance threaded through her at the sight of them together. They made a handsome pair, both light-haired, attractive, and titled, should a marriage happen between them, they would be a highly placed couple in society.

So would you, should you marry Lord Gordan.

Sarah did not move, merely watched as Lady Rackliffe leaned up to whisper something in Giles's ear. He nodded before striding away.

Her hold on her crystal flute tightened before she took a calming breath, reminding herself that Giles had asked her to trust him, let him court her, not Lady Rackliffe. He would not play her the fool.

Her brother strode over to her, and she schooled her features, not wanting him to know anything about her muddled thoughts on Giles. "Sarah, my dear, I'm glad to catch you on your own. I wanted to talk to you about yesterday. You seemed a little distressed when I came upon you with Lord Gordan."

Sarah shook her head, wrapping her arm around Hugh's. "Nothing at all is wrong. I was merely tired after attending my horse in the stables. How did your billiards game go? I hope you won, as you wished to."

He smiled down at her, his eyes bright with happiness. "Of course. Whitstone was all talk when it came to his ability." Hugh chuckled. "Are you enjoying yourself? We have not left you alone too often, I hope. I do want our first Christmas together again to be a pleasant one."

"Not at all. Surprisingly, despite my earlier concerns, I have enjoyed myself immensely. Everyone has been kind and not bold enough to bring up Henry and what he did. Have you found the same?"

He nodded, his face clouding a moment at the reminder of Henry and what he had done to Miss Cox and Hugh, especially. "I have. Molly seems to be the most accomplished hostess too. How lucky we are," he said, smiling down at her, the love he had for his wife shining in his eyes.

"Molly is simply the best choice you have ever made. If I have not said before, Hugh, I am so very happy for you both."

"Thank you, Sarah. Your words mean a lot to me." Hugh gestured to the dancers. "I hope you're going to partake in a jig or waltz this evening. The most handsome sister in attendance should not be a wallflower."

"Perhaps I will." She grinned, hoping that Giles would move over to where she stood and ask her.

Hugh studied her a moment, a small frown between his brows. "You have been spending some time with Lord Gordan these past few days. Each time I look up, you're together partaking in conversation. Is there something that I should be aware of between you two?"

Heat rushed to her face, and she prayed he did not notice. "What? No, nothing is happening between his lordship and myself. We're friends, just as we once were."

"If I recall correctly, you had a falling out just after I left. Lord Gordan wrote to me and told me of his disappointment."

"What? He wrote to you and told you? What did he say?"

Hugh stared at her as if she had lost her mind, which, if she found out that Giles had told Hugh of her kissing him, she may very well do.

"That you disagreed over a trivial matter, and you refused to speak to him. That is all he said."

Sarah sighed, swallowing her fear and mortification that what she had done to Giles others may know about. And not just anyone, but her brother. "That is all in the past now. I have moved on from that difference of opinion."

Hugh's lips lifted into a half smile. "I am glad for it, for I do believe Lord Gordan likes you, Sarah. More than you possibly know."

Oh no, she knew how much Giles liked her, and she had enjoyed every second of him showing her so yesterday in the stables. Even now, her body yearned for his touch, his kiss, his breathy gasps against her ear when he'd undulated against her flesh.

"We're friends. Of course, he admires me." She sipped her punch to stop from having to say any more.

"I'm not blind, sister. I have seen the way he watches you, waits for you when you're not present. He thinks that I do not discern, but I do."

Sarah made the mistake of being caught in her brother's penetrating stare. She bit her lip, thinking it best not to say anything at all lest she blurt out her fear that she was falling in love with the marquess. If it were not love, it most certainly was already lust.

"He does not look at me so. You're too overcome with Christmas festivity to see clearly," she teased.

He chuckled, the sound mocking. "I'm not blind, no matter what you may think. I ask for one thing if there is anything between you. Do not cause a scandal by doing anything untoward. There are many eyes on our family, thanks to Henry. We must not allow the *ton* to have any further fodder to use against us."

Sarah nodded, shamed by her brother's words. Had

anyone come across her and Giles yesterday in the stables, she would have been ruined. Her family once again the main talking point of gossip in town. She would have been dragged down the aisle to become Lord Gordan's wife before she could explain what she was about.

Not that being his wife was ever so bad. There had been a time that she'd wanted that above anything else, but he had chosen another. That that other person happened to be at this house party was merely an inconvenience. Even so, it did not change the fact that he was now courting her, not anyone else.

If she behaved, waited to see where her newfound friendship with Giles led, maybe they would be married before the next Season. "I will not do anything that could cause you or Molly harm. I promise," she said to her brother, just as a shadow fell before them both.

Sarah glanced up, her stomach fluttering, and she knew who was before them before observing him for herself.

"Lord Gordan," she said, dipping into a curtsy. "I hope you've come to our little impromptu dance ready to escort many a young woman onto the boards."

His eyes bored into her, the heat that she could see swirling in his blue orbs sent a frisson of desire to pool at her core. The man before her was determined to throw her life into a delightful turmoil.

"I am, Lady Sarah." He held out his hand. "Will you do me the honor?"

Sarah looked up at her brother, and the knowing look he bestowed upon her told her all she needed to know. Her brother had seen and approved. All that was left was for her to decide if she also did.

Sarah placed her hand atop of Giles's arm. He covered her hand immediately with his own, leading her onto the dance floor. "What is the next dance, do you know?"

The strains of a waltz started, and he grinned, a devilishly wicked light in his eyes. "I never leave anything to chance, my lady. Now, come here," he said, pulling her into his arms.

Sarah went willingly. At this time, should he ask her of anything, she was sure she would do it.

Even say yes to this handsome marquess.

CHAPTER 10

Giles made sure he danced with every woman present at the impromptu ball that the Duke of St. Albans had organized. The Christmas ball was still a week away, but with the need to keep those in attendance happy and occupied, a small dance did not hurt any of the plans.

The main Christmas ball would have the families of the nobility who lived close by in attendance, a much grander and more formal affair.

He had danced with Sarah twice already and knew he should not ask again. His interest would be noted and would only bring more eyes watching them.

He didn't need that annoyance. He wanted to spend as much time as he could with Sarah without everyone watching their every move. He needed to make her trust that he was in earnest. Explain to her, when the time was right, why he'd not thrown Lady Rackliffe aside when Sarah had kissed him.

That his betrothed had thrown him over had been a welcome reprieve from a choice he had not wanted to make in the first place.

Nothing stood in his way of having Sarah as his wife now. As much as he loved and missed his parents, they were no longer living, and he could choose whomever he wished.

The night was coming to an end, and he bid those about him goodnight, having already done so with Sarah before she took a turn about the floor with her brother.

Giles left the ballroom, heading for the servant's stairs over that of the main staircase. It came out just beside his suite of rooms, and there was less of a chance of him being accosted by Lady Rackliffe, who appeared determined to take up as much of his time as she could.

He pushed through the servant's stairwell door into the passage near his room, the paneled door unsuspecting to anyone walking up the corridor. A feminine gasp sounded, and he closed the door quickly to see Sarah looking at him as if he'd accosted her.

"Apologies, Sarah. I did not think any of the family were headed to bed as yet."

She clasped her chest, her eyes wide with fright. "You startled me, that is all. I wasn't expecting anyone to barrel through. What are you doing using the servant's stairs again?"

He glanced down the hall to ensure they were alone. "Avoiding Lady Rackliffe. She's quite determined to catch me under a bough of mistletoe."

Sarah's delightful mouth twisted into a mulish line. Was she jealous? Did she not like the thought of someone else vying for his attention? He could well understand the sentiment. He, too, did not want to think of Sarah being with anyone else but him. It had only been by chance that he'd stood by all the years to take over the title that she had not married.

Had he been a man, stood up to his father and

demanded he was marrying whomever he liked, they could have possibly been married for several years by now.

But he had not. He'd been a coward. Had allowed his father's prejudice and threats to keep him away from her. Thank bloody Christ that he did not have that issue any longer.

He was a bastard to think that way, to be now able to court Sarah meant that his father was gone. Even so, his sire had been wrong to demand such from him. He would not do it to his son when the time came.

"Lady Rackliffe does seem determined. Now that she is a widow, you do not wish to try your advantage at winning her heart a second time?"

"Hell no," he said, his tone more severe than he'd meant to project.

Sarah started at his words, staring at him. "She will be disappointed," she said after a time.

Giles stepped closer to her, placing but a hairsbreadth between them. "Let her be. She is not the woman I want, as you well know."

Sarah's eyes twinkled with a knowing light, and his body yearned to pull her against him. Kiss her soundly until they were both sated.

"Did you enjoy dancing this evening? You were quite the popular gentleman."

"I aim to please." Giles reached out, the urge to touch her sweet face overwhelming. Her skin was soft and warm, and he ran his thumb along her jaw, swiping it over her bottom lip. Her lips opened on a sigh, and his body hardened. "I want to please you."

SARAH SHIVERED AT HIS WORDS. She wanted him to please her, too, in all ways. Thoughts of being with him as they were yesterday afternoon flittered through her mind, made her body yearn and ache.

His stormy, blue eyes darkened, enticing and wicked as ever. She had been so very angry at him for so long, how was it that a mere kiss, a sweet word, and roguish touch could make her let go of what had happened between them?

Because you were old friends, you loved him once.

All true of course, she had loved him, had been his friend, until he tried to marry a woman even Sarah could have told him would not make him happy. Sarah had long believed it was only she who could make him so, and now, after all these years apart, it would seem she was correct in that estimation.

What was she to do about it?

"Please me as you did yesterday in the stable? I do believe that was teasing, not pleasing, my lord." Her naughty words were unlike anything she'd ever spoken before. But she could not stop herself. Her body was not her own. Not anymore. She wanted the man before her to finish what he had started in the hay.

A growl emitted from him, and her breath hitched. "You're playing with fire, Sarah. Do not tempt me. I'm already at my limit when it comes to you."

She raised her brow, wanting to stir him more. See where their interlude could end. "Really? So if I were to step closer to you..." Sarah did as she suggested, her body close against his, her breasts grazing his chest. Her nipples pebbled, and moisture pooled at her core when his hardness settled into the dip of her stomach.

Sarah bit her lip, reaching up to drape her arms about his shoulders. "Your tolerance would snap?"

"Fuck, yes, it would." He picked her up, walked two steps, and pushed her up against the paneled wall. His mouth settled over hers, deep and commanding, taking her lips with a punishing edge.

Sarah clasped his shoulders, let go of her inhibitions, and drank from his desire. Let it spark hers to a flame. His hands slid down her back, clutching at her dress as if to rip it from her person.

Desire and need thrummed through his actions, his strong hands shaking against her body told her without words what she did to him. He hoisted one of her legs against his hip at the same time he ground against her, reminiscent of yesterday.

Oh yes...

They moaned, and with a nip to her lip, Giles pulled back, staring at her as if he were unsure, uncertain of what they were doing. Sarah knew exactly what they were about, and she wasn't going to let him end this interlude before he finished what they had started.

"I shouldn't be doing this, Sarah. Not until we're married."

The word marriage acted like a balm against any fears she may have held. Sarah kissed him quickly, a light brushing of lips. "Make love to me, Giles. I do not want to go to bed alone."

He leaned his forehead against hers, his eyes pools of uncertainty and need.

"We cannot," he gasped as she rubbed against him, using him to soothe the ache between her legs.

Sarah pushed him away with one hand before sauntering toward his bedroom door. "Yes, we can, and you will. I've never heard the Marquess of Graham being a man who did not satisfy. Do not start now. Not with me."

CHAPTER 11

Giles followed Sarah into his room, shutting and locking the door to ensure they were not disturbed. She was a goddess, her gold silk gown with gauze shimmering over the fabric gave her an air of decadence and privilege, of beauty that was both outside and in.

She sat on the edge of his bed, her wicked, come-hither look she threw him threatening to buckle his knees.

Giles strode over to her, wrenching his cravat and jacket off, dropping them to the floor without a second thought. Within a few moments, he stood before her with nothing but his breeches, his bare feet refusing to move from the soft Aubusson rug.

"I'll need help with my gown," she said, leaning over and giving him her back.

He drank in the sight of her straight spine, her swan-like neck, and sun-kissed hair pulled up into a decorative motif.

Thoughts of pushing her onto her hands, racking up her gown, and taking her from behind bombarded his mind. Giles pushed down his baser, harsher needs. Sarah was a maid, her first time with him could not be so, but one day. Soon, he promised himself. They would enjoy other ways of being together.

Giles made short work of the small, decorative buttons down her back. He slipped the gown down her arms, taking the opportunity to kiss her slight shoulders, the tops of her arms. She smelled divine, of flowers and a unique scent that was wholly Sarah.

Goose bumps rose on her skin, and he quickly pulled at the ties of her corset. Undressing Sarah was akin to unwrapping a gift. Having Sarah, such as she now was, willing in his arms and his, was the best Yuletide present he could have possessed. Her gown pooled at her waist, and Giles ripped her shift over her head, her corset next, discarding it somewhere about the foot of the bed.

She stood, and her dress fell to the floor. Giles took her into his arms, tumbling them down onto the soft linen. They bounced, and she chuckled, the throaty tenor of her voice hardened his cock.

He pulled back to admire the view of her before him. Her cheeks were flushed, her breasts full and heavy, all but begged for his touch. His mouth watered and, unable to deny himself a moment longer, he gave in to the desire thrumming through his blood like a raging torrent.

Giles licked her beaded nipple before taking her into his mouth. She moaned, her fingers spiking into his hair, and he kissed and paid homage to her breast while his other hand kneaded and teased the other.

"Oh, yes," she sighed. "You have no notion of how long I've wanted you this way."

He inwardly cursed all the missed opportunities, the years they were not together so. He'd wanted Sarah for as long as he could remember, and from this day forward, he would not be separated from her again.

Nothing would deny him her hand.

"Marry me." Giles kissed his way down her chest to her stomach, paying homage to the little freckle that sat beside her naval. He went farther, running his hand down the inside of her leg before touching the wet heat between her thighs.

He felt her start at his touch, and he looked up along her body, meeting the question in her hooded gaze.

"Lie back. I want to show you what we can have."

She bit her lip, sending desire straight to his cock. He pushed down his own needs, promising himself his turn would come. Soon, she would be his, and they would be one.

Giles kissed the inside of her thigh, breathing deep the sweet, musky scent of her mons. She undulated beneath him, and he held her legs apart, wanting to see her wet, pink lips that were his to enjoy.

He licked her swollen nubbin, and she gasped, her hands no longer pushing at his shoulders, but wrapping into his hair, holding him in place.

A dark, hungry need tore through him. He licked along her cunny, kissing and lathing her honeyed flesh to a fever. He made sure to stroke and frustrate her nubbin, running his thumb between her lips and tantalizing her where they would soon be joined.

She mewled, gasping with each of his tongue's strokes. His balls tightened, his cock heavy and erect, his release taunting deep in his gut.

"Yes, Giles. Ohhh, please, more."

He'd give her as much as she liked. He slipped one finger into her scorching heat. Her body tightened, contracted about him, and it took all of his self-control not to wrench up, placing his aching cock at her entrance and take her.

Soon. Soon, they would be one.

She lifted her bottom off the bed, undulating against his mouth, and he knew she was close. Without fear or shame, she rode his face, took pleasure from him, and never would his life be the same.

He would marry the woman beneath him. From this day forward, he could not live without her. How he had survived all the years was beyond him.

He kissed her fully, lathing her to a writhing frenzied, begging lover before he suckled on her clitoris, and she gasped, moaning as her release spiraled through her.

An overwhelming sense of power thrummed through his veins as he milked her of her pleasure. With ragged breath, and only when he was sure she was satisfied, did he move.

He came up over her, wrapping her legs about his hips. She watched him, her eyes pools of satiated desire and expectation. A small quirk tilted her lips. He placed himself at her entrance, meeting her eyes.

Sarah reached up, wrapping her arms about his neck, and he thrust into her, taking her virginity, and finally, they were one.

Lady Sarah Farley was his.

Sarah had thought Giles taking her would hurt. How very wrong she was. After his wickedly clever mouth had brought her to such pleasure that even now she could not catch her breath, his intrusion into her body only brought more pleasure.

With each thrust, it teased, thrummed, and reignited the climax she had just experienced.

She wanted him deeper, harder, faster. With a wantonness that she did not know she possessed, she spread her legs wider, hooked them higher on his back, and gave herself over to him.

To pleasure.

"Sarah," he gasped against her lips. "I've wanted you for so long."

"And I you." She held him against her, needing him to take her. To give her the soul-shattering pleasure he'd just bestowed. Once would never be enough. She needed more. Now.

"Take me," she panted. He did not disappoint. He thrust hard and deep. The sound of their flesh meeting, of creating pleasure echoed throughout the room and was music to her ears.

He kissed her, and she took the opportunity to run her hands down his back. Sweat-slicked skin met her fingers as she ran them down the taut, flexing muscles beside his spine. His bottom thrust against her and she clasped him there, enjoying the feel of him within her, taking her.

She would never get enough of this man.

The pleasure his mouth wrought teased her yet again, and she rose to meet his every move, and then she was there, spiraling out of control. Pleasure rocked through her, more pronounced, coarser, and overwhelming her soul.

"Giles," she cried.

He moaned, taking her, their bodies a burst of needs and wants, of receiving and giving.

"Sarah," he panted against her lips, kissing her softly. "Please tell me you will marry me now?"

She grinned, snuggling into the crook of his arm when

he rolled to his side, pulling her up against him. She lay one leg over him, idly playing with his chest, which rose and fell in quick pants.

"Yes," she said, looking up and meeting his gaze. "I will marry you." And finally, he would be hers. Always.

CHAPTER 12

Sarah stuck her head out into the darkened passage just before dawn, glancing up and down to ensure no one was about. The servants would be up soon, and if she were to sneak back to her bedroom without being seen, now was her chance.

She turned, taking one last glimpse of Giles as he slept in the bed they'd shared. He lay on his back, his arm sprawled out over her pillow where she'd rested. Her heart fluttered in her chest, and regretfully, she turned, slipping into the hall and closing the door behind her, taking care not to make any loud noises.

"Good morning, sister."

Sarah squealed, slapping a hand over her mouth before she woke any of the other guests. Footsteps sounded in the room she'd just emerged from, and the door wrenched open.

Giles stood at the threshold, hastily tied breeches his only attire, his chest, one she'd never tire of looking upon flexing with each breath. The moonlight from the window at the end of the hall, the only illuminating light.

"What is wrong?" Giles's words faded at the sight of Hugh glaring at them both.

Her brother pushed Sarah out the way and, with a sickening crunch, his fist connected with Giles's nose.

Sarah gasped, watched as Giles flayed backward before he fell with a crashing thud on the floor. Sarah kneeled at Giles' side, checking him as best she could. He pinched the bridge of his nose, blood seeped between his fingers and onto his lips, staining his teeth. He held up a hand, stilling her brother from doing any more damage.

"I suppose I deserved your wrath, but I'll not be hit a second time," Giles said, letting Sarah help him to stand.

Hugh shut the door to the bedroom, enclosing all three of them in the room. "What the hell do you think you're doing with my sister?"

Hugh glared at them both, his eyes wild with temper. Never had Sarah seen Hugh so incensed and shame threaded through her that she'd caused him such distress. If this were to get out to the other guests what she had done with Giles, the scandal would be all the *ton* would talk of next Season. Marriage or not.

That Hugh had asked her not to cause a scandal was the veriest dishonor.

"I asked Sarah to marry me, and she has agreed. I would never touch her had she said no."

Sarah raised her brow, unsure that was true. She was certain that if she wished it, she could have seduced Giles before last night.

"Is this true, Sarah?" her brother asked, pinning her to her spot, the anger and disappointment shimmering in his eyes, eliminating any ire she felt at being caught. At receiving a thorough set down from her brother over her conduct.

"Giles has asked for me to be his wife, and I want that

in return." She met Giles's gaze, her heart taking a little leap at the warmth and adoration she read in his blue orbs.

"How long have you been behaving in this manner?" Her brother shook his head. "I should have guessed yesterday when I caught you both upstairs, looking as guilty as you do now."

"Excuse me, Hugh, but I'm not a child. I'm eight and twenty and quite capable of making my own decisions."

Her brother pointed his finger at her nose. "You can make decisions, Sarah, but this one is what I specifically asked you not to."

"No one needs to know. You're the only person who has seen me this morning. If we leave now, announce the betrothal in the morning, all will be well."

Hugh glared at them both, his balled fists flexing at his sides. "I ought to call you out, Gordan." His jaw clenched, and he took a deep breath. "But I suppose since you're to be my brother-in-law by choice not by my decree, I shall let you live."

Sarah sighed, and Giles reached over to take her hand. She stared at the blood that marked his chest and face. Sarah moved over to the pitcher of water and bowl in his room, poured some water and rinsed out a washcloth.

"Here," she said, handing it to Giles. He gave her his thanks and set it against his nose, wincing a little as he did so.

"I'm sorry you had to find out about Sarah and me in this way, Hugh, but I love her. I want her to be my wife. I promise that later today, I was coming to ask you for your permission to make her my wife."

Hugh rubbed a hand through his hair, the dark circles under his eyes telling Sarah her brother was weary.

"We are sorry, Hugh. Please don't be angry. I want this

time to be a happy one." It had been so very long since she'd been so content.

He stared at them both without a word before he nodded, once. "Very well. I give you my consent, and I do wish you both very happy. You can be married as soon as we can gain a special license." Her brother met her gaze, some of the anger dispelling from his dark orbs. "Congratulations, Sarah."

She went into his arms, holding him tight. "Thank you, Hugh, for being so understanding."

"Yes, well," he said, relenting and pulling her tight in his arms. "You may not have gone about this the way that I asked, but it is done now. All will be well, I'm sure." He set her back and started for the door. He paused, turning to watch them both. "Come, Sarah. I will escort you to your room."

Sarah met Giles's eyes, and he nodded, winking at her. She smiled, bidding him goodbye, her words but a whisper, and followed her brother from the room.

He didn't say anything to her as they made their way back to her room. He opened her bedroom door, pushing it wide. "In you go, dear sister. Do not let me catch you out and about the house again. Not until you're a married woman. Do I make myself clear?"

She swallowed her retort, wanting to remind him that he wasn't so very well-behaved when Molly was in Rome. Sarah was privy to how they came together, so her brother's high-handedness was a little galling.

Even so, she would do as he bade because, in the end, she would marry Giles. The sacrifice would be worth the wait. "Perfectly clear, brother. I shall do as you ask."

He watched until the door to her room closed. Once more alone, she ran over to her bed, slipping under the soft sheets and heavy blankets. She smiled, contentment thrumming through her veins. She was engaged to Giles, Marquess Gordan. Excitement somersaulted her stomach, and the day could not start soon enough. She wanted to shout it from the rooftops that they would be married. Her husband and she his wife.

How well that sounded to her ears. A dream that finally came true.

CHAPTER 13

Before dinner the same day, Sarah sat beside Giles in the drawing room, an overwhelming sense of happiness consuming her as her brother announced that she and Giles were engaged.

Congratulations sounded loud in the room. An array of guests came up to them to wish them very happy.

Sarah laughed, thanked each one in turn. Giles pulled her into his side, watching her with an expression that made her stomach twist into delicious knots. "I hope you're happy, my lady?" he asked, his eyes dark pools of an emotion she hoped would be voiced again soon. She wanted to hear him say that he loved her as much as she had always loved him.

"So happy," she said, meaning it more than anything she'd ever said before in her life.

Dinner that evening was a boisterous, excitable evening. Everyone seemed to be in a rush to speak, drink wine, celebrate the Christmas season, and Sarah and Giles's betrothal, which only added to the celebrations.

The after-dinner drinks were no different. Sarah sat on

a settee watching as Molly and Hugh toasted her and Giles yet again, her brother's wide smile and laughing eyes telling all in attendance how very pleased he was for his sister. Even if this morning, he'd been so very mad.

Sarah caught the eye of Lady Rackliffe, who excused herself from her small social circle and strolled over to Sarah.

The forthcoming conversation, as awkward as it would be, had to be had. Lady Rackliffe was, after all, once betrothed to Giles. No doubt, the woman would, at the very least, have to remind Sarah that she was asked first, no matter what the outcome had been for them both.

"Lady Sarah, may I say how very happy I am for you and Lord Gordan? You shall be very happy, I'm sure," she said, sitting next to her and sipping her wine.

"Thank you, my lady. That is very kind of you to say." Sarah almost rolled her eyes at the banality of their conversation. Even so, she did not wish to extend their little tête-a-tête any more than she had to. They had never been friends in the past. Certainly, Lady Rackliffe thought herself above most within society, even within her own circle of friends.

"I must say the news of your betrothal to Giles has shocked me. I did not even know there was anything representing affection between you both. From knowing Giles all these years, how he lived his life in London, I'm surprised you accepted him so quickly."

Sarah stiffened her back, refusing to let this woman's words deflate her agreeable mood. "Lord Gordan," she said, reminding Lady Rackliffe that she no longer had the right to use his given name. She threw that away the moment she threw his lordship over for Lord Rackliffe. "He is an honorable man. I have little concern about his life before me. I think him the best of men and one who'll make me extremely happy."

The idea of days and nights in his company, to wake up in his arms, have his children, sent a thrill through her she'd not felt since the moment she closed the space between them and kissed him on a moonlit terrace in London ten years before.

Lady Rackliffe's mouth pinched into a displeased line. "Oh, I'm sure he will not stray, my dear. But," she said, biting her lip, "it does seem odd that his morals would allow this change of heart. You know why, do you not, he never offered for your hand during your first Season. Why no one offered."

Sarah was not sure she wanted to know, certainly not from this viperous, gossiping snake.

"I do not know, no." Nor did she wish to be privy to the details. What was in the past as far as she was concerned needed to stay there. If she were to endure the *ton* and re-enter society, she had to be able to let go of their wrong-doing to her brother and move forward without hate in her heart.

Lady Rackliffe chuckled a high-pitched cackle that made her ears hurt. "The scandal, of course," she whispered, making sure no one else could hear. "Giles's father was friends with your late mama. He did not approve of the scandal Lord Hugh had bestowed on the family. Of course, even knowing the truth as we do now that it was the duke, and oldest brother Henry who was at fault, the late Lord Gordan did not know that.

"He saw his good friend, the duchess heartbroken that her son had acted in such a way and refused to counter a friendship between Giles and Hugh. Had demanded Giles remove himself from your family and cease all contact. Of course, he did. Giles was always a good son to his parents.

He set off to London, courted me, and asked for my hand before the first week of the Season had ended."

Sarah swallowed past the lump in her throat at Lady Rackliffe's words. Was this true? Had Giles thrown them aside like trash to appease his father? She took a sip of wine, needing at that very moment more fortification than this. A hard whiskey or brandy would do very well to dull the ache in her chest.

"You are mistaken, my lady. Giles would not have forgone a lifelong friendship with my family regarding a scandal that was of the duke's making."

Lady Rackliffe shrugged, smirking. "Well, did he visit Lord Farley when he lived in Rome? Did Lord Gordan travel down to Kent and visit you here at the Abbey? I think the fact that he did not is proof enough, no?"

Sarah fought to breathe. She looked up and met the contemplative stare of Giles. Not wanting to confront him here, she threw him a wobbly smile. He grinned back at her, and her heart broke in her chest.

He'd believed the lie? Had towed his father's line and thrown them out with the scandal. Had ceased his friendship with Hugh and her due to not wishing to dirty his name by the association.

How could he have done such a thing? She and Hugh were innocent of the crime. Certainly, she had nothing to do with what her mother and elder brother had concocted to hide.

All the years she never saw or heard from him came rushing back, the pain his absence had caused in her heart. The past week with him here at the Abbey, she had allowed him to make her forget his wrongdoing.

She was a fool to have let his pretty face and words trick her into disregarding the truth that now having been told was blatantly obvious.

"Lord Gordan was busy elsewhere, that is all." It was all Sarah could say in defense of Lady Rackliffe's words. What else could she say at hearing such a devastating truth about the man she had agreed to marry?

"I know that you held a tendre for Giles during our first Season, and you must know that I did not mean to steal him from you. Our family was not going through a troubled time as your own, and the late marquess thought I was the better match for Giles. He agreed, of course, and offered for my hand. I hope you weren't too heartbroken, my dear, for look at you now. You have won him in the end."

Lady Rackliffe's tone was lathed with sarcasm and hate, each word dripping with scorn. Sarah met her ladyship's gaze, her own narrowing in inspection.

"Which begs the question as to why you would throw him over for the ancient and decrepit Lord Rackliffe? I know that if I had the choice between Lord Gordan and Lord Rackliffe, I certainly would not have picked a gentleman who was old enough to be my great grandfather." Sarah downed her wine in one swallow. "You must have loved him a great deal to have married a gentleman fifty years your senior." Sarah waved her empty crystal glass before Lady Rackliffe's face. "If you'll excuse me, I need another glass of wine. A lot more celebrating to be had."

Sarah stood and, without a backward glance at the gaping Lady Rackliffe, joined Giles, who was speaking to the Duke and Duchess of Whitstone.

Tonight was not the time, Sarah reminded herself. Later, she would sneak to Giles's room and ask him the truth. Only then would she know what she would do and what her future would encompass.

CHAPTER 14

Sarah paced her bedroom late that evening, the skirts of her pink silk shift and dressing gown billowing about her legs. The house the past hour had been quiet. Was Giles in his room? Or was he still downstairs with her brother and celebrating the impending wedding? An event that she was not certain would take place, not now that she knew why he'd abandoned them all those years ago.

A light scratch sounded on her door, and her pacing ceased. She flew to the door, cracking it open a little to see who was there. Giles's handsome, smiling visage greeted her, and she stepped back, letting him in. He smiled at her, reaching for her the moment she shut and locked the door. Sarah stepped back, holding up her hand. "We need to talk. Before anything else is settled between us."

He frowned, his face a mask of confusion. "Very well. What is it that you wish to discuss?"

Sarah walked over to the settee before her fire and sat. Giles joined her, taking her hand. She didn't pull away as she should. Instead, she allowed the small gesture, if only to will herself to what she must ask.

"I spoke with Lady Rackliffe tonight, and she explained your betrothal to her with a little more clarity."

"Really." His brows drew farther together still, his eyes narrowing. "What did she say?"

"Did you push me away the night I kissed you because of the scandal that was ripping my family apart?"

He ran a hand over his jaw, and Sarah could see he was choosing his words carefully. An inkling of fear rippled through her. So there was truth to Lady Rackliffe's words.

"When you kissed me, I wasn't prepared for what that kiss would mean."

Sarah frowned, knowing only too well what that kiss meant to her at least. It had changed her world, made her realize to the very core of her soul that she wanted him, and no one else. For all the years she'd pined for him, longed for him to look her way had not been an impossible dream. Had it meant anything to Giles? Or had she been nothing but an annoyance, a walking scandal that he did not want to be associated with?

"What do you even mean by that?"

He gestured between them. "Your kiss unraveled the world that I convinced myself I wanted. I was betrothed to Edith for only one day and could not cry off. I was trapped, furious at myself that I had chosen the wrong woman."

She met his gaze, wishing that were true, but it was not all of his truth. There were parts of his story he was keeping from her. "Did your father command you cease your friendship with our family over what Hugh was accused of? Even though you of all people, one of our closest friends, should have known Hugh could not be guilty of such a crime."

He was silent a moment, a muscle working in his jaw. He stood, striding to the mantel, leaning on it as he considered the roaring flames in the hearth. "My father was not an easy man, Sarah. Certainly was not one whom a son would go up against." He turned, meeting her gaze, and the fear that lurked in his eyes made her stomach churn. She hated to see him so fearful of the truth. Only someone guilty of the crime, understood the ramifications, would be troubled. "My father demanded me to marry Edith, or he would cut me off. Leave me to rot, I believe, were his words."

"Your father was my mother's friend for years. How could he hate her son so much as to demand this of you?" To be so cruel did not make sense. The late marquess could not have been so blind and wicked.

"They remained friends, even though he ensured the association did not sully his son and only heir. When Edith did not show up at the church for our wedding, my father's fight to tell me what to do seemed to dissipate from that point onward. He became an old man overnight, and within three years was gone."

"What about all the other years you stayed away?" She shook her head, fisting her hands in her lap. "Why? If I meant so very much to you, why did you let me rot in Kent? Left me under the protection of a brother who gave no security at all."

"I thought you shunned me. I did not think that you wanted anything further to do with me after the way I treated you after our kiss."

"I did not like you at all, that is true, but if you came to me then, explained why you had acted as you did, it would not have been so bad, but now..." Sarah stood, coming before him. "I could not have meant any great deal to you if you stayed away. You believed the scandal, didn't you? You knew Henry was a rogue, hell-bent on causing and living a debauched life, and still, you believed Hugh was guilty of the crime against Miss Cox."

"I did not believe that of Hugh. Never." He clasped her hands, squeezing them. "Please, Sarah, you must understand."

"No, I do not need to understand anything. I do not need to believe you at all." She tore her hands away, putting distance between them. "You lied to me, and worse is that your ex-betrothed threw the truth in my face." How many others in the *ton* would laugh at her for being so blind? Had Lady Rackliffe told her knowledge regarding Giles and Sarah to everyone at the house party? Were they laughing at her behind her back?

Humiliation tore through her and anger thrummed in her veins that the *ton* was once again laughing at her family. Snickering and speaking about them behind their backs.

He stared down at her, a shadow crossing his eyes. "I did not tell Lady Rackliffe anything. If she knew anything at all, it was at my father's doing."

"You've made a fool of me, Giles, and I won't stand for it. I promised myself years ago that I would never allow the *ton* to laugh and criticize my family. I have not, to this day, missed the society that I once graced. I cannot marry a man who believed Hugh was guilty. A man who allowed his father to dictate whom he should marry all because of a lie. Did you try to contact Hugh at all when he was in Rome?"

Giles dropped his hands at his sides, his face paling. "I did not."

Sarah shook her head, not believing what she was hearing. How had she not seen the reason why Giles had cut them off? It was not simply because she'd thrown herself at him, and he did not feel the same way. It was because he'd been told to stay away, to remove his oldest friends from his life. Do as he was told or else.

"I cannot marry you, Giles."

Sarah started for the door, needing him to leave. A hand clamped about her arm, wrenching her back. "You're crying off from our understanding? Even though I love you as much as you love me?"

His declaration sent a frisson of pleasure to course through her, but she pushed it down, stomped on it until it was no more. Her heart ached in her chest, her throat tight with unshed tears. She would not give in to emotion. She'd learned a long time ago to remain calm, don't show a response to situations that could cause her pain or give others power over her. "I will not marry a man who treated my family so poorly. Did you know how I suffered here in England without Hugh? Without you?"

The pitying look he bestowed on her fired her temper. She paced before him, her mind a whirlwind of thoughts. "Henry was awful after he schemed his way out of ruining Miss Cox. He threw parties here, lived for nothing but debauchery and strife. I had no one. Society shunned me, so I stayed here, hiding like some felon who had committed a crime. His friends would come from town, the gentleman I had danced with during my first Season. I soon learned to be wary. They were wont to follow Henry's etiquette. Whenever my brother came to stay, I fled to the dowager house."

He took a step toward her, and she put out her hand, stopping him. "I do not need your comfort."

"I did not know, Sarah. I would have come had I known. I'm sorry."

"Everyone knew what Henry was like, you more than anyone else, but you chose to stay away. I was not important enough to you that you would come and visit like you had when we were younger. I allowed myself to be swept up in your attention to me the past week. Allowed your sweet words and even sweeter kisses to taint my recollection of the past. How fortunate Lady Rackliffe reminded me of my failing."

A muscle worked in his jaw, and she looked toward the fire, not wanting to see the sheen of unshed tears in his eyes. "I made a mistake, do not punish us both for the rest of our lives by doing this, Sarah."

"Leave," she said, her voice cold and emotionless, just as her soul was right at this very moment. He'd left her before. Surely she would survive if he left her again.

"This is a mistake." Giles started for the door, pausing at her side a moment. Sarah willed him to leave. To go now. If he stopped, if he pulled her into his arms, she wasn't certain she would be so strong to deny him.

Sarah did not respond, merely listened as her door opened and closed quietly behind the one man in the world she did love and who, for the second time in her short life, had broken her heart.

CHAPTER 15

The following morning Giles waited in the Duke of St. Albans' study, needing to speak to him before the day commenced. His gut churned, his eyes itched with a lack of sleep. Would Hugh aid him in winning Sarah back, or tell him to bugger off after hearing why he'd distanced himself for so many years from Hugh's family?

The duke strode into the room, his steps slowing when he saw him seated before his desk. "Gordan?" He came the rest of the way into the room, slipping his tall frame into his leather-back chair. "To what do I owe the pleasure?" His Grace asked, smiling.

Giles wondered how long the comradeship would last, considering he'd lied to the duke's sister, and Hugh also. Giles could only hope his old school friend would let the past be. They had all made mistakes, granted this was one of the biggest that Giles had made. And one he wanted to right before he lost the only woman he'd ever loved.

Something about the knowing depths of the duke's gaze told him he may have already heard why he wished to see him this morning.

"St. Albans," he said, nodding in welcome. "I need to speak to you quite urgently. It's important."

"I believe it is." His Grace narrowed his eyes, leaning back in his chair. "Sarah did not appear to be the incandescent happy bride of the evening before at breakfast. Have you quarreled?"

Giles cleared his throat. *You could say that.* "Sarah no longer wishes to marry me, and after what I'm about to tell you, I would not be surprised if you wish for me to leave the Christmas festivities."

The duke raised his brow, throwing him a contemplative inspection. "Well, that does sound ominous. What happened?" he asked.

Giles told him of his engagement to Edith. How the union came about at the behest of his father. How his father had wanted to distance his only son and heir from Hugh, his closest friend after the scandal, citing bad influence and being tainted by association. The kiss Sarah bestowed on him at a London ball and his reaction to the said kiss. He told Hugh all of his shame, his regrets, and mistakes.

A muscle worked on Hugh's jaw, his eyes narrowed, but he didn't utter a word. Giles met Hugh's eyes, hard, dark pools he could not read, and he waited for the demand to leave to be spoken. For him to declare he ought to let Sarah go and find another woman to marry.

Instead, the reaction Hugh gave him was not the one he expected.

He laughed. So hard, in fact, his eyes watered.

"Well, you have made a mess of things, have you not?" Hugh stood, striding over to a decanter of whiskey, pouring two good portions into crystal glasses. He came over to him, handing him one. "Drink. If you are to win my sister back, you'll need your fortification."

Giles did as Hugh bade him, the burn of the amber liquid down his throat reminding him he was alive and being so, there was the opportunity, the possibility, to win Sarah back.

"You're not angry?" Giles asked, unsure how he could not be so. "I ceased a lifetime of friendship simply due to what my father and the *ton* believed to be true. I should not have. I knew you better than anyone, I should have guessed that Henry was behind your downfall."

Hugh waved his concerns aside. "Henry and my mother were to blame. Not you. Nor are you responsible for your father's reaction to the scandal that rocked my family. Sarah should understand this."

Giles had hoped that she would, but it was not so. "I should not have allowed my father to dictate my life. I lied to her, and she knows that I did. In her opinion, I chose to follow the *ton*, let their response, and opinions guide me away from my friendship with you both. I did not go to her after my father's death as I should have. She cannot forgive me."

Hugh sighed, leaning forward and crossing his hands on the desk. "Why did you not repair the friendship after the marquess's death?"

Giles cringed, wishing he had. "I had not seen Sarah for some years by then, and our parting did not give me the sense that she wished to know if I were alive or dead."

Disappointment lurked in Hugh's gaze, and Giles knew that particular point was his downfall. Why he could lose her. He should have gone to her immediately. Begged for forgiveness and made her remember how very much they liked each other. "I know," he groaned. "You do not have to say it. I know I buggered up."

Hugh nodded. "On that point, yes, you did, but we've all made mistakes. I more than most. I should not have allowed my family to push me from the only home I had, and yet I did. I took their financial support, moved to Rome, and started a new life. All the while, I let an innocent woman suffer in England at the hands of my brother's treatment."

Giles did not know what to say to such a declaration. Since Hugh's return, they had not discussed the scandal or outcomes of the time but had been happy to put it all behind them. Move forward, pick up the friendship where they once were, and forget the duke's brother and his mistreatment of those he was supposed to love.

"Sarah dislikes the *ton* and their treatment of her and me. While I understand why she's reacted in such a way, I also know that she will be thinking clearer in a couple of days. Do not give up on her, Giles. I've known that since we were boys on the brink of becoming men, there was a special bond between you two. I would like nothing more than to welcome you into our family, to become my brother. I always saw you like one, more than the actual blood brother I was saddled with."

Giles took a calming breath. The duke's comforting words went a long way in dispelling the gnawing worry he'd been plagued with ever since Sarah told him their understanding was no more.

"She does not want to marry me. How do I win her back? I have waited years to be with her. I cannot lose her now."

Hugh threw him a pitying look. Giles knew he was pitiful at this very moment, but panic threatened to seize him at the mere thought of walking away. Of hearing months or years from now that Sarah had married another. Loved another. He would not let it happen. She loved him, not anyone else. He simply had to remind her of that fact.

"Let me talk to her, Giles. As her brother and the one person she trusts most in the world, let me see if I can get her to see another point of view."

While Giles doubted it would be successful, he would try anything not to lose her. "Thank you, Hugh. I cannot thank you enough for this kindness."

Hugh stood, coming around the desk to clasp his shoulder. "While I cannot promise success, I will do all that I can. As you know, my sister can be quite stubborn with independent thought, that is hard to sway at times."

Giles chuckled, knowing how true that was. It was one of the reasons he loved her as much as he did. She was no wilting flower, his love. "She is a rare beauty." And he would win her back, losing her simply was not an option.

CHAPTER 16

Sarah sat in the duke and duchess's private parlor, not for use by the other guests at the house party. She sat on the settee facing the fire, waiting for her family to join her.

She had requested they come to see her, to hear of her change of circumstance, where it regarded Giles.

The thought of him made her skin chill, and she rubbed her arms, pulling the woolen shawl about her shoulders, her light-green gown not warm enough on this cold day.

She had not seen him at breakfast this morning, had not reveled in his company, his wicked glances across the table and lively conversation.

How could he have pushed her away and discarded her when she needed him the most? His actions were unforgivable.

Molly and Hugh strode into the room. Molly came over to her, kissing her cheeks in turn, before sitting beside her. Hugh stood before the fire, warming his hands.

"Sarah, I must say that I'm pleased you asked to speak to me, for there is a matter we need to discuss."

"There is? What was it that you wanted to talk to me about?" She had not mentioned anything to anyone about her and Giles's parting ways. Had she been too sharp with one of the guests? Lady Rackliffe, perhaps, who had a way of getting under her skin.

Hugh turned, facing them, his hands clasped behind his back. Molly took Sarah's hand, giving it a comforting squeeze. "What is wrong? You're both starting to frighten me."

"Be assured there is nothing wrong, but I have spoken to Giles this morning. He has told me everything that happened between you."

Molly threw her a look full of pity, and Sarah sighed. Not wanting anyone to pity her for standing up for what she believed. If Giles truly loved her, he would have fought for her. Came to her the moment his father had passed. He did not.

"No matter what your choice, we're here for you, Sarah."

Sarah thanked her kind sister-in-law, but turned back to her brother. "He spoke to you? I hope you made it clear that his actions toward you and our family were unacceptable. Hurtful and not those of a friend. Which, I had to remind him of the fact, he was supposed to be."

Her brother's lips thinned into a displeased line. "Come, Sarah, you know it is not always as easy as that. I am proof of such, am I not? What mother and Henry forced me into was perhaps a time when I should have shown the remnants of a backbone, but I did not. An act that I will forever regret, but one that I did to save what little was left of my life. Giles kept his distance as per his father's decree. Such action may well be displeasing. It is hard to deny one's sire when they threaten you."

"He's an only child, Hugh. He could have refused, and there would be nothing the late marquess could have done. He may have lost the access to funds, but what is that when you have stood by your morals? Your friends?" *People who loved you.*

"That is unfair, Sarah. Not everything is so black and white. There are portions of gray in life."

"If he liked us so very much, why did he not come to see me after his father had passed? Why wait until you returned from Rome? Why not write to you and keep your friendship a secret?"

"You know why, he told you himself. While we men may pine for a woman who has captured our heart, realize that we're only living a half life when we're not with those we love," Hugh said, looking to Molly, his face softening with affection for his wife. "It does not mean we do not have pride. And Giles did write to me, Whitstone too. They never abandoned me to my exile completely." Hugh paused, a frown between his brow. "Can you remember the last words you spoke to Giles on the night you kissed him at the London ball?"

Sarah gasped, heat blooming on her cheeks at the fact that her brother knew of her kissing Giles and their following argument.

She thought back to that night. She could still smell the freshly cut grass, the flowering roses, and the ivy prickle against her back as she tried to hide in the greenery.

"I told him I did not wish to see him again. That our friendship was at an end, and nothing would persuade me to think otherwise on the matter." She swallowed the lump that wedged in her throat. Giles had looked devastated at her words, as if she had ripped his heart out and thrown it into the gardens.

"How can you stand it, Hugh, what the *ton* did to us, not Henry and Mama, but you and me? We're the ones who paid the price for their deception other than Miss Cox," she said, whispering sorry to Molly, who was the young woman's cousin. "They shunned us, talked about us, and did not hide the fact that we had fallen from a great social height. I do not care what they thought. I do not. I could let the *ton* go hang and not glance back, but Hugh, Giles was one of those whispers. He agreed with their views, left us alone and without friends. How can you forgive that? How do you expect me to marry such a man?"

Hugh came and sat beside her, taking her other hand. "He never spoke of us. I'm certain of that. He merely went about his own business and got on with things without us to keep his father happy. I suppose when the marquess passed, Giles thought too much time had gone by for there ever to be forgiveness between you and him. But there can be. You can be happy, Sarah, if you let the past go. Truly let it go and stop it from festering inside of you." Hugh winked at Molly, and out of Sarah's peripheral eye, she could see her sister-in-law grinning. "You can love and live as you've only dreamed. I want that for you too. You're my sister, let us not let Henry and Mama ruin our future and our past. They do not deserve the power."

Sarah sniffed, swiping her damp cheeks at her brother's wise words.

Could she forgive Giles? Did she want to have a future with him after knowing all that she did? Sarah only had to think about that fact a moment or two before realizing the truth. Yes, of course, she did. She wanted him in all ways, even if he had acted a total fool and almost lost her forever.

She stood, striding for the door.

"Where are you going?" Molly asked, standing.

Sarah wrenched the door open and stopped, turning to face her family. "To catch myself a marquess before he does something foolish once more, like ask Lady Rackliffe for her hand again, and I lose him forever."

Hugh chuckled, pulling Molly down beside him. "Close the door on your way out, sister."

Sarah rolled her eyes at her brother's wickedness with his wife, only too glad not to be privy to their love. They were worse than anyone she'd ever met, and she too wanted the same.

With Giles.

CHAPTER 17

Giles stood looking out his bedroom window, watching as the carriage came around from the stable. Behind him, his valet packed his belongings in his trunks. A maid came out from the house's front door, handing warming bricks to his driver, who placed them on the carriage floor.

It would be a cold trip back to London, but it was one he must take. He could not stay here any longer, not with Sarah wishing for him to leave.

He clutched the back of his neck, rolling his shoulders to dispel the tension that plagued him after their last words. He had tried to make her see his position, right or wrong, he had obeyed his sire and, to his detriment, had lost Sarah in the process.

That they could be together now caused frustration and impatience to run through his veins. If only she put the past behind her, stopped allowing others' actions to guide their lives, they could be happy together. Have a life, a marriage.

"Excuse me, my lord. We're all packed. I shall have the trunks carried down and will meet you at the carriage."

"Thank you, John," Giles said, turning from the window, unwilling to leave the Abbey without one last chance of winning Sarah's trust and love.

He beat his valet out of the room, striding toward Sarah's bedroom door when he spotted her all but running down the corridor. His steps slowed, and he schooled his features, unsure of what, if anything, seeing her running in the direction of his room meant.

He stopped, bowed. "Lady Sarah." His eyes devoured every morsel of her, her fitting, complementary gown that showed off her figure to its full advantage. A body he had savored, enjoyed, and worshiped only two nights before. The light-green muslin with pretty darker-green flowers embroidered on it, making her eyes seem fiercely olive.

"Giles," she breathed, fighting to catch her breath.

That she used his given name and not his title sent a frisson of hope to course through his blood. Had she changed her mind? Had Hugh talked her 'round to forgive him? Or was she merely coming to ensure he did, in fact, leave?

Two footmen entered his room behind him, and within a moment, walked out into the passage, carrying one of his trunks.

Her face fell, along with her shoulders. "You're leaving?"

He nodded. "I think it is best, yes."

She watched him a moment, and he could see she was choosing her words carefully. He wanted to take her into his arms, pull her close, and tell her that he was sorry. That he'd never meant to hurt her. That he was simply obeying a father that he never wished to disappoint.

Sarah clamped her hands before her, raising her chin.

"We need to talk." She clasped his hand, pulling him down the hall and toward where the picture gallery ran. He'd not been in this part of the house for many years, and following Sarah as quick as he was, didn't allow him to take in the most recent painting of her that Hugh had commissioned.

They stopped at the end of the long hall, the bank of windows overlooking the side of the house's gardens, allowing light to flood the space.

Giles looked back to where they had come from and noted how very alone they were in this part of the house.

"I do not want you to leave, Giles." She stepped against him until the hem of her gown slipped across his hessian boots. "I was wrong to judge you as harshly as I did. While I will not forget or forgive what society did to my brother and myself, I will forgive you. I love you, and I'm sorry for blaming you for all my anger. I will never do so again."

Giles reached for her, pulling her against him, breathing deep the sweet smell of berries from her hair. "You have nothing to apologize for. I'm the one who is sorry, Sarah. I should have declared to my father that I would be friends and love whomever I pleased. Love whomever I wanted. It was one of the reasons why I was so angry with you the night you kissed me. I knew the moment I had you in my arms that we would never be. That through my foolishness, allowing others to dictate my actions and life that the one woman I did want beside me for the rest of my life would not be you. I had offered to Edith, and it was too late. I lashed out, blamed you for my own failings. Please forgive me."

Sarah reached up, running her hands over his jaw. Her eyes shimmered with unshed tears, and he wiped them away with his thumbs when they fell. "No tears. No more looking back. Walk beside me now, into our future. Will you marry me, please? I cannot live another day without you in my life." Never had he ever said anything so true or had wanted anything so desperately in his life.

She was his everything, and from this day forward, if she said yes, his sole purpose in life was making her incandescently happy.

"I will marry you, yes. Now please tell me you will stay. I cannot be without a dance partner for the Christmas ball."

"Wild horses could not drag me away from you." Giles leaned down, stealing a kiss, reveling in the feel of her again in his arms.

He did not let her go for a very long time...

EPILOGUE

They were married Christmas morning under a steady fall of snow. The small church that sat on the St. Albans estate was full of local gentry and those who stayed at the Abbey for the Christmas festivities. The ball that night a time to celebrate the nuptials of Sarah and Giles and Yuletide.

She stood beside Giles, her arm wrapped about his as they watched some of the guests take part in a waltz.

Warmth blossomed in her chest, and Sarah was sure her heart might burst with happiness at being married to her one and only love. She glanced up at him, caught him watching her, and her stomach flipped deliciously.

"You look like you're scheming something, my lord."

He chuckled, a deep rumble that spiked her need of him. It had been so very long since they had come together, Giles wishing to wait until they were married, and Sarah had to admit she was well past ready to have him in her bed once again.

"I'm simply happy." He paused, leaning down to

whisper in her ear, "And looking forward to having you in my bed this evening."

Heat bloomed on her cheeks, and she could not stop a grin from forming on her lips. "Maybe we could slip away? No one will pay any heed to us, leaving early. I should think it would be expected."

A wicked light entered his eye, and he took her hand, pulling her along through the guests as they made their way out a side door that would take them toward the back of the house and near the servant's stairs.

Instead of going up the stairs, however, Giles turned them down a small passage. He moved them toward the conservatory and one of Sarah's favorite places at the estate.

The smell of summer bombarded her senses, roses and foliage of earth along with the trickle of water from the large, circular fountain.

The room was warmer than other parts of the house, as it had a constant source of heat from the two large fires that burned beside the wide glass doors leading into the room during winter.

Giles shut the doors, the snip of the lock echoing about the space.

Sarah turned and watched as he gestured to the space. "The first night that you kissed me in London was warm, and although we cannot sneak outside and kiss against the ivy, I can kiss you properly here, in a room reminiscent of that time."

Her heart lurched, and she went to him, wrapping her arms about his neck. "A new beginning, since you made such a mess of things ten years ago," she teased, chuckling.

Giles growled, hoisting her up against his side. "Kiss me, Sarah, and see if you're rid of me."

Sarah did as he asked, and finally, the marquess was hers, and in no way would she lose him again.

"Merry Christmas, my love," he said, pulling but a breath away from her.

Tears welled in her eyes at how happy she was. How happy he made her feel. "Merry Christmas."

Thank you for taking the time to read *League of Unweddable Gentlemen box set, books 4-6*! I hope you enjoyed the stories.

I'm forever grateful to my readers, so if you're able, I would appreciate an honest review. As they say, feed an author, leave a review! You can contact me at tamaragillauthor@gmail.com or sign up to my newsletter to keep up with my writing news.

If you'd like to learn about book one in my To Marry a Rogue series, Only an Earl Will Do, please read on. I have included the prologue for your reading pleasure.

Tamara Gill

ONLY AN EARL WILL DO

To Marry a Rogue, Book 1

The reigning queen of London society, Lady Elizabeth Worthingham, has her future set out for her. Marry well, and marry without love. An easy promise to make and one she owed her family after her near ruinous past that threatened them all. And the rakish scoundrel Henry Andrews, Earl of Muir who's inability to act a gentleman when she needed one most would one day pay for his treachery.

Returning to England after three years abroad, Henry is determined to make the only woman who captured his heart his wife. But the icy reception he receives from Elizabeth is colder than his home in the Scottish highlands. As past hurts surface and deception runs as thick as blood, so too does a love that will overcome all obstacles, unless a nameless foe, determined with his own path, gets his way and their love never sees the light of day...

PROLOGUE

England 1805 – Surrey

"You're ruined."

Elizabeth stood motionless as her mother, the Duchess of Penworth, paced before the lit hearth, her golden silk gown billowing out behind her, the deep frown between her eyes daring anyone to follow her. "No. Let me rephrase that. The family is ruined. All my girls, their futures, have been kicked to the curb like some poor street urchins."

Elizabeth, the eldest of all the girls, swiped a lone tear from her cheek and fought not to cast up her accounts. "But surely Henry has written of his return." She turned to her father. "Papa, what did his missive say?" The severe frown lines between her father's brows were deeper than she'd ever seen them before, and dread pooled in her belly. What had she done? What had Henry said?

"I shall not read it to you, Elizabeth, for I fear it'll only upset you more, and being in the delicate condition you are we must keep you well. But never again will I allow the

Earl of Muir to step one foot into my home. To think," her father said, kicking at a log beside the fire, "that I supported him to seek out his uncle in America. I'm utterly ashamed of myself."

"No," Elizabeth said, catching her father's gaze. "You have nothing to be ashamed of. I do. I'm the one who lay with a man who wasn't my husband. I'm the one who now carries his child." The tears she'd fought so hard to hold at bay started to run in earnest. "Henry and I were friends, well, I thought we were friends. I assumed he'd do the right thing by our family, by me. Why is it that he'll not return?"

Her mother, quietly staring out the window, turned at her question. "Because his uncle has said no nephew of his would marry a strumpet who gave away the prize before the contracts were signed, and Henry apparently was in agreement with this statement."

Her father sighed. "There is an old rivalry between Henry's uncle and me. We were never friends, even though I noted Henry's father high in my esteem, as close as a brother, in fact. Yet his sibling was temperamental, a jealous cur."

"Why were you not friends with Henry's uncle, Papa?" He did not reply. "Please tell me. I deserve to know."

"Because he wished to marry your mama, and I won her hand instead. He was blind with rage, and it seems even after twenty years he wishes to seek revenge upon me by ruining you."

Elizabeth flopped onto a settee, shocked by such news. "Did Henry know of this between you and his uncle? Did you ever tell him?"

"No. I thought it long forgotten."

Elizabeth swallowed as the room started to swirl. "So, Henry has found his wealthy uncle and has been poisoned by his lies. The man has made me out to be a light-skirts of little character." She took a calming breath. "Tell me, does the letter really declare this to be Henry's opinion as well?"

The duke came and sat beside her. "It is of both their opinions, yes." He took her hand and squeezed it. "You need to marry, Elizabeth, and quickly. There is no other choice."

She stood, reeling away from her father and such an idea. To marry a stranger was worse than no marriage at all and falling from grace. "I cannot do that. I haven't even had a season. I know no one."

"A good friend of mine, Viscount Newland, recently passed. His son, Marcus, who is a little simple of mind after a fall from a horse as a child, is in need of a wife. But because of his ailment, no one will have him. They are desperate to keep the estate within the family and are looking to marry him off. It would be a good match for you both. I know it is not what you wanted, but it will save you and your sisters from ruin."

Elizabeth stood looking down at her father, her mouth agape with shock and not a little amount of disgrace. "You want me to marry a simpleton?"

"His speech is a little delayed only, otherwise he's a kind young man. I grant you he's not as handsome as Henry, but…well, we must do what's best in these situations."

Her mother sighed. "Lord Riddledale has called and asked for your hand once more. You could always accept his suit."

"Please, I would rather cut off my own hand than marry his lordship." Just the thought was enough to make her skin crawl.

"Well then, you will marry Lord Newland. I'm sorry, but it must and will be done," her mother said, her tone hard.

Elizabeth walked to the window that looked toward the lake where she'd given herself to Henry. His sweet whispered words of love, of wanting her to wait for him, that as soon as he procured enough funds to support his Scottish estate they would marry, flittered through her mind. What a liar he'd turned out to be. All he wanted was her innocence and nothing else.

Anger thrummed through her and she grit her teeth. How dare Henry trick her in such a way? Made her fall in love with him, promised to be faithful and marry her when he returned. He never wished to marry her. Had he wanted to right now he would be on his way back to England.

She turned, staring at her parents who looked resigned to a fate none of them imagined possible or ever wanted. "I will marry Viscount Newland. Write them and organize the nuptials to take place within the month or sooner if possible. The child I carry needs a father and the viscount needs a wife."

"Then it is done." Her father stood, walking over to her and taking her hand. "Did Henry promise you anything, Elizabeth? The letter is so out of character for him, I've wondered since receiving it that it isn't really of his opinion but his uncle's only."

"He wanted me to wait for him, to give him time to save his family's estate. He did not wish to marry a woman for her money; he wanted to be a self-made man, I suppose."

"Lies, Elizabeth. All lies," her mother stated, her voice cold. "Henry has used you, I fear, and I highly doubt he'll ever come back to England or Scotland, for that matter."

Elizabeth swallowed the lump in her throat, not wanting to believe the man she'd given her heart to would treat her in such a way. She'd thought Henry was different, was a gentleman who loved her. At the look of pity her father bestowed on her, she pushed him aside and ran from the room.

She needed air, fresh, cooling, calming air. Opening the front door, the chilling icy wind hit her face, and clarity assailed. She'd go for a ride. Her mount Argo always made her feel better.

It took the stable hand only minutes to saddle her mount, and she was soon trotting away from the house, the only sound that of the snow crunching beneath her horse's hooves. The chill pierced through her gown, and she regretted not changing into a suitable habit, but riding astride in whatever they had on at the time was a normal practice for the children of the Duke of Penworth. Too much freedom as a child, all of them allowed to do whatever they pleased, and now that freedom had led her straight into the worst type of trouble.

She pushed her horse into a slow canter, her mind a kaleidoscope of turmoil. Henry, once her father's ward, a person she'd thought to call a friend, had betrayed her when she needed him most. Guilt and shame swamped her just as snow started to fall, and covered everything in a crystal white hue.

She would never forgive Henry for this. Yes, they'd made a mistake, a terrible lack of decorum on her behalf that she'd never had time to think through. But should the worst happen, a child, she had consoled herself that Henry would do right by her, return home and marry her.

How could she have been so wrong?

She clutched her stomach, still no signs that a little child grew inside, and as much as she was ruined, could possibly ruin her family, she didn't regret her condition, and nor would she birth this child out of wedlock. Lord Newland would marry her since his situation was not looked upon favorably by the ton; it was a match that would suit them both.

Guilt pricked her soul that she would pass off Henry's child as Lord Newland's, but what choice did she have? Henry would not marry her, declare the child his. Elizabeth had little choice. There was nothing else to be done about it.

A deer shot out of the bracken, and Argo shied, jumping sharply to the side. Elizabeth screamed as her seat slipped. The action unbalanced her and she fell, hitting the ground hard.

Luckily, the soft snow buffered her fall, and she sat up, feeling the same as she had when upon her horse. She rubbed her stomach, tears pooling in her eyes with the thought that had she fallen harder, all her problems would be over. What a terrible person she was to think such a thing, and how she hated Henry that his refusal of her had brought such horrendous thoughts to mind.

Argo nuzzled her side as she stood; reaching for the stirrup, she hoisted herself back onto her mount. Wiping the tears from her eyes, Elizabeth promised no more would be shed over a boy, for that was surely what Henry still was, an immature youth who gave no thought to others.

She would marry Viscount Newland, try and make him happy as much as possible when two strangers came together in such a union, and be damned anyone who mentioned the name Henry Andrews, Lord Muir to her again.

America 1805 – New York Harbor

Henry raised his face to the wind and rain as the packet ship sailed up the Hudson River. The damp winter air matched the cold he felt inside, numbing the pain that hadn't left his core since farewelling the shores of England. And now he was here. America. The smoky city just waking to a new day looked close enough to reach out and touch, and yet his true love, Elizabeth, was farther away than she'd ever been before.

He rubbed his chest and huddled into his greatcoat. The five weeks across the ocean had dragged, endless days with his mind occupied with only one thought: his Elizabeth lass.

He shut his eyes, bringing the vision of her to his mind, her honest, laughing gaze, the beautiful smile that had always managed to make his breath catch. He frowned, missing her as much as the highland night sky would miss the stars.

"So, Henry, lad, what's your plan on these great lands?" Henry took in the captain on the British Government packet; his graying whiskers across his jaw and crinkled skin about his eyes told of a man who'd lived at sea his entire life, and enjoyed every moment of it. He grinned. "Make me fortune. Mend a broken family tie if I can."

The captain lit a cheroot and puffed, the smoke soon lost in the misty air. "Ah, grand plans then. Any ideas on how you'll be making your fortune? I could use some tips myself."

"My uncle lives here. Owns a shipping company apparently, although I've yet to meet the man or see for myself if this is true. I'm hoping since he's done so well for himself he can steer me along the road to me own fortune."

The captain nodded, staring toward the bow. "It seems you have it all covered."

Henry started when the captain yelled orders for half-mast. He hoped the old man was right with his statement. The less time he stayed here the better it would be. He pushed away the thought that Elizabeth was due to come out in the forthcoming months, to be paraded around the ton like a delicious morsel of sweet meats. To be the center of attention, a duke's daughter ripe for the picking. He ground his teeth.

"I wish you good luck, Henry."

"Thank ye." The captain moved away, and he turned back to look at the city so unlike London or his highland home. Foreign and wrong on so many levels. The muddy waters were the only similarity to London, he mused, smiling a little.

Henry walked to the bow, leaning over the wooden rail. He sighed, trying to expel the sullen mood that had swamped him the closer they came to America. What he was doing here was a good thing, an honorable thing, something that if he didn't do, Elizabeth would be lost to him forever.

He couldn't have hated his grandfather more at that moment for having lost their fortune at the turn of a card all those years ago. It was a miracle his father had been able to keep Avonmore afloat and himself out of debtor's prison.

The crewmen preparing the packet ship for docking sounded around him, and he started toward the small room he'd been afforded for the duration of the trip. It was better than nothing; even if he'd not been able to stand up fully within the space, at least it was private and comfortable.

Determination to succeed, to ensure his and Elizabeth's future was secure, to return home as soon as he may, sparked within him. He would not fail; for once, the Earl of Muir would not gamble the estate's future away, but fight for its survival, earn it respectably just as his ancestors had.

And he would return home, marry his English lass, and spoil her for the remainder of their days. In Scotland.

Want to read more? Purchase Only an Earl Will Do today!

LORDS OF LONDON SERIES
AVAILABLE NOW!

Dive into these charming historical romances! In this six-book series by Tamara Gill, Darcy seduces a virginal duke, Cecilia's world collides with a roguish marquess, Katherine strikes a deal with an unlucky earl and Lizzy sets out to conquer a very wicked Viscount. These stories plus more adventures in the Lords of London series!

LEAGUE OF UNWEDDABLE GENTLEMEN SERIES AVAILABLE NOW!

Fall into my latest series, where the heroines have to fight for what they want, both regarding their life and love. And where the heroes may be unweddable to begin with, that is until they meet the women who'll change their fate. The League of Unweddable Gentlemen series is available now!

LEAGUE OF UNWEDDABLE GENTLEMEN

THE ROYAL HOUSE OF ATHARIA SERIES

If you love dashing dukes and want a royal adventure, make sure to check out my latest series, The Royal House of Atharia series! Book one, To Dream of You is available now at Amazon or you can read FREE with Kindle Unlimited.

A union between a princess and a lowly future duke is forbidden. But as intrigue abounds and their enemies circle, will Drew and Holly defy the obligations and expectations that stand between them to take a chance on love? Or is their happily ever after merely a dream?

ALSO BY TAMARA GILL

Royal House of Atharia Series

TO DREAM OF YOU

A ROYAL PROPOSITION

FOREVER MY PRINCESS

League of Unweddable Gentlemen Series

TEMPT ME, YOUR GRACE

HELLION AT HEART

DARE TO BE SCANDALOUS

TO BE WICKED WITH YOU

KISS ME DUKE

THE MARQUESS IS MINE

LEAGUE - BOOKS 1-3 BUNDLE

LEAGUE - BOOKS 4-6 BUNDLE

Kiss the Wallflower series

A MIDSUMMER KISS

A KISS AT MISTLETOE

A KISS IN SPRING

TO FALL FOR A KISS

A DUKE'S WILD KISS

TO KISS A HIGHLAND ROSE

KISS THE WALLFLOWER - BOOKS 1-3 BUNDLE

KISS THE WALLFLOWER - BOOKS 4-6 BUNDLE

Lords of London Series

TO BEDEVIL A DUKE

TO MADDEN A MARQUESS

TO TEMPT AN EARL

TO VEX A VISCOUNT

TO DARE A DUCHESS

TO MARRY A MARCHIONESS

LORDS OF LONDON - BOOKS 1-3 BUNDLE

LORDS OF LONDON - BOOKS 4-6 BUNDLE

To Marry a Rogue Series

ONLY AN EARL WILL DO

ONLY A DUKE WILL DO

ONLY A VISCOUNT WILL DO

ONLY A MARQUESS WILL DO

ONLY A LADY WILL DO

A Time Traveler's Highland Love Series

TO CONQUER A SCOT

TO SAVE A SAVAGE SCOT

TO WIN A HIGHLAND SCOT

Time Travel Romance

DEFIANT SURRENDER

A STOLEN SEASON

Scandalous London Series

A GENTLEMAN'S PROMISE

A CAPTAIN'S ORDER

A MARRIAGE MADE IN MAYFAIR

SCANDALOUS LONDON - BOOKS 1-3 BUNDLE

High Seas & High Stakes Series

HIS LADY SMUGGLER

HER GENTLEMAN PIRATE

HIGH SEAS & HIGH STAKES - BOOKS 1-2 BUNDLE

Daughters Of The Gods Series

BANISHED-GUARDIAN-FALLEN

DAUGHTERS OF THE GODS - BOOKS 1-3 BUNDLE

Stand Alone Books

TO SIN WITH SCANDAL

OUTLAWS

ABOUT THE AUTHOR

Tamara Gill is an Australian author who grew up in an old mining town in country South Australia, where her love of history was founded. So much so, she made her darling husband travel to the UK for their honeymoon, where she dragged him from one historical monument and castle to another.

A mother of three, her two little gentlemen in the making, a future lady (she hopes) and a part-time job keep her busy in the real world, but whenever she gets a moment's peace she loves to write romance novels in an array of genres, including regency, medieval and time travel.

www.tamaragill.com
tamaragillauthor@gmail.com